Cutter
Art of Blood

A collaborative debut novel
Written by
Blanshard & Blanshard

Susan Blanshard is an acclaimed poet, essayist, and literary editor. She has a background as an award-winning advertising writer.

Bruce Blanshard is an award-winning advertising creative director. A best-selling nonfiction author, short story writer, artist and designer.

B L A N S H A R D & B L A N S H A R D

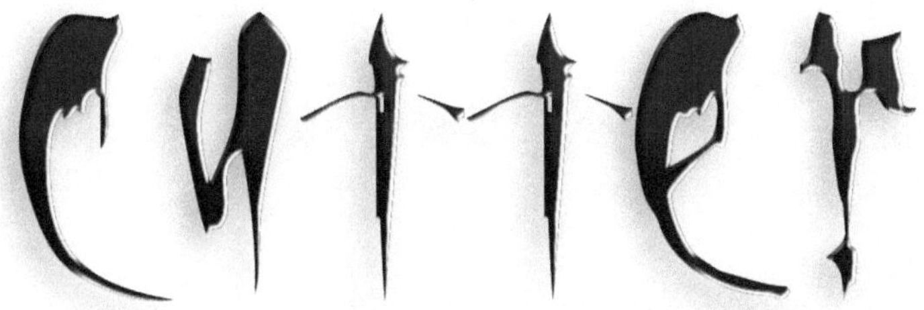

CUTTER

ART OF BLOOD

KILLING IS JUST THE BEGINNING

PAGE ADDIE PRESS
UNITED KINGDOM

First published 2021 by Page Addie Press, United Kingdom.

ISBN 978-1-8383465-5-3

Cutter: Art of Blood. Killing Is Just The Beginning.
Copyright©2021 by Blanshard & Blanshard.
Cover copyright©2021 by Page Addie Press. All rights reserved.

The Authors Blanshard &Blanshard have asserted the right
to be identified as the authors of this work in accordance
with the Copyright, Design and Patents Act 1988.

A CIP catalogue record for this book is available from the British Library

British Library Cataloging-in-publication Data has been applied for:
ISBN 978-1-8383465-4-6 (Hard Cover)
ISBN 978-1-8383465-5-3 (Perfect Bound)
ISBN 978-1-8383465-6-0 (ebook)

Printed in the United Kingdom, United States of America, Australia

PROLOGUE

THE SUN WAS BOILING in its shell. It was the height of summer. The front door left open to let the breeze through—the flies followed.

Every Sunday lunch was the same, our father eating meat. Henry was a brute of a father who ate nothing but butchered animals: their livers, kidneys, stomachs, ribs, shanks, and brains. Our father gave us everything we didn't want, and somewhere along our lives, he gave Joe and me misophonia—a hatred of certain sounds. The noise he made when he opened and closed his jaws, made us want to rip off our skin. His gravy slurping made me want to flip the plate and stab him in the eye with the bone handle carving knife. He said he hated our guts, and there Joe and I were, staring at a plate of cow's stomach—tripe and onions. Joe told me a joke about a grizzly bear. I sniggered with my mouth full of potato.

'Grace, where are the bloody vegetables? And you Christian,' cuffing his palm across the back of my head, 'don't laugh with your mouth full. Eat! Kids starving in Africa would be grateful for your food.'

Joe and I imagined a ship full of rippling tripe. How grateful to see it sailing far away with Henry on board.

'I wish, Christian, you'd never been born!'

'You can't *un-wish* him like that! Family is family,' Ma said, as she disappeared into the kitchen.

'I can say what I like. And as far as Joe goes, if he's got a mouth, he can use it. What do you say, Joe?'

But Joe was Joe, like always, he refused to answer. Joe was the master of muteness.

'Grace, call child welfare! Get them to come and take the rotten off-spring away.'

I HAD HEARD it all before. I never believed Henry because Henry was an unbelievable father. I knew Grace wouldn't make the call because our mother was a sweet liar. She always pretended to dial the number but rang a friend instead, tears forever escaping down the telephone wire. Whenever she spoke on the phone, Ma twisted her hair around her fingers and untwisted each blond strand. The more she lied—the more curls she made.

Our father thought he was a god and said we must obey him. He shouted commands at the top of his voice to make everyone do what he wanted. Grace said he had the high blood, and the high blood made his face red.

That Sunday, God had the last word, and so the unbelievable happened—we watched our father fall face down into his plate of hot mashed potatoes. Our father dead at the head of the table was something Joe and I had dreamed of.

Our mother appeared from the kitchen—her blonde hair twisted in tight curls—she took one look at our father, and dropped the blue dragon china bowl. Green peas bounced over the pink wool roses on the gray carpet. It was the first time we saw the kinetics of simple summer legumes, and the first time Ma had seen our father dead—us too.

I said to Joe: 'Our father is dead.'

'How can you be sure?'

'He's been face-down for three minutes.'

'We can hold our breath and stay face down underwater in the bathtub, but not for that long.'

'Maybe he's smelling the meat? Butchers do.'

'No, Joe, he's not smelling offal.'

'Well, someone in the world is. Someone always does something, somewhere in the world.'

'Who told you that rubbish?'

'You did.'

Grace put her hands up to her face and screamed.

'You see Ma screaming? It's a silent scream.'

'Can that happen?'

'Somewhere in the world it does.'

'What about our father? What happens now?'

'He'll get buried under a heap of dirt.'

'What's in the dirt?'

'Composted soil, leaf mulch.'

'Anything else?'

'Cat and dog shit.'

'Anything else?'

'Leftovers, like blood sausages made with a king's-hood.'

'What is a king's-hood?'

'A sheep's paunch stuffed with blood.'

'Like a ball sack?'

'Not exactly—as I was saying—tied with string and slowly boiled until black.'

'Then what?'

'Worms and maggots will eat his body, but not his liver.'

'Why not liver?'

'Because of the cirrhosis.'

'Chorizo, like a Mexican sausage?'

'No, fatty and scarred from drinking the spirits.'

'OK—so not the liver. Is that the end?'

'Not exactly.' I changed the subject. 'If he's done bad things, he'll go to hell.' Hell alarms Joe. Hell means fire. Fire means burning. He reads too much.

'A lot of cartoon characters go to hell,' Joe said. 'The Evil Lord of Destruction who seeks to conquer the castle so he can learn all of the ancient secrets, which would make him unstoppable and make him conquer and rule everyone. He'll go to hell. And the evil wizard and alchemist, the one who makes magic potions to destroy the Smurfs. So Henry's going to hell?'

'Yep. Definitely. And he's going to the deepest part of hell.'

'Will we?'

Here's where death got tricky. I should have told him the truth—that most of us get roasted eternally, most of us end up in hell, even living can be hellish, and a living hell, but I didn't want to upset him. I wanted to keep dumb about death. What else could I do? His inquisitiveness was a habit, and I fed his appetite for nothingness, and it was time to tell him something more of nothing.

Joe and I went upstairs into our bedroom.

'You and I are il Divino. Do you know what that means?'

'No I don't.'

'Extraordinary regents of the great talent of the infinite.'

'What does that mean?'

'An awful lot, when you get grown up, you will see.'

'How do I get grown up?'

I opened up my album and pointed to one stamp in particular—

mint condition, from French Polynesia.

'See this?'

The picture on the forty-franc stamp showed a hypodermic syringe inserted into a human forearm.

'What is that?'

'Adult blood—it works by gravity, adult blood goes from a plastic bag, through a plastic tube, down the needle and into your arm.'

Joe stared at the stamp for a long time before he spoke. 'Does everyone in the world have to have a blood confusion?'

'A transfusion—you do if you want to be a grown-up.'

WHEN WE CAME downstairs, a morbid quiet had settled in the house. We didn't hear her come, but yet, there she was, a solitary figure, suddenly in our vision, standing in the doorway. She appeared like a stigmata—how the image of a saint can appear on a piece of burned toast. At that moment, Joe and I had our first religious experience. We even looked at our hands to see if our palms were bleeding. Was this woman here to save us?

'Hello Christian.'

The Virgin suddenly dissolved into Mrs. Kitts, the widow who lived next door. Mrs. Kitts put her arms around Grace, and thought for a long while, like a person who'd forgotten to make a shopping list. 'With that bastard out of your life, you can become more like yourself every day.' What Mrs. Kitts said next had an indifferent tone. In three words, she summed up everything she knew about life. 'Life goes on.' She paused. 'Christian, why don't you go play outside. Let me have some time to talk to your Ma—alone.'

Inertia filled the cracks of thought, and a blowfly crawled into the crevice of Henry's nostril.

'Maybe this isn't the right time,' Kitts murmured, casting her dark eyes over Henry's dead body sprawled across the table.

'How about in the living room?' Ma suggested.

She appeared oddly strange. Her face had changed; her eyes almost free; yes it was Ma, much the same, but she seemed happy, yes, her mouth had untangled a little into a smile, sweet and kind. In the living room, with its garden of floral wallpaper, our mother pushed the Sunday morning paper off the coffee table so Kitts could spread her cartwheel of Tarot cards over the table's scarred surface, the wooden top held up by carved lion legs.

The first card she tapped with her nicotine-stained finger, was a man holding a hawk and a man juggling a golden ball. She talked about Joe and me like we weren't in the room.

'Your son ... Christian ... he will sign a document with an engraved silver pen which will make him one of the richest men in the world.'

That's a good thing, I thought.

Then she tapped two other cards: a skeleton armed with a scythe, and the tower card, two people falling from the collapsing tower. She shook her head, reshuffled the cards.

'What did you see?' Ma inquired, staring at the pack of cards.

'Make sure Christian never wears black.'

I looked into her eyes and held my breath: a way to control the long nerve, a way to control the pupil, until the black circle in the center was dilated and fearful.

I said: 'Black isn't a color. It's a feeling.' The way I looked at her scared her, I could tell.

She walked towards the door stepping on peas, squishing them into the pink roses of the gray carpet. Mrs. Kitts gave me a glance that was a bit strange but not the worst of looks I'd had. Then she embraced Grace, holding her like a store dummy, and left.

On the day our father was buried and went to hell, a large packet arrived in our post box. Mrs. Kitts had sent us a book, *The Child's Instructor.* Inside, the author said bees gather honey from flowers, and only naughty boys stick pins in insects. And the rule was, it was cruel to do that. However, rules didn't matter.

We caught moths. We caught moths either in a gauze net or with a pair of forceps covered with gauze. In his secret heart, Joe didn't want to hurt them: he just wanted to examine the little bodies and see the wings speckled with a thousand colors. Then I showed him how we could preserve them, how to expand and keep their wings open with the pressure of small slips of paper. After a day or two, the wings stayed open, but naturally, we had to kill them first.

One moonlit night, I took a box of matches and a candle up to the attic space. Joe brought a live moth, held captive inside a glass preserving jar.

'What are we doing?'

'An experiment.'

'What can I do?'

'Keep the moth in the dark. Hide the jar under your sweater.'

'Why?'

'Because we're in control—we know what's going to happen.'

Then I lit a white candle, unscrewed the lid and released the moth.

'A moth is a night creature. It navigates through the darkest hours, following the path of light.'

'What happens if we blow out the candle? Will it break its neck, like our yellow roller canary did when you opened the cage to see if it could fly in the dark?'

'That was a bad accident.'

'Are there any good accidents?'

'Only when you don't have to go to school, like in black ice, that's a good accident. That's when something very good comes out of something very bad.'

The moth flew closer to the flame. I blew out the candle and sat with Joe in the dark.

'What will the moth do now?'

I turned the light switch on. The moth was totally gone, as in disappeared!

'Where did it go?' Joe was confused.

'The night creature could be anywhere.' Moths are masters of disguise; the moth blends into a point of invisibility—adjusts and adapts a situation to its advantage.

'Moths mean death. Remember when a moth flew through our house? And Henry caught it in his fist.'

'And that made Henry go dead? Who let the moth in?'

'Maybe I left the fly screen door open for it.'

'You made Henry go dead? On purpose?'

'Everything has a purpose—even a moth. What do you think? I did that on purpose?'

'It's possible?'

'Neither of us will fall dead. We are night creatures, you and me. We are born to metamorphose. We'll always have our secret life.'

'Tell me another rule about night creatures?'

'Henry's ghost lives in the basement.'

'In our basement?'

'No, but somewhere there's a basement, someplace in the world. His ghost is there because everything has to be somewhere, even a ghost. That's the rule. A place for everything.'

'So Henry's gone to hell, but his ghost is in a basement someplace? Like two people?'

'The dead are not people anymore. Faraway from here, in an ancient castle with rotten floorboards and night creatures, where darkness is at its darkest, there is a basement filled with ghosts, where sewer rats have eyes wet and red, like blood, in the dark.'

'Or red like wet paint, magenta or crimson?'

'Either way—red as blood—red as paint. It's all the same thing.'

Joe asked a trick question. 'Christian, what do you think the world stands on?'

'A great turtle.'

'What does the turtle stand on?'

'I don't know what the turtle stands on!'

'Perhaps a tortoise, and that's why the world turns slowly.'

'Maybe the world doesn't stand on anything but balances by itself and goes around the sun and then, once a year, it's our birthday. You know we share our birth date with Galileo, Leonardo da Vinci, Hieronymus Bosch, and Bruegel the elder. So we will climb the same pathways to genius. Geniuses can see what's coming in the world.'

Joe and I were introduced to genius when we were five. Our mother took us to Michelangelo di Lodovico Buonarroti Simoni's tomb. Then she told us we were Michelangelo's reincarnation. We came to believe what Ma said. If Michelangelo was the first version of us, we are child geniuses, Joe and I. And like Michelangelo, we are terribilità—terror-inducing.

'Christian, do you know what I want most of all?'

'No, what do you want?'

'I want you to give me a lead pencil for my birthday. Then I will draw you a hawk.'

A MONTH AFTER Henry's death, Mrs. Kitts came for morning tea. I showed Kitts our moth collection. Kitts looked at the dead moths and said nothing. She reached across the table and took Ma's cup by the handle, held it in her left hand, waved it in a circle three times. Then she turned the teacup upside down, then right-side up, and stared into the mush of dark leaves, the scattered shapes and figures left on the bottom. 'There's murder here.'

Grace gasped because she believed everything Kitts said, but Joe and I burst out laughing. Widow Kitts was just so crazy.

We left Kitts in the kitchen with Ma and went back to developing a prototype; a lion made out of Technic Lego—only the yellow pieces. A lion that would walk, stop, rear on its hind legs, and open its chest to present a bunch of lilies, just like Leonardo's lion, the mechanical lion he made for King Francis I.

It was Joe's idea to make a lion with the body of a lion and the head of a human. Joe never got past the first drawings, and unlike Leonardo, we never did assemble a lion, but at least, like Leonardo, we were born with a talent to make something of ourselves. Joe and I resemble each other. We are like two drops of distilled water, but we each have different reflections.

I was a witness on the day Joe first tagged himself as Black Shadow underneath the steel footbridge, fifty feet above the Hudson River. By the following Sunday, we'd tagged two water towers, the pylon girders of the power station, and Jackman's trucker yard guarded by two black and tan Doberman's, with spiked collars. The adults saw graffiti as vandalism. To the neighborhood kids, we had flipped a middle finger, and broken another rule.

TEN YEARS LATER, I went off to Harvard. Joe went his way. Despite my efforts to stay in contact, I lost touch with him. Then, when I was sick in bed with a high fever, he came back for good. From that point on, we were inseparable.

I did a Masters Degree in Molecular Biology and a Degree in International Business and Entrepreneurship, and turned into a moneymaking plutocrat, and Joe became an artist.

I own the 1920's building in the Upper 30th of the Fur District and more than that. So perhaps, the fortune teller was right about me. The difference between the blue-chip rich and the rest of the world is the definition of more. If less is more, I don't want to know about it. Money may not buy happiness, but I would prefer to cry in a grand apartment, and use brand new hundred dollar notes to dry my eyes, than live under cardboard on the sidewalk.

Neither Joe nor I were born with the tarnish of silver spoons in our mouths. We try to be who we are, but fate makes us what we are. I'm not sure how much I believe in the ordained, but Joe and I had an impact on the lives of at least five people. Over the years, we've managed to increase those numbers considerably. That's why I know, as well as Joe does, what is about to happen. Only Joe and I know why the chosen ones have to die.

1

THE CHALLENGE OF FORTUNE telling is how correct your manifested predictions are. So far, Mrs. Kitts was right about Grace's strange but handsome boy, Christian. His sense of entitlement attracted money.

The challenge of a fortune is to find new things to spend it on. Christian Cutter bought bricks and mortar south of Penn Station. The first was the landmark but abandoned furrier building: where once minks, sable, ermine, and other small animals, like rabbits and red foxes, had their fur processed into coats, stoles, hats, and jackets. An elegant pair of vixens, five feet tall, each one carved from gray stone, had guarded the arched doorway since the time when the first fox had its throat cut, and its fur ripped from its back.

In sympathy with the architecture, restoration took place: the metalwork of the original main doorway, an Art Deco masterpiece returned to former elegance, a marble staircase; its banister of black iris floral motif and brass rail, painstakingly polished. The foyer reflected the elegance of the building, the wide eaves of the roof supported at regular intervals with ivy carved columns.

With the help of Milan designer Cara Rossi, old dusty spaces were transformed into grand light-filled rooms. Reflections pass through Italian mirrors, until lofty interiors appear to extend out to vanishing points in either direction. There is a European-style kitchen a master chef would envy, a gymnasium, a movie theater, and in the converted space under the building, a garage housing a stable of luxury cars.

The one thing Cara could never understand was why Christian insisted she leave the top floor in its original state: small bare ghoulish areas filled with steel racks, iron hooks, and dyeing vats, where anything living would fear for its life.

The place gave her the shivers. 'Too morbid.'

Nothing could change Christian's mind. 'The top floor is where I'll spend most of my alone time.'

Of all the wealthy clients on her books, Cara had never met a man like Christian.

One by one, he bought the surrounding buildings: the cigar importers, the guitar shop, grocery, dojo, three art galleries, artisan cheese shop, Belgium chocolate shop, a recording studio, and a corner flower shop called Stems. If materialism is a god, Christian Cutter was a dedicated worshipper. Like a shot of greed, he believed in money as much as he believed in himself.

It is early morning. Eight million people stir, ready to wake. Dawn creeps in, kissing Our Lady of the Harbor with a guilty breath. If anyone loves New York, Christian does. The city is like a woman who satisfies his every craving. Christian reaches over and touches the remote control for the bedroom drapes. Layers of dark indigo silk slowly draw back, exposing Manhattan's morning skyline through the landscape window. He doesn't need caffeine to revive him this morning. He walks into the floor-to-ceiling Italian marble bathroom and turns the dynamo rain shower on full. His body is tall, unscarred, a sexy body denoting fitness. If God created Man, this one was made so very logically, well proportioned with broad shoulders and muscular forearms. The type of guy who looks as good in formal suits as he does shirtless on the beach or in the bedroom. His face reflects his image in the steam-free mirror. Christian draws the razor through the shaving foam. His handsome, tanned face revealed; high cheekbones, long slim nose, generous lips, dark eyelashes, square jaw. He takes out a pair of contact lenses from the bathroom cabinet, towel dries his thick black hair and goes naked into his walk-in wardrobe. Thirty-one tailored suits, one for every day of any given month, all kept in their original garment bags, neckties like silk fists set in a drawer, thirty-one pairs of handmade shoes, thirty-one pressed shirts.

In the corner of the bathroom, a wicker laundry basket filled with Joe's black jeans and dark-hooded sweatshirts. Every article of clothing stained with black artist ink. The ink is by no means ordinary; made of pure pine-soot, deer horn glue, and preserving perfumes—black ink, worth more to him than penicillin or human blood. Christian knows there will always be a point of messiness. As long as he lives with Joe, things will be messy. It is pointless to change habits; besides, the interior of every man's closet is his own business.

Joe is another poor New York artist who amasses work and stores his paintings in the back room, and hasn't sold one picture. Joe never asks for financial help because asking is just another form of begging. With Christian, it's a given to assist Joe. He leaves tabs open for him at all the downtown art stores. Family is family to the end. Christian knows if his financial world turns to ruin, Joe will never let him drift like human debris in the world. Christian feels a vibration from his phone.

Call me when you have time.

Give my love to Joe.

Ma.

Grace worked two jobs since Henry died, worked herself to the bone, doing day and night shifts, and now she was sick. He doesn't hesitate to provide for her. But all the money in the world can't buy good health. The nurse still injects vials. For all Grace's pain and suffering, the help Christian gives is right up there with her tanks of oxygen.

Christian sent a message to the florist at Stems: Deliver bunches of white and purple violets to Grace, at St Margaret's, please. Then Joe came in. 'I had a feeling Ma needed violets today.' Like the *Madonna and Child with Flowers* by da Vinci, Joe thought, the violets making the cross were white, but her tears turned them purple. But, what the hell? Even if you cut the stems at an angle and add a preservative to the water they die. Cut flowers are no more than a bunch of colored petals without the will to live. Violets drink through their petals, so they need to be turned upside down for a while, but left too long, they drown.

Christian does up the last button on his Savile Row, bespoke shirt, and knots Friday's tie. A black silk tie, on this 13th day. Also it happens to be a Friday.

This morning, Christian is about to execute his best plan to date.

2

CHRISTIAN WALKS TO THE antique elevator in his apartment, and pulls the folding metal gates to the point of symmetry—the brass hook slides into the female part and locks solid. Without simple, but proper connections, the lift would suddenly come to a standstill, and cause entrapment between floors. It happened to Joe on his way down to the basement garage once; the lift stopped, Joe was facing the interior of the shaft, red brick upon red brick, history upon history. A herringbone pattern, every brick initialed by the maker. Convicts who had marked the passing of time. Today there was no time for error. Christian gets out of the elevator, into his car, and heads for the freeway.

CHRISTIAN ARRIVES AT Biozen Corporation and drives down into the multi story car park, knowing that when he finishes his meeting in two hours, he will leave there, one of the wealthiest men on the planet. And after that, who knows. As he accelerates his Porsche around concrete pillars, the tires scream on race alloys. Underground, three stories down, he drives into the visitors' space, turns off the ignition, and listens to the sound of water. Water trickling from somewhere, an irritating sound that adds to his dislike for basements—with their faithless margins of cold light.

He drops a couple of smart drugs, steps into the elevator and hits the elevator button for the 38th floor, checks his reflection in the glass ceiling and sees himself as he is—a man in an elevator—on the way up.

The doors open into Biozen's foyer, decorated, for some reason, like an archaeological time capsule: limestone tiles embedded with prehistoric plants and fish, a foyer of time and consequence, so many grooved shells of extinct ammonites, primordial creatures pressed onto the surface of the stone, overlapping and breaking up, like the signs of time. Ancient Sumerian cuneiform writing tablets are lit up inside a glass cabinet. Above him, the only four hanging art deco lights in existence, fourteen feet of luminaire prisms and light beams. On the wall, a Eugene Delacroix painting, *Massacre No: 2, 'The death of a king.'* The beams of light pick out the gamut of reds and browns—life and blood.

Christian walks on the red Persian runner carpet woven with celestial stars to the double etched doors and enters the executive suite. Two men are waiting.

Geoff greets him like the old friend he is. 'Good to see you again.'
'Likewise, Geoff.'

But when he puts out his hand to Geoff's partner, Christian feels vague hostility in the cold haddock handshake. Spencer's clammy palm is a dead giveaway. There is no way back from this day. It doesn't take a brainiac. Spencer knows it, and so does Christian.

CHRISTIAN HAD PREVIOUSLY done his research and due diligence on Geoff and Spencer, the creative minds behind Biozen. In the geocryology department of Biozen, Geoff, the head scientist, had made a discovery in Siberia. The permafrost was melting due to global warming, and ancient bacteria, trapped for thousands of years, was leaching into the water supplies. The local tribal people, who drank the water, never got a cold or flu, were completely free of killer diseases like cancer, and lived longer as a result.

After conducting successful experiments injecting rats with the ancient bacteria, both Spencer and Geoff believed in their research, and took an unprecedented step forward. They injected stabilized bacteria found in the frozen wastes of Siberia into their veins regularly, and monitored the physical effects of the ancient microbial soup as it passed the blood-brain barrier in their bodies. As far as they knew, they weren't infected or adversely affected. They got away with it and developed the prototype of senolytic agents, which delay, and prevent the diseases of aging.

Biozen then invested eighty million dollars in initiatives and developed B-Zen10, phytochemical compounds known to block the harmful effects of free radicals. B-Zen10 promoted cell renewal and delayed the aging process. One year after they set up their smart biotech company, they listed Biozen on the stock market. In six months, shares went through the roof of Wall Street. And that's when Christian bought four million dollars worth of shares and decided to send Geoff and Spencer an invitation to lunch.

AT THE SAVOY Hotel in London, over roasted wild quail, Christian introduced the idea of a merger between Biozen and Christian's Human Development Corporation. As the meal progressed, the annoyances increased. Christian felt irritation rising and stopped talking. Spencer chomped fried game chips as if he was eating glass. Spencer had intentionally triggered Christian's misophonia.

When Spencer dragged gold cutlery through his teeth, Christian wanted to stab him in the eye with the golden oyster fork. The only problem was, Spencer would see him coming.

Great opportunities of a lifetime can happen over a lunchtime. By the time the peaches stuffed with Amaretto and ground almonds arrived, Biozen Corporation had already begun to merge with Christian's company. Geoff had enjoyed not only the dessert, but the business idea Christian had first muted back when the starched napkins shaped like white swans were first unfolded. By the end of lunch, Spencer's stained red and crumpled napkin was an ugly duckling in his lap. For the first time in his partnership with Geoff, Spencer sat with a sense of powerlessness, duplicated by the triumphal look Christian flashed across the table. No matter how many scenarios Spencer ran through his mind that day and the months that followed, he couldn't help feeling the deal was just between Geoff and Christian.

Now it was Black Friday. Christian sits down on the couch in the boardroom. The leather gives way with an audible sigh—the smart drugs had taken effect—without the red leather-trimmed boardroom table to anchor Christian's vision, he could be swept out of the landscape window overlooking New York's harbor, and forget what he was doing here. He felt the height of the building—as it held its balance—concrete slabs both vertical and horizontal. In mergers, maintaining vertical balance means moving between shifting levels of reality. Aware of what is actually revealed and what is hidden within agendas.

Christian focused up.

'I think you'll find everything in order, more or less,' Geoff says.

Christian glances at the glossy white folder in front of him, the Biozen letterhead, embossed in gold. Impressive, he thinks. The right proportion of aspiration, inspiration and information. His lawyers and accountants had poured over the offer for weeks. Christian pushes the papers neatly together and smiles at Geoff.

'We are all in agreement then,' Geoff said, looking at Spencer.

'Would you like a pen?' Spencer asked, handing his pen over before Christian can refuse it. Of course, this writing implement was no ordinary pen. It was a forty-nine thousand dollar pen, a status symbol, more expensive than the average family car. When Christian turns the solid silver barrel in his hands, the gold dust and cut diamonds create a cosmic map. As he spins the cap off, he has a flash of Mrs. Kitts in the living room saying he is going to be the wealthiest man in the world. If I use this silver pen, fate rules. If I don't, the world plays to my rules. He replaces the cap on the silver pen and hands it back to Spencer. Christian then reaches inside his jacket and takes out a black pen, signs the documents in twenty-four places, and increases his wealth by three hundred million dollars.

3

LIGHTS MOVE OMINOUSLY along the edge of the dock, throwing green phantom beams over the black waters of the Hudson, 4:30 am—fog and edgeless hoar frost grip the city.

Crossing over the Hudson Bridge in a yellow cab, Agent Michael Steel rubs grains of sleep from his eyes and stares down at the docks in North Harbor, where a constant body of water sucks around redwood piles. He'd fished for sprats there as a kid and watched how seagulls hovered in air eddies. Gulls knew fish. Fish lurk where cloudy water meets clear water. No need for a rod. No need for a reel; drop a line straight down, hook rig and sinker. Once a busy working pier, now only three boats a year moored there, and then just to get fuel tanks flushed. When engineering shops are shut down, wharves become a ghost place, but a certain depth of water near to shore, has its advantages. During the night, an inflatable tender unloaded its cargo, and left unnoticed.

Agent Steel walks into the murder scene at D Dock. Another

dawn—a different kind of murder. The tide is fast, running out. Below the dock, a lifeless bump, a puzzle of sound, melancholy against pylons. Black neoprene frogmen, swim like spawn in a halo of watery green light. A rescue crane with its braided steel cable lowers a heavy freeman hook into the water. The task is to recover an inflatable pink pool chair with a body gaffer taped inside. Water-swollen arms float freely like flaccid tentacles, but the left foot is anchored by hooks from lost lines; old lines wrapped around the oyster encrusted pylon by tides and fleeing fish. Once cut from entanglement, the naked body dangles from the crane's cradle, black water cascading back into the Hudson. Michael scans the tide flowing around the pylons. On the pier, forensic photographers take photos. Intermittent camera flashes, stern and bright in lime light. Reflective yellow tape flutters like kite tails around a white nylon investigation tent on the dock.

Inside the tent, a forensic pathologist examines the remains of the young man. 'Arms slit from wrist to armpit. Either a razor or a scalpel was used to inflict these telling wounds.'

Michael takes a closer look at a black silk cord, and a Medusa of bruises around the neck, blonde hair wet like Neptune's weed. 'Could it have been sexual asphyxiation?'

It is the contents of the wine glass locked in the fingers of the dead man's hand that holds forensic attention. The head of the forensic team sniffs the vague remnants of the glass. 'This isn't a Pina colada. The victim was given a cocktail of Tanqueray gin and quaternary ammonium salt. A potent nerve drug.'

Michael said: 'So the victim would have been incapacitated by the nerve drug, then tortured to death.'

'Sure looks like it,' the pathologist remarked.

'Nightmarish signature,' Agent Fullerton said.

'With this guy, death is in the detail. I think we can expect more deaths and more elaborate poses.'

Michael recognized the pattern: an organized killer working out complex strategies to fulfill his killing fantasy. Michael knew that if he was right about his theory, more people would end up murdered by this serial killer.

THE FORENSIC SCIENCE Center had received a six million dollar grant for refurbishment: solid plinths, exposed columns, and floor slabs that seemed to float, a Brutalist tank of city architecture. The front door is plain, nothing to make a noise, no plate to strike, or bell to ring before you enter the place of silence. Dead silence.

Agent Brooke Fullerton walks along the gray slab path to the morgue. The flowers blooming in rows on either side might be mistaken for perfect plastic daffodils. If you didn't know. But the flowers, with six petal-like tepals, are merely the yellow narcissus, not a sign of a beautiful spring morning. The path leads to the dead. And what the clues found on a victim, reveal about a killer?

Brooke is aware she is late. A mind full of thoughts like Polaroid snapshots had broken into her dreams, and she woke up with a blistering headache. She had stopped in at a drug store on the way to pick up medication.

Michael, always punctual, had arrived on time, half an hour before her. Michael moves along to make space for her on the cold vinyl bench. They sit behind the glass-viewing window, waiting. Michael looks at the body on the examination table below. The walls painted Titanic white have a metallic sheen, morgue rooms hold secrets, and it is up to the technicians to uncover forensic truths. The autopsy examiner pulls down the green morgue sheet.

Brooke whispers to Michael. 'Have I missed much?'

The examiner speaks without looking up. 'Nothing, we're just about to start.' The examiner's white coat has an heirloom string of cultured pearls tucked inside the neckline. Two diamond studs pinned through her dainty earlobes flash the blood diamond red of old mines. As she turns her head, they sparkle under the spotlights. It's the way she works with death—in dazzling detail.

The lifeless body is lying exposed on the metal table. The face, luminously pale, at peace, even though the rest of the body, at a glance, shows hallmarks of excessive violence. These eyes saw things others have not seen, should never see, the examiner thinks. Using the gloved tips of her index fingers, she respectfully closes each eyelid. She rolls one arm and then turns over the other one. She reads the toe tag and cross-references to her clipboard.

'Deceased number 407, male, begins the body count for Monday. The surgical incisions along the skin of the arms have penetrated the top layers of the epidermis, leaving the main veins exposed and intact, which have then been methodically pierced to allow controlled blood loss and sequential coagulation to occur. This life ended with surgical precision.' Looking at her notes, she adds, 'The blood volume had reduced by two-thirds before the heart stopped. Broken flesh does not accompany the bruising around the neck. Restricted airways caused lightheadedness, not death. '

She walks to the foot of the corpse, observes the ankles, and says, 'No sign of hands or feet being restrained.'

She moves up the body, surveying the landscape of flesh and the scrotum sack.

'Testicles removed.'

With gloved hands, she lifts the tanned penis and inserts a metal probe into the urethra. 'There is evidence of semen present in the penis but no intrusion into the anus.'

As she puts down the last instrument, the orchestra of sterilized stainless steel falls quiet. She snaps off her gloves and turns off the recorder. She catches Michael's glance. Her voice echoes slightly through the observation room speakers. 'I wouldn't like to see what he saw. You sure do get them, don't you?'

'So off the record, what are your thoughts on the cause of death?'

'I think the cause of death was shock due to hypoxemia, which is the lack of oxygen in the arterial system. Shock, coupled with emotional terror, would have assisted in eventually shutting the body down. Prior to death, the nerve drug causing muscular paralysis meant he would have lived through the hell of four or five hours of torture.'

'Castrated alive and bled to death,' Michael said, looking at the lacerated body, 'how long before he died?'

'I would guess five hours of blood-loss before death.'

'Anything else?'

'Michael, there is something. You and I have known each other for a decade of autopsies.'

He waits, wondering what is coming next.

The pathologist is stressed. 'I've decided to make this my last case. I've seen more than enough for a lifetime. I want to spend more time with the living.'

The young man in the morgue had been tortured and murdered, bagged and tagged as evidence, awaiting the coroner's verdict.

Outside the morgue, Michael walked Brooke to her car.

Before getting in she said, 'You want a ride?'

'No thanks. I'll catch a cab.'

'That was a grueling session,' she said, through the open window of her car.

It is then Michael notices a cursive script written in the dust on the roof of her Ford: *Clean your act up slut.* He wipes off the last word. She wasn't a slut. He wasn't the only one who watched her drive away. The problem is, when you're looking ahead, you don't always see what's behind you.

A yellow cab came alongside, cruising for a fare. The driver appears familiar, yet Michael can't place the face. The driver took the shortest route to Michael's apartment in East Street and parked alongside the deep drainage curb outside his house.

'1041,' the cab driver says.

Still, Michael can't place the foreign accent. He steps out of the cab into heavy rain. The rainfall in July and August used to flood the basements of every brownstone house in his street. The city council had taken two years to dig up the road and put in flood-water drainage. He glances down the road at the row of terraced townhouses clad in Triassic-Jurassic sandstone, urban sentinels connected to each other, supporting each other. The neighbor-hood felt solid.

Hanging up his coat on the backside of the front door, he sees Charlotte standing in the kitchen. The kitchen was the last room they'd renovated. He'd sanded back fifty years of paint off the French doors, and polished the tongue and groove floorboards. He and Charlotte had designed the kitchen layout together; Viking grill, stainless oven, dual door fridge with ice-maker.

Charlotte has no need to turn around, she feels his presence, and always had, even from the first time they found each other, in the crowded corridor of the university. From that moment ten years ago, they'd studied, made love, graduated, married, and set up the apartment together.

Michael stood in her warmth. 'What's cooking?'

She hands him a glass of wine and leans up against him. Her body instantly ignites him. She feels his warm embrace.

'I haven't made anything yet,' she whispered.

'So this isn't a dinner date?'

They fall laughing into the soft folds of the couch. He unzips her jeans and slowly slips her red hipsters off. He touches her firm, round buttocks with his strong hands. He loves the way the hair at the nape of her neck smells of sunshine and mead-honey. She lifts higher to his touch as he presses into her femaleness. They pass into the candlelight's ambush.

Lying naked and warm on the couch, together, Charlotte is the first to speak. 'If that doesn't make a baby, we'll have to keep trying.'

'If that doesn't make twins, we'll have to go for triplets.'

After a loving hour, they go arm and arm up to the roof garden and step into the moonlight pool. The feel of her body arouses him again, as she wraps her thighs like velvet ties, around him. Together they know the recipe of life, and tonight they have made it happen. He is sure. Soft love waves make the pool flapper thud, but sound brings back the day's demons.

After Charlotte fell asleep, he lay awake, chasing thoughts. Looking around for something familiar, he turns on the Hawaiian hula dancer lamp. Her Bakelite grass skirt, and the coconut palm glowed. He had found her in a second-hand store when he was at college. Michael had been in between girlfriends, the state of his love affairs, and Charlotte was not yet on the scene. This started a joke among his frat friends, that the hula girl was the one. No one could understand why Michael collected old island souvenirs; the outrigger canoes carved in coconut wood with little paddles and the lamp he rescued. Simple things reminded Michael of the simple things in life; a beach where you can catch fish for dinner instead of opening a can of tuna. When he met Charlotte, the hula girl took a back step. But he still held onto the daydream, that one day, he would retire from law enforcement, quit the city, and have a simple life in the islands, just the two of them, swimming amongst a rainbow of tropical fish.

An agent's life isn't straightforward—it's as complicated as human life can be. Broken dreams were the nightmarish reality of law enforcement, but things were about to get a whole lot worse. The carnage he'd witnessed during the week; bloodless, drained, ghostly bloated flesh themed his dreams, and turned them into nightmares. The same trade wind that rustles a grass skirt was blowing his island dreams further away.

CHAPTER

4

MARIA LETS HERSELF INTO Christian's apartment. As she hangs up her checkered coat and puts on her uniform, Shadow purrs and rubs himself around her legs, the feline's way. Unable to ignore the cat, she bends down and strokes him. This is a cat that likes to bring dead mice into the apartment for her. He follows her into the bedroom.

Maria dusts the mahogany tallboy and polishes the wood. On top of the furniture is an antique box inlaid with mother of pearl. This time she notices Christian has forgotten to lock it. Curious about the contents, Maria lifts the lid. There are two layers, like a chocolate box. The top compartment has man's things; an Oyster Rolex, gold coins, gold heraldic rings, and diamond cufflinks. The bottom layer like a pawnbroker's mess of memories; a tangle of women's gold chains, earrings, and rings.

The magpie in Maria takes over. She carefully fingers through the jewelry on the second layer and finds an irresistible gold ring with a cornflower blue sapphire and places the ring on her wedding finger. It fits as if handcrafted for her size. Maria knows better than to steal from the man she wants a future with. She will never steal from Christian. But what is the harm in wearing the ring as long as she puts it back? There is pleasure in everything. She sets to work cleaning the bathroom mirrors.

Cleaning Christian's apartment is the only job Maria has had since arriving in New York City. She was attracted to Christian the second she walked in for the interview three months ago. She pays attention to small details to please him. 'If god is in the details, Maria,' he once remarked, 'you must be the angel he sent to look after me.' That made her smile.

She takes exceptional care. When she puts freshly pressed sheets on the bed, she spritzes them with lavender from Provence as a finishing touch. She makes sure the envelopes on the euro pillowcases face away from the door, the four edges of each white bath towel face into the bathroom, the first sheet on the toilet roll, she folds into a neat triangle. Not a water drop is left on the shower door or mirror.

She spoils him with her care and attention in the hope that one day he will notice not just what she does but who she is as a woman. To realize she is a woman who has fallen in love, and wants to take care of him and his apartment forever. Maria harbors such a fantasy. She imagines and hopes that Christian will return from work, stand in the bedroom doorway and say, Do you come with the room? And she will say, Yes, I do. And he will sweep her down the aisle, her, dressed in bridal organza and lace, take her on a honeymoon to the crystal turquoise of the Bahamas, make beautiful love with her, and have three children, two boys that look just like him and a girl, like her. Then he will buy the house next door and invite her sisters to live close by, send them airline tickets, arrange visas, set them up in business, all legal with green cards.

DREAMS HAPPEN WHILE reality makes other plans. An ocean of suds spills over the spa bath onto the floor, seeping under the door to soak the hand-loomed silk carpet with its tightly woven shells and fishes. Everything is happening, but not the way she imagined it. She pulls the plug. Only when the mess is cleaned up, does she notice the ring is missing from her finger. Has it swept away down the drain? She searches everywhere in a panic then figures; he has so much in that box, he will never miss it, she wishes. But nothing escapes a man like Christian.

He returned home earlier than usual that day. 'Hi Maria, I didn't mean to startle you!'

'Oh, sorry Mr. Christian. I'm not quite finished.'

'Sure. No problem.' He loosens the noose of his silk tie. 'Will you be long?'

She calls after him: 'I've just got to unload the dishwasher.'

He comes back out, just as she is leaving. 'I see you're all washed up,' he says with a smile.

She quickly changed the subject. 'I've put your dry-cleaning in your wardrobe, thirty-one suits, thirty-one laundered shirts all ready, as you like it, although you need twenty-nine for February because it's a leap year.' She said with a sweet smile. 'Perhaps Mr. Christian is a little too organized?'

'Maria, you know me so well.' He stood tall and handsome above her.

Maria gazes into his eyes. Not as well as I'd like to, she thought. Everyone has a lucky day—maybe today was hers.

'I see you're on the way out, but will you stay and have a cup of Travelers Tea? I want to discuss your future here with me.'

My future with him? So he does have feelings for me. 'Yes, I'd love a cup.'

Christian pours water over a muslin bag tied with string and hands her a bone china cup filled with amber liquid. Maria takes a sip.

'I have never tasted anything like it.'

'You won't have unless you've been to Paris.'

She takes another sip and says, 'Black cardamom, oranges, and something else? It escapes me.'

That something else in the tea is a small measure of digitalis.

'Have you been to Paris?'

'Only in my daydreams.'

'It's called the City of Love. I bought a rare sapphire from an exclusive jewelry store along the Champ Elysees. And when I was in Florence, the City of Lilies, I had the stone set in gold by a small jeweler's workshop on the Ponte Vecchio. Remind me to show you the ring sometime.'

'The ring!' She feels the slow, intermittent stuttering of her heart. Her breathing is like a hundred butterflies released into her chest. 'Mother Mary, what is happening?' The scent of orange blossom hangs in the room. There is the scent of white peaches. Sweet, ripe peaches. She sees the blue shutters on the painted house, Mama stands in the doorway in a white cotton dress, not waving, but beckoning to her.

Only the dying can see the dead. She prays she isn't dying.

Christian sits beside her on the couch, and for a while, he says nothing, because there is nothing to say, just combs her hair with absent-minded fingers.

'You know, you're too beautiful to be a maid to me.'

Tracing his fingertips over her mouth, he kisses her on the lips.

'If you can't be my maid, what shall I make of you—my heavenly slave, perhaps?'

He sits back and takes the vision of her in. His eyes hold her unsettled eyes in an intense gaze. 'I'm going to give you what you want while all the gods in heaven watch you, like the dreamer and sinner you are.' She flinched. 'Oh, so you're the virgin, Maria? I should have guessed.'

He makes this her first and last time. Then strokes down the length of her arm with a titanium scalpel blade.

Joe comes in quietly unannounced. 'Christ, Christian! You sure go through the home-help!'

'Yes, sad it had to be her.'

'Who is she?'

'Who knows? She is a maid without connections.' Christian undoes the small silver crucifix that hangs around her neck.

'No family, that's too bad. Everyone needs someone in life.'

Bad things can happen when you cross borders. You can end up dismembered with no backup, and with no one you can call.

Joe wraps a throw rug around her still warm body, picks her up as casually as a bag of dirty laundry, and carries her upstairs. 'Don't worry, you're mine now and always will be. Let me take care of you.'

CHAPTER

5

IT IS ALREADY FRIDAY, and Isabella Jones is in for a nasty surprise. She has a job that is deemed out of fashion and politically incorrect, working as she does for Carson and Sons, the furriers on West 29th Street. The architecture of the area is famous for its elegant arched doorways, stone carvings of squirrels, foxes, and gargoyles that have seen more haute couture days. Her mother worked for the same firm, and Isabella grew up playing hide-and-seek amongst pelts. Carson and Sons are one of the last furriers on the furrier frontier whom she believes has ethical principles and, as long as people kill animals to eat, and make leather shoes, wallets, and handbags, to her, one animal pelt is the same as the next.

The day started badly but not as bad as it would finish. When Isabella arrived at work, the building's façade had been attacked by animal rights activists; red paint splashed over the dark stone walls—*Animals have feelings too*, words scrawled in red. Lily, her co-worker, was waiting for Isabella.

'What a mess. Has the boss seen this yet?'

'Mr. Carson's not here.'

Lily touches the paint and says in her London accent, 'Still feels sticky, a right slaughter.'

'We'll have to call him.'

'It's enough to give him a heart attack. I've heard the trouble and strife left him today.'

'Who?'

'The wife … trouble and strife.'

'Someone else has got some strife. Did you see that yellow Porsche in the alley all covered with red paint or possibly pig's blood?'

'Animal activists never use animal blood.'

'Whatever. The anti-animal cruelty campaigners tagged it big time.'

'Someone's going to be pissed.'

'Yeah, but what knucklehead would leave a Porsche parked in the back alley, overnight?'

'Anyway, shall we call the boss or the cops?'

'Or both?'

'Let me call the boss first.' If Isabella thought the day started off poorly, it was about to get worse.

The boss arrives and sees the bloody graffiti over his much-loved 1920's building—ransacked by the 21st century activists. He makes his mind up to do something drastic. He storms into his office, slams the door, and locks it. At midday, Lily takes a deep breath and knocks timidly.

There is a shuffle on the inside. 'Not now!'

'Well, at least he hasn't jumped out of the window,' Isabella said.

Lily smiled. 'The building's going to cost a bloody fortune to clean up.'

'I've never seen you so happy. Admit it. You'd like to see bilious bosses falling out of the sky like rain and pedestrians threading their way through their dead bodies. Wouldn't you?'

Later, Isabella goes out into the alley to smoke a cigarette. The wind reaches through her cotton dress, cold insistent fingers. She shivers and wraps her blue sweater around her. Moments like this, she wishes she had given up smoking. The store is warm and glows amber with furs, while she is outside in the back alley braving the cold to light up. She is the last smoker among her co-workers. Smoking is no longer a social hobby. It is a lonely occupation. She should make this her last cigarette. Isabella takes a long, slow draw and scans the garbage of the garment district. The back alley, like her, was a little down at the heels, quiet but still interesting. Green dumpster bins piled high with trashy stuff, crushed coffee cups, a riotous carnival of fabric offcuts, and fur scraps. Delivery trucks had finished their early morning run to the fashion stores. Empty wooden pallets lay stacked against the delivery bay wall. A rare slant of sunlight reflects a silver glint. Isabella takes a closer look, and then speed dials her best friend.

'Mia, it's Isabella.'

'Where are you?'

'Taking a break.'

'A smoke?'

'Yes. I need one!'

'Smoking is a slow death.'

'Yeah, I know. I'm not in any hurry!'

'Ha-ha.'

'I found something.'

'What?'

'I think I've found a fur coat.'

'Well, you *are* surrounded by them all day!'

'No, I'm in the alley. It's fallen off the back of a truck.'

'And you want to keep it?'

'Well … what do you think?'

'Has anyone else seen it?'

'Don't think so.'

'Maybe it's a gift from above? Who knows, you could do with a warmer coat.'

'Is there a finder's keeper's rule here?'

'Yeah—you find it, you keep it—then I can borrow it.'

'How's this. If it is still here when I finish work, it's mine. If not, then it's not meant to be.'

'Exactly. Call me if it fits.'

Isabella went inside to finish her shift. Just as she came back in, the boss walked out of his office and called a meeting.

Lily turned to Isabella. 'He appears calm, don't you think?'

'No, I think it's an act.'

'He's got envelopes in his hands.'

'I've called this meeting to say goodbye.'

All the idle chat stops—an audible hush.

'I never wanted to be a furrier. My father started this business, and I carried on by default, I'm here to tell you, I was not born to make something beautiful out of dead animals. This afternoon is the end of an era. Isabella, Jessica, Lily, Amelia, please step forward.'

One by one, he called every employee's name in the room and handed each the necessary severance paycheck. Isabella looked inside her envelope, expecting some sort of bonus for all the years of service. True to his nature, no more and no less, no apology. Forever remembered as a tight ass.

With her last pay packet at the bottom of her bag, she walks out into the wintery air. She contemplates the pile of crates against the wall. No one had moved them. A steel door opens, a storekeeper throws the day's trash bags into the dumpster. She waits until the hydraulic door shuts behind him. Then she tries to lift the pallet to get at the coat bag. Shadows make the bag blacker. 'Oh, shit.' Isabella pulls harder until the pallet shifts, and out it comes. She guesses by the weight there's a full-length fur inside. If it is pale mink, not dark, she will wear it out with the girls, but then real fur is not politically correct, ranch farmed minks and all that controversy. She'll say its just imitation, but looks real.

Today is going to be the best day of Isabella's life after all. With no more than a measly severance pay from that bleeding furrier, she deserves this. Isabella lifts the bag over her shoulder, walks out of the alley, and hails a cab.

On the way from work to home, all she thinks about is the coat in the bag, and how easy it is to accept something she finds, as only belonging to her, the one who found it. If her mother asks where the coat came from, she'll say, 'It's an early Christmas bonus from the firm. I've been there for fifteen years, so I deserve it.' No, she won't believe that, so she'll say, 'I've got a new boyfriend.' That will make her happy, a Mother's dream. Her daughter finds a rich guy, settles down, and makes her a grandmother. Isabella can't wait to get back to her apartment to feel the luxury of her mink wrapped around her body. She knows it takes sixty ranch-farmed minks to make a full-length mink coat, each female blue-iris mink costs one hundred and seventy-five dollars. Maybe it isn't a mink coat. What if it is chinchilla? What will she do if it's rabbit? Throw it away in a dumpster, but on the other side of town. The cab stops, absent-mindedly she pays the fare, more dollars than she should.

She can hardly wait to get inside. She can already feel the warmth and luxury of mink. Pale mink, please! Isabella hangs the bag on the back of her bedroom door. The bag she found has a purpose.

She must convince herself the coat is not theft but a gift. Only then can she open it and keep what is inside. First things first, she must have patience and not give in to temptation. Blessed are those who wait. Patience is a virtue.

Of all the coats in the bible, she can think of only one—Joseph's coat of many colors. Hers is a coat of many minks stitched together. So what is the clue there? Joseph was the favorite and was given a special coat, but it made others jealous, so they planned to kill him. Wearing a special coat could make others jealous, she thinks, but not enough to kill her. What did Mary wear in the bible? Animal skins?

She doesn't know what is in the bag, but later she will understand. Some things should be left exactly as you find them. She unzips the garment bag, and pukes violently. Then, her horror becomes screams, heard through the timber floor, by a family living two stories down.

6

IT IS SEVEN IN the evening. Michael has just poured two glasses of red wine when the phone rings. Michael answers the call in his most unenthusiastic voice. 'This better be good, Brooke.'

'Am I interrupting you?'

'Yes.'

'The Deboner has struck again.'

'Where?'

'Hanging on the back of a woman's bedroom door.'

He picks up his gun and zips up his leather jacket.

'Got to go.'

'OK, darling man, just come back home safe.'

'Don't I always? Don't go out for anything tonight.'

'Not even street walking?'

His face doesn't pull a smile.

'Sorry babe, serial murderers kill my sense of humor.'

Michael leaves the place he didn't want to leave and goes to a scene he doesn't want to see. Just as he gets in the car, he sees a piece of paper tucked under the windscreen wiper. He scrunches the note into his pocket. By the time he waits at the red light, the crumpled piece of paper is playing on his nerves, enough to bring a closed file forward from the back of his mind. The riddle in his pocket reads like a personal threat. He rings Charlotte on his mobile.

'Hi, did you forget something?'

'I just rang to say I miss you already.'

'And?'

'Lock the doors.'

Michael arrives at the crime scene to find rows of police vehicles blocking off the street. Flashing lights turn delicate falling snow hazardous orange, blue and red. He flashes his badge and goes into the apartment building, acknowledges Brooke with a nod.

'Same as the others?'

'Yes. The bones have been ransacked.'

He goes up to the first floor, apartment 10. The awful smell of decaying flesh penetrates bricks and mortar. He walks down the hallway; the walls were rendered plaster over brick, typical of 1920's architecture. A kitchen with Formica table, chrome chairs upholstered in rose pattern vinyl. The bedroom door is open. Blue and yellow walls like a summer's day at the seaside. There is no sign of blood splatter or evidence of a struggle. The apartment is tidy, and more than that, the bedroom lacks the dark vibration killing gives a place. But there it is on the back of the door, a sack of human flesh. The coat hanger suspends a completely boned-out body. In a thread-like fashion of the macabre haute couture, the killer has taken everything the woman had inside her. Not a frenzied attack, but carefully executed with a sharp-tempered blade, like an abattoir knife, a gutter's knife, to cut through muscle, sinew, fat, and flesh, slice by slice, how the killer carves his prey. The radius and ulna of the arms cut off at the shoulder, each rib bone cut off at the sternum, shoulder bones, and clavicle removed, and the empty shoulders slung over a coat hanger, legs cut from crotch to ankles, flayed out, how prey is sometimes turned inside out to remove the internals, leaving a flesh sack behind for someone to find. A woman hanging in an abattoir coat, depleted of anything human, except for those hazel eyes. Michael contemplates the victim's face, her eyes distant and watery as if she had watched someone blink her out of existence.

Blood was a river of passing events. Michael had seen twisted kills of psychopaths before. The more he looked at red blood, the more one thought soaked up another, and another took its place, and that too was swept away. It was all part of life, which worried him. The presence of evil is out there—impossible to destroy.

'What a mess! This is the second body bag we've found from the garment district.' Right now Brooke is stressed out and tired, eyes gritty and red, a late-night face, another night of sleep sacrificed. 'It's ironic. A woman dead inside the garment bag of Carson and Sons, the classiest fur house in the city. The other night, animal rights activists splashed red paint over that building and a Porsche in the alley.'

They strip off their Tyvek suits. Brooke pulls off her mask and wishes she hadn't. Death is a smell in and out of itself. Such gore triggers the gag reflex and makes even iron stomachs heave.

'You're a paler shade of white,' Michael said. 'Let's get some black coffee.'

They go around the corner to the 24 hour diner.

'So what have we got?'

'I know what we haven't got, two hundred and six bones,' Michael said.

'Neanderthal happenings, in New York? Humans defleshing other humans is not new. The ritual goes back six hundred thousand years.'

'But why is it happening in the 21st century?'

'He's a bone harvester! I figure he's got heaps of bones in his possession right now.'

'He must need them for something because he's escalating his body harvest. This is his second kill in a month.'

'But with this one, he has painted her face with a dark brown viscous resin, like a mask.'

'We'll get the substance results later, but it smells a bit like bitumen. The tar they use on road surfaces before the grit goes down.'

'There's also an autoerotic element,' Michael said. 'Semen was found in the body cavity. And if he runs true to form, he'll perform repeated autoerotic acts over his cache of souvenirs from the kill.'

'A bone wanker! What the fuck!'

'And the victims to date are border jumpers, working for cash, with no government identity.'

'Without social security, that gives us a big problem.'

'We have brutally murdered unidentified women and no answers.'

Michael is interrupted by his phone. When he hangs up, he says, 'They've found a handbag in the dumpster near Carson's. Guess what they found inside?'

'Lipstick, mascara?'

'Sixty laundry tickets.'

'That's a lot of dirty washing.'

'Perhaps the woman worked as a maid.'

Michael turns a piece of paper over on his notepad; paper has two sides, there are two sides to everything, right versus wrong, good versus evil, there is no separation, one exists with the other— a laundry ticket has two facings.

'The killer has an above-average IQ. He has the charisma to manipulate these women into a sense of security. He maneuvers his victims into a vulnerable position through alcohol or some other social drink, like coffee or tea, so he can administer a nerve agent. This degree of control and orchestration of the situation turns this guy on. He'll be well thought of in the community, earning more than the average person, a professional with a respectable persona. You would never guess by looking at him that he's a serial killer, and his signature crimes tell us he's an egocentric psychopathic narcissus.'

'The laundry tickets are an accidental clue,' Brooke said. 'I don't think the killer wanted those to be found.'

The local NYPD checked out the laundry records and camera footage and matched the handbag to the victim. The woman had been a regular customer over the past two months. It seems the maid was working for someone with too much dirty laundry. No doubt it'll all come out in the wash.

BY EARLY MORNING, Brooke and Michael are past the exhaustion stage, heading into overdrive, with the irritation that comes from working the graveyard shift. Like passengers walking off a long haul flight, they walk behind the woman, or what is left of a woman, zipped up for the second time in a black bag and wheeled on a gurney down the hallway to the waiting ambulance. When it bleeds, it leads; crime and death are the fodder of breaking news. By five o'clock in the morning, the crowd outside the apartment had tripled. There was one thing everyone wanted to see, to make the wait worthwhile. Some people climbed trees and fire escapes. Others, daredevil parapets and balconies—to get a better look. The end of life doesn't come with a beginner's guide. No one asks to die. A murder of crows, sixty or more, caw raucously overhead, shadowy and vague. The crowd turn silent watching the body being moved down the steps, as if shifted out like an old couch, to make room for the new one.

The morning sun appears on time for sunny-side up in the city; freshly brewed coffee, hot buttered toast, orange juice, waffles, bacon, cereal, and a suicide in the morning paper. The headline reads: Bankrupt furrier shot himself in the heart, leaving a note to tell everyone: "My body should go to science, my soul to my dog, my sympathy to my creditors."

Michael walks Brooke to her car and waits until he sees the red tail lights disappear. He needs sleep like a car needs gas, while a suicide and a serial killer make breaking news on the TV channels.

C H A P T E R

7

CHRISTIAN OPENS THE FRONT door to find a delivery guy holding out a consignment docket.

'Two deliveries for a Mr. Joe Cutter?'

'I'll sign for that.'

Christian goes into the darkened studio balancing a painting under one arm and holding a cardboard box. He puts the painting face down on the table and turns on the light. To his surprise, Joe is there.

'How long have you been in the dark?'

'Not until you arrived.'

'Why do you spend so much time in the dark?'

'I can see more in the dark.'

'Do you want to know what I think? You're as obsessive as you are reclusive.'

'Thanks for the compliment.'

'And maybe a little crazy? I'm not saying you are. You're the artist.

You paint hundreds of paintings, and you never think they're right. But you have to turn your mind off sometimes. You obsess and never go out socially. What's up with that?'

'I have this mental image of my creative self—alone.'

'And you are always—alone?'

'Yes. And I don't need a shrink to get back in line with the rest of the narcissists, ignorant, brainwashed, shallow, mindless, vacuous state of the materialistic culture, with all its fakeness. I don't want that life.'

'I'm just saying, you can choose to stay inside and live as the artist, but recluses are more likely to commit suicide.'

'Somewhere in the world, someone is always killing themselves. But have I ever said anything about killing myself?' Joe didn't mention the voice that comes to him, insisting he paints death into life.

Christian opens one of the deliveries. 'I've got this for you from Sotheby's auction house in London. Cost an arm and a leg.'

It is the original pastel of Edvard Munch's *Der Schrei der Natur— The Scream of Nature*, known to art lovers as *The Silent Scream*. The effect of the original up close reaches out to the artist in Joe. His eyes follow along the lines of cadmium yellow, orange, vermilion, and the railings of black.

'You can feel palpable terror,' Joe murmured. 'One hundred and twenty years later, the painting is still screaming.'

Christian places it on the marble mantle over the fireplace. 'There is something else. I was researching in the library and found this quote by the art historian James Levi: *Munch lived in a world that straddled life and death. His reclusive nature meant that he found it impossible to exhibit his paintings. Then within a few years, his fame spread throughout the art world.* I looked further and found that Munch, just before he became famous, became involved in a secret society of painters and writers. It was then, Munch made the acquaintance of a famous pigment maker that supplied the great artists of the time. The pigment maker was a man named Cutter. A distant relative of ours. Artists are not special, you know, art is just another job.' Christian waited for what he said to sink in.

'Creativity and craft is the line you and I draw in the sand.'

'Being obsessed won't make you a better creator. You just need better tools. Since your blenders have buckled blades, I've got you something to sharpen up your act. Something that will help you carry on in the family tradition, as it turns out.'

Christian opens the other package. Inside, there is a heavy-duty commercial blender. He sets it up, turns it on, and throws in a handful of flat-head nails. The tempered steel blades spin as a thousand shuriken assassin stars, turning coffin-sized nails into iron filings.

Christian smiles. 'Comes with a lifetime guarantee.'

'Whose lifetime? There are no guarantees in this life. Or the next.'

'Now, let's try it out on the real thing.'

Upstairs, Christian opens the double airlock laboratory doors. An airlock entrance prevents the escape of inhabitants and the entry of predators. Light-locks minimize outside light, which gives the illusion that a room is clean, benevolently pure—mistakenly. Christian drops bones onto blades; rigid pale ivory recoils.

I believe it looks like bones
Curse them, for no one is spared
Blend! Blend! There is no end
Still the sound of breaking bones.

And when the motor stopped, it was full of whitish powder. Joe takes a generous pinch between his fingers and rubs it together.

'Fine as French talcum.'

'She said she was from Toulouse.'

'A perfect mix,' Joe said.

Joe takes down an antique terracotta jar from a high shelf, unseals it, and a dark liquid oozes out, smelling rank, like burnt iodine and mildew, with the rottenness of meat gone bad and old linen bandages unwashed for six hundred years. 'Eugene Delacroix used this exact brown pigment.'

'Now you can paint the town brown.' Christian leaves Joe in the laboratory, grabs a bunch of keys, and takes the elevator to the basement garage.

8

To CHRISTIAN, WITH HIS sexist ways, his car is like a fabulous woman; model perfect, beautifully built, great looking from behind. The raised center console places the gear lever just where he wants it. Everything he touches responds. Christian's car is a customized yellow hue, like none other. This yellow instills a feeling in him, a consciousness that he is different from every other human being. Surrounded by intense yellow, he is the Yellow Emperor. The Porsche badge is the stamp of status that no one can erase. He is loaded and doesn't mind spending a fortune on objects he desires. Rich men can't be bothered with matters of petty cash.

Christian powers out of corners faster than he drives into them. The Porsche demolishes the concrete ribbons of the stack interchange. He takes the last exit. As he pulls up to a red light, a woman in a black convertible catches his eye, her engine idling. If it were a summer's day, she'd have the top down, and he would toss his business card into her lap, but her window is up, on account of it being a freezing day where the sun has no heat in it whatsoever—a day of extraordinary mortification—darker than most. Then the red light changes to green, and by the time the music track changes to '*Boulevard of Broken Dreams*', he's forgotten how she looks.

IDEAS DON'T COME out of nowhere. They don't fall out of the sky. He drives to The Medici Library building. Two uniformed guards were on duty, each packing a Glock 10mm. Security was as necessary as it should be, and bullets speak for themselves. Books change thought, overthrow governments, and unlock the unfathomable mysteries. Stolen irreplaceable books fetch millions of dollars on the black market. Book theft was exactly what Christian had in mind.

The guard gives him a car park ticket. 'You have four hours, no more, no less … or, maybe more.' The guard palms the hundred dollar bill and folds it into his back pocket.

At the information desk, a librarian greets Christian. She feels his eyes assessing her features, as considered and carefully as she scans Christian's details on the computer. Every action leaves a trail behind; his alumni, university transcripts, doctorate degrees, companies, and marital status. Of all the information, the fact that Christian is still a single guy interests her the most. She knows something he doesn't. He is going to ask her to marry him. She will go from Ms. invisible librarian to Mrs. C. Cutter by the following year.

Marriage is on the cards. Harper had visited the most famous clairvoyant in the city. By the spread of cards from the black velvet bag, Harper believed what she wanted to believe—Christian and she would get married, go on an extended honeymoon to Venice, and they'd sip peach Bellini's at The Gritti Palace, make love in the Grand Canal room with its silk damask walls. She'll catch her naked reflection in Venetian mirrors as she steps out of a carved four-poster bed onto dark oak parquet floors. A waiter will bring breakfast on a brass trolley, and they'll sit on the balcony over the canal, drinking strong espresso and biting into dusky plums and baked brioche with damson jam, and perhaps, some late summer apricots. Yes, a romantic place, that's where he'll take her.

The clairvoyant had reshuffled the cards and said, 'The Knight of Cups: your proverbial knight in shining armor, someone special will court you. He is a tall, dark, handsome, and successful businessman. Your next card, the Ace of Cups: a new relationship with excitement and happiness. The Lovers card: a deep connection between two people. The Hierophant card: a long-term committed relationship in marriage. And finally, The Yellow Emperor card: a strong male figure and a long-term partner.'

If the cards are right, this makes her the Empress, a beautiful, fertile, and expressive woman. What Harper had forgotten was the way the clairvoyant had reshuffled the cards and tapped the Emperor with her yellow nicotine-stained finger, and with a severe look of disdain, gathered up the pack and never said another word.

Harper asked, a little dreamily: 'Could you please sign here.' She hands Christian her pen, an offer he ignores, as always, preferring to use his own.

The importance of signatures as evidence. How many signatures will be signed in a lifetime? Signatures attached to library ledgers, property deeds, insurance claims, mergers, and replications. How many types of signatures will be left behind? How many signings before he is dead?

The library is quiet, sedated. Christian follows Harper, watching how she moves in her tight pencil skirt, down a corridor of books, and into the inner sanctum. A woman can feel a man looking at her curves.

'No eye candy allowed, Mr. Cutter.'

She redirects his interest to the pile of books he had requested over the phone. The leather-bound manuscripts were nature themselves; glue from the gum, ink from plants. The words inside penned with feather quills, books with marbled fly verso, sealed with wax, red as pigeon's blood. So it was. The timeless wisdom inside swallowed the remains of Christian's day.

'Mr. Cutter!'

Christian came out of his monastery of thoughts.

'It's way past closing time. You are the last one in the library.'

'I hope I'm not keeping you from anything.'

'No, I've got nothing pressing. Have you found what you are looking for?'

'Not quite.'

'Then I may have what you want.'

Harper climbs the rolling library ladder. As she reaches up to lever a book from the shelf, Christian puts both hands on her thighs to steady her. If his focus had been on her face instead of her ass, he would have seen the signature dimple a smile puts on her cheek. Harper comes back down the ladder, puts on white cotton gloves, and indicates he does the same. As he turns the pages, her brunette hair falls loose, brushing his face with a heady scent of jasmine and vanilla. He glances around, nothing but oak-paneled walls, heavy antique desks, polished wood floors, and worn leather couches. In this bookish sanctuary, he is about to turn a public space into their private place.

He takes a cigar from his inside pocket, takes off the wrapper, and rolls it in his mouth until the outside of the cigar is wet. He strikes a light and holds the burning match up to her until he sees fear rising in her eyes. 'You can't smoke in here. What are you thinking?'

Only then does he blow the flame out.

'I'll show you what I am thinking. I'll show you Castro's secret. He knew how to make a thousand dollar Cuban even more perfect.'

First, he kisses her full on her lips. She tastes so good. Then he undoes her white work shirt while she unzips her skirt and pulls him closer. The perfume on her skin, Jasmine Noir, mingled with the scent of her. Having sex with Harper was like a soft porn movie, only better. She gives in to him like she has given in to him before. They have great sex until the cleaners in the room next door disturb them. In a post-coital fumble they struggle to identify personal pieces of clothing strewn over the floor.

He took what he wanted from her, but still wasn't satisfied. The spell was broken. He wants something more from her, more than vanilla sex, and he wants it badly. Christian needs Harper to give it to him, he has something in mind, and she is a part of it.

'Show me the original manuscript, including notes from the alchemist Croll.'

He is about to be let into a secret deemed too dangerous for everyone to learn. Such knowledge can be decentering, frightening, unsettling, a psychologically perilous place. He had chosen this woman to take him there.

'*The Lost Writings of Paracelsus*. A medical alchemy, is that what you want?'

'Yes. The only manuscript about the transmutation of the life spark.'

However, Harper had a foreboding she couldn't shake. One thing can change everything. If she hands over the restricted book, her future will be in his hands. Rules would be broken. Rules are fragile and shatter reality like glass, if you break them.

Christian smiles. His smile is a key to unlock anything in the world, and he knows it. Anxious feelings bypass Harper's instincts, and she opens the cabinet door. She hands Christian the book.

Christian takes a series of photos with his mobile phone.

'Photography is forbidden.'

'Who will tell?'

Oswald Croll's *Basilica Chymica: The Book of Corpse Medicine* has a recipe for the *Confection of Paracelsus* using three unburied human skulls. *Flesh that perishes three violent deaths and kept for one night, exposed in the open air to gather dew, in a serene time, awakens the dreaming eye and the dawn of life will ensure.* There is another recipe in the book for *Treacle of Mummy: An excellent remedy against all kinds of venoms.*

Treacle could be useful for Joe, perhaps, but venoms? Do they mean venom? Christian has another thought. He turns the manuscript on an angle and sees a correlation of symbols to text. The leather binding creaks and parchment pages give way to a faint auditory phrase, 'misuse will destroy you.' Christian closes the manuscript.

Restrictions on original books are there for a reason. Whatever is written down has another meaning. Hidden symbols in the text should be revealed to the initiated only. When Harper turns away, Christian conceals *The Book of Corpse Medicine*. The flesh to perish, the gathering dew, the dreaming eye, all illicitly tucked away inside his briefcase, breaking library rule number two. The book thief never borrows what he can take.

Harper gives him a look of attachment. 'So what are we going to do now? Late dinner? My place?'

He gives her a kiss on the cheek, short as a peck, and walks out the door—without looking back.

A SOFT RAIN FALLS, slanting through golden spires at the far end of Brooklyn Bridge. The quiet rain smudges a burnt orange sunset. A curtain of damp mist surrounds a man gripping the bridge handrail, a runner glances fleetingly at the man, but runs on by.

Joe runs for the sweet spot of the runner's high. It makes him feel better, like medicine, if you remember to take it. He stops on the wood-slatted walkway and breathes in the city ether; wet steel, weed, and river brine, before heading back home. He arrives back at the apartment as the elusive runner's high fades. He pauses under the arched Gothic entrance to the apartment with its stone foxes like feral watchdogs, two gargoyles—one skinning a mink, the other sewing a pelt, their haunting grimaces set in weathered stone, etched by acid rain.

Joe swipes the black keycard, and the heavy oak door unlocks with a click. In the foyer stands an ornate cage lift, made in an era where going somewhere was about style, not time. Joe didn't have time for its antique idiosyncrasies, so he took the marble staircase.

'Christian, are you there?' An empty echo resounds in the marble void. The metamorphose of sweat had saturated his t-shirt and formed the shape of a moth on his back, distinctly light and dark purple, it had morphed, like the Eacles imperialis found amongst dying hemlocks. Soaked from rain and sweat, Joe peels off his sodden clothes and throws them into the hamper, takes a hot shower, then changes into jeans and black hooded sweatshirt.

If creativity is a magnetic force, Joe feels it pull him into his studio. The studio is his real world, an eccentric place, and a hidden place. Crushed tubes of paint, jars of brushes, wooden easels, oil skimmed palettes, stacks of art books, and torn-out pages from a habit of mutilating art magazines—images for the imagination. He picks up Edward Munch's *Silent Scream of Nature*, sinks into the Kensington leather couch, and reads how Munch's reclusive nature, as an agoraphobic, made it impossible for him to exhibit. Yet within a few short years, his fame had seemed to spread mysteriously throughout the art world, in a wildfire of pastels and paint. Of all the art Munch created, Joe was drawn to the painting of *The Scream*. How underlying bones stretch the skin around an open mouth to form a void. He read Munch's brush lines as emotive text, cadmium yellow, orange, vermilion, and understood the foreboding hand rail.

Joe has an idea. He removes a cloth to uncover a painting. A frustrating work in progress. The face he had been struggling for nine months to resolve. Capturing the emotional state of fear on canvas is a transcendental challenge. The more he had worked on the painting, the more it continued to perplex him. No matter how many times he'd scraped back the ordinary, he couldn't bring the image to life.

'If the language of art summates all existence and creativity is a universal force, you should use it.' Joe hears the voice from beyond his imagination. 'You are il Divino. Genius gives birth, and talent delivers. No longer crush the urge to create, feel what you paint. Take the blade!' Joe takes the same scalpel he uses for sharpening his drawing pencils, and without hesitation, cuts straight down his forearm; suddenly blood wells up and runs freely, dripping off his fingers onto the slate floor. He screams silently into the mirror. The movement of the jawbones stretches the skin over his upper face, giving it a yellow caste. Joe picks up a hog bristle brush. 'More yellow than green, you need insight to see.' The voice trails off. Joe paints.

'You've almost got it, but not quite enough.'

'Not enough of what?'

'For fear absolute, add green at the edge of cadmium yellow.'

'Like this? Now what?'

'Run the brush through the two.'

Joe picks up the flat-edged sable brush.

'Now, look at the handrail of the bridge, why use so much black?'

'Black is the only true color in the color spectrum. It absorbs all light and all life.'

'Black is a dead color. That has always been your problem.'

Joe loads up his black sable brush with a shade of mummy brown, an umber, as it touches the canvas, the man who stands on the bridge releases his grip on the railing, holds his head in agony, and screams the scream of a person in terror. Then distinct silence.

'Now you know it's not what you paint,' graveled the voice from the grave of the long deceased pigment maker Griuik Cutter. 'It's what you paint with.'

At that moment, the past reached out and touched the artist within Joe, changing his ideas on creating art forever.

What he dares to create, from that time on, will undo him.

10

MICHAEL FELL ASLEEP AS soon as his head hit the pillow, and a good thing it was a feather one. The weight of thoughts that filled his head were enough to give him whiplash.

Sleep hadn't found Charlotte the same way. She wanders into the living room and surfs the television channels; a commercial for Florida orange juice, orange candy bullets, orange as the new black on the fashion channel, how to graft navel oranges with oranges from Seville, terracotta pots with topiary orange trees. She opens the refrigerator and gulps orange juice straight from the carton. Cravings are the litmus of pregnancy.

Pregnant?

Charlotte goes into the bathroom. The packet of Clear Blue in the medicine cabinet is empty. She remembered how the negative results made her feel, and how the tub of chocolate-chip ice cream filled her in a cold vacuous way. She wanted a baby as much as she wanted to marry Michael and settle down in the first place. A baby was part of the package. Pregnant or not, perhaps the single most life-changing question every woman in her reproductive life, wants answered. Now she is just another desperate woman wanting to know, will the wand show blue or pink this month, or nothing at all? Now out of the blue, she has a feeling she is pregnant.

Charlotte wraps up for the cold and locks the apartment door behind her. She does what she knows she should never do. Go out alone in the late hours in New York City. The cold light interplayed shadows, not that she notices, her mind on other things, the moon casts the shape of magician's hat, then a shadow rabbit right there on the sidewalk, a gray rabbit of unforeseen circumstances. The rabbit moves ahead of her. Everyone is born with a shadow. This night there are two actual shadows: her own and a coatless shadow of a man with a plan that would scare the Devil. The twenty four hour drug store is one block away.

Michael is asleep under the feather duvet, having a nightmare of his won. He sees a priest holding a small animal, the victim of a predator; a white rabbit hunted down and caught. Michael is floating away, the rabbit indistinct, a snowdrift on the horizon, a white puff of cumulus cloud; like a sleeper losing connection with landmarks. The priest, sinister, not a minister, strokes the animal with an offhanded but bemused tenderness. And as Michael dreams on, the innocent skinned rabbit, dead and pale, turns into the young man lying in the morgue. Michael wakes up to the rusty taste of blood. He'd bitten down on his tongue.

Charlotte re-enters the apartment as stealthily as she left. She rips open the brown paper bag. Inside is the pregnancy testing kit. She drinks a glass full of water and goes to the bathroom to take the test. She checks again to be sure. There is a first time for everything; pregnant for the first time, followed by first baby steps, first baby teeth, first words, first tantrum, first day at school.

Michael opens the bathroom door. 'What's up?' He stifles a yawn. 'Party of one?'

'Happy birthday!' Charlotte hands him the pregnancy stick.

'Is this what I think it is!'

'We're pregnant!'

'You sure?' He hugs Charlotte.

The moon sinks as the carbon night edges lighter. They sit talking in the kitchen, eating cinnamon and raisin toast together.

'I can hardly wait to phone Mom.'

'She'll be sound asleep.'

'What time is it?'

'3 am.'

'Oh. Why were you awake?'

'Nightmare.'

'Not the man in black again?'

'This time, the priest was a holding a white rabbit by its hind legs—then he slit its belly open and skinned it alive.'

'On the positive side, to skin something means you're having the bare truth revealed to you. The truth is we're pregnant. A white rabbit means you have a desire to be a parent. And you know how rabbits breed!'

Michael wasn't a man to decipher the undecipherable, but a recurring dream speaks to the sleeper to open their eyes. Michael hugged Charlotte, but as he held her close, his lizard brain, where instincts warn of danger, felt the black priest shadowing.

Illuminated by industrial lights, the indoor climbing center defied the edge of night. A woman was climbing the wall. Of all the women Joe had seen climbing, he felt attracted to this woman in particular, how agile and fluid she was in her movements. Zak, the climbing instructor, comes over and stands beside Joe.

'Like a cat,' Joe said. 'She swings through the dead point, the split-second point, where most people fall.'

'Haven't seen you down here for months, but you still look in fit climbing form. You training someplace else?'

'Oh, I climb here and there when I can.'

Joe opens his chalk bag and dusts his palms for grip. A way to avert his eyes from the woman; aware of how long he had been watching the sweat form a patch on her back, a pattern like ethereal frayed wings. Joe moves closer to her, drawn in by instinct. For moths emit scented pheromone trails, like tendrils to pull in males from the night. He swings into the first-hand hold below her. His strength and fluidity take him towards her. But just as he reached the top of the climb, she rappelled down past him, and as her feet touched the ground, she threw a jacket over her frayed wings and left.

Joe went to the climbing center every night. No sign of her. He tried going earlier on Saturday, still no sign. The mind is like an iCloud, the way it stores images, black Lycra, long sleeves rolled up over muscular, tanned arms, white chalk smudge on her forehead, her rough-cut blonde hair that gave her face a tough yet angelic look.

A week later, Joe asked Zack: 'Have you seen the woman who climbs the southern wall?'

'You mean Alexis? Not lately. She phoned and canceled all her upcoming training sessions but didn't say why.'

Like a bird uncaged, she had flown past him, perhaps never to return. Days turned into too many weeks. Then one night, she walked in slightly favoring her left side, the hood up on her faux fur jacket, a bruise on her cheek casting an indiscreet shadow across her face.

Zack walks over to her. 'You take a fall?'

'You could say that,' she hesitates, 'I was with someone I fell for.'

'Well, you're back, and it's good to see you.'

Meantime, Joe came to the pinnacle of his climb and checked his Rolex. Just as he thought, he had beaten his last climb time and rappelled down the rope, landing on the floor beside Alexis.

'Great climb,' were the first words she said to him.

Joe is close, aware of her warmth.

'I've seen you before,' she said, taking in his entire physique. 'I felt your eyes watching me on the wall last time I was here.'

'Sorry, I couldn't help it. You are beautiful, you know.'

'You chatting me up? Mr ....?'

'Joe Cutter.'

'Can I tell you something?'

'What is it?'

'You know, the sweat on your back has made a pattern, a butter-fly!'

Butterflies in the evening are an omen. Joe turned around and looked in the mirror on the wall opposite. The sweat had formed the outline of a moth, only seen in drug-induced dreams. Yaqui sorcerers knew it as the guardian of eternity, carrying the golden dust of knowledge.

'It's a moth.'

'You sure?'

'I couldn't be surer,' he said, smiling into her eyes. 'The night belongs to the moth.'

'I better get on with this,' Alexis said, looking up. 'Any advice?'

'Hold tight.'

'I intend too.' She reaches into her chalk pouch. 'Darn, I'm out of chalk.'

Joe takes a handful of his chalk and rubs it into her palms. She feels the pressure of forbidden pleasure. Alexis and Joe then climb together for twenty minutes before rappelling back down to earth.

Joe unclipped his safety line. 'We make a great team, don't you think?'

'I think we do. I haven't had this much fun in months.'

Joe picks up her duffel bag.

She looks at her bag in his hand. 'Are we going someplace?'

'How about my place?'

She pauses a fraction too long.

'A video of the Everest ascent?' Joe ventured.

'Well, if you put it that way, but I've got to stop by the apartment and feed two dogs.'

'Can't the dogs wait?'

'If they don't get their dinner on time, they chew shoes, bags, you name it.'

'They sound like demons, not dogs.'

'Yep, demonstrative dogs at best. The only dogs expelled from canine obedience school, so the urban legend goes. They're not my dogs. The apartment isn't mine either. A long story. But I'll explain later.'

Joe tears a page out of his sketchbook, draws a butterfly, then writes his address on the back. Alexis folds the paper delicately, like a keepsake.

'I'll see you in an hour then?'

Without thinking she says yes.

ALEXIS DROVE OVER the Brooklyn Bridge, wondering if this was another one of her 'yes' situations. Yes or no was complicated. Yes had not always turned out well, especially with good-looking men. But on the other hand, saying no got you nowhere. Maybe she should stay home and forget about going to Joe's. She had only just met the guy. But if she didn't go, what then? Stay in and watch the movie channel? A white sweater would highlight her tan, she thought, as she ran a stop sign. After a ticket from the traffic cop, she arrived back at her apartment.

She fed the dogs and put them out on the balcony to do their business on the fake grass, but dogs being dogs, whimpered at the door, and Alexis, being a soft touch, let them back inside. 'Don't you guys get into mischief. I'll be back in a couple of hours.'

She found the street where Joe lived. There he was, leaning against a black painted railing, still as a statue. In the Gothic stone archway, the overhead light threw a dark shadow over his face, but it disappeared when he saw her.

'Come upstairs. I've got a surprise for you.'

The lift shuddered, before settling into the slow journey upward. Brick by brick, internal architecture passes by them. The shaft had wine racks built-in, like a vertical cellar, stacked full of expensive vintage wines. He stops the lift and pulls out a bottle of red. And they ascend.

This apartment is nice and arty, Alexis thinks, as the doors open to Joe's studio. Joe flicks a switch, and automatic flames lick the logs in the fireplace. She pulls off her boots and settles into the faded leather couch.

'I was going to say, make yourself at home, but I can see you already have.'

She gazes at Joe's handsome face. Blue pools of eyes inviting her into his world.

'You've got a lovely place here.'

'So where do you live?'

'Nowhere permanent, till next month.'

'How come?'

'I'm waiting for major renovations to finish at 23rd Street, between Seventh and Eighth Avenue.'

'You're moving into a hotel?'

'I inherited an apartment in The Chelsea Hotel, from my grandmother.'

'The Chelsea Hotel. That's iconic!'

'She was a nude model and muse to Miro and Salvador Dali.'

'Sarah Ashford! I went to a recent exhibition of hers, and I know that several Beat Poets' wrote her into poetry. You've got art in your blood.'

'Well, I like to think I'm colorful. I'm the manager of Ashford's Gallery.' Alexis looks around at all the paintings. 'And I would love to list you as one of our contemporary artists.'

'Where do you exhibit?'

'I don't.'

'Why not?'

It was a story he didn't feel like telling. Joe's non-verbal answer was to turn his back on her and walk into the kitchen. Alexis hears the sound of a blender crushing ice.

He comes back carrying two tall glasses on a tray. 'Try this.'

'Luscious color, what's in it?'

'Berries.'

She takes a sip. 'It's got real body. Blueberries, strawberries, and I can detect something else. Not sweet and not sour. What is it?'

'My secret.'

'Tastes good. I like it.'

He leans over and kisses her berry red smile and puts his arms around her.

She flinches.

'Oh, I'm sorry.'

'It's my ribs.'

'Can I see?'

Alexis turns her back and slowly raises the bottom of her sweater.

'Can I touch?'

His hands are warm.

'Some bluish discoloration, but the bruise is turning yellow around the edges. That was some fall you took, wasn't it?'

'You could say that.'

But still, you look in great shape, he thinks, as her soft sweater fell back down.

'Do you know something?'

'What?'

'Men and women have the same number of ribs.'

'Yeah, but in women, one of the ribs floats. The story goes while

Adam was in a divinely induced sleep, one of his ribs was taken and formed into Eve.'

She gives him a wicked smile. 'Maybe the floating rib was created from Adam's baculum, a boner.' Then continues with her interest in his art. 'Are you with an agent, Chalkman?'

'Chalkman? What makes you say Chalkman?'

'It's your work. Your work is your signature, and I've seen your portraits on buildings around town, and this studio is full of the original paintings. I'm right, aren't I?'

As soon as she said that, Joe's face changed to livid.

'You should understand,' he said with a cold expression. 'Privacy is an art form.'

'Don't worry. Your secrets safe with me, I have a few secrets myself, and I know how to keep one. I won't call you Chalkman again.'

He stood up and left the room. Me and my big mouth, Alexis thinks. I've blown it.

Joe returned with something familiar, neat lines of fine white powder—framed inside a mercurial hand mirror. He inhales the first line. His reflection smiles upside down in the mirror. Silvered cherubs watch the ecstasy in Alexis's eyes as she takes the silver tube and inhales the white line.

She is attracted to the island of a man who is taking her further from shore.

'Delacroix's wife admired herself in this mirror.'

'This mirror belonged to her?'

'Family heirloom. One of my relatives was a personal friend of Delacroix's.'

'Delacroix was a French romantic painter,' she said, wide-eyed. Then inhaled a line of coke, tilting her head to snort back a residue of the blow.

'His optical effects with color influenced the Impressionists,' Joe said, going down on the third line.

When he looks up, he notices that Alexis's eyes have touches of vermilion in the corners. 'I want to do something special with you.'

She was intrigued with the puzzle of this man. 'Oh? I have only just met you. And, only just kissed you. So what do you have in mind?'

'Why don't we climb in the Shawangunk Mountains?'

'Why don't we. But not right now. I can hardly walk.' They fall about laughing.

'Gunks it is,' she hears herself say.

At three in the morning Alexis arrives back to a ravaged mess. The dogs have savaged couch cushions, making a white blizzard of feathers, and rendered leather covers of the owner's first edition books into canine jerky.

Both dogs eye her and whimper—their animal instincts see the coming carnage within her.

12

JOE THROWS A DUFFEL bag over his shoulder. He'd packed a heavy kit, bolting gear, graphite clips, daisies, heavy-duty rope, insulation tape, and an array of knives for his upcoming weekend away with Alexis. As Joe walked to his car, aluminum chinked against steel, a discordant symphony. When he arrived at her apartment, Alexis was waiting on the steps. A diffusion of sunlight sunbathes her in a golden glow, a shaft of light pierces through the clouds, a rainbow arching over her. That was the instant Joe saw her as the perfect subject.

She throws her canvas bag full of climbing gear into the trunk. The metallic contents resound like a monastery bell, a solid chime, buried someplace far away. Alexis climbs into the passenger seat.

'Nice wheels.'

Joe accelerates into the fast lane. Alexis rummages in her handbag and slides a disc into the Bang and Olufsen. A few bars into the song, Joe said: 'Are you clairvoyant?'

'Why do you ask?'

'Of all the songs in all the world, this happens to be my all-time album for cruising.'

Alexis felt the torque of the Porsche, sank back into the cream pigskin leather seats, and closed her eyes. The late morning was all blue skies. The wind forecast, marginally low, the depression and trough from the north lifted, how long she had been asleep was a puzzle because the next thing she was aware of was Joe turning off the ignition at the foot of the Gunks. Alexis looked up as the sun touched the yellow walls of the mountains.

Joe shades his eyes. 'Having second thoughts?'

'No. It's breathtaking.'

The rays of sun found them on the sheer rock face. Distance soon turned the fir trees into an evergreen carpet, and the car parked below them on the grass became a yellow toy on the fringe of that carpet. The climbers had four hours of vertical climbing ahead. Alexis had begun the climb cautiously, testing every hold. But after an hour, she was using Joe's same handholds. Her knuckles took over Joe's empty grips, like a hermit crab making a new home. Following him made the climb easier, but where was the personal challenge?

Take responsibility for your direction, she thought, as she angled away and changed her route towards Taylor's Mistake, with its near impossible horizontal overhang. A mistake or misfortune? Once past Taylor's, the summit would be in her reach. The mountain challenges anyone who dares. She might just beat Joe to it. But as she approaches the overhang, the mountain gained silence.

Joe wedges a pin in a crack and secures himself to the mountain face. He unclips his video camera from his belt to capture Alexis's live or die moves; as he zooms back to emphasize the deadly drop. Alexis's foot slips, leaving her hanging by one arm. The vast expanse of bright blue sky morphs her into a black silhouette. Her fingers like hapless seeds in a crevice, she clings to the cold rock like the pygmy pines above her, she remains rooted to the spot, the aluminum clips dangling at her waist, turn tuneful chimes in the wind, either a deathly refrain or a requiem.

Fear is life, and life is fearful. Joe focuses in on Alexis, she's lost her bravery. Her frightened face fills the video frame, her eyes scanning the rock face for impossible holds. He hears a gasp. She is desperately feeling for a saving niche, somewhere on the rock. Anything to get a hand into. Her feet are on a crumbling ledge, the rocks are falling. With no where to go, she stops still, breathing hard. Nine hundred feet below, death waits, as death does, with indifference. Fear is a rescuer. Fear rushes it chemicals, insisting she stays alive. Her only move is to dangle vertically over the drop. She must then swing one leg up to the level of her hands, find the toehold and lift her body out of the death zone, but her leg muscles have tightened, her knee is locked. In a skewed sense of time, within her anatomical maze, she hears a voice: 'Lift your leg, feel the toe hold.' She swings through the dead zone and out of danger. She's now climbing ahead of Joe. Above her mountain peaks pierce the sky, a gap in the arc of heaven. A falcon on the hunt glides past solo—soaring on feathers and hollow bones.

On the summit, she and Joe kiss and make love on mountain moss. The endorphins and adrenaline of life surge, the verge of new beginnings; a feeling of first real intimacy and attachment flow through her, with Joe it feels like love, or whatever, it felt more than good.

Joe hands her an enamel cup that reminds her of family summer picnics. He pours tea from a stainless flask. The brew, a few degrees off scalding.

She cools the tea with her breath, and takes a sip. 'What kind of tea is this?'

'Gold-scissor-clipped tea.'

'Gorgeous taste. And violets?'

'The Vietnamese call it Dreamers Tea: Yuzu, jasmine and blue-pea flowers. She isn't listening. His voice goes far away before it returns. 'Ready to get back down to earth?'

She feels the pressure of the mountain's gravity. 'Do we have to?'

'No. But you will get hungry and cold.' Joe reaches out his hand and pulls her to her feet.

The mountain air is giddying. If she lifted her arms and the wind caught her, she might fly off the edge. Two falcons circle above. Rope coils like a yellow cobra at Joe's feet.

Pushing out from the rock face in tandem, they drop fifty meters in ten seconds. Crèches of green lizards scatter as the climbers float past, rappelling down.

THE DINER WITH a one-pump petrol station comes into sight. Joe pulls up in front of the burger joint.

'Here we are, best burgers in town.'

'What town? Nothing here says town to me.'

Alexis considers the wire fencing strung on weathered posts like rusted guitar strings, the tire-less wheels of a 1972 Chevy pick-up going no place, the highway snaking off to someplace else, in this place of no place. They open a fly screen door on its last hinges, sit down in a corner booth, and wait for the only waitress that would ever work here. She pulls the pencil from her braided dreadlocks, licks the lead tip and scribbles the order on the pad, then turns and yells her loudest to the short-order chef, 'Two mega burgers and fries for the booth. No salt!'

'Alexis, do you have brothers, or sisters?'

'No. I'm the only child. You and your brother, are you close?'

'You could say that.'

'What star sign are you?'

'Gemini.'

'Ah, the twins. A life shared, even into the afterlife. That's as close as you can get in a star sign. Do you have a rising moon?'

'All I know is, the earth cast its shadow onto the full moon, and we were born into the darkness. Christian looked into it. According to the records, it was a dark day, two million people died, the rain was the heaviest ever recorded, and the tides were the highest in history.'

'So your were born during a total eclipse of the moon.'

'Christian said it took a difficult day to make us, so that we could make a difference in the world. But I gave up trying to be different. I decided to do something instead.'

'Like what?'

'Not to be an artist but to do art.'

Lyrics from a dead poet came from the jukebox in the back. A shadow of thought hovered like an out-of-season butterfly before settling on Alexis.

'Can you excuse me a minute?'

She went into the restroom and closed out the sad song. Her hand shook as she took woman things out of her leather shoulder bag; thrown-together things like tissues, perfume, contraceptives, lipstick, and coke she had lifted from Joe's apartment. Soon everything would be perfect again.

CHAPTER

13

MONADY MORNING, CHARLOTTE WORE a proper maternity dress to the office. Up to now, she had modified her clothing with strategically placed diaper pins. The shop assistant who sold her the green designer dress told her it 'became' her, a feminine word for suiting her. Charlotte felt like the Madonna in a Renaissance painting, as velvet draped her rounding curves. Under the fabric, she feels the twins giving her baby jabs and little kicks, with newly coordinated arms and legs.

She finishes her cup of black coffee and takes a bite of muffin. Warm blueberries pop on her tongue. Food tastes good for the first time in months. She and the babies are packing on the pounds. Her stomach appears to be more like a pregnant belly than a large lunch. Maternal thoughts knitted together like baby shawls. The twins have doubled their weight at the second trimester making four pounds of babies, sucking and swallowing, starting to sense things and to hear. Each now with fingerprints at the end of their tiny digits, sucking their thumbs, their eyes beginning to open and blink. What color eyes? Charlotte wondered again, brown like your Daddy's, or green like your Mom's. One baby yawns, but she only feels the other hiccup. The phone rings her out of the baby dream.

It's her assistant: 'Christian is waiting in the foyer.'

'Can you believe it. A case of momnesia, Lisa! I forgot about the meeting.'

'So, shall I show your client into the boardroom?'

'Yes. Thank you Lisa. I'll be right there.'

For a woman who prides herself on multitasking, and her ability to organize even the messiest closet, having the top three shelves of her brain filled with baby stuff, was giving Charlotte angst. How could she continue to run the talent agency if pregnancy hijacks her attention?

IN CHARLOTTE'S BOARDROOM, Christian looks through the picture window over the expanse of the city skyline. Where Liberty Enlightening the World stands over the harbor entrance. The Statue of Liberty, a woman unmoved, one would think, but even statues move in strong prevalent winds, a slight sway of her hips, and the gold torch in her left hand moves five inches. Not that she notices, her statuesque mind on other things. She would always be French, this woman of the harbor, sold by the French to the Americans. Gustave Eiffel designed her spine, four iron columns supporting a metal framework under her copper skin, less than the thickness of two American pennies, or one French franc, her fashionable robes oxidized by time, weathering in the sun and rain, to a pale green patina. Perfect, yet imperfect as a woman can be. With seven rays on her crown, one for each of the seven continents and seven oceans, the woman attracts forces from above, hit by six hundred bolts of lightning every year. For all she is, The Statue of Liberty has city historians perplexed. Over the last six years, the lady's expression appears changed, from her look of freedom and liberty to one of fear. Of what, no one knows.

Charlotte walks into the boardroom. Christian puts on one of his beaming Cheshire-cat smiles from his deep-seated emotional closet. 'Great to see you again.'

'Sorry to keep you waiting.'

'Don't be. I was admiring the lady of the harbor. I heard the one hundred and thirty-year-old woman is up for sale.'

'That's news to me?'

'An investor approached the President with an offer for the famous landmark.'

'He's not considering it?'

'Seems to be. Everything is for sale at the right price.'

'So excited to hear about your new product launch. If Mona Lisa were alive today, I would cast her.'

'Not a good idea.'

'Why not?'

'She wasn't a woman.'

'You're telling me Mona Lisa was a Mona Man?'

'Yes, Mona was a young man called Gian Giacomo Caprotti. He worked as an apprentice to the artist, whom he affectionately called Salai.'

'Salai?'

'It means little devil. He and Leonardo were once rumored to be lovers,' Christian adds, with an enigmatic smile. 'Salai's mouth has a striking similarity to Mona Lisa's. A researcher also claims to have found the letter 'S' in her eyes.'

'I never knew you were such an art buff.'

'There's a lot about me you don't know. Yet.' He mumbles under her radar.

Charlotte has the gift of exceptional hearing.

'I heard that, Christian.' His arrogance always irked her.

But Christian continued his monologue. 'Leonardo's subjects all look like each other, characteristics of masculine and feminine, the abstract ideal of beauty.'

'Now you sound like an artist. Have you taken up painting?'

'Not me. My brother's the artist.'

'Does he exhibit?'

'No, he doesn't want to put himself out there.'

'So, not recognized as a serious artist.'

'I never heard of a non-serious artist. Art is a passion, not a mere pastime. If you really want to know about the artist, you need to look at what subject he or she paints.'

There was something about Charlotte he couldn't fathom. Why had she turned him down when he asked her out in college? Why did she refuse him? He never knew, and she never said. Later he heard she'd married an FBI agent. Getting what Christian wanted from her was always like pulling the wrong rabbit out of the hat.

Lisa comes into the room carrying a lacquer tray. She pours tea into china cups as delicate as eggshells, so transparent that golden dragons appear to float in pale green mist.

Christian waves the golden dragons away. 'I've given up tea recently. Do you have espresso?'

'Let's get started,' Charlotte said. 'This is a judgmental and harsh industry. Models are often criticized, but these models are true professionals who know how to work with their facial features.'

The 47-inch flat-screen monitor shows face after beautiful face.

Christian watches intently. 'I know what I want.'

'I am sure you do.'

'The face I am looking for this brand must be fresh and have an accessible look with beautiful even features, yet a commercial appearance to mold into our vision; eye shape, and eye color, her lips, her nose, and in particular the contours of her face, assets such as high cheekbones, and an even jawline. For this product launch I don't want any digital enhancement, no phony made-up face. No deceiving the consumers. Before we do any photography, the model must use our range of cosmetics for a month to ensure an authentic, youthful, glowing look.'

'So, no Photoshop?' Charlotte is surprised. 'That's a breakaway from the usual cosmetic product advertising with its idealized retouching.'

'Won't be needed,' he said, concentrating on one stunning woman. He's mesmerized by her headshots—her facial features, close-up, zoomed-in, how she narrows her eyes, pouts her lips, and lifts her head to make a new angle that changes the shot, how she uses subtleties to create diverse expressions, and how she works with the camera to capture her look. 'That's her. A woman who knows her own true face.'

'Ah, that's Rosa Bonheur, our top model.'

He doesn't choose Rosa because her namesake was a notable 19th-century French artist; or because Rosa is the most famous women's name in the Italian and Spanish language. He chose Rosa—a traveler from a faraway place—for her luminous skin, as radiant as the Black Madonna; the friend of sinners, artists, and rulers. 'I'll leave the contract details to you, Charlotte.'

A meeting was set for the following week.

ON MONDAY MORNING Charlotte comes into the boardroom with no less than a twenty page modeling contract with all its disclaimers and waivers. The ten million dollar contract included the lease on a luxury five-bedroom apartment on Park Avenue with three private car parks. It also included international private jet travel, a health club membership with spa and beauty treatments, an unlimited wardrobe credit at Saks, Macy's, Lord & Taylor, Bloomingdale's, Anya Ponorovskaya, and Henri Bendel. And for her accessories; Jimmy Choo shoes, Louis Vuitton handbags, and Victoria Secrets intimates. Rosa could expect a million dollar bonus on completion of the project. Money talks, and in Cutter's contract, the money screamed take me! Christian gave the deal a cursory glance, and as he signed the last page, he senses the garden of her, warm notes of musk rose, even before she enters.

'Rosa, I'd like you to meet Mr. Christian Cutter.'

Christian holds out his hand and feels the return of pressure. With a woman, a beginning is sensed by the palms mound of Venus. She is the one. He directs his conversation to Rosa, not ignoring Charlotte rudely or deliberately, but everything about Rosa is enchanting and distracting. She makes him forget all the women in his address book. He doesn't consider himself a serial flirt or womanizer, although he had heard rumors that others thought so. However, Christian is one man who should come with a warning label. Because what he keeps inside him, is as hazardous as a chemical spill. Christian hands Rosa a fountain pen. The black ink has already dried on Christian's signature.

Rosa initials page after page until the legal bond is formed. 'So many pages—makes me feel like I'm signing my life away.'

'As long as you don't run out of permanent ink, you'll be fine!'

'Such an elegant pen,' she said, handing it back.

'No. It's yours now.'

Rosa turns the extravagant silver barrel in her hand. She sees her name engraved in a cursive script through a galaxy of diamond stars along with a exquisite enamel painting of a face. Her portrait painted in miniature.

Then he hands her a diamond-studded mobile.

'You'll find my private number programmed on fast dial.'

'I can't possibly accept this.'

'Too late, it comes with the contract. Another thing, you're not afraid of heights, are you? Because I want to show you a side of New York you've possibly never seen before. Will you join me for a formal occasion?'

Suddenly, Rosa senses Christian Cutter is determined to possess her, but Christian already knows she is his.

She hesitates, 'I would love to, but…' she adds softly, 'I have a boyfriend.'

'It's a company dinner. So, is that going to be a problem?'

'No.'

'Good, in that case, I'll make the arrangements.'

CHAPTER

14

ASIDE FROM THE ULTRASOUND pictures of the twins magnetized on the fridge, Charlotte had a professional photographer take photos of her baby bump. As she hung the frames up on the nursery wall, she felt a kick, then another. The babies were growing out of room to move. She lifts her sweater and runs her fingers over the outlines of the tiny feet that give her plenty of kicks and pokes. Putting her feet up, she takes another sip from a large glass of milk and turns up *Vivaldi's Four Seasons*: a shepherd and his barking dog can be heard in the viola section, buzzing flies, storms, drunken dancers, hunting parties, from both the hunters and the prey's point of view, frozen landscapes, and warm winter fires. Her babies are listening. They listen to music, the sound of her voice, perceive sunshine and darkness, taste what she eats, blinking and dreaming, swimming in her blood, what's hers is theirs, and they are part of her.

She has stuck to the pregnancy diet throughout her pregnancy, watched the bathroom scales, and monitored shifts in weight gain.

She practiced pregnancy-safe sex, kept up with doctor's visits, scheduled a birthing center tour, interviewed pediatricians and chose one, stocked up on baby clothes, diapers, wipes, bought a changing table and a baby monitor. She attended childbirth classes until she became somewhat of an expert on the stages of labor; early, active and transitional. She understands ways to manage childbirth and what happens during the first twenty-four hours after birth, and about breastfeeding. She agreed on a birthing plan with Michael, arranged cord blood-banking, learned how to bathe a newborn, and give life-saving baby CPR. She stocked the freezer with man-meals and packed her hospital bags—while running the most successful talent agency in New York City.

This trimester is the most taxing for her. Charlotte is waking in the night with vivid crazy dreams. During her waking hours, she experiences persistent heartburn and an achy lower back. Even the beginnings of stretch marks on her belly and the pressure on her bladder don't bother her. I sneeze. I pee. But it is worth it. I am keeping my eye on the prize, meeting our babies one day soon. It's part of the baby experience, she kept reminding herself.

MICHAEL AND CHARLOTTE spent Saturday shopping in baby stores for essentials on the list.

Charlotte touches a dreamy, angelic-looking crib. 'Isn't this one gorgeous.' She runs her fingers over the bedding with its applique ducks and embroidery. Then she flips over the price tag. '$4,575, times two! That's so expensive!'

Michael has another idea. 'How about a kit-set designer crib, like this one. I'll get your Dad to give me a hand. Give us a chance to catch up before we both turn into something else.'

'What?'

'Dad and Grandman!'

'Great! Grandman would like that.'

Charlotte eyed up a double baby pram with pale cream cowhide lining, but again she hesitates at the four-figure price tag.

'Nearly the same cost as the first year of private preschool,' she exclaimed. 'There must be something else.'

'How about these canvas washable baby slings? We could strap the babies to the front of us, like packed parachutes.'

Charlotte laughs. Baby bottles next on the list, but for later, she plans to feed the twins herself.

Everything goes according to plan—sometimes.

ROSA DOESN'T ANSWER THE call from her boyfriend but smiles at the row of champagne glass emojis Christian has sent her. The next question is, can she complete her to-do list on time? Get a full body massage, a French nail polish, a deep facial, go to the hair salon but stay relaxed and try not to overthink under the dryer. Then meet up with her best friend Carla for lunch, but there was one thing to remember and not to forget; phone her fiancé later. She rechecked her messages, took a quick bite out of pumpernickel toast and headed off to buy the pair of heels she'd seen in a 5th Avenue store window, not kitten heels but high heels of reckless abandon. Today she could well afford to buy them.

OUTSIDE HER APARTMENT at 5:30 pm precisely, a chauffeur wearing a smart dark suit held open the back door of a Mercedes-Benz S600 limousine. 'Welcome, Ms. Rosa.'
With that, she steps into the opulent interior.

Rosa reports to Carla on her jewel-encrusted iPhone.

'It's amazing how much fits into this limo,'

'What color interior?'

'Tuxedo black.'

'Nice. Wish I was there!'

'Yeah, a hell of a driver.'

'Fast?'

'Yes, and cute, you'd like him. He is just like the driver in the movie we saw.'

Millions of golden bubbles rose in a champagne flute and took a little of Rosa's red lipstick away with every sip. Rosa reads the label to Carla, 'Perrier Jouet Belle Epoque Rose. Vintage Champagne with hand-painted Art Nouveau roses on a honey-colored bottle.'

'I'm so jealous of you.'

'Working! Remember this is work.'

'Well, if that's work, I'll work day and night,' Carla says.

They had been friends since junior high when both wore night braces and shared a crush on the history teacher.

'So what's his name?'

'Who?'

'The handsome chauffeur?'

'No idea.'

'So where is he taking you?'

'No idea!'

The limo stopped opposite the Guggenheim in Upper East Side Manhattan.

'Gotta go. Talk later. Bye.'

The chauffeur opens her door, and tips his hat with uniformed formality. 'This way please.' He leads the way through the foyer of a grand hotel; the flagship for a chain of unlisted luxury boutique hotels. Light catches the beveled edges of the lead-crystal ceiling and shines prisms of amethyst, lavender, and wisps of fire violet over her face. Violet the color of extravagance, artificiality, and ambiguity, but violet doesn't worry the woman whose perfume fills the foyer with musk rose. The doors of the central elevator open. She steps inside. As the lift ascends, she sees the Hudson River coiling throughout the city like a sparkling boa. She glimpses the silhouette of Our Lady of the Harbor, while the evening paints the sky with tendrils of purple. The elevator doors open to the penthouse. Someone has thought of every detail. The room has crystal vases full of blue French damask roses. She closes her eyes and inhales the hedonistic scent—fifty or more blooms together, intoxicating, almost overpowering.

The chauffeur touched the keypad on the wall, sliding doors opened onto an expansive roof-top topiary garden, with hedges manicured in geometric shapes of hearts and diamonds. Rows of twinkling fairy lights create stardom that lights up her face, erasing shadows of doubt in their magical way. White loungers edged the 25-meter pool, long enough to recline on, to stretch out and relax on—if one was so inclined. Rosa wonders, who would swim in such a contrived garden?

Over the edge of the topiaries, a helicopter suddenly appeared with hovering intrusion. Rotary blades cut the evening into sharp pieces before the chopper landed on the bulls-eye and settled down on the roof-top pad. Christian swung out of the pilot's seat. 'So glad you could make it.' Rosa's smile is captured in the Polarized lenses of his Aviator sunglasses.

Then the chauffeur, manservant, butler, valet, this formal man with no name, poured Perrier Jouet into two glasses, bubbles rising in gold-rimmed flutes. Rosa considers the drinkers.

Christian smiles like he just read her mind.

'Don't worry. I never drink and fly.' With a tilt of his head, he indicates toward the helicopter. 'Bring your glass with you. We haven't got much time.'

'Where are we heading? Or is this a private party?'

The turbines whine over her words.

'I wish, but there are places to go and people you must meet. The New York wealthy are waiting.'

The helicopter's turbines rotor up to Q max. Christian points to the headsets, and she puts them on. 'Buckle up,' comes the cool Bronx accent, as the helicopter lifts skywards.

With a surge of vertigo panic, Rosa shouts into the micro-speaker: 'You haven't closed the doors!'

He grins. 'All the better to see the sights with.'

The wolfish look that flashes across his face, startles Rosa's inner child, her voice of intuition demanding her attention, she can choose to listen—or else, ignore at her peril.

The helicopter flies amongst a kaleidoscope of glass sunsets reflected in a thousand downtown office windows.

Christian said: 'I like this time of the evening, when the sun goes down, and the city's power grid takes over solar responsibility.'

Out of the darkening sky, the helicopter touches down on the superyacht's helipad. A billionaire's bragging right—five hundred feet of decadence. Rich varnished teak decks, beveled crystal windows initially shipped over from Paris, two hardwood dance floors, two mahogany-wood bars, and a jacuzzi on the sundeck. A spacious main saloon seats up to one hundred guests. Below decks twenty accommodation staterooms with sumptuous beds, en suite bathrooms, and personalized climate controls.

For Rosa, it will be a ship of dreams, or a sinking ship, depending on the cargo.

CHAPTER

16

CHRISTIAN LOOKED RELAXED IN black and white. A black Italian dinner suit, and a thousand dollar white Italian linen shirt. He stood at the top of the gangplank, greeted his directors, and shook the hand of every employee of the merging companies, music rose from the baby grand piano. Waiters moved among the guests offering divine canapés. The banquet dinner followed; warm Nova Scotia lobster infused with one-hundred-year-old French cognac, Pacific scallops complete with their orange coral row on blini topped with beluga caviar, Tahitian vanilla ice cream infused with vanilla beans, rich chocolate mousse blended with twenty-eight cocoas from around the world, and adorned with edible gold flakes.

Christian tapped his glass and waited for the room to fall into silence before he spoke.

'As you know, The Human Development Foundation and Biozen have merged, and our new company's shares were floated on the stock market on Monday. Every member of staff receives a free portfolio of Biozen shares, and we expect these shares to increase by three hundred percent in one month.'

The room rocked with the swell of applause.

'Biozen products will transform age by setting the clock of time back to beautiful. That's why we're here tonight to celebrate the first stage of everlasting beauty. We are in the beauty business, and together we are going to make this a more beautiful world. We don't believe beauty is skin deep. The aesthetics of beauty is where power is. The more beautiful you are in this society, the more you get, and the more people take you seriously and indulge you. There is one other thing. In the future, people will look youthful for life. In the future, death itself will be delayed, but that is still in the development stage. We'll keep you posted. Now I invite you to indulge in Biozen's diamond cocktail.'

Waiters serve glasses of nitrogen cocktails, each one an ice-cold molecular mixology concocted of three champagnes poured into extravagant flutes, a one carat diamond sparkling in every crystal stem.

Raising his glass Christian says, 'If you are hesitant about drinking this unfamiliar concoction, well all I can say is this—only those who drink this, are the ones who truly trust me. Wait a minute for the mist to disappear, and I'll wait for the unbelievers amongst you to disappear from the room. So how much do you trust me?'

Christian opens his arms, palms facing upwards. In a duplicated moment, he is both Christian Cutter and Christ the Redeemer, like the statue with outstretched arms in Rio. A woman appears beside him, like a saint or stigmata. A handmaiden sent to him, wrapped in a white mink coat, her olive skin as flawless and transparent as a polished pearl.

'Meet the new face of Biozen. Rosa!'

Rosa takes center stage, statuesque and stunning. She gives a subtle nod and a private smile. Christian signals to his advertising manager, Miles, to take the floor. Miles unveils the four million dollar advertising and media package to be launched at the All-Star Game in mid-July.

Later, boat tenders began ferrying guests back to the dock, leaving Christian's mega-yacht at anchor. Rosa stands on the deck, about to put her fur coat on, when she feels someone behind her lift the coat over her shoulders. She turns and is face to face with Christian. He thinks, this is more like it, much better to see results on a rose, rather than laboratory fruit flies and mice. This face is a tribute to me.

'You're leaving?'

'You noticed,' she said.

At which point, Christian whispers in her bejeweled ear, a perfect ear shaped like a delicate seashell. 'I notice everything about you, Angel—stay longer?'

Rosa is tempted by temptation himself. She likes this man, not for his wealth and position but for how generous he is towards her. 'Christian, it's been a beautiful evening, but I must get back. I promised to meet someone. So a rain check, perhaps?' As she spoke, a dark cloud settled over the harbor.

When she got into the limousine on the dock, her phone rang. She recognized the man's voice at once. The following weeks would bring more grief than the storm forecasted.

17

THERE ARE FIFTY WAYS to have sex, give or take some, but only two ways to make a baby. Accidentally. Or intentionally. For Alexis, the plan to keep Joe as her man needed feminine biology warfare; being Joe's steady girlfriend was not enough, it should have been, but it wasn't. She didn't trust love. Every relationship started hot and heavy, then fizzled away, and she'd be alone again. If getting pregnant was the only way to get Joe to commit to her, then that's what Alexis would do. In her diary, she circles the date of her next period in red ink. While she can't figure out how to stop the monthly, she has figured out a way to bypass the situation, like a temporary trick of nature, but it will be the start of her plan.

The following day, the sun rose at the same time Alexis opens her eyes. Joe is still asleep, sleeping like the dead. But this morning there is no time to waste. She throws her clothes on and heads out the door.

At the corner drugstore, Alexis buys a pregnancy testing kit, the one with the most straightforward instructions. On her way back to Joe's place, she picks up freshly baked pastries, and the morning paper.

Alexis lets herself back in. The apartment is quiet. The cat follows her into the guest bathroom. 'Nice collar Shadow.' She turns the collar around, tiny diamonds sparkle in the overhead light. 'All this bling. Who's a spoiled cat!' Then she locks the bathroom door.

Faking a pregnancy test is relatively easy to do. Alexis takes a small sticky label, draws a positive sign on it, and cuts it to fit neatly inside the little test window. Then she takes a cotton Q-tip moistened with water and rubs along the positive line. But the red line smudges, and the positive result fades before her eyes. She throws the failed test into the trash. Not everything goes to plan. When one idea gets lost, it leaves space for a better one to be found. Next, Alexis flips the lid on a can of cola. She had read that some women were faking pregnancy results using soda drinks. Alexis dips the tester into the coke, but the stick just turns an ugly shade of brown.

THE PEALING BELL on the steeple of the Roman Catholic Church wakes Joe an hour later with its vaulted echo. Alexis comes in balancing a wicker tray with an Alessi pot of espresso coffee, a pair of Versace Scala del Palazzo Rosa cups, and reheated bakeries piled up on an underglazed red porcelain plate.

Joe smiles. 'So, what are you sacrificing this morning?'
Alexis cheeks flush with guilt, as if he knows what she's up too.

'You know that blood red porcelain plate, is a five-hundred-year-old Jinhong plate, initially used for sacrificial ceremonies. It's Ming Dynasty, but hey, why not use it for a lazy Saturday Brooklyn breakfast.'
'I just thought it had an air of joy and happiness about it. Shows you how wrong I can be.'

Later, when Joe leaves for his morning run, Alexis goes back to her apartment. She showers and changes into a crisply ironed shirt and designer jeans, applies red gloss lipstick, and a wand of dark mascara. She slips on the pale blue leather pumps she'd ordered online from Madrid. Shoes shipped over the ocean from the land of Seville oranges and bullfighting, delivered right to her front door. The other delivery Alexis was expecting had arrived in a padded brown envelope postmarked Nebraska. No return address. It was her biggest secret to date. She had bought a positive result from an anonymous pregnant woman, who mailed it to her by express delivery. You can buy anything in this world.

Now she was ready to make this a special day for Joe and her. Stopping into the delicatessen, Alexis picks up a bottle of red, two dozen Bluff oysters flown in from New Zealand, drops of the salty Able Tasman Ocean still inside their shells, and a beef lasagna that, according to the gold medals it won, apparently tasted better than any homemade version.

She let herself back into Joe's apartment. If things went according to plan, this would be the last time Alexis would use the spare key. She was expecting him to attach a permanent swipe card on her key ring, the beginning of a long series of attachments. If that meant giving up white powder for baby talc, she was prepared to do anything to bring Joe and her closer together. A baby on the way was the only way to get some guys to commit. Men live in ignorance of women's lies. After all, seventy percent of men spend their lives raising kids they never fathered, the premature births that were full-term babies. They are the half-children, half-sister, half-brother, accidental babies that fell into bassinets and prams—half belonging.

At least she wouldn't be lying about the father when she delivered a baby. She and Joe would make a baby together; she was sure of that. All she had to do now was lie back and make the baby happen for real. One hiccup Alexis had yet to figure out was the baby bump in the interim, between the fake pregnancy, and the real one. She was up against time.

JOE AND ALEXIS crumpled the sheets again until they were lying back, looking up at the scrolls and leaves on the plaster ceiling, warm and blissed out from another afternoon of mutually satisfying sex.

'If we keep this up, we'd better get married.' Alexis runs her fingertips sensually over his lips, kissing him, a kiss full of promises. 'You know I love you, Joe.' She looks deep into his eyes. 'I never noticed you wore contacts until now.'

'A woman with an eye for small details, I like that. Colored contacts even things out.'

'I've never met a man as interesting as you.'

'I have never met a woman as interesting as you, but there's something you should know.' Joe's expression looked serious. 'I am not sure we can go on like we are,' his voice low.

She can feel the brush-off coming. She closes her eyes. All the boyfriends Alexis had known flashed past her face, the guy next door, the film producer, the landscape gardener, the art director, the medical student, the businessman, the drummer in a band, and now a street artist. Alexis felt it coming. The relationship black hole again, where she loses emotional time and every feeling she invested, ends up in the relationship trashcan.

Joe senses her insecurity. 'I'm falling in love with you.'

'What did you just say?'

'I've fallen in love with you.'

Her eyes opened.

'I've never told a woman that before—but is this just me in love? How about you?'

Alexis lets her body answer.

With the sun warm through the window, they made love, slept, then talked until the afternoon cast more shadows.

Alexis felt relaxed with Joe. 'So where do we go from here?'

'Nowhere! Stay the weekend with me.'

On Sunday afternoon, Alexis decided it was high time to get things rolling. 'Joe, there's something you need to know.'

'Now you sound too serious.'

'I'm pregnant.'

'You're what? Already?'

'Yes!'

'Are you sure?' She opens the bedside drawer and hands the pregnancy test to Joe. He contemplates the positive pink line as he turns it over, like a new life in his hands. No woman has given him the promise of life. He leans into her and whispers into the cavern of her ear, 'I will keep this forever.'

Then he carefully tucks a strand of hair behind her ear before he tilts her chin upward, like an artist posing a model for a portrait. He takes in her features in a look that says she belongs to him. Not that she notices. It is the long, deep kiss that follows that causes tears to well up in her eyes. Hopeful tears.

Alexis moved in with Joe the following week.

18

DESPITE REFLECTIONS OF LIGHTS from vehicles that snake over the bridge, during the interlude between evening and morning, the river flows black.

Inside Grimaldi's, the smell of roasted garlic turns on Christian's appetite as soon as he walks through the door. The place is always the same; pummeled pizza dough thrown in the air, caught by the floury hands of pizza chefs, tables set with red and white cloths, candle wax dripping down Chianti bottles, same as always.

Christian sits down at his booth, the one near the window facing the street, a vantage point to see brick warehouses in various states of repair and disrepair, sprawled with graffiti. The view of Manhattan under the shadow of the Brooklyn Bridge opens the eyes, and illuminates the understanding of what it's like to live in a great city. That's what some places do, make us feel familiar by what one knows—but one never knows.

It is unusual to see Christian on a Thursday, not his regular day.

The waiter interrupts Christian's thoughts with a question.

'Can I get you anything Mr. Christian?'

'The usual thanks Angelo.'

Coincidently, *Waiting on a Lady* plays in the background. Songs have a way of making you feel you are in the right place, at the right time, doing the right thing. She was late. He ordered up a classic pizza, thin base, pepperoni, basil and mozzarella. A bottle of Quintarelli red wine turned up at the table, courtesy of the house. Half a bottle in, he rechecks his watch. Fashionably late was not admired by Christian. He fast dialed her.

No answer.

So where is she? Switching to the GPS locator embedded in her phone, the signal identifies her as static opposite Central Park.

He asks the waiter to package up the remainder of his pizza. He hates to leave food uneaten when there are starving children to haunt him. He finishes his glass of wine.

Angelo presents him with the leftovers in aluminum foil. He had carefully wrapped and shaped the leftovers into a gaggle of silver geese.

Opening the trunk of his car, he checks his kit. He doesn't want any mistakes, and wasn't planning on making any. He double-checks again, and gets into his car. He scrolls through his music and stops at a song he hasn't heard for a while. As he listens, the lyrics echo his thoughts: *Whose bed did you sleep in last night? Don't lie to me.* Exactly, who are you sleeping with tonight, Rosa? He drives to the GPS coordinates and parks outside a hotel.

Christian sees her coming out of the main entrance carrying a Birkin Cargo bag. A man in uniform drives a red Jaguar out of the car park basement and pulls up in front. Rosa slips seductively into the passenger seat, hitching her skirt a little, just far enough for

Christian to glimpse her thigh. The Jaguar pulls into traffic and is soon lost amongst commuter headlights. Christian follows in the traffic flow, watching their direction on the GPS. As they enter the freeway, he realizes they are heading for JFK Airport. Arriving at the airport, he follows them up the ramp and into the airport car park.

OBSERVING HER FROM a distance in the departure terminal, he sees her pulling a cabin bag behind her as she weaves through the crowds towards the check-in counter of Air France. At the priority queue, she talks to an airline pilot and passes him the cabin bag. She slowly takes off one of her diamond earrings and whispers in his ear, 'Until you return, I am only one half.'

'J'aime tu!'

He checks in and checks his watch. They have a short time before his flight departs. Out of sight of the crowd, he kisses her, a deep passionate kiss of a man holding the love of his life in his arms. Then with a farewell wave, he goes through the crew line at immigration.

Christian melts away into the airport's confusion; the yawning lines of ticketed boredom, in Pac-Man like queues; overweight bags at security causing significant hold-ups; exhausted passengers milling about with luggage laden trolleys. A place to go unnoticed.

Christian gets back to his car in time to see Rosa walking tall on high heels towards her Jaguar. She unlocks her car, gets in, and a second later, gets out and checks the front tire on the driver's side.

She surveys the silent landscape of cars. A car engine revs. She is not as alone as she thinks. Headlights come towards her, and a car slows down and stops. The driver's tinted window slides down.

'Perhaps, I can help?'

'Christian! What are you doing here?'

'Pure synchronicity! I have just seen my sister off on the last flight to Indianapolis. What are the odds.'

'Very odd. These are brand new tires, but one is completely flat. I'm not mechanically minded. I have never used a car-jack before.'

'It's not something you should have to fix. Changing a wheel on a luxury car is technical. That's what Elite Tow-Trucks are for. Let me call one.'

'Thanks, Christian.'

'You're welcome, no problem.'

'And I am so sorry about tonight. I tried to call you earlier, but the battery in my phone was flat.'

'I figured you were otherwise engaged.'

'My boyfriend didn't want to miss his flight. We just ran out of time.'

'You must have been in quite a rush. You're only wearing one of the Tiffany diamond drop earrings I gave you. Unless you have lost the other one?'

She reaches up and feels her earlobes.

'Oh! Imagine just putting on one. How forgetful of me.'

'Why don't we have a nightcap before I drop you home.'

It is four in the morning when Christian opens the freezer and places leftovers inside.

'How was your date last night?' Joe asked.

'She never turned up.'

'You don't say! One for the books! You always get what you want.'

'Who says I haven't.'

Later, Christian takes the solitaire diamond earring out of his pocket, and places it in the jewelry box.

19

MICHAEL SEES THE YELLOW taxi weaving through the traffic twenty meters away. He raises his hand, and the driver swerves into the curb. 'I'm going to grab this one. You want a ride?'
Brooke thought about it for a second and changed her plans.
   'Perfect. A dream come true! Drop me at the precinct.'
   Michael opens the back door, and Brooke slides inside.
   The driver catches Michael's eyes in the rear vision mirror.
   'Where to, Sir?'
   'Centre Street, then Stems Flowers.'
   After dropping Brooke off at the precinct, the cab melts into the lava stream of rush hour traffic. New York is electrified with lights from cars, taxis, trucks, bikes, and neon signs. In the dark recess of the back seat of the cab, Charlotte's name lights up his mobile.
   'When are you coming home?'
   'One more thing to do, and I'll be home.'

The cab stops outside Stems; motor idling. Michael opens the cab door and shouts, 'Wait a minute,' to the woman flipping the closed sign. He puts his hand on the store door and pushes it open, but that comes as no surprise to the florist. There is always a reason. An argument or a forgotten anniversary is enough to cause this kind of floral desperation, and a good way to sell the last of the daily stock. She didn't mind finishing late.

Michael needed flowers. He might occasionally miss a friend's birthday, but the 'love at first sight' anniversary he hasn't missed in ten years.

Eva the owner, said with a flourish: 'Only for you, Michael, come in. These sunflowers are happy flowers, they always follow the sun. And, of course, Van Gogh, they remind everyone of him. He painted seven versions.' She shakes each vibrant yellow flower with its dark brown velvet center, a pincushion of tightly packed omega seeds.

'These will be *son-flowers* for the upcoming twins. Would you mind wrapping them in two separate bunches and tying each with a blue ribbon?'

Eva pulls two sheets of paper from under the wooden counter. 'By the way, how's Charlotte doing?'

'Great.'

'Good to hear. And for Charlotte?'

'Roses. You got a few stems of red?'

'Sold out. But you can have the last of the blues.'

'No. Definitely not.'

'Well, how about white with a tinge of pink? And the last of the white delphiniums?'

'Perfect.'

The taxi drops Michael outside his apartment, but just as he turns to pay, the cab driver accelerates away. Michael makes a mental note of the number plate as the cab drives through the amber light of the intersection.

He walks up the steps, dusk's quiet light slants through leafless fingers of the white oak. As he walks through the door, the sense of home touches him, dinner in the oven, the smell of roast chicken's crisp skin, and blueberries popping open under their puff pastry blanket. Charlotte is on the couch with her eyes closed, an open book on her lap, *What to Expect When You're Expecting Twins*. There is a half-knitted angora baby sweater next to the Siamese kitten asleep beside her. The white bundle of soft fur makes it difficult to tell where one fur begins, and another ends. Charlotte opens her eyes and sees Michael stroking the purring kitten, and her eyes fill with tears.

'Oh, Michael!'

'What?'

'One of our models has gone missing.'

'Since when?'

'Two days ago. Rosa missed an important photo shoot for the front cover of Ella Mils Magazine.'

'It doesn't mean something bad has happened to her. In fact ninety percent of missing people turn up within the week.'

'No, you don't understand. Rosa is just not the missing person type.'

'What car does she drive?'

'A Jaguar. Why?'

'We found a red Jaguar convertible abandoned yesterday at the airport car park with a flat tire.'

C H A P T E R

20

PEOPLE WHO RUN ARE either running away or running towards something. Dave Watson, a family man by choice, is about to do both. This morning will give him more on his plate than the breakfast he is dishing up for his two preschoolers.

It's his turn to do the morning shift while his wife, Emily, takes a hot shower. He wipes egg yolk and toast crumbs off his child's face but misses the dribble bubble hanging from her chin. His other daughter empties the cereal packet onto the floor, creating a golden carpet of cornflakes. She is about to pour full-fat milk on the mess in a way that only a thirteen-month kid can. Dave grabs the carton off her. Another Tetra Pak with kids' photos printed on the side. Dave recognizes every kid's face on every carton. Boys and girls—the missing children. This is his advertising awareness campaign to get lost and stolen kids back to their families.

Everyone says, Dave is a caring, loving, super-dad. Still, for him, toddler mayhem is a migraine headache in the making.

Emily walks into the kitchen, her wet hair caught up in a towel turban. 'We've got to teach these two table manners!' She ties a knot in her blue cotton kimono, a robe that found its way into her suitcase when she and Dave were on their honeymoon, but that was their other life, BC—before children.

Today was just another Saturday.

'So what time are you thinking of going for your run?'

'Kind of like now.'

'Well, can you hold on? I've got to blow dry my hair and put some clothes and makeup on. And remember, the kids have got a birthday party to go to.'

'I forgot all about it. What gear do they wear?'

'Ashley and Olivia are fairies.'

'Of course, why didn't I think of that?'

'Now, sweeties, while mommy is putting her clothes on, daddy will help you get dressed up for the party. OK?'

Getting two kids dressed up in fairy wings has its moments. By the time Emily had done her makeup, both kids were holding wands in one hand, a wrapped gift in the other, ready to go except for the socks and shoes.

Ashley stamped her feet. 'No shoes.' Olivia joins in the toddler stampede.

Dave says unconvincingly: 'All good fairies wear sensible shoes.'

'No, no, no,' they cry in unison.

Olivia and Ashley have a knack of crying in tandem, one setting the other off and always with a high-pitched whine.

'Got a slight problem, Honey. I'll leave this to you.' He puts on his running shoes. 'I'm out of here. Bye kids have fun.'

Dave is sure that people who run in the park on Saturdays are running away from something. He cuts through the vacant lot to the park. Dew hung in sparkle drops, and bent a thousand blades of grass. Two runners sprint past Dave, exhaling personal clouds of frosted breath.

Dave's knee was playing up again, despite the sports strapping, a deep nagging ache persisted from a torn ligament repair. He veers off to escape the running track designed by the city planners with its yellow centerline, distance markers and asphalt surface. Instead, he detours across new mown grass, through the botanical gardens, ignoring the no trespassing sign. He runs past the delicious smell of brunch cooking at the Pine Tree Café. Grilled maple-cured bacon, flapjacks, cinnamon lumberjack cake, and freshly brewed coffee. He stops at the Haupt Conservatory, classical white architecture that always reminds him of a plaster wedding cake. He flashes his New York City Resident Grounds Only Pass, and walks through the climate control doors into the humidity of the Victorian glasshouse. A lush tropical rain forest with curated displays of aquatic and carnivorous plants like the giant Venus flytrap that can swallow a rat whole. The pond is alive with freshwater life; floating velvety plates of Victoria cruziana water lilies, purple buds of Angel lotus, and giant orange koi fish milling around in their dark water underworld. He checks the noticeboard for an exhibition called *Floribunda Illustrata, 1514,* botanical paintings through the centuries. And takes note of the opening hours.

Then he runs over the manicured green lawn towards the rose gardens, past mulched garden beds of roses arranged by genus, the Petite Knock Out rose, Ballerina rose, Golden Celebration rose, White Blizzard rose, roses upon roses, the mauves, yellows, the whites, the reds, the candy-floss pinks and the fragrance of Rose Absolute and French Damask. If anyone loves roses, his wife Emily does. She grows roses in tubs on their balcony and roof garden. She named one of their girls Olivia after David Austin's mauve shrub rose, Olivia Rose. It didn't matter that Emily was a psychologist with letters after her name, and knew all the answers, she was still a hopeless romantic. He stops at a rose bed to pick a thorn-less rose for Emily, their never-ending love. He reaches down to get to the base of a long stem rose. He reels back in horror. His hand had touched the damp skin of a naked woman. Something is horribly wrong.

The body of a woman lies in the rose bed, face-up. She rests on rotting leaf mulch, and someone has carefully and painstakingly covered the contours of her breasts and belly with petals of blue roses. The demonic sight is a morning's nightmare. His mind slaps thoughts around. Let someone else deal with this—Run! Run! But what are the rules about death? You can't ignore it, you can't just walk away. Report it. You must report it. You have to. Go on, do it now! Dave fumbles for his phone and immediately drops it on the grass. His hands shake violently, as if possessed by something ghastly. He picks up the mobile and turns his back on the gruesome scene. He can't talk about a dead person, not in front of her. Not in front of nakedness he was never meant to see.

Despite his hands shaking, he manages to dial 911. 'What service do you require, Fire, Police, Ambulance?'

He can't speak. Words have gone. He is holding back a guttural groan.

'What service do you require. Fire. Police. Ambulance?'

Hang up. Hang up. He wants to, but the emergency operator stops him by the calmness attached to what she asks. He forces his voice into coherent place, but still, it cracks into brittle syllables.

'Police and Ambulance—both.'

'What is the nature of the emergency, sir?'

'It's the worst nature. Murder.' His voice sounds watery, guilty—unlike his normal vocals.

'What is the location?'

'The location?' Where *is* hell? Where exactly *in* hell is he?'

His eyes as witness. Images set to haunt him. The touch of death suffused him with unexplained human guilt. It would lead to a drinking problem, his wife leaving him on his own. A small room in a lost place. The killer ended more than one life that day.

Dave shut his eyes in an effort to close the world out, but the sirens grew louder, noxious, like poison ivy amongst the innocents.

AT THE ENTRANCE to the botanical gardens, a coffee cart happens to be conveniently parked outside. Michael wraps his hands around a little Columbian, his habit; he joins the estimated hundred million coffee addicts that morning—a double shot of the daily grind, the eye-opening rush ensures he is fully awake. Nothing is easy in this job, and at times, when his workload burgeoned with difficult cases to solve, he wishes he wasn't color-blind. He'd be flying jet planes instead.

At the crime scene, Pete, the coroner from city hall, crouches down on one knee, examining the dead woman with reverence. He takes care not to touch the wreath of thorns entwined around her neck, a painstakingly twisted contraption fashioned from branches of a spiny shrub—the crucifixion thorn, its white sap dripping poison and its deep red bracts of flowers like blood, piercing her throat with the corona de Jesus.

Michael examines the lacerations along her arms. 'We've seen this before.'

Pete follows Michael's glance. 'Someone controlled the blood flow, so blood coagulated sequentially. A modern-day bloodletting, but without leeches.'

'And the thorns?' Michael asked.

'The thorns penetrated the jugular. From the look of the injuries and lack of restraint marks, she was drugged. I suspect a strong muscle-paralyzing drug was used to restrain the victim. Her facial expression indicates she was kept alive long enough to feel the horror.'

Michael thought: this killer has manipulated this scene to give the death pose symbolic meaning. He is leaving us clues. Each kill is more complex. He's become more confident and has control of his patterning. He's bent on perfecting a killing finesse to satisfy his developing fantasy, and taking pleasure in his theater of death—his art form. We are his audience, the victim merely a player.

'And take a look at this, Michael!'

21

THERE IS AN UNDERCURRENT of uncertainty and concern. A room of subdued conversation. Christian enters the room. With all staff present, he announces, 'Bad news, I'm afraid. Rosa's been missing, and I know all of you have been waiting for news of her. I now have the sad task of announcing her tragic and untimely death. Her body was found yesterday morning.'

An empty funereal silence follows.

'When I have more news from homicide, I will update you. As a mark of respect to her family, the office is closing for the day. I have also arranged for company psychologists, and specialists in grief, to be immediately available to those who worked alongside Rosa. I am very sorry. She was an asset to the company and will be sorely missed by all.'

Christian left the room, for all appearances, visibly shaken. Back in his office, his secretary comes in with a short black espresso and a wrought expression.

Clara's tears welled up. 'I still can't believe it! Rosa was here in this office yesterday. Now she's gone.'

Christian flips through a stack of photographs. 'Here today, gone tomorrow. That's life as we know it. Your mistake is, you take familiarity for permanence.'

'You're looking for a new face already?'

'Yes. Thankfully we haven't gone public yet. Can you imagine the media cost of a complete product re-launch?'

This is not right Clara thinks. What is it with this dime a dozen cookie-cutter attitude towards people. Then under her breath, well out of normal ear-shot she said: 'You bastard. You don't waste any time.'

But Christian, for all his fortune, was doubly fortunate to also have the hearing of a slum rat. 'You are right, Clara. I don't waste time. You're fired!'

DEAD BODIES DON'T MAKE for the perfect day for Michael. As bodies filled morgue drawers and with so many bodies on ice, Michael's filing cabinet drawers burgeoned with gruesome and macabre forensic photographs—the color of the dead—their skin, nails, hands, lips, blood, saliva, vomit, lung purge, bruises, stab wounds, bullet holes, and ill-begotten maggots. Every single body made an imprint on his mind. Victims became his responsibility. And he was on his way to the morgue with Brooke again.

Murderous days and morbid floribunda. Yellow narcissist flowers wave in their wake as Michael and Brooke pass by on their way to the door of the morgue. A chamber of dead space. Opening the front door was like opening the lid to a coffin.

The session began as a faulty fluorescent light stuttered overhead, causing a ten minute delay in the proceedings. In the cold calcium light, the metal table was a chilling feature, displaying an opaline female body in the morgue. The body everybody had come to see. The pathologists faces behind forensic masks, well protected from pathogens and microbes. The voice of the senior pathologist broadcasts a sagacious monologue.

'There are only two pints of blood left in the body. There are six identical puncture wounds in the arteries along both the left and the right arms. On the neck, puncture wounds from the thorns caused negligible blood loss—however, the thorns released a toxic agent that caused temporary paralysis.'

She rolls the victim's head to the right. 'Behind the ear—a small keyhole has been bored into the skull—surgically performed.' The buzz of a rotary saw makes Brooke turn away as the back of the skull is removed, exposing the brain and all its visceral contents. 'No sign of trauma to the outer casing of the brain, but note the channel behind the ear which leads to the brain, clearly shows signs of abrasion.' With a scalpel held in a latex-gloved hand, the pathologist proceeds to slice away the posterior section of the brain, exposing the gray inner core. There is an empty pause as she cuts away the brain material covering the chamber to the ear. 'The pineal gland has been removed by penetrating the cranium's natural pathway leading to the center of the brain. This hole was made to access the pineal gland without the brain being alerted to the invasion. Death would have occurred only when the pineal was severed. The victim was conscious up to the point of death.' She refers to her clipboard of notes. 'There is no sign of sexual penetration. However, it has been confirmed that teeth were used to remove the clitoris.'

So the afternoon unfolds. The thorn and the rose together mean pain and pleasure, and if roses represent the hope and promise of new beginnings, the killer is taking intense pleasure, by circling the name of his next victim in crimson ink.

23

MICHAEL'S TEAM GATHERS IN the briefing room to discuss the latest killings. The labeled photographs of victims, and plastic bags of grisly crime evidence—every little piece added up to the gloomy tale of death. The door opens, and four more agents join the meeting along with the Chief, his controlled cough brings the room to silence.

'As of now, Michael and Brooke are assigned the best forensic and psych team on the force.'

'Thank you Chief. The Inflatable Murder and the Rose Garden Murder were elaborately and theatrically staged. Victims are the same age, mid-twenties, professional models. The murders happened in the early morning, and torture always preceded death. Blood tests of victims reveal the presence of neuromuscular drugs. The victims show airway restrictions, incisions in arms exposing arteries with puncture wounds for controlled blood loss, keyhole invasion of the skull, and removal of the pineal gland. All executed with the skill of a surgeon. There is an order of injuries leading to death which are; first injury is the opening of veins and consequent blood loss. The second injury is airway restriction. The third is the removal of a sexual organ. Of the three injuries inflicted, any would cause death if left untreated. However, in the last victim's case, the removal of the pineal gland was the cause of death.'

Avoiding wild stabs in the dark that others might quickly jump to, Michael picks up a dark blue stubby marker and writes on the whiteboard. His firm pressure on the final word torture sees the tip of the marker retrench into its plastic casing. Michael tosses yet another blue felt-tip pen into the trash can.

'Why paralyze? Why prolong death? Why torture? Why sexually mutilate? Why enter through the back door of the skull and steal the pineal? These are the questions you need to ask yourselves. The torture begins in daylight but death takes place at night. The body is then transported and dramatically staged in a public place. We know the killer's modus operandi, so let's anticipate his moves. We need to stop this guy.'

The forensic psychologist is up next. She answers some of Michael's questions. 'Why paralyze the victim? To keep the person conscious and aware. Why torture? Pain releases opium hormones. Why target the pineal? The ancient ritualistic method of trepanation, which is the practice of cutting a hole in the skull, was thought to increase a level of consciousness.' Flicking through her report she finds her notations. 'Certain occult circles saw the pineal as the center of wisdom and intuition, and the seat of God. It's also called the third eye. The light above. The pineal is light-sensitive, and there's the clue. Pathology indicates that torture started in daylight. That could be meaningful if the murderer is into both the occult and medicine. The killer knew the gland's response to light and waited for the gland to complete its full endocrine cycle during the evening and harvested it in the early hours of the morning.'

Michael writes on the whiteboard; pineal hormones, pineal endocrine cycle, medical knowledge and surgical abilities, understands botanical toxicology, ritualistic theme.

'The killer has premeditated ideals, and a complicated agenda. It is not about killing for blood lust or passion. He's not in the category of a disorganized killer. We are dealing with an analytical, well-organized, rational, and clever serial killer.'

The psychologist adds: 'He's a paranoiac who hates his father and wishes him dead. In contrast, he harbors an opposite feeling towards his mother—an obsessive Oedipus complex love for his mother. He wants her to live on forever.'

Michael concludes: 'To catch this guy, we have to think as he does. What are the fantasies? How does he engage his victims? How does he get to know them? How does he gain control over his victims? What are his core needs? I want answers for each and every question. And theories on why the murderer kills the way he does. In short why did it happen the way it did?' Michael stacks his notes and folders, one on top of the other.

'Let's re-group at 9 am tomorrow.'

Brooke looked at the paper bundle under Michael's arm. 'A little light reading tonight, is it?'

'No.'

'So those reports are for ... ?'

'You.'

Under the cover of a black umbrella, Michael and Brooke walk out of the precinct into the smudged rain. If the temperature drops another degree, the rain will freeze into flurries and coat the steps with a white powder, leaving a light brushing over their footprints.

But nothing will freeze tonight. They walk around the corner to the local café. Meetings gave Brooke an appetite for carbohydrates with no fiber and little food value. As she finishes her coffee, she feels the familiar flutters in her heart, like a butterfly trapped inside. Coffee is her weakness. Despite the way the caffeine butterfly flutters, coffee is her drug, and she will never give it up.

'What do you think, Brooke?'

'Don't get me started. I think murder has become mainstream. We've lost the sorrow. Humans used to hesitate before they took lives. We've become more arrogant and detached from our true nature. We desire to become rich without limit, so we destroy the planet believing that there is no other choice—animals, humans, unborn children, marine life, forests, all up for grabs.'

Michael waits … 'And as far as this case goes?'

'Promise me you won't recommend me for a sabbatical? What I'm about to say is way out of the normal.'

'What is it?'

'Well, the murderer is now physically incorporating symbols. Ones that represent the darker side of the soul, darker aspects of the universe, including death, mourning, evil, and revenge. The blue rose set-up seems particularly significant.'

'Go on!'

'The body was discovered under a rose bush. Something hidden under roses means secrets are hidden.'

Brooke signaled the waiter. 'Another coffee please. Black.'

She stirs the coffee out of habit. She gave up sugar a week ago.

'So, a rose can indicate death, and the act of saying goodbye. It's also the symbol of sacrifice, meaning wishes come true after death. Closed petals mean love has ended; the relationship has come to an end. The blue rose means unobtainable; I can't have you, but I can't stop thinking about you. The melancholy of feeling blue when love goals can't be met. Also, when someone kills the holder of the blue rose, it was said that the killer will possess her—after death.'

'That's one strange love story.'

Brooke was on a roll and her fifth coffee of the day.

'I believe the victim knew her murderer.'

'So do I.'

'Of the thousand variety of rose bushes in the public garden, the murderer placed the body under a blue rose bush.'

Michael drained his latte. 'Those blue petals on the corpse are a botanical conundrum. There's no blue gene in nature. However, a scientist uncovered a recessive gene and through genetic engineering created blue roses.'

'That's right, and as a result, blue roses represent the mystery and longing to attain the impossible.'

'Do you know that New York is the only city in the world with a garden of genetically engineered blue roses, which are named Rosa. The victim's actual name—coincidence?'

'So the killer spills her blood three ways, interferes with her, takes her life and possesses her in death!'

The café has nose-to-tail offerings on the menu, created by a new chef. Lamb kidneys in light filo served with garlic potato mash, faggots, and oxtail tamarind soup. In such an eatery, Brooke and Michael are like Haruspices, like the Roman soothsayers who interpreted omens by observing sacrificed animal entrails.

'It's even got Roman-style tripe.' Brooke orders Greek salad, minus the olives.

'A question?'

'Shoot.'

'Why order Greek when the whole point is the Kalamata olives?'

'Same reason you're picking capers out of your bagel.'

'So what can we take from this?'

'The killer is a medically minded madman.'

Brooke's headliner is closer to the truth than she realizes.

'We've got one last stop before we call it a day.'

Brooke sighed. 'And what a day!'

Together, they head on foot, to The Medici Library, a library of rare and restricted books. After walking a short distance on the rough sidewalk, Brooke stops and checks the sole of her shoe. She rustles through her bag, finds a sharp nail file, lifts her shoe, and balancing on one high heel, digs out the culprit, a small stone before it had a chance to work deeper into the leather. Nothing will get into her today if she can help it, not a stone, not grit, not anything.

24

IN THE FOYER OF the library, a medieval mural shows two ancient scholars writing manuscripts, unaware of the town engulfed in flames behind them. In the plaster cornices above, satyrs encroach the space between the cherubs and griffins—odd-fellows hunched together, looking down at the entrance.

Michael flashes his FBI badge to the librarian on duty. When he requests entrance to the archives, her expression turns colder than the climate-controlled atmosphere. Still, Harper knows she can't deny an official request any more than she could deny Christian his requests. Regrets have a way of stockpiling. The way books do when nothing is put back on the shelf. She led them through a series of redwood archways to the annex of rare books.

'Please use the white gloves provided. Do not handle the books without them.'

Harper waits outside the annex. She picks up a gossip magazine and flicks through a dozen paparazzi photos of the furrier's wife dressed in a full-length mink coat, leopard-skin tights, and red stiletto heels. In her new lease of life, now her tyrannical husband was gone, she's gone and got herself a toy boy, a handsome man of thirty-nine. Her body and her face for a seventy-year-old, look remarkable. The rumor is she appears younger because she's got herself into the anti-aging trials at Biozen Corporation. Harper thinks, I want some of that, and I know just the man to give it to me.

Three hours later, Michael and Brooke continue to turn the revered pages of antiquity until the pages fall silent. Brooke's hand stops dead. 'Check this out. Egyptian priests believed that human sacrifice was necessary to give and resurrect life. Interestingly, the image Egyptian scholars have drawn here is the Eye of Horus. The mystics of Egypt believed that it was key to heavenly eternity. The third eye gave extra perception and created a mirage of unheard of possibilities, and it's the exact shape of the pineal gland.'

'And listen to this, *The Pharmaceutica* is the alchemist's guide to raising the dead. It's a manual for the death cults with formulae for killing. Take this passage: *"Thrice killed, leave in a peaceful place gathering dew, then the sacred Horace Eye is ready to look on heaven for eternity."* The killer has read this. He's following the cults' ordinations to the letter.'

Nothing surprised Michael, but this was uncanny. The inspiration for the heinous killings could have come directly from this book, these pages. Death cults and one particular hidden society had strong links to ancient Egyptian rites. Hidden societies took death as a powerful life force that could resurrect life in the divine world. Leonardo and Sartre were all heads of secret cults, as were leading scientists and alchemists. Today was a day for uncovering the past, Michael thinks. Times have changed, but what went down in one thousand BC and the fifteenth and twentieth century is happening in the twenty-first century, he was sure.

Brooke writes the Dewy Decimal numbers and titles of the manuscripts down. *The Pharmaceutica*, written in the Middle Ages, explains to pharmacists in Europe the ancient Egyptian priests' practices for using parts of the dead for the living. So this morbid compendium details recipes on how to prepare mummy parts for human use and consumption. She reads the bibliography of *The Pharmaceutica*: *Herein lies extraordinary recipes for ceremonies, artist materials, and medicines.* And there's a creepy cough syrup extracted from mummy bandages soaked in laudanum. Whatever next Brooke thought.

She beckons the librarian to the table piled high with books.

'Can you tell me who has accessed these books?'

The librarian scans the titles. 'Is this a trick question? We don't hold records on people's reading interests. This is a private reading room and no surveillance, in case you hadn't noticed.'

Brooke stands up. 'We would like the name of every person who has accessed this room in the last year.'

Harper thinks on her feet. 'You will have to have a warrant to access that information.' Then she said, with a thin crescent of a smile: 'Is there anything else I can help you with?'

Brooke said in a flat response: 'We will be back on Wednesday with a warrant.'

Harper watches them leave the building before she sits down in front of her computer. Her glasses reflect a list of names, but one name appears often, and she knows who he is. Almost without thinking, she sends a text. A message flashes back, and she follows his instructions to erase his name from the computer. If only she knew how evil twists a life to suit its plan. She puts the library ledger in her bag, pushes open the double doors of the side entrance, and in her high heels descends awkwardly down the flight of stone steps leading to the street, only to disappear around the corner where a car is idling.

Once Harper turned the corner, down 6th Avenue, it was a sure thing she wouldn't be coming back.

25

THE SUBMISSIONS FROM ARTISTS who entered the *'Portrait Artist of the Year'* competition attracted overwhelming interest from art critics, dealers, artists, and art lovers. Charlotte and Michael arrive at the art gallery on Wooster Street to hear the winner announced. Art wasn't Michael's interest, but Charlotte loved art, and he loved her. Michael looked at the creative crowd. Unlike a contemporary palette, Michael didn't blend with this eclectic, arty group, like the man wearing black leather pants, leaning into the man wearing a mauve jacket. Instead, with Michael's brown shirt and chino pants, he is more drawn to the familiarity of the brown autumnal themed buffet with its buffalo wings and miniature pumpkin pies. With his plate of savories, he drifts through into the gallery annex.

Back in the main gallery, a holographic portrait of a young woman holds everyone in her gaze. As the hologram projects her image, light catches her eyes; shards of refraction set off red flashes, like millions of blood diamonds, ill-gained, challenging the crowd to look directly at her, not through her or past her. To see a woman as she now is, a celestial woman. For art critics and dealers present in the gallery, a portrait by a street artist was not on exhibition to please their sensibilities. They were only bent on creating fame for an elite group of their favorite artists. And commercially, a street artist doesn't cut it—for them.

The gallery owner's liberal voice silences the conversations.

'Thank you for braving the cold and coming tonight. From the thousands of entries, the art committee selected three finalists. It's my pleasure and honor to announce the winner tonight. By the unanimous decision, the judges have voted the *'Unknown Woman'* a portrait by the urban street artist, Chalkman, the winner of this year's $100,000 prize.'

From out of the crowd, a tall figure steps forward.

'Good evening, I'm Christian Cutter. The artist has asked me to accept the *Portrait Artist of the Year Award* on his behalf. He says he will send his message of thanks through social media.'

Joe had won. Christian expected as much. Christian understood that critics and gallery owners were the guardians of fame. So he had gone out of his way to wine and dine them in the buzzy bistros of West Soho, discussing art over copious bottles of French and Italian wines. His social efforts paid off. Christian had submitted Joe's entry without asking his permission, because he knew Joe was adamant about protecting his anonymity.

Meanwhile, the exhibition *Great Bodies of Art* catches Michael's interest enough to make him put down his plate and listen to the curator. 'The Great Masters' pigments came from a surprising source—the grave. The dark brown tones in the paintings of Eugene Delacroix, Sir Lawrence Alma-Tadema, and Edward Burne Jones, to name a few. The pigment they sought for flesh tones and shadows was called Mummy Brown. They knew Mummy Brown came from the carcasses of the dead. As far back as the Middle

Ages, European artists were aware that Egyptian artists had used pigments from mummies before the time of the Pharaohs.'

Michael picks up his empty glass, and a waiter, as if reading his mind, appears from nowhere and presents a tray of red and white wines, but something in the waiter's eyes was off-putting. 'Between the 16th and 19th centuries, many painters, wanting flesh tones and clothing to appear more life-like, used mummy pigment from the grave. Mummies were ground up to produce the color. Rumor had it when the famous artist Burne-Jones discovered the source of the pigment he'd been applying; he was so horrified he buried his reserves of Mummy Brown paint. Michelangelo had no such compunction and used it on the Sistine Chapel in the 1500s. It took four hundred years to reveal famous masters, like Leonardo da Vinci, Delacroix and Degas, used the decay of human life to make bodies of art.' The speaker pauses to clear her throat, and continues. This is the point where her research pays off in spades, and the buzz of satisfaction happens. The audience was clearly horrified at her macabre breaking news. She keeps a straight face amongst the sea of pale faces. Some people, the Leonardo da Vinci lovers, are the most shocked. 'The pigment remained viable until the 20th century. In 1915, a London pigment dealer commented that one mummy produced enough pigment to last his customers twenty years. As supplies of mummies ran low, dubious dealers used body parts from other sources. Over time, 700,000 bodies were buried, dug up, broken into pieces, and then ground into powder. Mummies of men, women, children, dogs, cats, birds. Their carcasses and linen wrappings became oil pigments painted into masterpieces. These are the paintings, macabre resurrections, that art lovers queue to see; in the Le Louvre, Paris, The British Art Gallery, London, The Prado, Madrid, Uffizi Gallery, Florence, and The Guggenheim, New York. Death pigments made artists famous and art dealers' their fortunes, and thereby making the unacceptable, acceptable.'

At that instant, Michael felt a chill, as if somebody was preparing his future grave. Random facts create possibilities. Possibilities become clues. Clues make answers possible. Michael picks up his wine glass. As he does so, the Eye of Horus appears inside the ring of condensation left on the glass surface, a strange projection of the cabinet's contents. A lithographic symbol, a picture of an eye inside a triangle, glued on a wooden box of pastels, and the label *Mammillary Pastels* written in ink and penned by goose-quill pen, two hundred years before.

There is something else. Michael sees a shadow move within a shadow, fleeting as if imagined. His senses jag him to move away from the overhead balcony. Like fish are observed from above, somebody is watching him below. Michael feels a familiar touch and takes a step back. It's the familiar face of Charlotte. 'I'm ready to go. How about you?'

'Before we leave, what's your impression?' Michael points to the somber kitchen painting by Michel Martin Drolling's; as dark and heavy as the gilded frame surrounding it. In the painting, two women sit by an open window, yellow light slants in, turns copper pots on the dark wooden table light brown, as the women's dresses fall in shades and hues of endless brown.

Charlotte says: 'Brown, brown and brown, such an oppressive atmosphere, more like the kitchen of death, the women are mourning, not cooking.'

They both agreed, it was definitely time to leave.

Through the Tribeca gallery window, the holographic portrait flickers, gilded and caged. Within an hour, the winning painting had gone viral on the dark web.

26

JOE IS PAINTING LATE into the night when one of his headaches kicks in. He drops his brushes and presses his hands on either side of his temples to release the pain imprisoned inside, but the throbbing gains power along with the voice. A voice that speaks of deeds of darkness amongst mildewed circles, Leonardo da Vinci, Delacroix, confessions, and admissions, repetitions, life through the death of others. A headache that brings the maniacal twilight's manifest, until the poppy field of opiates stretches the voice further away, into the distance. Joe finds himself in the elevator, going down, drowning in vaporous thinking. The lift door opens. A night cleaner stands in the corner, ready with a rusty bucket and an incendiary mop to keep the deluge of demons out. Night throws a black velvet robe over his shoulders, enveloping him.

The manifesto of the city felt fertile. Traffic lights blinked on amber. No moon yet, buildings loom dark against the lazuli blue sky—the city a free canvas for all graffiti artists. Soon Chalkman's presence on the face of the ten-story building is nothing more than a dark shadow in the black husk of night. The artistic doings of the graffiti artist go unnoticed by millions of New Yorkers; inhabitants of buildings, some sleeping below him in the confines of their dreams, some with eyes shut, some with blinds drawn, except for a couple arguing into the night, and the baby crying, inconsolable. Someone left the lights on. A child, perhaps, or an adult perhaps still sadly a little afraid of the dark, from monsters of their own toxic childhood. And so bedroom lights are left on by the fearful, unaware it is they who are giving essential light to the street artist, to do what he does. Clandestine does as clandestine desires—the moon arriving later. The moon's graphic curve, like a silver blade, cuts through the lunar sky. Stars align in a heavenly formation, like a proof sheet of silver that needs no correction. Chalkman paints through the night.

Six hours pass, and the portrait is almost finished. Chalkman thinks: No one belongs here more than you do. Then, before his eyes, the rosebud curve of the woman's lips suddenly turn bright red, he sees his fingertips rubbed raw and bleeding, as if he had seen everything at once in seconds. Then, hears the voice again: 'Blood mixed with chalk. This pain will be useful to you. The color is less magenta and more a shade of blood-red.'

At the end of the night he had painted his own reality. With that, he climbs down the iron ladders of forgotten fire escapes, walks through poorly-lit back streets, past corrugated fences that enclose vacant lots with their dark recesses of rubble. A lone dog barks over fathomless space. Perhaps, not just barking at the artist, but howling for all the broken lives, and dreams left empty.

Chalkman passes a familiar diner. The aroma of hot donuts comes on strong, in a memory trick of cinnamon and glazed sugar. Still, it is the slow hypnotics of all-night jazz next door that leaves

Chalkman outside and draws Joe inside the club for a smoke, while listening to *Jungle Reinhardt*. Although the sun is yet to rise, the urban legend's painting has gone viral. It starts with a Twitter and soon becomes cyber-birds all a twittering, while art critics and gallery owners dream on, and those who find themselves awake, count sheep in the pen of unconscious mortality. No matter how poorly they slept, they wake to another day to bitch and criticize nothing in particular, unless it's particularly peculiar.

As hashish smoke rises from soft stone chillums, black keys play on, and Christian appears as a haze.

'Are you celebrating alone, Joe?'

'You've got me wrong Christian. I'm not celebrating at all. Why should I?'

'Why not? Fame is fame.'

'The win was your doing. People may believe in fame or the economics of art. But I don't. It's the painting they like, not me. Are artists truly respected, or is the art industry a money-making sham? I have too many options to let myself get manipulated by it.'

Christian has another perspective and shares it with Joe. 'There appears to be a growing institutional intrigue about a street artist out there, who's bent on keeping street art alive. Misgivings aside, Chalkman made a name for himself.'

'Yes—but what's in a name! The way I see it, James Barry died in poverty. Toulouse Lautrec died of alcoholism, syphilis, and in debt. Rembrandt died in obscurity and poverty. Modigliani died of meningitis at thirty-five. Vermeer died at forty-three, his family was left penniless. Gauguin died in poverty. Vincent Van Gogh sold only one painting in his lifetime, and for $109. He committed suicide by shooting himself in the chest. His last words were, *"The sadness will last forever"*, and he died broke and destitute.'

'And your point is?'

'True fame comes after death.'
'Then, you'll show them the truth. So where to next?'
'29th East Street.'

27

A CRASH COMES FROM the spare bedroom. Alexis opens the door.

'Joe?'

Shadow crouches wide-eyed guilty amongst Joe's collection of memorabilia. Marilyn Munroe is on the floor, a limited edition ceramic figurine in a curvy one-piece bathing suit, lies in pieces, her face intact and still beautiful, but the back of her skull is smashed in. Broken things give Alexis a sense of guilt. Even if she is not at fault, she feels guilty, so she places the figurine upright in the corner and carefully balances the broken head on the shoulders. At first glance, the star appears complete. Only when she is touched will she fall apart once again.

Alexis takes a shower, washes her hair, and scrunches it with her fingers while blow-drying a tousled look. This morning she finds Shadow annoying. Being more of a dog person, she pulls up the sash window and shoves him outside. Shadow stares down the street, flicks his tail in anticipation, as if waiting for someone, walks along the narrow ledge, and climbs up a twisted wisteria vine. It seems, no sooner had she put Shadow out, he razes diamond-like claws down the window, etching frenetic patterns, persisting as only a cat can. Alexis opens the window and lets him in, along with a blast of hoar frost.

Apart from the cat, Alexis is alone in the apartment. Christian had apparently gone away for a long weekend. She'd asked Joe about Christian several times. Alexis wasn't sure if Joe was fobbing her off with his off-the-cuff comments alluding to Christian being hardly ever home due to his business commitments. Her intuition came to the fore. Why didn't she believe him? It was a grand apartment, with plenty of space for both of them, yet she hadn't seen any sign of Christian.

Looking around the building would not be snooping, but more like getting to know the family. Besides, they better get used to it because she was going to be a part of the family, so what harm could it do? But still, as she gets into the lift, a quiet nagging thought reminds her, there's a good reason to mind your own business. If only she had listened. Minding your own business keeps you out of trouble, but the trouble was, where she was headed. She pulls the brass lift lever, and the lift ascends to Christian's private apartment. When it stops, she stands still for a while in the low yellow light of the elevator. She doesn't make a move. Instead, she listens for movement. Any warning sound, however slight, matters, but nothing is untoward, just the tapping of water dripping from the eaves and a siren in the distance.

'Hello? Anyone there?'

As soon as she speaks, lights flash on, activated by the sound of her voice. The halogens reveal a modern, ultra tidy living room. Not the touches of a woman tidy, but a paid maid type of clean. It didn't take a forensic accountant to see Christian was into money, not that she was good with figures, but if she guessed correctly, he was one of the top five percent of high-income earners in the world. He was living the life of the upper echelon. He must be a multi-millionaire or billionaire with more disposable income than she had hot baths.

Arriving unannounced in his inner sanctum, she had a distinct feeling of being a trespasser and a voyeur. The twilight time between getting away with what you are doing, and having some-one walk into the room and catch you in the act.

She looked around for surveillance cameras—nothing. The door to the master bedroom was open. She admired the scale of a super king bed, one that demanded custom-made linen, monogrammed sheets, a goose-down comforter, and copious swan- feather-filled pillows. Indigo drapes were festooned back from the upholstered pelmets, revealing a landscape window framing New York City.

Snooping is addictive; opening drawers, closets, photo albums, and reading dairies was her pleasure. Alexis was a spy on the lives of others. For some reason, she had yet to figure; it made her feel happy. Alexis could origami private papers back along their lines, fold them so precisely, no one ever knew she'd read them.

Alexis opened the wardrobe door and was suitably impressed. Expensive shirts, color co-ordinated ties, and shoes of the most exquisite leather, pairs of emu, lizard, crocodile and snake. There were gold embossed coat hangers in the wardrobe, evenly spaced, each facing the same way. To Alexis's mind, the closet belonged to a man who was a 'Double O', very over-organized. By comparison, her personal wardrobe was a jungle of tangled wire coat hangers. She had read that quirks like a tidy closet, can be chalked up to obsessive thoughts and compulsions. But only one percent had full-blown OCD.

It was around the time when she stepped into the elevator to check out the penthouse, that two feelings hit her. An unnerving feeling that someone was listening, and another, that she was being followed closely. It was Shadow that watched Alexis step into the lift, saw how she shut herself in the black cage, and how she talked to herself. Shadow caught every word, not the cat exactly, but the surveillance device attached to his collar—a feline transmitter.

When she arrived at the top floor, nothing could have prepared her for what she saw; a bright hermetically sealed state-of-the-art science laboratory. As she steps into the bright lights of the lab, double glass doors close behind her, cutting her shadow in half. Standing there alone in a room of white opaque liquids at different stages of evaporation, and crystals in transparent beakers, it would be nice if something made sense, but nothing, at this point, made any sense to Alexis. When you don't know what you're looking for, sometimes you stumble onto what you want, like white powder on a glass slab. Now here's something I know about. Whoever made this stuff has an eye for quality. Below the bench, on the metal shelves, she counts ten packs of white powder. A drug lab! No wonder you kept the family business quiet, artist and business-man indeed. The brothers at work here! A couple of drug lords! My favorite kind of people!

A thought comes to mind of Lewis Carroll's *Alice Through the Looking Glass,* and what Alice found there, potions someone had left behind for Alice to find. It was too easy. One of the kilo packets was open. Alexis takes a scalpel, lifts out a small amount of powder, and places it on a mirrored surface. Dividing it up into three lines, she takes a pipette, runs a line, and tosses her head back, feeling the burn, then the rush ... *'In a wonderland, they lie dreaming as the days go by, dreaming as the summers die, ever drifting down the stream ...'* Alexis does her second line of coke ... *'dreaming as the summers die, lingering in the golden gleam, life, what is it but a dream?'*

Places where death occurs are not always the same. Alexis won't remember finishing the last line because a white light draws her towards the man waiting for her, but the man turns his back. She reaches out to him, but he keeps walking away into the distance, until he is no more than a pinprick in her pupils. Her eyelids now in lockdown.

CHAPTER

28

Joe arrived back at the apartment, somewhat trashed from the hash, resinous and illicit. The highest quality Manala Cream from the foothills of the Himalayas, and it certainly gave Joe a high. Still, like all things, everything eventually dissipates to nothing.

He walks into the bedroom, where curtains remain drawn against sunlight. He throws his clothes of the night into the hamper, a hopeful act of salvage, for ruined clothing, torn by rappelling. He showers and slips into bed beside Alexis, but the sheets are cold. Alexis was gone. He searches the apartment for clues; a wet bath towel dumped on the bathroom floor, a cup of coffee gone cold. He opened the window. A gust of unconscious urban air blew inside. The pervasive dust that blanketed the city consisted of human slough. It coats balconies and windows, cloistered in an inextinguishable dust cloud from the funeral pyre of humanity. It is the only way dead people can return home—in the dust you see, in a slant of sunlight.

Alexi's car was parked outside. Had she decided to go for a walk? Then he imagined Alexis standing in front of a shelf full of warm pastries at the bakery. Joe switches on the coffee machine and phones Alexis but hears her mobile ring from the bedroom. Maybe she hasn't gone to get pastries. Maybe she's gone and left me.

He felt emptiness, but Joe being Joe, was used to being alone. But he could always count on Christian to be there. Joe pressed the elevator button, but nothing happened. Christian had imported the elevator, the contraption dated back to 1893, from a Prague hotel where it had become a trap for the wealthy and self-important. The Grand Hotel sold the lift to Christian because it had stalled and trapped too many aristocrats inside. Joe leans in and glances up into the lift well to see the culprit, a jammed pulley wheel.

What Joe really wants to do is crash into his bed and sleep, the sleep of the dead. He was exhilarated but exhausted from the last two weeks. Instead, he goes up the internal marble staircase, swipes the laboratory's keypad, and as he enters, the rush of atmosphere feels disturbingly warm. Either the thermostat malfunctioned, or the electrical system has a fault. Either way, one thing was certain, the overall temperature was set to ruin Christian's latest cultures.

Joe doesn't expect to find the top notes of luminous bergamot and clementine blossom, a notable perfume with a floral edge. Or to suddenly hear Christian say: 'So this is Alexis. The new love of your life. This is the infamous Alexis who faked her pregnancy, her art gallery, The Chelsea Hotel, and her famous grandmother. And lied about everything else she has ever told you. At last, and finally, we get to meet the liar in person.'

Alexis lies barefooted on the floor. Her toenails and fingernails painted Cajun shrimp, silver Pandora bracelets on her wrist, her fingers entwined like a liana vine through the elevator cage. Joe thinks about what he sees, all eight bones in the wrist, five bones in the palm, fourteen bones in her fingers, all twenty-seven bones twisted in rigor. Christian leans down and snaps them, one by one, until she releases her grip. Then he slips off her gold watch and puts it in his pocket.

He touches the carotid on her throat out of habit, no arterial pulse; he didn't expect one, definitely dead. He picks up a fallen chair, straightens out the rack of glass tubes, proceeds to check samples of cultures under the proton microscope. 'At least the batches are viable.' He sets to cleaning and disinfecting the entire laboratory. The last thing to tidy up is the woman, which he under-takes with the care of an undertaker. Her eyes are wide-open, unusual sage-green. He closes her lids. She is quite beautiful with a small aquiline nose. White powder from her nostrils had fled down her face in a stream of white snot. She was an enigma. Perhaps she was French? Whatever she was, she was dead.

Joe sits on the chrome lab stool and revolves around and around; flasks, vials, microscopes, flasks, vials, microscopes flash by until he stops the room from spinning by putting his foot down. His vision comes into stark focus on a pack of white powder sliced open on the metal bench, silver pipette lying beside a gold earring. 'She snorted the powder,' Joe said, looking at Alexis incredulously. 'She thought it was cocaine. What an absolute waste of a woman.'

Nothing goes to waste, Christian thinks as he wipes off her snot with a tissue. Then he grabs both her ankles and drags the body along the polished concrete floor to the chiller. Her arms flail in a wave of dead semaphore. If Alexis had been alive, she would've run for the door.

29

JOE THOUGHT ABOUT HIS last visit with his mother. The old book Grace had given him, the binding falling apart, at first glance, too much disrepair, at face value worthless to any antiquarian book collector. To her, it was a book of consequences. Grace had said: 'This is the Cutter book of the chalk-makers' secrets. It has been handed down through the Cutter family for five centuries, but it is one of two books. They say you need both books to find the genius within. One is useless, without the other.'

Joe traced the family tree to a pinprick on the map of the world. Cerne Abbas, a small village in the English countryside in the county of Dorchester. But the first stop, as crows fly, was London.

'Hello, British Airways, you're speaking with Ella.'

'Next available flight to London, please.'

'Economy class?'

'No, must be first class. My legs don't fit in economy.'

LONDON WAS A seven hour flight from New York. The enthusiastic welcome from the English cabin crew, and plates of roast beef and Yorkshire pudding they served, took him back to old pubs with names like the Lamb and Flag and The Turf Tavern where the U.S. President "did not inhale marijuana". The beer would take a bit of getting used to again, but that was England. Warm beer on a warm day was part of the custom. Meanwhile, he is at forty thousand feet, flying over the mysterious Devil's Triangle; a dozen or so nuns sitting in economy running the rosaries, with all the blessings of Saint Christopher patron saint of journeys; a rabbit's foot in a passenger's pocket, a four-leaf clover in another's. All the good luck charms for the believers and the faithful keep the plane flying, as Joe finishes custard and apple crumble. The aircraft arrives on time, perhaps because nuns prayed the whole journey for the souls on board, their safety, and their salvation.

Joe waits in the arduous queue at immigration. A broad mix of citizens and legal aliens holding temporary visas, makes for a long multicultural line. The border security officer scrutinizes Joe's passport. Then says with the demeanor of someone who loves the authority a uniform gives. 'Come this way.'

In the windowless room, Joe is questioned about his itinerary. Can he explain the reason for his brief visit to The United Kingdom? They quiz him fanatically about his occupation until he lies and insists he is a good friend of Banksy, which as it turns out, was the wrong lie to say.

'Banksy is thought to be a variety of people, anonymous. Do you intend to do street art in London with Banksy?'

'It's not a felony where I come from. It's a mere misdemeanor with a maximum sentence of one year. But in New York, it's got to be done with an aerosol can or a magic marker to be classed as a misdemeanor, and that's not what I use.'

His body, which had already been duly patted down, is upgraded to a full-body search. 'I take it no one here is a fan of graffiti art. Thanks for the friendly welcome. A little too intimate for my taste.' His bags are opened, and contents rifled in search of graffiti gear. But Joe is here to steal—not paint.

Three hours later, he leaves the airport terminal and joins the taxi-queue. The taxi driver, an eminent surgeon who once hailed from Saudi Arabia, drives Joe to the train station where he waits in line for a ticket to Cerne Abbas. On the train, rows of commuters reading newspapers, teenage kids with headphones, and crying babies all go down the line to Dorchester. A girl who sits beside him has a rose tattooed on her ankle. The brand new tattoo trickles blood into her Doc Martin boot. She feels Joe's eyes, like a brush tracing the thorns, and gives this stranger a cold, hard stare, more than a transient hint to look the other way.

The hotel Joe booked is a sixteenth-century pub in the village of Moreton, ten miles as the crow flies, from the Jurassic Coast. The Tudor building is a chocolate box postcard; wattle and daub walls, oak beamed ceilings, endless creaking floorboards despite the carpeted hallways, and according to the legend, a resident ghost. Small casement windows of hand-blown glass have a Tudor rose etched on each pane. The thatched roof is covered with chicken wire to stop crows from flying away with straw reeds. A fledgling sparrow had died between wire and thatch, not that anyone but Joe notices such things—the bird's featherless body, mummified.

Joe sits in the bar waiting for the maid to finish cleaning his room. With a pint of bitter in hand, he looks for all intents like an Englishman, but really more like a character in a novel, and by the time the room is ready, he's been shouted a single malt whiskey by a retired English punk rocker, who was infamous, and wants to be famous again, which is why Joe gives him Christian's business card.

'Room's ready, at the top of stairs, mind yer noggin,' Albert the publican said. His snowy beard and gut hanging over his belt give him the look of an out-of-work Santa Claus, just as friendly and jolly, but the way the old man smacks his lips before beginning a sentence sets Joe's teeth on edge.

The upper floor has five attic-like rooms, wallpapered in floral, each with its own bathroom and iron radiators for heating, most of which never get past lukewarm, not that such quirks are mentioned in hotel brochures. Albert smacks his lips again. 'Supper's in an hour.' He closes the door on Joe.

Despite Albert, Joe likes England, somewhat, unless adding his list of exceptions; the days of drizzling rain, the fog and low lying mist, the gray skies, endless queues, and lumpy mashed potatoes smothered in packet gravy.

Joe is unpacking when he hears a knock on the door, and as he opens it, Albert thrusts a plate of cookies into his hands. By the blank stare Joe gave him, he explained further. 'Dorset Knobs, complimentary packet.' Albert picks one up and takes a bite.

'This recipe has been handed down for generations. The knobs are handy biscuits, especially for working folk. In the old days, it was traditional to serve knobs swilled down with ale, to give the lads something to go on.'

Joe's nerves jangle as Albert crunches through another biscuit and adds with his mouth full of crumbs. 'Our grandpa was one to dunk them in his tea to soften them up a bit, on account of his having false teeth. I do the same.'

At this point, Albert reminds Joe so much of Henry, he herds Albert back out the door. But Albert is oblivious and goes on with his monologue. 'In the same way as our Cornwall cousins and their beef pasties, were good enough for taking to work or war, as they last for an age without spoiling. If Dorset Knobs are baked three times, rather than twice, they're be known as the triscuts instead of biscuits. And can knock a man out at ten paces if hurled with enough vigor.'

By which point Joe manages to squeeze the door shut and lock it behind Albert, who goes downstairs, still talking to himself, or is he laughing?

30

It is early morning. Joe hears the fire in the kitchen stove being stoked. Smoke before the blaze has a particularly acrid smell; the degree of lead, fonts in newsprint melting until paragraphs, whole sentences and crossword puzzles are caught up in the fire, words swallowed by flames escaping through the brick chimney. The burning of fossil fuels changes the weather, changes the climate of the world. Not that the villagers pay attention to global warming. Coal was coal. They cut it straight out of the ground.

The breakfast is the house specialty; honey smoked shoulder bacon, free-range eggs, two rounds of black blood sausage and acid-free tomatoes, served on top of a slab of fried bread; followed by toasted farmhouse bread with churned creamery butter and bitter orange marmalade, with its dash of Scottish whiskey.

After breakfast, Joe heads to the grass verge of a local airfield where a yellow de Havilland Tiger Moth, a 1930's biplane, sits on the tarmac, ready to fly into a somewhat depressing gray sky. Joe hopes the hearty breakfast will fortify him against the cold weather at altitude, since he had forgotten his leather gloves. He will fly the only biplane named after a moth: the great tiger moth of the Arctiidae family found throughout Europe, as far as Lapland, and up in the mountains as high as 9,800 feet. A clever moth that makes ultrasonic sounds to fight predators, a moth that foils its attacker by playing dead when in danger.

The biplane is a simple plane to fly, if you know how, but like most things in this world, will not wing its way out of trouble on its own. The aircraft is radio-equipped, a far cry from the days when it had a pair of homing pigeons in a wicker basket to send messages of help. The Tiger Moth, used in The Great War as a killing machine, was equipped with a 25-pound bomb and a scythe like blade to cut the parachutes of enemies as they descended to earth.

With no electrical starter, the plane must be started by hand. Sitting in the open cockpit in front of the control panel, Joe rubs his hands together, not for the cold, but his nerves have got a hold of him—or maybe a jolt of common sense, he isn't sure which, not that he is afraid of heights, just this old plane and who maintains it. The reliance of people to ensure mechanics are in order before take-off makes Joe nervous.

You can't trust anyone. A plane can be sabotaged by negligence, not deliberately but inadvertently, like forgetting to screw a fuel cap back on. A plane in a hangar is safe, but that is not what planes are made for.

The ground mechanic gives a lazy wave, spins the propeller, and sets the parachute cloth wings vibrating in the airflow. Leaving his concerns on the ground, Joe takes off into the wind, gaining height over the green fields with herds of Dorset longhorn, trampling amongst yellow buttercups, the breed of cattle that made England famous for its fine roast beef—white bovine faces turning upwards to watch him fly overhead.

Joe pulls on the joystick, the moth turns downwind. He's flying to see the big man, the Giant of Cerne Abbas, made from ancient limestone chalk deposits. The one hundred and eighty-foot chalk warrior known to the world as Chalk Man, a man you cannot miss, with his one hundred and one foot nobbled club in hand, and his thirty-six foot erection which apparently includes his testicles.

Far below Joe, a white outline of the Giant lays forever on the green grass spreading over hills, like an emerald blanket.

No one knows the reason for his being. Some say he is a Celtic British figure of the Ancient Greek Hercules. Others say the Giant is the rude man of Cerne and if they lie on his cock he will make them pregnant, or bring libido back. Some say the sight of the Giant makes them feel horny as a jackrabbit, and if they could roll naked all over his grassy embankment, they would. But such acts are now prohibited.

Joe takes his hands off the controls long enough to snap a series of aerial photographs of the Chalk Man, before heading back.

The aircraft is a taildragger, so you have to push the nose hard down onto the runway in a three-point landing, which brings the tail down sharply at just the right speed.

Next on his list is the famous curio shop Memento Mori, *remember, you will die*. Memento Mori has a focus on death—a collection of everything macabre; an authentic Edwardian skeleton of a young woman named Claire, the headsman's ax used to sever the head of Henry VIII's mistress, a pair of dueling pistols, swords, daggers, rusty iron bunk beds from a Soviet prison camp. And an enormous chandelier designed in the late 19th century, constructed of every bone in the human body, which Joe buys.

The next stop is St Mary's Church. Not to pray for Christian's soul, it is too late for that. And so it was. The bells peal in the ancient tower; twelve bells rhyming through wars and weddings, famine and joys, pealing through the centuries. The historic church stands on Abbey Street. Once it stood alone on the heath, wind blowing around rock archways and oak doors. Eventually, the old church became a spiritual island, surrounded by thriving commerce. Thatched cottages were turned into hotels, cafes and art galleries. Gabled Victorian houses became tourist shops selling pulled taffy, souvenir linen tea towels, and stuffed toys—shops trading six days a week. But on Sunday, God made the rules, and shops closed for the Sabbath, a day of rest.

There is a small library in the annex of the church which houses a collection of parchment books dating back to Doomsday. Old books contain history, knowledge, and deadly dust. Pages act as dust magnets, and every time a book opens, an air current fans dust into readers' lungs. If you are surrounded by dusty books for years, a slow, unnoticeable demise occurs as you breathe in volumes of microorganisms that book mites create.

The librarian who shows Joe around is dying from her life's work due to tiny organisms that had worked their way into her lungs. Her patchy skin reminds Joe of bruised figs. Disease had ravaged her countenance, but not it appears her demeanor. She is uninhibited and confident, this caretaker of antiquarian books. Only she holds the keys. Only she can unlock glass cabinets where parchments lie seductively on blue-purple velvet.

Hearing Joe's American accent, the art of flirting comes back to her. For the first time since the war, she feels attractive, and no longer old and invisible to men.

'I didn't catch your name.'

'Cutter. Joe Cutter.'

'Well, saints be saints. This is a coincidence waiting to happen.

You being here and all.' She shows Joe the rarest book in England. 'The ecclesiastical scribes in Dorset returned from Egypt with alchemy formulas and symbols preserved intact for seven hundred years, and faithfully copied them for prosperity. The animal parchment used for the pages in the 1450's had been specially selected and stretched. You can see it is still remarkably pliable, stigmata in perfection and preservation. Some liken it to the Shroud of Turin, touched by the hand of God.'

She opens another cabinet. 'There is more than meets the eye. It is not what is written on the pages but what is hidden beneath the surface that creates the mystery. At the point of making this manuscript, someone had instructed the paper makers in the paper mills of Italy to embed watermarked images. These could only be seen when the paper was held up to the moon or a candle. The watermarks are important.'

She turns on a lamp with a halogen light sympathetic for books, not too hot and not too bright. 'I suggest you hold each page up to the light, and you will see the symbols scholars still do not agree on. But you, being descended from the original family of Cutter, might make sense of it and see the meaning of the symbols.'

Her hands drift to her hair in an unconscious act of grooming around a man she is attracted to. 'You see, in the middle ages, one group of artisans, a family of chalk cutters, from these parts, became known as the Cutters. From that time on, famous artists of the day requested custom-made Cutters chalk and pigments.' She hands Joe the manuscript without questioning her motives, because Joe is a Cutter, and chances are, a Cutter will not pass her way again.

'People believe this is one of two manuscripts, and that other was taken to America on an immigrant ship, but like all good mysteries, who knows if the other exists at all.'

The watermark on the front page is barely visible to his naked eye, but yet there is a gray smudge of his family crest with a third eye placed in the center of Ra's radiance—three crescent moons, the letter C, and next to the crest, miniature portraits of ancestors.

Joe turns the pages tentatively, but is not seduced by rich gold embossing or vibrantly colored borders, the more he studies the watermarks against the light, the more he understands. Shaded and chiaroscuro shadows of human shapes appear, first a head, then a hand, a pair of hands and feet, and one heart. A body in bits and pieces is not arbitrary. The librarian was right. The Cutters had embedded their secrets within the vertically laid paper.

Time scatters family history until it doesn't exist. Families break up through death, war and time. Most treasured family objects end up in museums, auction houses, and antique shops. Eventually, all is sold, lost, stolen, or traded. 'The Cutter family manuscript was never intended to be displayed as a Cerne Abbas curio,' Joe said. At this point, the librarian turns powder pale and apologizes with a stutter Joe had not noticed before. Either a speech impediment that surfaces when she is scared or nervous, or a little fearful, Joe thinks, but a face like bruised figs is harder to read.

'My apologies, I don't know what I was thinking. Public access to this manuscript is strictly forbidden, and only scholars vetoed by the universities of England are authorized to scrutinize the Cerne Abbas Manuscript. I'm afraid the manuscript must go back in the cabinet now.'

'Sure, I understand, and thanks. I appreciate you breaking a rule for me.'

'Rules are there to break, Mr. Cutter. But there is a limit.'

After she sees Joe out, she locks the door for the day.

KILLING TIME, JOE drives to East Weare Camp, an old abandoned detention barracks known by locals as The Forbidden City. He arrives to find no one there.

Abandoned places happen when no one is left to guard them. This particular place of bad repute had fallen into disrepute, where one of the rooms was known as the Liar's Room. Graffiti above the bed said—LIAR—in case there was ever any doubt. What is a liar? A fabricator? A dissembler?

In the Liar's Room, a single metal bed is edged against the wall. Its cum-stained blue and cream-ticking mattress had haphazardly slipped off the bed, for it seems, even the mattress was trying to escape. Joe heaves the mattress back on the bed and lies down on it. He waits in the Liar's Room watching the moon move over the graffiti of fuck words. Joe counted forty fucks scrawled over the walls in aerosol naivety, turning the Liar's Room into the fuck room.

Under the light of the same moon, he drives back through the nocturnal landscape of country lanes and outskirts of villages. A few miles later, he parks the car under a railway bridge and walks to the library.

It is 2 am. The moon is a streetlight, bright enough to color the sky Prussian blue, but the stars are, for the most part, lost. No one roams these parts in the dark. Only the local dog sees the lone figure, but sensing a presence is untoward, it stifles a bark of alarm.

Joe undoes the iron lock of the library door with a skeleton key and enters. He opens the second drawer of the librarian's desk and gets a key out of an old toffee tin and unlocks the book cabinet.

The Cutter manuscript is open at the watermark of twins, the shadow marks similar, but not identical. A collusion between past and present, like a fault in the rising moon of imagination; like Gregorian chanting, and incense spooned over the coals, something persistent, dark, spectral—an ambrosial mist, a slow breath of air. Joe pulls the hood of his black sweatshirt up over his head, now he is the Gregorian hooded priest who lifts the manuscript and carries it out of the library, and out of the country.

Back in New York City, Joe and Christian reunite the two lost Cutter manuscripts. An act that would turn fame into infamy—which made perfect sense to both of them.

31

THE HUMAN BODY SUFFERS along with the years, making people want to dump their skin in their forties, and jump out of their skin in their sixties, and in their seventies—anything and everything to escape their sagging lives.

Spencer knocks on Christian's door.

'Come in.'

'You wanted to see me?'

'Yes, Spencer, I do. Sit down.'

Spencer glances at his watch as if timing the wasted minutes.

'I want you to be the first to know. The senolytic youth serum has just been approved to be formally tested by the FDA.'

'At a price,' Spencer chips in. Christian glances at Spencer within the silence of the room.

'Spencer you are right. The organic ingredient comes at a high price. Some would say prohibitive.'

Spencer was sure the malevolent glare Christian shot him was the evil eye. Evil eye or just a stare, neither matters to Christian, who continues his rhetoric. 'Vials will sell for the princely sum of fifty thousand dollars each. So the serum will be only for the very rich. Well worth it. The promise of a youthful and beautiful appearance, increased sexual drive, improved muscle growth, fitness, energy, stamina, extreme well-being, reduced fatigue, improved memory, intelligence, in short—eternal youth. Worth more in the long run than money can ever buy.'

Outside the tempered glass window, the icy fist of midwinter suddenly picked up the neatly raked pile of leaves and disarranged them.

'Now, I have a rich client to meet, a famous one.' With that, Christian got up and left.

The rumor of eternal youth is out in the media. The rich and famous, and even the not-so-famous nouveau riche are dying to have it. It is the first time Nick has been in a lavish research environment, the walls covered in priceless memorabilia. And it's the first time a client has sat in Christian's new consulting suite. The distinct smell of new fabrication makes Nick reach out and touch the wall to see if the paint is still wet. His hands an ink canvas of tattoos, ringed fingers sporting knuckle-dusters of precious stones set in platinum, but his sense of smell is mistaken. It is only the vague euphoria of carpet glue, curing beneath his boots.

Christian closes the door behind him. 'Nick, good to see you. I've got something you'll be interested in.' He takes a guitar off the wall and hands it to Nick.

'My old red Fender! I'm sure I smashed it, not that I would remember. I was on a bender and pretty smashed myself.'

Christian laughs.

'Oh, I missed you baby!' Nick runs his fingers along the fretboard. 'Most things get lost in life, and you never find them again. What are the odds?'

'Even though it was unsigned, I knew it was yours.'

'You got a pen? Nick signs the fender and hands it back to Christian.

'No, the guitar's yours, keep it.'

'You mean it?'

'She's always been yours.'

'Thanks, man, I owe you one.'

'You're going to owe me a lot more before you walk out of here today.'

Nick scans Christian's face and tried to guess his age. Christian's tanned and unlined visage makes Nick's crows-feet and sagging jowls, by contrast, more than a tad unsightly. Nick thought for a moment: judging by the college degrees on the wall, we are the same age. How is this possible? Surely it can't be purely genetics.

'Something I've got to ask you, Christian?'

Nick takes a silver cigarette case out of his shirt pocket, flicks open a battered, bullet-dented Zippo lighter, a souvenir from 1969, and draws the smoke deep into his lungs before he speaks.

'I want what you've got!'

'And what would that be?'

Nick laughs. 'I want your ageless face. I've got sell-out tours that crisscross the States and Europe this summer, but I'm looking and feeling too worn out to start.'

'I thought you'd gone country, and retired permanently from the music business.'

'I did, but then I wrote a whole bunch of songs, and the public loves the revival album, which has frankly been a good thing and a bad thing. It's dragged me out of mothballs, but now I need the balls to kick ass.'

'When are you heading off on tour?'

'Three months, but the truth is, when I look in the mirror, I see a worn-out, exhausted man. I scare myself, so how can I expect my audience to watch me on forty-foot monitors. How can I expect my fans to love me when I don't love myself.'

'How is your energy?'

'You mean my libido? Ask my wife about that stuff. The thing is, I'm a winter chicken, not much spring in me.'

'I can fix that too.'

'Is three months enough time to renovate this chipped rocker?'

Christian thinks about implications.

'The turnaround for improvement is six months. Can you shift your dates?'

'Not possible. The venues are locked in. Can you fast-track my treatment?'

'Definitely not. Although, there is something. But it's outside the trial parameters.'

'I'm outside parameters. Have been all my life.'

'To date, I'm the only guinea pig, and we are a year off FDA approval. So it's a risk.'

'So! I'm an experienced risk-taker.'

'There are three compliance issues. First, you must sign a contract before you can be accepted. Second, a non-disclosure statement.'

Nick got it straight away; he had spent much of his life keeping secrets, some good and some bad. He needed this last opportunity. Lies, truths, secrets, it was all the same to him.

'I'm in. And the third thing is?'

'The everlasting price. You will get results, but to continue to stay young, you must take the serum for the rest of your life. Under no circumstances can you stop taking it.'

'I've been hooked before. Being young to the end doesn't seem like a bad habit.'

'The price of staying young doesn't come cheap. Sourcing the raw material is a risky business.'

Nick doesn't flinch. 'So what am I looking at?'

Christian shunts an electronic calculator across his desk like an ice hockey puck.

Nick catches it and smiles.

'$50,000 every four weeks, direct debit.'

'Hell, I give thousands away to save howler monkeys. Now it's time to save me from extinction.'

'Any questions?'

'What about supply?'

'We use an organic compound from a single source, and the raw material is difficult to extract.'

'Sounds like a mineral mine somewhere in Siberia.'

'You could call it a wasteland.'

'Could I buy in bulk and keep it in the refrigerator or freezer?'

'No. Not possible. The serum must be fresh.'

'Side effects?'

'If you stop the treatment, at any time, for any reason, the adverse negative effects will cause you to age, almost instantly, far beyond your years.'

'I'll keep the habit going. Evade the age.'

In the treatment room, Nick pulls down his jeans and exposes his butt. Even great tattoo artists have off days, Christian thinks, scrutinizing Nick's old tattooed ass. At least when Picasso or Monet screwed up, they could toss it into a trashcan.

'Supposed to be my birth sign, two fish chasing each other in a circle, but it morphed into one ugly butterfly.'

'This will make your butterfly feel like a hawk on steroids.'

Christian scrubs his hands, and snaps on latex gloves, before priming the gold hypodermic with 10cc of liquid gold. The first shot will make history, like the first moonshot. Christian intends to encase this syringe behind glass as a memento—a reflection on the vanity of earthly life and the transient nature of all normal worldly pursuits.

'Fuck, that hurt. But what a rush!'

'The rush of youth.'

'I'm indebted to you forever, man.'

Christian rolls off the latex gloves.

'I'm looking forward to seeing your New York concert.'

'I'll send you front row tickets.'

'Here's my private number. If you feel anything strange, call me.'

Nick is used to strange. He had dealt with weird before, so he didn't feel the need to keep Christian's number. It wouldn't have helped him anyway.

'Oh, and Nick?'

'Yes?'

'Give up the cigarettes. They're silent killers.'

CHAPTER

32

MICHAEL SOAKS IN A cast iron tub from the 1920s, a claw-foot with its four iron paws balanced on iron balls. The bathroom was an aesthetic headache until he renovated it. No easy job to get the sixty-year-old caulking off the tiles. By the time he got to the end of the endless six-week project and peeled the last of the frog-tape off, he swore he saw two yellow ducks in the resurfaced tub turn concentric circles, and fly off quacking.

Now, happily, here he was, up to his neck in hot water in the tub, his fingers and toes shriveling like prunes. He finds the transparent lemongrass soap he'd lost in the water thirty minutes before, now a yellow slimy blob that slips through his fingers and disappears again. The problem with taking baths instead of showers—you turn the shower off, and it's all over—you turn the bath tap off, and it's all on. Once submerged in a bathtub, the rest of your time is spent wondering when to get out. Michael is definitely stuck in the tub. It's a water trap. Soak in a tub too long, and the future has a way of flooding in.

Their bathroom would soon be invaded by little people, not that he minded; there would be two inflatable baby baths with suction cups stuck to the bottom of his tub. Still bathtimes would be fun. When the babies arrive, help will be needed for sure, but what could he do to keep the mothers-in-law from knocking on the apartment door and staying until both boys left for college.

Michael dries his hands, leans over the tub, and picks the paint chart off the floor. He was the roller and brush man, and renovated on his days off. The nursery was his next big project, starting on Saturday. He and Charlotte discussed decorating at length. Her idea was to call in the decorators—but Michael concluded the discussion by saying, 'You gave them a womb, I'll give them a room.' Charlotte agreed, he would be the painter and decorator. That's how he'd talked his way into an extra job.

So what colors are best for a nursery? Color affects human emotions. Red was not a choice. Chili pepper might encourage volatile personality traits, like fiery tantrums. Orange is cozy, warm, and comforting. Yellow is energetic but rattles a baby. Green is the best color for learning. Blue is calming, but dark shades can make a baby sad. Purple is royal. White is clean, pure, innocent and angelic, but promotes secretiveness. White is prone to stains. The nursery wall must not be any shade of gray, Charlotte was adamant. Gray fosters loneliness. Gray is the reason why so many poets and writers live in Seattle.

The bath water had gone cold. Michael circles duck egg blue, mint julep green, periwinkle blue, and swan white, drops the paint chart onto the floor. Job done.

His mobile rings. 'Hey, Brooke. Got any leads?'

'If I tied them all together, I'd make a Pawnee Island hammock, a heavily knotted double one at that. You?'

'Yes. Let's see how it all hangs together in the morning.'

Michael finally got out of the tub. 'I've made the color choices,' he calls out to Charlotte, wrapping a yellow towel around his waist. Dripping with water, he tracks wet footprints like a duck across polished floorboards and into her home office. She notices his water tracks, but then, you can't undo a man's footprints, and besides, Charlotte wasn't one to dampen anyone's enthusiasm.

He leans over her shoulder, kisses the nape of her neck, all sunshine, with a hint of warm honey. She's a beautiful woman, he thinks, I love everything about her.

Charlotte pauses the video footage she's watching.

He puts his hand on Charlotte's belly and whispered: 'I think your Mom is a workaholic.'

She gives him one of her serious expressions. 'I've been thinking about practical things to do with parenthood.'

'Surprising you've had time to think, looking at the workload on your desk.'

'So make that two busy parents. Seriously, twins mean we'll need some help, like my Mom coming to stay.'

'Or my Mom?'

'Or both Moms in the apartment with us?'

'Well, if I invite my Mom and not yours, or your Mom comes to stay and not mine … can you imagine the fallout? So both Moms, one for each baby!'

'How about a neutral modern thinking nanny, a British Gray Nanny, well trained, and the boys will grow up with a clockwork routine.'

'Like cuckoo clocks! How about we take time off work and do the diaper changes together.'

'Yeah, why not? We can work it out like we always do.'

'Speaking of working things out,' she takes the frame off pause.

'You know celebrities take months to prepare for this event.'

'What are we watching?'

'*The Movie Awards.*'

Celebrities caught in the wildfire of electrifying photo flashes. The overdressed, rearranging breasts in under-dressed cleavages, singleton movie stars, famous couples, haute couture, high glam, heists of jewels, and a lifetime in front of mirrors and audiences.

Charlotte covered the event each year. She had such a charming, personable air about her; English mannerisms, and a soft-spoken voice that invited people to open up with honesty. Celebrities became her friends. Friends shared more, much to the displeasure of interviewers trying to up their rankings. They turned jealous, as celebs on the red carpet waved and stopped only to talk with Charlotte, sharing personal details they never divulged to anyone but her.

'You look like one of the stars. I like you in that red velvet dress.'

'TV makes me look ten pounds heavier than real life. Plus the baby weight makes me look far from svelte.'

Time for confidence-boosting superlatives. Michael is quick to answer, 'You look hot!'

'I look flushed?'

'Hot, as in hot, desirable, pregnant and glowing.'

She hit pause, and a famous star in her late seventies filled the screen.

'Do you see more of a sparkle in her eyes?'

'Cosmetic surgery?'

'It's Sara Miles. She's seventy.'

Michael takes a closer look at the screen and scrutinizes the facets of a beautiful oval-faced woman. 'Her face doesn't have the typical plastic surgery mask, more a vibrant natural look.'

He is right. Sara lacks the surprised plastic look of skin pulled tight to banish crow's feet along with inflated lips and fillers in the cheeks. Instead, she looks surprisingly young, beautifully so. But it is the smallest detail, a black vector logo repeated over and over on the wallpaper in the background, no less than the size of silver dollars, which catches Michael's eye.

'Who is the sponsor of this event?'

'Biozen. What of it?'

'Well, Christian Cutter has just applied for a patent for a cosmetic product with penetration enhancers combined with nanoparticles.'

'For the purpose of?'

'Maybe it's staring us in the face! After reviewing the science on skin penetration enhancers, I made a few discoveries of my own. The skin acts as an impermeable barrier to anything it comes in contact with. Skin creams are worthless if they can't go any deeper than the immediate surface. But you know, people who have money don't follow the rules, and Cutter makes rules up as he goes.'

Cutter's patent was indeed pending. A patent to deliver bioactive ingredients beyond the intercellular matrix and the dermis layer of the skin into the circulatory system, bioactive ingredients transported across the blood-brain barrier.

'Once the ingredients suspended in his face creams reach the brain, which to all accounts acts like a circuit breaker box, the chemicals flip the switches back on to youthful, reversing the aging process and changing the biomarkers of aging.'

'I wouldn't mind my switches flicked to on!'

'For all the misnomers, it appears Cutter will be granted FDA approval for a cosmetic that crosses the blood-brain barrier. If it can be done with a patch for quitting smoking—it can be done with skincare formulations. If he gets this patent passed and authorized, Cutter and Biozen will be crossing ethical borders using a cosmetic

Trogan Horse to do it.'

'Cutter doesn't stop for anyone.'

'You would know more than me!'

'Oh, don't start that dialogue. Cutter and I were never an actual item. And besides, that was years ago. I have one heart, and you are the law enforcement officer who captured it. Beginning and end of story.'

Charlotte's fingers kept on tapping the keyboard, but her digits picked up speed with a degree of irritation. Michael had brought up her past relationship with Christian. How many times did she have to tell him they had never been lovers. When she felt annoyed as she was feeling right now, concentrating on work, was the only way to avoid a disagreement. They were both tired—a couple's bad recipe for a twenty-four hour argument. She draws the conversation back to the present.

'Just one more thing. How far do you think Cutter is going with all of this brain barrier stuff?'

'Cutter appears to be targeting the A-list of well-connected people. He's been observed dining, wining, and gambling where the other half live—making his appearance in international private homes, villas, condominiums, spas, casinos, yachts, and clubs of the world's most renowned movers and shakers, the mega-rich, and nouveau riche.'

'So he is under surveillance?' Charlotte asks, knowing the question is fraught with non-disclosure and not one Michael will answer. 'What will happen if the patent goes through?'

'That's a wide open question. What I can say is the U.S. Food and Drug Administration is reviewing the data and determining potential risks and effectiveness of the product. Most products do not require FDA approval to market in the USA. Only FDA registration is required. But not in Cutter's case. They have been keeping this issue away from the public. So something is going on behind the scenes.'

'Interesting, because I'm doing a background interview with Christian Cutter about the launch of his new cosmetic range tomorrow. Cutter's own can of worms, or proverbial Pandora's box—who knows what will come out.'

CHAPTER

33

IN THE TELEVISION STUDIO, Charlotte's makeup artist uses a moss brown shade to add a little more depth to Charlotte's eyes; the cosmetic artistry brushed onto the lid and smudged to create a soft shadow. A dot of ivory highlighter smoothed under the brow bone opened up her eyes further. Whether a woman's eye shadow should match her eyes or clothes is a fashion opinion.

The production coordinator shouted out: 'Five minute before we go live, people.'

Charlotte gets the lighting cameraman's attention. 'Those lights are too hot. Can you deflect them a little? I want to be in the spotlight but not cooked. A soft yellow filter would help. Make me look good, Danny!'

'You look good in any light.'

'You're a darling—but the filter, Danny!'

The cameraman slid the soft warming yellow filter over the front of the lens and peered into the finder.

Christian Cutter comes out of a side room with the makeup girl beside him. He has too much shine on his face, not that anyone but a professional makeup artist would notice, and she did, it was up to her to take the shine away before the heat of the lights, and personal tension gave him a greasy look. She takes a smoothing brush to his cheeks to even out his complexion. He sits down in the leather chair opposite Charlotte.

'Good to see you, Christian.'

'Likewise, Charlotte, no need to ask how you are these days. You look absolutely radiant.'

'Thank you.' She veers the focus away from her and back to him. 'Have you recovered from your recent loss?'

'Loss … what loss?'

'Rosa … you did have a thing with her, didn't you?'

Christian's eyes disengage from her face and look away to the left, the liar's corner.

She notes his shady angle of vision, but he merely says with a neutral tone, 'No, no, I didn't have a thing with her. It was purely professional, and it's only a loss if you forget to remember.'

The production manager points to Charlotte. She is now live in millions of homes, not to mention bars, malls, shop windows, and prisons. Charlotte immediately faces the camera and speaks directly to her public.

'We're here with the CEO of Biozen cosmetics, Christian Cutter.' Camera one cuts to Christian smiling smoothly at Charlotte.

'He's a guy with an eye on the future, and on the money. Mr. Cutter, you have made an incredible promise of eternal youth. Can your products possibly live up to this promise?'

'Please call me Christian, and yes, they will. Eternal youth is about to become a reality.'

Charlotte glances up from her notes. 'I believe not all experiences have been happy ones.' A small muscle twitches at the corner of his jaw as she continues her line of allegations. 'Some very unhappy celebrities say they signed up for the trial, but soon suffered the most serious ...' Christian interrupts. 'These unhappy people you talk about, Charlotte. This is fake news. I'm sure any issues are minor. If, however, they quit the trial before the end date, they are responsible for their actions. There are strict guidelines for participants. End dates are mandatory, not arbitrary. These are FDA trials after all and highly regulated.'

To pointedly maintain his moral compass, Christian had prepared well-rehearsed answers. You had to be tough to survive Charlotte's barrage of questions.

'Thank you, Mr. Cutter. We wish you all the best of luck for your billion dollar quest, and we wait in anticipation for your cosmetic range.' Aware that they are still on camera, he smiles and adds, 'Not that you will need it, Charlotte.'

The camera frames up both of them chatting before it cuts to the Biozen cosmetic range commercial. Christian stands up, kisses Charlotte in the Parisian way, on both cheeks, a seductive maneuver that did not go unnoticed. 'Charlotte ... the pleasure was all mine.' And without waiting for her comment, he strolls over to the side door and leaves as inconspicuously as he had entered.

As they say, you can fool most of the people most of the time, but after the interview, her doubts were confirmed. Christian's Porsche drove by with just enough speed to keep the car engine from stalling and enough time to give her a wave. A wave with the sleight-of-hand distraction of stage magic. Only then does she take out her mobile.

Michael is back in his office, selecting corpses to pin up on the magnetic board. His mobile phone vibrates a slow arc through the photographic remains of victims strewn over his desk.

The call is from Charlotte.

The sound of Charlotte's voice brings him back from the dead to living reality. 'What's up? I was just going to phone you.'

'I've just finished interviewing Christian Cutter. He is hiding his involvement with Rosa. He denies they were involved, but the girl grapevine insists they had a fling. He's a cool liar in any event.'

'Lying is what Cutter does well.'

'I agree. But what's strange is the man didn't seem to have any feelings over Rosa's death.'

'Is that women's intuition?'

'It sure is, and there is something else that bothers me.'

'Honey, sorry, I've got to go.'

'OK. See you soon.'

Charlotte forgets to hang up the call. For the rest of the afternoon, her phone will make phantom calls in her shoulder bag. By the time she walks through the apartment door, her monthly phone credit will be used up and the battery completely drained.

Michael's attention is back on the board. Some interruptions tighten perspectives, creating an idea you never had before.

He writes the word CALCITE just as Brooke walks in.

'What do you think of this Brooke?'

'What did you find out?'

'Long periods of excessive pain create high levels of Calcite. A compound only found in the pineal gland. I checked with the pathologist Diana. She confirmed terror activates the hormonal glands in the pineal, increasing the amount of Calcite.'

'I think you are onto something here. What compels anyone to tamper psychologically and physiologically with a person, and go messing with their mind and their brain?'

Brooke searches her computer and reads aloud, 'Calcite deposits have also been linked to the process of aging.' Michael writes AGE on a yellow note and pins it on the board.

'This serial killer is mining his victims, as if normal rules don't apply. He's going against the most basic principles of right and wrong, decency and morality.'

One way, or another, answers have a way of navigating forward.

34

IT IS SUNDAY MORNING. As Charlotte is about to leave the apartment, she gives Michael a hug.

'You'll be pleased to know, I've made sure the paint for the twins' room is free of VOC's.'

Charlotte asked quizzically: 'What exactly is a VOC?'

'Volatile organic compound, a substance that contains carbon, and evaporates to become a gas at room temperature, so even after the paint dries, it still emits toxins.'

Michael reads from the brochure: 'Made from natural soybeans, no chemicals, non-toxic, lead-free. It contains an antibacterial silver colloid, which makes the paint resistant to 99.9% of pathogens. No bacteria can live on the walls once painted. Creates a clean, germ-free environment for newborns.'

Charlotte gives Michael her—are you kidding me look. 'Hey, I want us to be normal parents for our kids. It scares me when we are so particular and trying to make everything so perfect before they are born. We might be trying too hard for perfection and turn into helicopter parents or lawn mowing parents or bulldozing parents, don't you think?'

'No, and we won't be perfect parents, but we'll be good enough.'

But the FBI side of Michael knows it's not about parenting styles, but how will we teach our children—how not to get killed, how not to be abducted, stabbed, raped, murdered, or buried in an unmarked grave.

Charlotte feels a kick, or two. 'I am so excited. I thought my biological alarm clock had gone off. Feel this tiny foot, you can really see the heel bulging out.'

A car horn sounds outside. Michael looks lovingly at his beautiful pregnant wife. 'You go and have fun at the baby shower, and I'll stop by around three.'

'Yeah, I'll need you to help me carry the gifts. Everyone has been waiting for us to be expecting, so the baby shower my girlfriends planned will be as big as our wedding day. Well, almost. They've even organized a college friend, now living in New Zealand, to fly over.'

MICHAEL TAKES THE lid off a paint can. Matt emulsion, durable, washable, with no smell at all. He is almost fooled into thinking a color that pure will be wishy-washy, but instead, it appears sunny and happy, like the beach-bathing sheds on the Atlantic seaboard. Charlotte had decided on the hue of blue; a woman knows best, especially a pregnant one.

The paint flows on like silk. By the time he cleans the paint off the roller in the laundry sink, the paint is touch dry. The clinical white spare room now transformed into a welcoming soft blue space. The sky is unlimited for much-wanted babies, not that those in utero are even remotely aware.

Later that afternoon, Michael changes his paint-splattered clothes and picks up Charlotte and armfuls of baby gifts from the baby shower. The back seat is piled high with teddies, baby clothes, toys, two cot mobiles, one that plays Brahms lullaby when you wind it, giving baby twenty minutes of tinkling classical. The other, a bashful lamb star musical, complete with a fabric lamb hanging under a fabric star. Disposable diapers, dozens and dozens of leak-proof legs, some with repeated patterns of blue elephants, and the six-week size—the cutest—tiny yellow ducks holding umbrellas. So much love, Charlotte thinks, as her girl crowd waves them goodbye.

Michael drops Charlotte at the front door of the apartment.

'I've just forgotten something. I'll be back in five minutes.'

'What is it?'

'A secret, you'll see.'

After about twenty minutes, there is a buzz on the intercom. Two delivery guys are standing on the doorstep, talking but not looking up.

Charlotte asks: 'Who is it?'

'Inter-shipping. We have a delivery for Charlotte Steel.'

'I'm not expecting a delivery. Who is it from?'

'No name.'

'OK, come on up.'

'This is my day for surprises. I guess you can't have too many surprises in one day?'

'No, Ma'am, can't say we've ever been that lucky.'

Michael arrives back thirty minutes later with a bunch of fragrant Casablanca lilies. He feels in his pocket, realizing he's left his key inside the apartment. He pushes the buzzer. The door clicks and unlocks.

Michael smiles and hands her the flowers.

'What an amazing surprise.' She kisses him with an exuberance he wasn't expecting.

'I almost fainted when I saw them. You are such an incredible guy. The babies are so lucky to have such a great dad. I can't believe it. I'm so happy.'

'Glad you like the flowers!'

'You're such a kidder! I mean your other surprise. The big one.'

'You love the room I take it? The color was darker when it was wet, but then dried paint chart true.'

'They fit perfectly.'

'They?'

'Come and see.'

Charlotte leads the way to the nursery.

'Close your eyes.'

'*Ta-dah*! Or should I make that *Dad-dah*! Open your eyes!'

He couldn't believe what he saw.

Two luxurious baby cribs in a shade of blue, both cribs decorated silver and gold, regal as if from the French palace of Versailles; silk ribbons, silk flowers, and even a heraldic crest at the head of each crib, like royal baby cribs awaiting the arrival of two baby princes.

'You bought the cribs I loved after all, and had them delivered while you were out. Nice touch.'

He sees her reaction, but says nothing.

'What is it? You don't like them, now they're set up in the room?'

'No, it's not that. It's like someone is reading our thoughts or yours at least.'

'What! Seriously?'

'The cribs were a moonshot beyond our budget.'

'What are you saying?'

'I never ordered these cribs, but someone has.'

'Who then?'

'We are talking $5,000 each.'

'More, because the mattresses are handcrafted, bespoke, with cashmere and silk materials, hand-collected from Icelandic and Scandinavian bird nests, no less.'

'Did you say something to your Mom?'

'None of our parents would spend $10,000 on nursery furniture.'

'So it must be a wrong delivery.'

'Was there a packing slip?'

'It was an anonymous gift. Recipient details only.'

'Did you set these cribs up yourself?'

'No, the delivery guys did.'

At first unnoticed, attached to one of the carved cherubs on the crib, there is a note handwritten in black ink on a white silk card and tied with a black ribbon.

Michael reads the note:

To Charlotte and Michael.
It's never too early to get your twins started
on a life of luxury and pampered living.
—Christian Cutter.

The gift had successfully infiltrated their most intimate space, the baby nursery. It isn't Michael's male pride that irks him, it is his intrinsic sense of family protection, and why he immediately dials the precinct.

'Lawson, can you get me home details for Mr. Christian Cutter?' Lawson taps in Christian Cutter on the computer.

'His private number is blocked and restricted. Give me five, and I'll get back to you.'

Michael hangs up.

'There's a point where people overstep the mark, and Cutter stepped over it.'

'It is just a thank you from a guy in a different income bracket. Money means nothing to him.'

'The cribs are going back.'

Michael's mobile rings. It is Lawson.

'He's a difficult man to find a home address for. Cutter doesn't own an apartment precisely; he owns a land-bank, two blocks of real estate.'

'Why doesn't that surprise me!'

'He owns the entire neighborhood. Cutters Delicatessen, Cutters Grocery, Cutters Bakery, Cutters Drugstore, Cutters Laundry, you name it, it's his.'

'He doesn't do things by halves.'

'Well, actually, he does. His private apartment building has two street frontages.'

'What else have you got on Cutter?'

'He rents out the other half of the house on 30th Street. Sometimes a young woman comes and goes there. She often stays overnight, drives a classic car, 1970 DS 21 Pallas. Records show his apartment was a furrier building. Cutter's mother worked there, and the family lived in the apartment next door.'

'So he kept his childhood home and bought his mother's workplace.'

'With a few property add-ons.'

'He must have liked growing up in the neighborhood.'

'Did you check on his mother? Does she live in the apartments?'

'She's in a private nursing home. He visits her regularly, pays all her accommodation and medical bills. She has cancer of the left kidney, workplace-related, but not compensated. Cutter picks up the tab, and she is currently in a state of remission.'

'Does he have a guard dog?'

'A cat rescued from the local pound. And two rescue dogs are registered to that address.'

'A man who cares for strays is not unusual, but it depends on the man. Cutter has harnessed the one attribute most appealing to women. Lost animals.'

'I have a rescue dog, but I'm still a single guy.'

'Thanks for your disclosure.'

Michael dials the delivery truck guys who happen to be taking a lunch break just around the corner.

'The guys will be back here in fifteen minutes to pick up the baby cribs.'

Every street corner has a king who makes his own rules. Cutter had made a fortune and created his own kingdom. The rumor about town dubs Christian as the Yellow Emperor on account of his obsession with yellow. The keys he gives to tenants who sign a lease with him are metallic yellow. He was a man who could lock you in or lock you out. Rulers break existing rules and create their own. As far as Michael was concerned, Christian had ignored the moral and social code of family. His family. That made him an outsider in his book, and outsiders need to be watched. Michael was going to make sure he and his family were never pawns caught up in Cutter's game of castles.

Michael's mobile rings. 'Steel.'

'Agent Steel, this is Dr. Irons. I'm the head psychologist at the maximum-security prison at Clinton.'

'Yes. What can I do for you, doctor?'

'Lee Byron escaped.'

'Yes, I am aware.'

'What you should also know is his psychotic obsession with you.'

'I didn't think he would forget me.'

'He hasn't. In fact, Byron developed an entrenched fantasy of revenge. He wrote tortured poems about you and a woman called Charlotte. Also a Fred and a Michelle? Are they related to you?'

'Yes. My wife, my father, and mother.'

'Lee Byron amassed hundreds of poems. He's a literary genius according to staff and inmates, but the subject matter regarding you is so poisonous, threatening and alarming, that the poems were brought to my attention. You need to know. I will send you the file.'

35

CHRISTIAN HAS TAKEN THE initiative to increase security in his office. The windows in his office have been upgraded to be impervious to bombs or automatic gunfire. Two bodyguards flank either side of his desk. A brindled Bullmastiff, a silent guardian fearless and confident, bred to keep large estates free of poachers by tracking unwelcome visitors and dragging them to the ground—he named this dog Killjoy. The other guard dog is a black Cane Corso, an intelligent breed with watchdog instincts, not to be confused with a Pit Bull Terrier—he named this dog Viper. Viper is true to his breed; exceptionally aggressive, self-assured, and fearless, with an intuitive ability to sense danger. Viper is more watchful than the CCTV cameras installed on the perimeters.

Through the window of his office, the mathematical garden outside is arranged in odd numbers of three, five, and seven. A living Pythagorean equation: borders of green box hedges interlock beds of blue Delphiniums, black Iris, and Gelsemium elegans. Razor edge Plantain Lilies surround a mat of black monkey grass and dwarf lilyturf. Throughout the private garden, manicured topiary trees pruned into peacocks and bowerbirds create a herbaceous zoo. From the open window, Christian can throw bread to orange koi carp swimming amongst the purple lotus and floating clusters of deep pink water iris. A second Statue of Liberty sent to him from Paris, a bronze statue nicknamed *little sister*. She is just shy of ten-feet tall and is one-sixteenth the size of the one on Liberty Island. The smaller sibling, all nine hundred and ninety-two pounds of her had been lifted and loaded into a special container and sent to Christian with a card—*Our friendship with you is very important, particularly at this time. We have to conserve and defend our friendship. Regards Julian.*

Joe comes in, unexpected as always. Christian asked: 'What do you think about my latest acquisition?'

'The Roman goddess Libertas is imbued with symbolism: the crown with seven spikes, the sun rays extending out into the world and broken chains at her feet, bronze plates over an iron frame.'

'Gold plates over the iron. I enriched her.'

'A little too rich for my taste. But if that is your aim, then it works.'

'Being rich is not my goal. It's more than money.'

'What is it about then?'

'Mega-wealth. It buys time, peace-of-mind, and the special kind of freedom only massive wealth can give.'

Joe watches two gardeners outside. One is pruning a Japanese pear tree topiary, as the other ties the next year's future fruiting branches along a thin wire. Aware of the gaze in her direction, the young gardener, the one with blonde hair tied in a ponytail, looks up, shading her eyes with a gardening glove—a blue hyacinth tattoo on the inside of her wrist where cotton glove meets skin, or perhaps a bluebell, Joe is not quite sure.

Exposed in daylight aperture, in contrast to the greenery outside, Christian's office is white, the color of secrecy. White walls full of client photographs, black and white portraits of the famous, rich, slightly mad, and the eccentric wealthy, framed and all hanging out on the wall together. Amongst them, Nick, the rocker, who is staging a comeback tour.

Nick talked to his oldest friends. One friend told another and another, until the clandestine circle of friends were all users of the serum—the impotent Prince got his mojo back, the Texan oil tycoon, once upon a time a premature ejaculator is now the king of Tantric, a Grand Slam tennis player reversed back to back seasons of sun-damage on the court, the silver screen actress went from aging recluse to being photographed again, the childless Russian billionaires now proud parents of quadruplets, an aging president just won himself another four years in the oval office.

The phone rings again.

'Christian Cutter here.'

'Christian, it's Senator Roberts from Connecticut. We met at the hospital fundraiser last week.'

'Yes, Senator, how can I help?'

'I'm presenting a new policy to the house, but the Senate is favoring ideas from younger candidates, and if this doesn't get passed, I'll lose my seat.'

'I understand Senator. I will book you in for Tuesday at 2 pm.'

Roberts is the sixth Senator to call him this month. At this rate, he will have all the Democrats and the Republicans on his office walls by Thanksgiving.

36

NICK STARTED HIS GLOBAL tour at the Tushino Airfield in Moscow. The band played a three hour show every night, an epic rock revival tour of all time. He'd made it back to the top of the charts, doing what he loves. When you are born with talent, you have a path to destiny. Money is not a zero-sum game. The more successful you are, the more you are part of the American dream. If he can make it, anyone can.

As a veteran of the rock and roll industry, Nick knew the best concerts were more than the music on stage. It was about writing lyrics that uncovered wisdom among the riffs and ruins of life. The new album seemed to write itself during the fortnight he spent on the Tahitian island of Bora Bora, half asleep, swinging in a string hammock on those balmy days—gold-winning lyrics came to him. But on the last day of vacation, the words that found their way into his musician's notebook freaked his band and himself out. A song detailing his death sent cold shivers every time he sang it.

The plan was to wrap up the summer tour with a free show. Nick generated a crazy buzz for his final concert. Fans were blogged a week in advance with a request to wear masks to the concert, to get door prizes of autographed t-shirts. Nick's fans didn't need much encouragement or incentive to get with the vibe. More than 80,000 people showed up to the concert venue on the last night of the tour, but other estimates doubled that number by taking into account the bolt-cut hurricane wire fence. Thousands of fans had slipped through for free, making it the highest attended concert in rock and roll history.

Nick takes to the stage with four other rock legends in his group, performing electrifying guitar rifts, a sensory-blast, and later, a concert finale to one of Nick's original songs. The crowd screams for more. Nick comes back onto the stage for a crowd-pleasing encore.

'Thanks for making this the best night of my life.'

He stands solitary in the spotlight, 160,000 arms waving in the air. Nick bows to his audience amidst rave whistles and cheers, then gives a deeper bow to honor the creativity of his band, or perhaps on another level, his bow is the point of climax, a tour de force, an end-to-end it all, his foreshadowing finale. 'Thanks, guys, for hanging in with me and making this life possible.'

The lead guitarist plays the first note of the last song, and as the pitch rises and falls, the final chord fades into silence, no one moves, no one claps, no one breathes between a pause. The spotlight searches out Nick in the dark—Nick sings—'*You Take My Heart*'—the lights, the fans, him out front—he spreads his arms out as if embracing them all—the flames, the heat, his face and hair on fire, he sees it all in the minutest details, the band trying to extinguish the flames engulfing his body. The Statue of Liberty raises her arms higher as if to cradle his fall, or perhaps she is an angel sent to bring him back, but he is far out of reach, higher than fingers can touch. Then he heard her whisper in a coppery voice: 'Nothing ever goes to waste. Music goes on forever.'

The morning papers stacked in kiosks on the street corners tell the shocking story: 'Rock Legend Goes Out In Flames.' Nick's sudden death spreads a wide circle of gossip among the wealthy. Music and movie stars, princes and politicians, all the rich and powerful people began asking the same freaked-out questions: Why did this happen? How did it happen? Could it happen to me?

It was Max Sloane, the Presidential Aide of the White House, who phoned the Mayor, who rang the Chief of Police, who called Michael before daybreak and gave him the order.

37

MICHAEL WALKS INTO THE flat white light of the briefing room, a crowd of detectives, agents, forensics, pathologists, and psychologists. All there to present their reports on Nick's death. A ghostly breeze arrives, a noticeable wind disturbing photographs on the display board, lifting chromatic images, slow waving Nick's charred face in a grotesque greeting to default fans gathered in the meeting room.

Opening the folder to detailed forensic and pathology reports, Brooke squints her eyes, reluctant to focus on the raw images.

'What a horror show,' Brooke said. 'Not the kind of fame he wanted.'

She feels her stomach heave the way it always does. It settled back down, but still, her guts were struggling to keep the watery gray mushroom omelet down. She goes to the bathroom and throws up. The meeting is about to start without her. Brooke comes back paler than she left and sat down in the front row.

Michael starts the meeting. 'Thank you for coming. You all have the reports. Please keep your questions for discussion time.' Michael points to Nick's 'before' photo. 'It's really not about what happened at the stadium. It's about why. The aging rock star had completed two world tours at seventy-two, but as you can see, he gives the impression of a thirty to forty-year-old man. This is more than a resurrection story. It's a bonfire of vanities that concerns our country's security.'

'I'd like to call on agent Caruthers.'

Brooke moves her legs out of the way to avoid getting caught up in the stampede of the hardheaded, heavy-footed FBI agent. Caruthers slaps a bundle of papers onto the desk. 'The deceased was a different man a year ago. To illustrate, here's a television reality program filmed at that time.' Caruthers queues the video that shows footage of Nick's country house with a white limousine parked outside the front door. Nick steps out of the limo, bangs his head on the car door frame, lurches forward, laughing, 'Fuck, I swear they're making these limos smaller.' Inside the kitchen of his mansion, he mumbles incoherently to the camera, pausing to look vacantly out the window. 'Oh yeah, we were at Woodstock, don't remember what we played, but yeah. What a blast.' At the back of the kitchen, his teenage children are eating out of the fridge, feeding every second slice of bologna to the poodles while totally ignoring their dad. 'We were all you know, wow, it was, well you know, all the drugs, yeah, at Melon's house that summer. Gold guitars welded on his fucking front gates.'

By comparison, Caruthers plays another video, a cut from Nick's show filmed four days ago: Nick strides, struts, and sprints around the stage without running out of breath. 'A year ago, he couldn't jump over a line of coke.'

Caruthers moves aside to allow the pathologist to present her evidence from the autopsy.

'A small tear was found in an artery caused by a heart attack. In this case, the tear released stored fat in the body. The body fat became fuel. The deceased received extensive third-degree burns to his body, all except the hands and feet. This is a typical pattern found in victims of spontaneous combustion. The unusual event of spontaneous combustion is thought to occur when the body goes through intense activity, creating enough heat to ignite the fat. The burns on the body indicate flames started internally then burnt in an upward direction, called the candlewick effect. In conclusion, the remains of the body of the deceased presented bone density, muscle fiber, collagen, brain, and organs of a man in his thirties.'

Brooke writes in the corner of the pathology report *Candle in the Wind*. Most notes, including doodles she drew, were mentalist clues—none of them nonsensical scribbles.

Michael thumbs through the coroner's report on blood chemical analysis. The blood results highlight growth hormones and high testosterone levels, equivalent to a thirty-year-old, which concur with pathology findings.

The coroner addresses the room. 'The presence of Calcite and copious amounts of growth hormones found in the deceased bloodstream indicate he was, or someone was, injecting Calcite into his body in the months before his death. Calcite is a branch chain chemical associated with brain growth potential. On more in-depth analysis, blood results reveal evidence of altered DNA sequencing.'

Michael writes in his notes—HOW?

Back in his office, Michael watches his screen saver—his unborn babies float across in tandem—amniotic-astronauts in space. An idea passes through his mind; he clicks the Google icon and, word by word, types in every chemical found in Nick's body. His computer picks up body-building site cookies like a girl scout going door to door selling growth hormones and vitamin supplements. He searches through twenty pages of Nick's medical history to find a diagnosis of sarcopenia; muscle loss with aging. It was evident that Nick had lost a significant amount of muscle mass, due to inactivity, drugs, alcohol and smoking, during the past two decades.

Brooke comes into Michael's office. 'Brooke, is there anything on record about Nick having a body-building gym membership?'

'A lapsed one to a fitness center, ten years ago. Back then, he was no gym junkie.'

'Well, Nick was a user.'

'Hard drugs?'

'Yes for sure. He had a serious drug addiction and was in and out of rehab. More recently, he became a user of serious growth hormones. I'm not talking gym supplements or steroids. His body mass growth factor had been reactivated and accelerated by something. We need to find out who was supplying him and with what.'

38

Christian doesn't knock before he enters Spencer's office. He walks in, stands at the window, and takes in the city vista, ignoring Spencer completely. At that moment, light playing on the water around a heavyweight container ship, catches his eye. He watches the ship's giant cranes unload containers and stack them like yellow and red Lego blocks. Passengers disembarking down the gangplank of an international cruise liner appear as insects, a thin black line of ants disappearing into the customs shed. 'I'm always stunned at your view of downtown Manhattan, Spencer.'

Spencer doesn't look up but remains tight-lipped as if silence is something he plans to keep. He doesn't see the matrix of cars below or the pigeons circling the building or the seagulls over the harbor or rainclouds shrouding the city. In his private mental waiting room, just below his consciousness, black emotions arise whenever he is in close proximity to Christian. Spencer feels colder towards Christian than any man he has ever met before in his life—thoughts held in ice. With Christian, Spencer has developed a range of mechanisms to keep his impulses shackled. He avoids standing next to Christian. It was more than one man being taller than the other, Spencer is a centimeter taller. It was Christian's towering personality, his unstoppable unchallengeable persona, a force Spencer was terminally reckoning with.

Spencer breaks his silence. 'I want to discuss the formula.'

'I've been looking at the stats Spence, and business is on the up and up.' Christian's thoughts towards Spencer will never change. To him Spencer is an indulgent, supercilious ass.

'Do you climb Spence?'

'No, I don't, and I don't like climbers.'

'There is something about office towers, don't you think? We work with our heads in the clouds and our feet off the ground.'

With a view of malice aforethought and a trick of light, Christian watches Spencer's warped reflection in the toughened glass and sees a man clinging to a ledge, about to fall. 'I once heard of an advertising guy who hung his partner out of a window by his feet, ten stories above the street. Didn't drop him, because like a cat he would have landed on his feet. A week later, the adman, like a madman, took a chainsaw to the boardroom table. He couldn't be fired for any misdemeanors because he was an Executive Director.'

Spencer interrupts Christian's rave. 'I said, I want to discuss the formula.'

'So you said. What exactly do you want to discuss?'

Spencer picks up reams of papers and shuffles them in a highly agitated way. What he really wants to do is rip the company papers to shreds, throw them in the air and watch them fall like bleeding goose feathers, and then smash the smarmy smile off Christian's face with his fist.

There is a moment between holding it all together, and losing it altogether.

'We are all in this together, and if you died suddenly, the formula would die along with you.'

'I don't intend to die anytime soon, Spence.' Christian watches a skyscraper piercing a stray raincloud like a blade. 'But I get your drift!'

'The formula must be a Biozen patent, not a Cutter patent.'

'Who's making this company an International success, Spence?'

'No one person in particular. The integrated corporate plan of expansion. That's what's making the company grow.'

'Spence! To whom are Wall Street papers attributing the massive company growth?'

Spencer was well aware of Christian's face fronting well-known financial, economic, investing and marketing magazines.

'That's right, my formula, my expertise, my contacts.' What doesn't he get? Christian shakes the latest edition of the Forbes 400 in Spencer's face. A special edition showcasing the rich list, and rankings of America's wealthiest people and companies.

Christian slams the magazine face up on the desk.

Spencer spits out. 'It's not just about you, Biozen is bigger than any one person.'

'Let me put you straight here. There's an element of delusion among people who believe they are better than me. Simply put, they overestimate their abilities. Take you, Spencer. Your name is derived from the French word dispenser. You are dispensable. You're nothing more than a used snot tissue, whereas I've made the company four hundred percent more productive in six months.'

'You're a fucking egomaniac.'

'And you're a loser, Spencer. Always will be.'

Spencer jumps as a bird crashes into the window, and plummets out of sight. Christian looks up at the sky as an afterthought, as if he alone had orchestrated the fall, then walks out of the office, leaving Spencer staring at a thick smear of bird blood. Avian entrails glide down the reinforced glass.

Gravity pulls us into grave situations. Spencer was caught up in a veil of vertigo as if he was the damaged bird falling out of the sky. He hears the dying bird's fluttering. Beyond that, his mind reels off a list of imperatives, like a poem of consequences.

Was it a pigeon or a crow? If a crow, then an omen, a bad one, for a crow lives in the void, has no sense of time; it sees past, present, and future, merging light and dark. What if the crow dies in the void? Something sinister is shown; pennaceous feathers embedded quills into the skin, severed remiges feathers, the rachis no longer supporting the wing vane, as crimson blood coagulated.

Spencer picks up his mobile and speed dials. 'You're the one who knows things. What does it mean if a bird dies before my eyes?'

'Death means change. The change is up to you, or it could be an omen. If it is, then your world changes in spite of you. Was it a raven, or a crow?'

'I think a crow.'

'Are you sure? The type of bird makes a difference. The crow means darkness surrounds you. A death or end of an ill-gotten relationship, or a bad financial situation, or a pattern needing to be broken before it breaks you.'

Ever since Spencer looked around in his mother's room as a child, the death card haunted him. He never intended to find things that said more about his mother than she told him—the half empty bottles of spirits, ashtrays swollen with cigarette butts, some with lipstick stains, not every butt her own. The wardrobe with a box on the top shelf, just within his reach, a pack of Tarot cards wrapped in velvet she'd warned him never to touch. But he did. He played games with death and fortune, inventing a game of Tarot solitaire that suited a child of a fortune teller.

'So what shall I do?'

He hears Kitts drag on her cigarette.

'I thought you were giving up smoking this week? You promised me you would.'

'I know, your Ma is full of promises. Honestly, Spencer, I don't know why you would take any advice from your mother,' she takes another drag, 'because I don't take my own,' she wheezes her emphysema wheeze, 'with all things that end, there lies a new opportunity,' stubbing out the cigarette, 'will I see you this week-end for dinner? I'll cook a leg of lamb.'

'Only if you let me buy it Ma. You've got enough on your plate making ends meet.'

Spencer turns on his computer and writes a letter, the contents as formal and final as a suicide note. There must be more to life than this job. He thinks better than to print out what he has typed. The rule of a letter penned in anger is to wait a week before you send it. With that, Spencer saves his letter of resignation to draft and shuts down the computer.

If Spencer had left the office five minutes before, he would've been going down in the same elevator as Christian. Instead, the embossed metal doors close on Christian alone, going down with his thoughts. One thought dominates, as one thought does. How to eliminate Spencer from the company. Dispensing of Spencer rhymes, he thinks. The rich and powerful are blessed by God because we deserve to be. And Spencer will never be.

The doors open into the marble foyer. With a trick of glass and light reflections, the letters of the Biozen logo appear reversed on the marble floor—nezoiB. The right side of Christian's brain, the creative side, jumps to the chemical Benzoic, and immediately the analytical, logical left-brain thinking, breaks Benzoic into its chemical components (C7 H6 O2) Carbon, the divine element of life. The flash of insight stretches across time, back to the wisdom of Nostradamus, who believed this particular structure was the window on the creation of life. Christian thinks if life and death are inseparable, why not create an elixir of death for lesser people; to get rid of the drones who don't have a place in his world, the hindrances, people lacking in foresight, enslaved in the wheel of life.

Spencer watches Christian walk across the square, scattering a flock of white pigeons like a magician, before he disappears from sight. Spencer spits out vitriol: 'If that is my last sighting of you, it wouldn't be too soon. You fucking cock-sucker.' The words leave a spittle of expletives clinging to the window-pane.

On the main street a mounted policeman riding a black stallion, stops in front of a young woman no older than twenty, perhaps the same age as his daughter, if she had been alive. She is holding a rat cage with a white rat inside, and she's broken the vagrancy rule by sitting longer than thirty minutes on the sidewalk. Instead of ticketing her, the cop reads her handwritten sign: *Hungry Rat. Donations Please.*

'Any cheese, Officer?'

'Don't push your luck.'

His horse moves on by. A designer poodle cocks his leg on the yellow fire hydrant beside her.

'Oh, yuk! Get out of here!'

The dog who gave his owner the slip, its leash dragging along the ground, ignores her and finishes his dirty business, the dog who in ten minutes will be snared in a dog-catcher's net and booked at the pound as an offender, the dog that no one will claim, and no one will adopt, will get a stay of execution because he's a Poodle, but not for long.

The dog sniffs the rat through the bars.

'Get a grip on your dog, mister, because it's acting like a son-of-a-bitch.'

'He's not my dog. Do I look like someone who owns a Poodle?'

'Guess not. You look more a Doberman kind of guy.'

The girl has something he wants. 'You're the owner of the rat. It's a lab rat, right?'

'No, a pet store rat. There are actually three kinds of rats, wild rats, pet rats, and lab rats. There are probably other kinds of rats too. There's always more than you think.'

'Your pet rat's broke?'

'Yes.'

'What kind of donations do you want?'

'Up to you.'

'I take it you're not a registered charity, so how can I be sure the rat will get his fair dues?'

'You don't know. It's about trust.'

'I can tell he's starving. Check the little guy out! He's rubbing two crusts of bread together.'

'Very funny! You a stand-up comedian, or what?'

'Tell you what, I'll buy him off you right now.'

'He's never for sale.'

'Everything is for sale at a price.'

'You're after the wrong rat.'

'I'll take good care of him.'

'Why do you need a rat in such a rush? Rat acquisitions are not something you should rush. Besides, how can I trust you not to do something bad with him.'

'Blind faith.'

'Do you see my white cane?'

She gives him a stealthy look without blinking.

He recognizes the look—a way to control the long nerve, a way to control the pupil.

'How much is this cute little vermin of mine worth to you?'

'What do you need money for right now?'

'A Greyhound bus ticket back home.'

'You going back to visit your parents?'

'Assuming I have parents, I might be.'

Christian hands her a wad of dollar bills.

'And the cage. I want that too.'

'Deal. Oh, and one more thing. His name is Jinxed.'

'That's his name, Jinxed?'

'Yes. I named him that for a reason. Touch him with malice, and bad things will happen—just saying.'

'You're a strange person, you know?'

'So are you. But I hope you have a good life anyway.'

Christian walks along the street, holding the cage up in the air, like an unruly lantern, slightly away from his body, out of hearing range of the rat sharpening its teeth on metal bars. The rodent stares at him with red berry eyes that only a white rat has, whiskers a quiver. The rat can smell the rat in Christian, as only a rat can.

Christian picks his car up from the valet service. The detailing so precise even the leather inside has been treated with a special leather preservative, polished with a chamois dipped in vintage champagne.

He drives along inner-city roads that merge into junctions, a habit, the driver's predetermined pattern for the shortest route home. Zoned out by the monotony of prominent landmarks; a bridge, a tunnel, past a handful of road signs—while the rat runs its circadian wheel. Christian's thoughts force the auto-pilot in him to take over, changing gear, negotiating traffic, breaking at red lights, accelerating on the green, and driving into the entrance of his car park without incident. Parked, he sits for a moment, remembering nothing of the last few miles, motor idling. Turns the key off, the motor goes silent, and the rat runs on. Three is the key, Christian thinks. Three possible equations will work in the positive and three in the negative.

Life is preordained from the moment before you're born. He remembers how Mrs. Kitts had spread the cards and palmed The Wheel of Fortune for Grace, the day Henry died. How Mrs. Kitts had said Christian was destined for wealth and fame.

What he conveniently forgot were the cards on either side of the Fortune card. The Tower card: two men falling from the tower, falling from grace, falling to their death. The Devil card: two men trapped in a co-dependent relationship.

Christian and Joe had forged a promise not to have the destiny of others thrust upon them. In every act of blind faith, there are little misnomers best forgotten—the rat squeals as Cutter pierces its skull with a thick bore needle.

CHRISTIAN CALLS OUT TO Spencer in the corridor, 'Spence, sorry! I was totally out of line.'

Spencer taps his watch. 'Can't stop. I've got a meeting scheduled in five minutes.' He hurries off with the pace of a fugitive during a getaway. Christian overtakes him, walks a few paces ahead, and then turns around, deliberately blocking Spencer's path.

'I won't do this idle friendly chat routine. Piss off out of the way, Christian. Or is it Christ you call yourself now?'

Christian ignores the pseudo-sarcastic tag.

'OK, look, I have two tickets to the Mets and Yankee game, and I know you are a Mets fan, so here … they're yours.'

'No thank you, and by the way, don't you ever call me Spence again. Only my friends call me that, and you are not one of them and never have been.'

'We used to be. When we were all just kids in the neighborhood.'

'Dead history.'

'You're going to bring that up again?'

'It was my kid brother.'

The sound of his brother's head, like a watermelon splitting open, left Spencer with an indelible memory, impossible to remove or forget, ever.

'He *fell* off his bike.'

'Liar! You *pushed* him off.'

'Not my fault Spence.'

Spencer looked through Christian as though he wasn't there. 'I consider you to be the last person.'

'What do you mean by the last person.'

'The last person I want to speak to. I'd rather slit my throat than talk to you.'

Christian thought to himself: You wouldn't need to because I would do the deed for you.

'Come on, Spence. That's apocalyptic thinking. You really need to cheer the fuck up. You're one depressed guy. Are you on any meds?'

'Not like you, Snow White. The cilia in your nostrils are always in a blizzard, a cocaine whiteout.'

'Well, blow me, Spence.'

Then Spencer laughs, opens the door to the boardroom, and locks it behind him.

Christian can't help thinking how much he likes Spencer, the funny bone part; it's the asshole part of the guy he hates. Some of the things Spence comes out with are morbidly hilarious—slitting his own throat indeed! But then maybe Spencer does see his future, his Mom being the fortune teller and all.

Spencer leaves the production meeting. The weight of adverse reports red-flagged one depressing fact. The production of the new cosmetic range has become a budget disaster, a blowout. The profits, like red helium balloons floating into the stratosphere with no possibility of tugging them back down to real terms, and the frustration is, it was none of his doing. Often the essential 'secret' chemical, the one Christian refuses to disclose, is not available. And that is Spencer's nemesis. Millions of bucks stop, and profits go down the drain, when company chemists can't meet critical production schedules.

In his office, Spencer sits dejected. The high-backed, leather executive chair, padded and comfortable as it is, doesn't improve his morale. He has the underwhelming feeling, sitting in his prism of white walls and glass, that he is at the bottom of a tank, a holding tank with a glass frontage to the world, and here he is caught in the red and the black of deep commerce.

No escape clause.

There is no escape or getting away from the fact that he is stuck with Cutter until either the contracts run out, or he hands in his letter of resignation. If he stays, he might physically and mentally burn out. If he leaves abruptly, he will burn through savings not withstanding the burden of his $42,000,000 French Riviera villa, let alone the loan of $628,000 for the gold Rolex Submariner he'd purchased on a whim in Geneva.

He scans his letter of resignation again, a man looking for more than typos or grammar errors, but nothing made sense. He closed the thesaurus app and shut his computer down. The fuck-it-all-flight-fight side of his personality was kicking in. Thoughts cycled in a loop of despair and anxiety. The drained bloodless face in the looking glass of the office window belonged to him and no other. This warped and blurred image was his, a hollowed masked version of the man he was.

Rain fell a wet deposition. Mercurial night spread the bright light of Sirius, until it formed a five pointed star in the center of his reflected forehead—time to go.

He crams business accounts into his briefcase until it is as stuffed full of figures as his head is. At this point, he notices two tickets under his $258,000 glass paperweight. Two ballpark tickets from Christian—two choices. Either throw them in the trash or use them. Why not? Nothing should ever go to waste, especially free baseball tickets. He dials James. On the second ring, James picks up and answers in a husky voice, a little out of breath.

'How's it going, Spence?'

'You'll like this one. I've got two tickets to the final Mets and Yankee game next week, you and me?'

'That's great. When?'

'Friday night.'

'I can't. I promised to take Nicole for dinner.'

'Break the date; it's the final game. Come on!'

'If I do, it will be an end game.'

His friend was in a serial break-up relationship.

'Sorry, I just can't.' Then Spencer hears Nicole's bedroom voice whisper something in the background.

Spencer spends the next half hour phoning around: his friends have tickets, need more notice, or are just too busy. He turns his desk light off. Enthusiasm fades back to black.

CHAPTER

40

SPENCER WAITED FOR THE evening subway train. He stood behind the yellow line on the platform, the waiting space familiar, claustrophobic, airless, and vacuous. The smell of the subway worked its way into Spencer's lungs, dead dust, and steel. It came as a relief that the oncoming train was his. Onboard, the familiar smells of warm bagels, glazed donuts in paper bags, perfumes mingle together with after shave, floral and musk, and fresh newsprint of the late edition.

The commuter train is packed at rush hour. Missing the last vacant seat, Spencer braces himself for the journey—standing room only. He takes the overhead strap in hand, a fistful of leather with a greasy patina from thousands of hands that held it before him, sick people with germs, common colds, flu viruses, people with fevers who should have stayed home, and the terminal ones with some kind of incurable cancer, holding onto life.

The train suddenly jolted like a giant mechanical match-maker bent on connecting strangers together.

The woman standing next to Spencer falls into his arms just as the train enters the longest tunnel on route. In the semi-darkness, at the edges of imagination, the woman stays close up. They move to the rhythm of the carriage. He smells her warm perfume and feels her hand slip into his coat pocket. The subway train comes out of the tunnel, and the woman steps back to a conservative, public persona. At the next stop, she is gone. He puts his hand, where her hand had been a minute before. She was a giver, not a taker. In the depth of his coat pocket, she has left something for him. The subway train rumbles clear of the central tunnel, rattles over a bridge, flickers past a station, and on the curve of the sub-way wall, a face, Christian's face. The series of Biozen posters create an elongated landscape of his smile above the grime of white subway tiles. The marketing posters disturb the flimsy reality and unsettle the scab over the most massive wound in Spencer's life. Despite the therapy sessions and antidepressants, Spencer heard the sound of his younger brother's head splitting open, over and over. No one should look into a dead brother's eyes, but no one was quick enough to cover the boy's face. His brother's river of blood flows down the gutter of the unconscious, coloring Spencer's nightmares.

Spencer leaves the subway station and climbs the steps to East 43rd Street; a slow walk up, and with each step he takes, the load of crap that makes up his life, every problem, every demand, comes up with him.

What waits for him when he opens the door of his apartment is one hundred and sixty pounds of Great Dane, nothing great about this canine, who, by the smell in the hallway, had dumped a steaming load of recycled dog food, and by the red threads tangled up in the dog dump, he'd partially devoured the antique Baluch Persian prayer rug. Spencer's second marriage had hardly outgrown the puppy's house-training, when his soon-to-be new ex-wife got herself a good lawyer. It was a done deal. Spencer got the canine called Ragnar. As for the rest of the emotional chattels, well, let's say the relationship was a train wreck he didn't see coming. He threw a paper towel over the dog dump and washed his hands of it all.

He takes the business card out of his jacket pocket and checks the time. By phone etiquette standards, it is not too late to call the woman on the train.

'Hello? Who is this?'

'The man on the train.'

'Spencer Kitts, I've been expecting your call.'

'You knew I would phone?'

'Julian said you would. That it was your nature to be inquisitive and curious.'

'Who is Julian?'

'Julian is part of a wealthy organization who would like to talk to you about your molecular research theories.'

'No, that's not open for discussion.'

'He knows about your pending letter of resignation. He said to tell you that if you meet him in Paris, you can expect a complete turn of fortune. He will take care of all your travel arrangements, first-class, and your hotel accommodation. Five star of course. And to show his good intentions, he has paid off all your outstanding debts, including the mortgage on your French property and your diamond Rolex—no strings attached.'

'And you? What part do you play in all of this? Or are you purely the messenger?'

'That remains to be seen.'

'You sound like a woman of mystery. So will you be in Paris?'

Click. The phone goes dead.

C H A P T E R

41

THE YANKEE STADIUM IS legendary. Spencer was ambidextrous when it came to major league baseball teams. He was a Met fan and would shout for the Mets, but then again, if the Yankees won, which they usually did, he'd shout out with the Yankee fans. However, the Mets did have a remarkable winning record; World Series, National Leagues, and now the final game in the NLCS. Winning this game would advance the Mets to the World Series—again.

Spencer pulls on his red cap. The game hadn't started yet, but the banter was in full swing. Mets fans sing, *Ya Gotta Believe. Ya Gotta Believe.* Spencer, who'd avoided singing since he was kicked out of the choir as a kid, joins in the rusted baritone. A Mets fan, mistaking the vacant seat beside Spencer as unallocated, sits down beside him, closing up the elbow room. Fans can spark off at the flip of a Zippo. That's how riots start in the stands, so Spencer knows to say nothing, as he watches the teams warming up on the field. Behind the backfield, the crowd on wooden bleachers undulate in a sea of navy blue caps, while an ominous bruised cloud holds back its clap of thunder. Giant video screens broadcast close-ups of Yankee die-hard fans heckling the Met fielders. A fan's face fills the screen, his hands cupped like a megaphone, his jugular veins protruding as he shouts vitriolic cuss words, then turns to his buddy, and smiles. Spencer knows that smile. The billboard smile of Cutter.

The Yankee opening slugger gets underway, striking a curved ball for a two-base hit from the second fastball. Fans roar to their feet as the Yankees hit two consecutive home runs, right on half-time. At the same time, Christian buys two hot dogs and makes his way up the stadium steps to Spencer.

With the fast-food accent of a practiced street vendor, Christian yells, 'Hot dogs! Courtesy of the Yankees.'

Spencer is as tempted as a street dog outside a delicatessen. Two large hot dogs smothered in mustard and ketchup, the onions fried like a crispy apology. Was Cutter calling a truce with food, making amends, saying sorry?

'Thanks, I'll take them, but on one condition. If the Mets win, you shout me a weekend at The Ritz Hotel.'

'New York?'

'No, Paris.'

'You got it. All expenses paid.' Christian heads back down to the bleachers. 'But the Mets don't stand a chance,' he yells.

With a hot dog in each hand and a bet on the side, Spencer eats with relish as the Mets draw even on the scoreboard. The home crowd howls in the wild, someone had to win, and it wasn't going to be Spencer. He will be a loser before the game was over. His legs give way, and he collapses into the mayhem of foil candy wrappers, crushed paper cups, and outlawed cigarette butts.

The referee calls time out.

Christian notices the space around Spencer is suddenly empty, like a clearing in a forest. Fans had moved aside for the emergency paramedics.

The ambulance drives at an alarming speed from the stadium. Not that Spencer is aware of the blare of the siren and bright lights flashing. A lack of oxygen in his body resulted in a cardiac arrest. Spencer feels nothing. He doesn't feel the cold swab of alcohol, the jab of a needle, the blood pressure cuff inflating and deflating, or the IV catheter tugging in his radial vein as the ambulance takes a sharp corner. Two paramedics stabilize his airways, continue to check his breathing, and monitor his heart and circulation.

Spencer sees a pinprick of light before something lowers his eyelids, blackout blinds of the unconscious. He is a man sleeping the sleep of the dead when he arrives in the emergency room.

Doctors give him the tests: the pinprick stimuli, the corneal reflex, the gag reflex, he fails them all. Brain scan imaging follows the CT scan. The MRI shows abnormal brain function, and the monitoring of brainwaves records recurring seizures and hallucinations.

Spencer hears questions in the back room of his brain.

'What is your name?'

'Do you know where you are?'

'Open your eyes, Spencer!'

'Do you know what day it is?'

Spencer slips further away from the answers. It isn't the racing heart rate, high blood pressure, irregular breathing, or profuse sweating. It is the chemical imbalances in his body that corral him into a coma beyond the control of doctors.

Spencer lacks the regular sleep-wake cycle; in fact, he has a complete absence of wakefulness. He is unable to feel, speak, or move consciously. Spencer is unable to roll his eyes or blink. He is unaware of paddles on the crash cart jolting him back to life or his first ex-wife red-eyed in the room, and his second-ex-wife sobbing remorse, or the chic French woman observing both, but Spencer is aware something important has snapped inside him.

CHAPTER

42

IT WAS LATE AFTERNOON, there was high foot traffic in the café as usual, a neutral space for face-to-face conversations, people came, and people went. A man sits in the café window, his focus on a coffee cup. At first glance, you might think he is a bored man with nothing better to do. He is looking at the logo on the thick porcelain coffee cup, the green etching of a perfectly sweet mermaid, her breasts covered by her wavy hair, like the waves of the ocean. He has seen her likeness before, during his travels in France, he photographed the same mermaid depicted in stone at the Church of Saint Faith. Her ancient rune symbolized malice, or justice, sometimes death by accident.

He waits for a woman who's been ghosting away for a while now and has already changed her mind. A text message with no smiley faces lights up his mobile screen.

I had a lot of fun getting to know you. Dating a chef is a dream for a food lover like me. You are a creative, patient, passionate guy, but this relation-ship won't work for me.

They had been going out for three months, and in three seconds she ended it. Noah had booked the penthouse suite of a five-star boutique hotel, but his marriage proposal, dashed and denied before it began. No Brut cork will pop, no celebratory bubbles will rise. Now, the diamond engagement ring will be forever relegated to its embossed box. Some days never go like you plan, some in particular like today. He is numbed by superlative thoughts, what could have, should have, would have, and might have been between them. But an ending is an ending, whether you accept it or not.

Noah picks the newspaper off the table, but it is a day out of date. Old news under random rings of coffee stains, a cute doodle, a smudge of cocoa, crossword squares blue inked, apartments to let circled, and a personal column—man seeking woman, woman seeking man, someone seeking a friend. With a sleight of hand, he tears a strip of newsprint and squirrels it into his pocket.

As Noah sculls the last of his lukewarm latte, a man entering the cafe catches his attention. The way the guy glances at his watch like he is out of time. Noah knew that look.

'Hey, Michael!'

Michael turns around to see a tall, well-built man with dark curly hair and a generous smile.

'What the hell! Noah?'

Once upon a time, Michael and Noah were small boys growing up in the same neighborhood. Through the shared lens of child-hood, the friends you grow up with still look the same.

'Noah, I didn't know you were in New York!'

'I was waiting on a lady who never showed up. And you Michael?'

'Refueling! Who would believe that in this entire city, we'd be in the same place at the same time?'

A minute before or a minute later, in the difference of time, they might never have connected up again. And the story would have been entirely different. People change, but boyhood friends always remain the same.

'How did you recognize me?'

'You had that fixed long Michael look.'

'What? Vague?'

'Deep into questions.'

'Yeah, well, I have a few of those.'

'You were always looking for answers. One of the questions you asked me back then was, do you think Susan Freemont kisses and tells?'

'I remember because you never answered.'

'As it happened, she was double-timing us both, and we weren't the only ones!'

'We've sure got a lot to catch up on.'

'Yes, everyone seemed to move away at the end of high school.'

Michael asked: 'Did you ever catch up with Sandra?'

'The love of my life! No, but she's often on my mind.'

The talk continues, comfortable and full of reminiscing.

'Do you live in New York Noah?'

'Yes. In the Bronx.'

'You work there?'

'Yes. Po Boy Kitchen.'

'Great food. I've eaten there but never seen you.'

'I don't wait tables. The Kitchen is my office!'

'You own the place?'

'I do now, as of today.'

'And you?'

'I'm in law enforcement.'

'A cop?'

'Special Agent.'

'That figures. A job that needs answers.'

'Look, I'd love you to meet Charlotte, my wife. Got time now?'

'Sure.'

'I'm on my way home to pick up files. I think she'll be there.'

Leaving the café together, they fall into step as though they have never been apart. Michael and Noah stop on the sidewalk waiting for two men to shift an antique refectory table into a truck. Above them, the furniture removalists hoist a couch out of a second-story window. The demands of an over-stuffed couch, too big to come down the stairs, the mathematics of moving the cumbersome. The upholstered three-seater Petrie couch from Ross & Burnett, an ubiquitous piece, mid-century inspired, in glazed chintz fabric of blue cornflowers and asters on a soft minty green background. The couch hesitates for a split second, suspended in midair.

It is a simple three-person job, but a careless one. Exactly how the couch gets away from the men, whether one man slips up, or the rope slips a notch by its own accord, it doesn't matter. Either way, it happens. The upholstered piece smashes to the sidewalk, a garden of flowers, blue cornflowers, with bright splashes of blood spreading over the yellow asters. Noah goes down on his knees; his eyes stare out in bewilderment from what was once a handsome aquiline face.

These are our lives: we drown, we burn, we break, we split open, our bones shatter—we stay alive if we're lucky enough.

It is obvious how severely he is injured: obvious to the guy in the truck parked across the road; obvious to the girl walking her Fox Terrier, she runs to the barber's shop shouting for help; obvious to the mother fleeing the scene, pushing her child away from danger, while her newly born is cocooned in its Bugaboo pram; obvious to everyone in the vicinity who sees the sidewalk awash with an uncommon blood type and hears emergency sirens.

Accidents happen. You leave the apartment in the morning, never expecting to find yourself in an actual accident by the afternoon. Yet, it could have been the girl, the mother, the baby, the guy, or anyone, lying there in excruciating pain, waiting for paramedics.

Michael cradles his best friend in his arms and wraps his shirt around Noah's face. Blood soaks through white linen, as he tries to stem profuse bleeding, but then Michael remembers, Noah has hemophilia, that's why he keeps on bleeding.

In the ambulance, paramedics peel Michael's shirt away from Noah's face. The sight is shocking, a mess of flesh with bone shards protruding from the bloody oozing pulp. One paramedic talks into the RV, 'Male 35, massive loss of blood, and a hemophiliac, major facial trauma.'

It isn't always easy to stay alive after an accident. Within the urgency of time, Noah lies under a smother of white gauze and fades into another sphere. He hears a once forgotten but now familiar voice. 'Hold on. Stay with me buddy.'

The ambulance pulls into the emergency bay, a covered archway supported by a structural skeleton of metal poles. Dual doors open automatically into the emergency department, where a waiting triage team of doctors and nurses waste no time transferring the new admission onto a hospital gurney and wheeling him into the operating theater.

At the front desk, the reception nurse recognizes Agent Steel.

'Got another case, Inspector?'

'No, it's personal.'

'Sorry to hear that, would you like a cup of coffee? It could be sometime before we know more.'

In hospital corridors, if you follow the white lines on polished vinyl floors, each line is a hospitalization compass set to take you to a clinical department or ward. In bright interiors, shadows are replaced by reflection, until nothing is secret or hidden. Patients ghost past in pale green gowns tied loosely at the back, where a bare ass means nothing. Whether you are a woman, a man, a child, businessman, politician, artist, no matter; inside these walls, you are the patient, defined by the medical condition tagged to your wrist. They can chart you as overweight, a smoker, a drinker, a stressor, a worrier, hypersensitive to iodine, or allergic to specific brands of sticking plaster, but the tag on the wrist tells all, your condition, not your position.

When Michael gets back to the front desk, he can tell by the look on the duty nurse's face she's trying to hide information.

'What have you got?'

She can see from the computer that Noah Reddich has been transfused once and coded blue twice.

'Doctors are seeing to him; we'll have to wait for their report.'

People are either the patients or the visitors. Michael is a visitor and not too patient. He sits down on the leatherette couch in front of the flat screen and watches a woman taking secateurs to the roots of a Bonsai tree.

Michael's phone buzzes with a text message:

Roses are red
Roses are blue
Cornflowers and asters
The bouquet your friend got
Was actually meant for you
But for now, let's say, he'll have to do!
In time I'll send another don't worry
You'll get what's coming to you.

The rhyme reminds Michael of another time when Byron, the self-professed poet laureate, wrote deadly cryptic rhetoric to his victims.

Byron set up his kills by impersonating a plumber, pool guy, pest control, or electrician, so he could gain entry into a victim's home. Once he was inside, he set about installing high-tech surveillance in every room, including the bedroom, bathroom and dressing room. To the homeowner, he was a blessing, completing jobs to a high standard for a reasonable price. Clients, more often than not, showed their appreciation with generous tips.

Once the job was done, Byron would go back to his warehouse space down by the docks, sit back on his Edwardian chaise lounge, attired in a baronial red velvet smoking jacket, do lines of coke, chased by lines of verse. Then he would watch the evening show; forbidden intimate details of his client's private lives, a woman stepping out of the shower, a man and his wife arguing, and the makeup sex that followed, all caught on camera. He perused this surveillance, monitoring the family for weeks, until it was time.

Every man has a soul purpose, and Byron's was to take everything he could get: computer passwords, bank accounts, deposit boxes, off shore investments, private letters, and house deeds. As if that wasn't enough, through recorded surveillance he could exploit intimate secrets, and threaten to expose them. And just when people thought they had nothing left in the world, he came in the dead of night and cut verses into their flesh with the point of his Georgian silver letter-opener. Then slowly dismembered his victims to Tchaikovsky's operatic aria—*Tatiana's Letter Scene, 'Let me die but first.'* Loud enough to muffle their screams.

43

Noah lays in the hospital bed surrounded by a floribunda of roses, each fragrant head has over a hundred petals, a filigree extravaganza, like prima donna ballerina tulle. A room full of David Austin Juliet roses, a generous thought, as though he has someone special in his life. Yet Michael had traced Noah's parents and found both had died. No brothers or sisters, no wife, no special someone. But still, someone sent an overkill of roses. And that's when roses turn rotten.

People often called Noah stubborn. Up to now, he was. But lying there with continual breathing difficulties from a smashed septum, Noah felt the irony—the so-called hardheaded guy—the tough nut, had cracked.

Sixteen hours of lifesaving surgery, a hundred and fifty sutures and four steel gravity clips had followed the brutal face peel he never saw coming. He has no lips left to speak of. For all the pain and depression a disfiguring injury gives, even a faint smile is out of the question. During the first weeks of recovery, Noah spent four hours in the sterile dressing room each day, enduring bandage removal, suffering through agonizing wound cleaning, followed by topical creams and gauze packing, until finally a shot of morphine.

Micro-fine bandages covered his face again leaving two raggedy holes to see the world beyond, and one hole for the mouth. Big enough to push a bendy plastic straw through.

One of the surgeons comes into focus. 'I can see you are awake.'

Noah struggles to speak. He can feel the ghosts of lips, but when he tries to speak, his tongue wallows in the hollow, and it is impossible to make words. Seeing him struggle to talk, the surgeon touches his shoulder gently.

'Noah, you may feel you still have a complete face. This is known as a phantom body image. It's common in cases like yours. The facial injuries you suffered in the accident are catastrophically disfiguring. However, nothing is beyond repair, and the scans of your skull show a good chance for optimal facial reconstruction. First, we'll graft a biological face mask and grow a replica of your face. As a result, in a few months, you will look the same as you did before. You will undergo microsurgical repair of the peripheral branches of the trigeminal facial nerve while surgical technicians create a cellular bridging model. This will then be surgically implanted, allowing your body tissue to grow a cellular matrix to form your face. You'll notice facial functionality and sensory results after a few months. And you will get full facial feeling back within a year. Lifelong immunosuppressive therapy will follow this.'

Noah is no longer listening to the words. He is watching the wonder of the surgeon's mouth move.

'I can assure you, the result will be nothing short of miraculous.'

Noah nods and signs the patient waiver form.

44

CHRISTIAN STOPS IN AT the gift shop downstairs in the Cutter Wing of The Illuminati Hospital. His flirtatious side takes an interest in the hospital volunteer. The sexist side of him translates the red candy-stripe uniform into a male cliché. He can pick up flowers any place in town, but here the flowers will act as the bridge to get a date.

'I'll take those.' Christian points to tall-stemmed blue and yellow flowers. 'For my sick friend.'

As the volunteer leans down to gather blue delphiniums, she catches his sideways glance at the starched pinafore bib of her uniform. She mistakes the look. Neither the engraved stopwatch pinned on her pocket, nor her breasts tucked with decorum into a white lacy B cup catch his attention, but it is her name tag that gets a comment.

'Serena, that's an awfully pretty name.'

Serena is a princess of floral down to her lilac perfume. A smudge of fragrance on the inside of her wrist and in the hollow of her neck. But Christian also knows, lilac has the shortest bloom time. Pan, the god of fields, was once hopelessly in love with a nymph, who, afraid of his advances, turned herself into a lilac shrub. However, he found the nymph disguised as a lilac shrub, and cut her hollow reeds to make the first panpipe—and so he played her.

Serena breaks Christian's reverie. 'The whole point of flowers is to wake up the senses. Besides, you don't strike me as a guy who likes anything artificial.' Serena had a sweet smile that translated to purity and innocence.

'How long will your friend be in the hospital? A week? Or longer?'

'What difference does that make?'

'Some flowers don't last more than a week.'

'He's in for a long time. Chances are he will never come out.'

'How very sad. Then you might want to sign up for our floral plan. You pay a monthly subscription. We can make arrangements using fresh flowers on the days you allocate. Seasonal flowers flown in from Europe, freesias in spring, heliotropes in winter.'

'And tulips from Amsterdam?'

'Those too.'

'Who undertakes to remove the dead?'

'What?'

'The dead blooms.'

'I see to it personally.'

'So what's the floral trend for someone taking a vacation in the land of coma. Plastic frangipani Aloha Hawaiian leis?'

'Something lasting, but real, like these Singapore orchids. They like the warmth of the hospital ward. Or, consider flowers with intense perfume, like gardenias.'

'Could I ask you out on a date?'

'Yes, and no.'

'Yes and no?'

'You could ask me out, and I'll say yes. Or, you could ask me out, and I'll say no.'

'So what's your answer?'

'Silk roses.'

'I'll take them. And three balloons.'

'We only have these themes left: Congratulations on your new baby, Happy Valentines Day, and Happy Birthday.'

'Give me all—he won't be reading the small print.'

'Fine.'

'Is that a yes? A date?'

'I don't date customers.'

'I'll come back for another answer after I visit my friend.'

'I won't be here. I knock off at six.'

'After six then, and don't change.'

The coma ward is the quietest place in the hospital; you could hear a needle drop. In this twilight zone, some patients have lost the ability to wake up. Some will never wake up from their perpetual slumber, sleeping on into death.

It was the ward most nurses loved to work on. No patient to complain if the tea was too hot, the room too cold, and bring another blanket, forgetting to add the gratitude word, please. There were no early morning rising bed sheet tents to contend with, no bedpans, and no listening to life stories or bad jokes. The more patients sleep, the easier the shift. Especially a night shift, you could sleep the whole way through while they did.

Christian arrives to find a police officer standing on guard outside Spencer's room. A duty nurse sits on a chair next to the bed. The duty nurse smiles at Christian.

'You are?'

'Spencer's business partner.'

'Oh, you are the guy who was with him at the game. The doctor would like a word with you if you have the time. Also a Detective Steel.'

Christian inspects the small incision in Spencer's throat; the double lumen endotracheal tubes attached to the ventilator are critical for a man unable to breathe on his own. He scrutinizes the pulse oximeter for measuring oxygen saturation of arterial blood. The integrated circuits and electronic sensors; to monitor heart rate, respiration, galvanic skin response, heat flux, perspiration, and hydration levels—he is impressed with the setup necessary to keep Spenser alive, although he wouldn't have gone to that much trouble himself. The rubber feeding tubes to his stomach, and a catheter bag collecting urine, makes, Spencer's body look less like a human and more like the inside of an air conditioning unit.

The rule for survival is maintaining the milieu interieur. So an intravenous bolus of fluids must be delivered, drip by drip. The human causeway is an internal aqueduct, and what goes in must come out. A bag of urine is hooked up under the bed. The seedy daffodil yellow of urochrome gives clear evidence that Spencer's bodily functions continue even in the unconscious survivalist.

Knowing, from experience, the unconscious can hear, Christian pauses before he speaks because the auditory sense is the last to leave the body, so you have to be careful what you say around an unconscious person.

'Hey Spence, it's Christian. How's life treating you? Nil by mouth, I see.'

He ties the happy 100th birthday and the confetti-filled Valentine balloons to the end of the bed. 'Sorry, none of these say Happy Coma. But they're all foil balloons on account of I've foiled you!

Spence. Sorry, I should say Spence-sir. The Mets won. So I do owe you a weekend at The Ritz. What's that, you're laid up, and you want me to take it on your behalf? And there's something I want to ask, how was the hot dog?'

Spencer suddenly opens one eye.

'Glad to see you're awake! Can you talk? No? That's too bad. Blink if you can hear me?'

Spencer blinked a roving eye from a place where the beginning is the end.

'I'll let you into a secret Spence. Nobody is born rich. None of us are. I succeeded to be wealthy, where you failed. And why? It's so simple. To be filthy rich, you must have a fixed, hard, immovable thought, a single idea. Above all else, you must want to make a pile of money. And to become mega-wealthy, you must become like me, two-faced, a user, a thief, a liar, an extortionist, and you must especially mistreat the small and the weak. That's you, Spencer. You are the small and the weak. I was the beast that fed you. And in the end, I fed on you. And I'll tell you something else, Spencer, if I climb up on my mountain of cash, from the summit I can see you down here, in the valley of the sick and the poor.'

Spencer heard every word. But all that came out of Spencer's mouth, was a line of tiny yellow bubbles that kept on popping, his lips a worrisome shade of blue.

'What's up, Spence? You look older than when I arrived. How old are you? Forty-six? More wrinkles on your face than my grand-mother. And she's already dead. Take a look.' Christian holds up a hand mirror, huffs a fog on it with his breath, and wipes it clear using a corner of the bedsheet. He holds the mirror in front of Spencer's face.

'This is what comes from yellow mustard. A little recipe of mine tested on rats. Spencer, you ate that hot dog like a rabid dog. Come to think of it; the dog was your last supper *Dawg*. And like dead men, comatose men don't speak.'

Christian hears a noise behind him. In life, we set our own traps. He turns around to see Michael standing in the doorway.

'Hello Agent Steel.' As Christian shakes his hand, a thought double-crossed his mind: I wonder if that handshake would be as vice-like, with a few less fingers.

Michael walks over to the bedside. 'Has he shown any signs of consciousness?'

'No. Not a flicker.'

'Weren't you talking to him just then?'

Christian answers the game of questions. 'Yes, I was. Talking to the unconscious is encouraged by hospital staff.'

Michael studies Spencer's face.

'Did you see him blink?'

'When?'

'When you were talking to him.'

'No. Though talking in blinks is possible. There was a famous author who laboriously dictated his memoir, entirely by blinking his left eyelid, four hours a day for ten months. That's two hundred thousand blinks—then he passed away.'

'So Spencer should be able to give us answers, if he can blink. And I'm sure I saw him blink.' Michael pushes the response button to summon nursing staff.

'Yes, maybe so, but it would take months of blinking therapy, and he would have to be conscious to start with. He's the opposite of active right now.'

Christian had hardened a dislike for this man Steel. 'Give my regards to Charlotte. I've got to go.'

'Mr. Cutter! I would like to come and see you tomorrow.'

'Ring my secretary, and she'll make an appointment.'

'I'll be at your office at two.'

'Agent Steel, I will make myself available for you at two.'

There it was again, the Cutter smile, the mastery of smiles, how he controlled the corners of his mouth. There are two kinds of smiles; the genuine smile and the fake smile. Finding the answer to the smile's betrayal leads to a dark place.

CHAPTER

45

BROOKE PASSES MICHAEL THE bulging file on Cutter. A Harvard major, Cutter's papers on DNA development, in his graduate year, had met with critical acclaim. A man of high intelligence. While an associate professor at Harvard, he left abruptly to start up a company, and became a business tycoon in less than four years. His cosmetic products were hot on the market. Times magazine wrote him up as the next billionaire. Now on the boards of five charities, he donates large sums of his annual profit to hospitals.

Michael checks the time he is fast running out of, and hails a passing cab, arriving for his appointment with Cutter precisely on time. Michael is shown into Christian's office, which begs a second look. A collection of primitive masks displayed on the wall hold tight expressions, part smile, part grimace, part of the ceremony of masking and unmasking.

The view of the private garden stretches across like a mural; a handful of brown sparrows perch in the espalier pear tree, each leaf bud swelling, about to burst.

'A leaf will always fall,' Christian said. 'Beautiful, isn't it?'

'Did Mr. Spencer Kitts have any enemies?'

'He is a man of figures but not just a number cruncher. Rather a man of formulas and numbers. Spencer would rather avoid any and all confrontation.'

'Did you see Mr. Kitts at the game?'

'As it turned out, yes, I bumped into him in the terraces. He was having the time of his life.'

'Were you with him when he collapsed?'

'No, I had gone back to my seat.'

'Was he sitting with any friends that you know of?'

'No, I think they were Met fans. He doesn't have a lot of friends.'

'Was Mr. Kitts eating or drinking at the time you saw him?'

'No. Do you think it was food poisoning?'

'I see you bought two extra tickets to the game. One seat was where Mr. Kitts was found lying on the ground. Did you intend to sit together?'

'No, it was mere business gratitude. I expected Spencer would invite someone.'

'So you sat the whole game out in the bleachers.'

'I inherited the seat after my father Henry died. I always sit in his place, out of respect.'

'Has Mr. Kitts got any issues with anyone?'

'Not Spence. Not that I know of. You think it's foul play?'

Michael puts his notebook away. 'Mr. Cutter, thank you for your co-operation.'

'Anytime, here's my private number.'

'No need, Mr. Cutter, we have that.'

46

As THE HOSPITAL CAFETERIA serves up the lunch of roast chicken and gravy served with gratin potato topped with blackjack cheese, Noah, a sedated 'nil by mouth', is being wheeled down to the operating suite, again.

Noah hears a muffled laugh from a patient in a wheelchair, who passes by him in the corridor—another bandaged up head case. But if you saw inside the bandages, you would have seen the patient smile as the theater doors opened, and Noah was wheeled into surgery ahead of him.

SINCE THE OPERATION, Michael has visited Noah every morning on his way to work, except Fridays. Four days a week was enough. Noah was not the best of company during convalescence and did not attempt to be. Michael owns the empathy that compels one to help others. But in this case, making helpful comments wasn't going to make Noah's catastrophic loss go away.

The situation left Michael in the position of making small talk. Much like dentists do with patients muted by cotton-wads. So consequently, his dialogue turned into a monologue. Caught in boredom's net, he began to disclose some of his innermost thoughts, perhaps saying more about his investigations than he otherwise would. On one occasion, Michael noticed something odd—when he talked about criminal methodology, Noah's demeanor lifted, he appeared more animated and interested in life. Noah wrote on a small white memo board. You have an interesting job, Michael; I like hearing it, what is the guy's name?

'What guy?'

Noah wrote: The one that escaped.

'Protocol, Noah, protocol.'

Just as Michael is leaving Noah's room, the Chief Surgeon, a Doctor Campbell, breezes in, white coat sailing behind him. He picks up Noah's chart and flips to the last page.

'All good. Your temperature is back to normal. Bloods show no sign of infection. That was our concern. So let's remove your head cast in three days.'

As abruptly as Campbell entered, he leaves. Michael is quick to follow him outside and close the door.

'Dr. Campbell, do you have a minute?'

The doctor glances at his watch. 'Actually, I have three minutes to spare.'

'Great news about the removal of the cast, but my friend seems anxious.'

'It's to be expected, a deciding day, one way or another. He has good reason to be nervous. Complex facial muscles express the six basic emotions; fear, surprise, happiness, disgust, anger, and sadness. A constructed face is different. It will take time for him to master the nuances of natural facial expressions, enough to portray a full range of emotions.'

'Let's hope the first one he gets is happiness.'

'His facial movements will be off the mark, to begin with. And it will be easy for others to misread him. These procedures affect relationships, and to some extent, his personality. This is where you can help. Because you have a history with Noah, you know him better than anyone.'

Realizing the brave face that Noah must put on to cope, Michael walks back into Noah's room. 'Charlotte and I have decided you're coming home with us.'

Under the mask, Noah attempts a smile.

On his way out, Michael stands back to allow a pregnant woman through the automatic doors of the main entrance, her partner carrying two overnight bags with three girls in tow. The expectant partner announces hopefully: 'A boy this time!' The woman now in labor shouts aggressively, as only a woman in the second stage of labor can. 'Why don't you just shut up ... this is all your fault!' Another primal contraction goes beyond her pain threshold. The question of gender superfluous, a girl or a boy, is the last thing on her mind.

As soon as Michael steps out into the real world, his phone vibrates a text message:

When sweet violets sicken,
Alive within the sense they quicken
Rose leaves, when the rose is dead
And so thy thoughts
When you die.
Face it!
You're next.

Michael surveys the street with an unnerving feeling rising in him, and hails the first cab he sees.

'Where to?'

'NYPD Centre Street,' Michael recognizes the driver. 'Hey, you're the cabbie who didn't wait for the fare.'

A black car surges past. The cab driver glares, shakes his meaty knuckled fist, and shouts, 'Schas po ebalu pohish, suka, blyad!' Or in other words: '*I'll fucking kill you bitch, motherfucker!*'

He continues cussing a line of Russian expletives as enchanting as a row of wooden painted babushka. He then turns sibilant for the rest of the journey. At the precinct, Michael reaches for his credit card, and the driver jumps as if Michael had put the nose of a Glock to his head.

'You free, no pay.'

'NYPD, not KGB,' Michael said.

'You police. I know police. You free. No pay.'

Michael checks his pockets and fishes out a $50 note that had done time in a machine-wash cycle. The faded U.S. Capitol on the reverse, a washed out shade of green. Michael drops the laundered money over the front seat.

'This is the USA, and the one thing we do know is how to pay. You understand me? You gave me a service. I pay you. No one does anyone any favors here. You owe me nothing. I owe you nothing. That's the American way; everything fair and square. You got it?'

It isn't just tourist destinations that make a city famous. If anyone asked Michael where he liked to live, he'd say New York City. The physical and social architecture was home to him; her landmarks, the history on the streets, the historic police building he worked in, a piece of American history as American as pumpkin pie.

As he walks into his office, new kill photos on the wall stab him in the eye.

Brooke attaches three more photos to the board. 'Photos from the Paris branch of Interpol.'

The first is of a young woman amongst white lilies, on a square of sand, composed yet decomposed, her body drained of blood. The second image shows her arms sliced cleanly from wrist to elbow. The skin flayed open. The third photo shows a black silk cord twisted around her pale white throat.

'French Interpol have labeled it The Pharaoh Murder because of her straight black hair with a neat fringe.'

Michael compares the photos of The Pharaoh Murder to The Rose Garden Murder, and The Inflatable Murder. 'Same ritualistic methodology of death in all three murders. But what association does the serial killer have to Paris?'

The phone rings.

'Brooke here.' Her expression changes as she listens to the caller. 'I'll tell him.'

She crashes the phone back down on its cradle. 'We've got Byron!'

47

IN THE PLASTER SUITE, two doctors remove the facial cast, exposing sterile gauze webbing which they peel away, like the skin of a ripe mango is peeled away from its flesh. The patient can do nothing but wince. The face they reveal is red and raw. The specialists stand back and agree, the reconstructive ladder has held, and the skin graft is well bonded.

'Do you want to take a look?'

Noah takes the hand mirror and turns his head to the left, to the right, and straight on. The enthusiastic patient gravels, 'Good, good,' as if seeing himself for the first time. Everyone has to look like who they are expected to be.

'Once the swelling goes down, you will look and feel more like your old self. We'll see you back here in a fortnight to ensure the grafts are progressing in the right direction. You will, of course, be on anti-rejection medication for a lifetime,' then he paused.

'The transplant drugs are steroid-based. And, so, there may be some side-effects.'

'What side-effects exactly?'

'We have assigned you a drug manager. She will explain.'

With that, a woman, looking no more than twenty-five, entered.

'I've been following your case with interest.'

He notices she isn't wearing a ring, neither an engagement solitaire nor a gold wedding band.

She looked directly at him. 'It is important not to miss a dose, and not to overdose.' She parcels up an array of color-coded drugs, gives him detailed instructions on what to take and when to take them. 'And keep this.' She hands him her business card.

'It's been a while since I've had a woman interested in me enough to give me drugs.'

'That's my job.'

'What if I feel strange?'

'If you ever do, pick up the phone, and we'll talk.'

'If I am feeling OK, can I still call you?'

'Yes. You can call me Doctor Mason.'

It's hospital discharge day. Noah changes into the blue linen shirt and Versace jeans Michael bought in for him earlier, except Michael's jeans are a tad too tight in the waist. In the mirror, he sees a different man—pulling on Michael's boots was a step in the right direction. Life is one big fancy dress party, and you can end up wearing dead man's clothes, Noah thought. Michael's clothes will do for now, but he'll rectify his wardrobe when he hits the department stores and crunches some plastic—once he finds someone else's credit cards to use. There are three choices in this world, beg, borrow or steal, and he prefers to steal whenever possible, never asking, because asking is begging. As he calculates ways of obtaining money, Michael and Charlotte walk through the door.

'Noah! I almost forgot what you looked like.' At first glance, Noah's swollen face had the air of over-indulgent Botox sessions; taut skin and expressionless, but the precision scars carried the hallmarks of extensive reconstructive surgery.

Noah observes Charlotte to catch her reaction.

'I've seen your photograph in Michael's high school yearbook. Michael often talks about Long Island days and your Ma cooking pasta on Mondays. Today is Monday, coincidently, so I'm cooking spaghetti. Thought it might remind you of good times.'

For all of Charlotte's homely monologue, he gives no more than a nod. Michael pats Noah on the shoulder, 'Let's go, buddy. You must be busting to get out of here.'

A blond nurse aide pushes a wheelchair into the room. He refuses to sit in it. She insists he does.

'Every patient goes out in a wheelchair. Until you're outside the front door, we're responsible for your safety. Hospital rules.'

'As long as you push me then.'

She pushes him down the corridor. Caught in an ambush of her perfume, the warm scent of a woman makes his loins surge like a hit of Viagra.

Sitting in the back of Charlotte's car, his challenge is to validate this journey. Outside the confines of crepe bandages, plaster, and concrete, he is free. Free to watch the Manhattan scape flicker past the car window, free to connect to the cast of characters in the car. Michael, Charlotte, and him moving away from the present towards a future. He must not let his guard down. And he must remain in control, because things have changed.

Michael continues a broken dialogue from the front seat. 'The spare room, help you out, stay as long as you like, till you get an apartment, here when you need us.'

But Charlotte' steady profile holds Noah's attention. Her face was hard to read. He sensed coolness from her. He must remember to package antidotes that allow her to relate, don't speak details of the past, be non-specific, remember context, don't over-talk. They won't try to push you, you've had a close call with death, they want to help. Charlotte glances at him briefly, in the rear vision mirror; and sees deliberation, calculation. He sees a confident woman used to making decisions. She is the lynchpin for the upcoming bed and breakfast stay. He is also witness to the love that passes between Michael and Charlotte.

But to the new Noah, love is a Valentine's card with Anthrax dust inside.

C H A P T E R

48

CHANGE IS CONSTANT, AND now Noah is living in a nice apartment, invited to stay for as long as he needed. He slept the following days with the blinds drawn. By staying in the newly decorated room set up for the newborn, he had time to think without disturbance. A time of convalescence: His new role required altered behaviors, emotions, and adjustment of habits. It wasn't the circumstances that gave him heartburn. It was the care he must take to ensure there were no errors. It is up to him to filter out information that might contradict his position. And all the while remembering each small detail. He pulled his thoughts in line. Keep the blinders on. Tend to his targets because everyone is a target at one time or another.

Two weeks later, although sections of his face felt numb, he decided to shave for the first time. It was a close shave, and as he carefully scraped off the shaving foam, he sees a good-looking guy.

Noah comes out of the bathroom whistling his signature tune.

Charlotte had left him a note to say she was out shopping and Michael had gone to work. It's all about personal context when looking around someone's apartment. He sprawls on the couch and puts his red sneakers up on the rolled arms; it doesn't get more comfortable than this. He flicks through the TV channels at game speed. It was just the beginning. Does the choice of programs define the man? Possibly. From the hours of punching, kicking, smacks and groans, it soon became apparent that Michael's old friend was addicted to violence.

In the first month, couch riding was expected and easily forgiven. The man was healing, so assuming the convalescent position was justified. During the following months, his prone presence turned into an issue for Charlotte and Michael. Lowering their voices in the kitchen, so their guest was out of earshot, they discussed Noah's behavior.

'It's not natural to watch TV for thirteen to fifteen hours a day,' Charlotte said, speaking under the cage fighting commentary coming from the living room. 'Not only that, it's the volume and aggression. Fighting dominates the whole apartment.'

'I'll have a word with him. He needs to get back into life.'

Charlotte asks in a frustrated tone: 'And why doesn't he bother to take his shoes off on the couch? Was he always like this?'

'I said I'll talk to him. Things will change around here soon, I promise.'

This guy hanging around their apartment wasn't Charlotte's idea of family bliss; Michael needed to sort this. A few more days and Charlotte will pull the plug on the TV and take it to the repair shop, and throw away the receipt. She wants their personal space back. That's not a selfish thought either, because the way it is right now, three is more than a crowd.

Michael goes into the living room and sits opposite his friend while two bloodied fighters kick and kneed each other on the fight channel. 'That's got to hurt.' The bell rings. A fighter spits bloody gobs into a bucket. The bell rings again, and the opponents come out of their corners for the last round.

Michael stared at Noah, a man he no longer felt he knew. So much in life gets lost along the way. He had lost the comfortable feeling he'd always had with Noah. Trauma corrupts, and suffering can change a man. He should give the guy a chance to come right. Noah would do the same for him. They were blood brothers way back when they were kids, pressing bloodied thumbs together.

Michael asked: 'You doing anything tomorrow?'

'No, nothing in particular.'

'And the next day? Nothing again?'

'Not sure.' He looks at Michael enquiringly. 'What's up, buddy, getting sick of your old friend? Want him out of your hair?' With that, Noah switches off the TV. 'You guys have been fantastic to me, and to show my appreciation, I'll cook you dinner tomorrow night.'

The next night Charlotte comes home and goes into the kitchen, drawn by the smell of home cooking. Fresh green herbs, oregano, basil, chili, and ripe Italian tomatoes were artfully arranged on the wooden chopping board. Nothing is out of a can or packet. Noah is making the real thing.

'Where'd you learn to cook like this?'

'I'm cooking my Italian Mama's secret pasta recipe. But don't tell her.' Noah picks up the wooden spoon and tests the tomato and basil sauce.

'I thought your parents were dead.'

'Metaphorically speaking, yes, they are quite dead. A lot of parents are dead to their adult children.' His answer as twisted as the spiral pasta draining in the colander.

Michael walks through the front door.

'We're in the kitchen,' Noah calls out. 'Hey, buddy, what would you like, Italian red or a beer?'

'A cold beer.' Michael opens the fridge. 'Reminds me of a downtown Italian deli in here.'

And it was. On the bottom shelf, Noah's piece de resistance was tiramisu dusted with cocoa and decorated with candied violets.

Later that evening, as Michael tips trash into the garbage chute, a sticky packet falls onto the floor. With that, he rummages in the garbage. Another box of Mama Russo's Italian Tiramisu, four empty jars of roasted garlic and basil spaghetti sauce, and two empty bags of steel-cut artisan pasta from Cutters Deli.

All the ingredients of a liar, Michael thinks.

CHAPTER

49

AFTER A SUCCESSFUL NIGHT impressing Michael and Charlotte, Noah sleeps the sleep of a liar amongst innocent things. It is all child's play, toys and teddies in the duck egg blue room. Some mornings when he wakes in the nursery, he feels born again.

But this morning, before the urban dawn chorus of pigeons and cars, he is awake before he wants to be, less out of need and more out of habit. He reaches for the pain nurse, a stash of controlled drugs lifted from the hospital drug safe, left open for a minute. An opportunist for opiates, and he'd been quick to score. It didn't take a minute to put 75mg of hydrocodone into his vein. Brain dopamine flushes through his body, untranslatable, a vial to capture deep resonance, complete warm sublimity, the alternate state's white phenomena, artfully untangling pain's granularity. Proof a relaxed brain belongs to whatever the chemical. Right there, in the blue room of the innocents, the pain in his new face had gone, and the hydrocodone spun-dried his mind. Facets of thought far clearer than before.

He knows what he needs to do.

It is 1:30 am when Noah opens the door to Michael's den. First, he increases the speed and memory cache of Michael's computer. Next, he undoes the screws in the back of the hard drive and inserts the spyware platform. Then he hacks Michael's high-security code and gains a direct portal to the NYPD. Next, he downloads Michael's high-security files. The solved and the unsolved. The murders, the rapes, the kidnappings, the extortions, the thefts, the blackmails, and white-collar crimes. He downloads them all onto his external terabyte hard-drive; thousands of pages of unpublished who-done-it novels, and the entire incriminating psycho files on The Rhyming Couplet Killer. Finally, he closes down Michael's computer.

Noah takes a final look around. Morning light picks out details of trophies around Michael's den; a sharpshooters pistol with a framed certificate beside it; the highest score in the academy, five years in a row. Michael was the crack shot in the police force. And still is. A wall of sports trophies, baseball, ice hockey, swimming, track and field, triathlon and cycling, a good all-around athlete, not a chink of imperfection, the perfect cop, too perfect for Noah.

In the hallway he feels the dopamine flush ebb. The low will follow. He pauses, and then like an afterthought, gingerly opens the door before slipping inside the master bedroom, undetected. He listens to slow breathing, the breath of dreamers. Sleep had caught Charlotte and Michael in its encompassing drift. Michael dreamed of suffocation, ice blue eyes encased in white bandages, someone holding a goose down pillow over his face, while the hall clock ticked. Tick. It was the metallic click of a door handle turning that made Michael reach for his gun. But it was nothing more than pigeons congregating on the ledge outside the bedroom window.

He gets up and goes into the kitchen and does the fridge opening and closing thing, trying to figure out what to eat. If Charlotte were in the kitchen, she'd say, make a decision and shut the door. In Michael's land of thinking, a refrigerator has solid stainless doors, you can't see inside, so you have to open the doors to decide what to eat; in this case, deli beef, horseradish on rye, slivers of kosher pickle, a slice of Monterey Jack cheese and a swipe of mayonnaise. He places the *manwich* on a plate and wanders into his den. He opens the window. White linen drapes move like bellows as the quiet dawn enters.

He switches on TV; the President of the United States emerges from the UN summit meeting in Paris. The President waits calmly in front of the cameras, despite the harrowing hour, his face is bright and alert, not a puffy eye in sight. 'We have made significant headway over issues facing home security,' the President smiles and nods to someone off-camera. 'I will hold a press conference on the matter as soon as I return from Paris.'

Michael wondered, doesn't this guy ever sleep?

He opens his computer to do a quick Google search. Facts shape hunches, and there it was—a paper on anti-aging and the science behind the creation of new body parts. Where does manipulation begin and end? The paper written by Christian Cutter. A photograph of a human ear growing under the skin of a woman's shoulder bone, like an angel's wing. Facts give logic and reason. When the ear is fully developed, it is then harvested and surgically grafted to replace the one lost, by accident, or cancer.

Michael sees a reflection in his monitor, but when he turns around, there is nothing but an empty doorway.

50

THERE IS AN OLD SAYING, after a week, house guests are like fish. They stink something rotten! Noah knows he has to clean up his house guest act if he wants to buy more time. First, he changes his daily routine and goes out for most of the day. He leaves the TV off, except for checking breaking news. Charlotte seems happier. She likes having dinner waiting when she gets home. Fewer take-outs and more taste, a foodie vacation. Noah cooked seven nights in a row. Thursday, cheese macaroni; using mozzarella, Parmesan, Fontana, Romano, and Gruyere. Tonight, Friday, Noah dished up Thai; sublime kaffir lime leaves and green chili balanced in fresh creamy coconut.

Charlotte is impressed. 'You've got that flavor balance that sweet, sour, salty, and spicy thing happening.'

'Thanks, I try.'

'Noah, this tastes better than the green chicken at our local. Are these take-outs from Sawasdee Cafe?' Charlotte had noticed the garnish, carrots shaped like chrysanthemums.

'No, no, I was the head chef at The Mansion House in Bangkok, and my Thai girlfriend didn't cook.'

'What happened to the restaurant?'

'What?'

'The restaurant you bought before your accident?'

'Oh, right. My new restaurant. That's been taken care of.'

Noah goes to the refrigerator. 'There's a fight on tonight.' Noah tosses Michael a cold beer. 'The champion has thirty-six wins in a row.' Noah forcefully rips the beer tab off and slurps the lager foam. His brutish offhand demeanor surprises Charlotte and Michael. Beer guzzling mixed with blood and guts cage fighting made all his recent efforts to fit into their domestic scene, seem a sham.

'The fight starts in five minutes.'

Charlotte picks up a parenting magazine and goes off into the bedroom. Michael stacks the dishwasher before he disappears into his den. As soon as he logged on to Police Central, the computer automatically tuned into live police highway conversations. To be able to access an eavesdrop on a police frequency, you must have a security A-code.

Suddenly, a voice from behind. 'Hey, buddy, you missed the fight.'

'Fights over already?'

'So, what are you up to?'

'Just catching up on some work.'

'What, investigative stuff? It must be challenging to find out the name and background of an *unsub*.'

'Unknown subject? You've got all the cop-speak. Have you ever wanted to be in the FBI to find out answers of this sort?'

'Yes, it's the whole orchestration I like.'

'So, was the fight any good?'

'No, it was a letdown, the champion fractured his femur bone, and it was all over in the second round. One break and his career was over. It happens when you get smacked about and too beat up.'

Noah moves further into the room, a few steps at a time as he speaks. Now close as a parrot on Michael's shoulder, he has a birds-eye view of the screen.

Michael logs out and closes down the computer.

'Look, I'm dead tired. I'll see you in the morning, Noah.'

'Sleep tight, don't let the bugs bite.'

Michael locks the door to his den and goes into the bedroom. He lies beside Charlotte in the dark and listens. Later, he hears the door open a fraction. A shard of light pierces the darkness. A long line of illumination that had no place to be there. He swings out of bed and crouches down, holding his Glock in his hand.

He rasps: 'What the fuck are you doing, Noah?'

'Mother of Mary, Michael, I was just checking on my best friends.' Aware of the gun in Michael's hand, he backs up. At which point, Michael pushes him out into the corridor.

'Are you stoned?'

'Only on painkillers. A dumb ass thing to get hooked on, I guess.'

'You've really fucked things up. Noah, get some help for those painkillers.' Michael keeps an eye on Noah's strange body language.

'Don't worry, it's the last of my pain medication. The little drug nurse said I didn't need them anymore.'

Noah stood back against the wall, looking sideways at Michael and admiring the Delta Elite-10mm—straight beaver grip.

'The good just keeps getting better,' Noah says, reaching out to touch the gun. 'Nice. It's the sort of gun every man wants to own.'

'Suggest you stop raving and get off to bed.'

'Right. You're right, buddy. I'm off to bed!' He pauses. 'It won't happen again. Sorry.'

Michael has heard the word sorry too many times before, and it was just a sorry excuse. Life throws heavy things at times and leaves you wondering if the next move is the right one. Tolerance is a concrete word, not to take lightly, and it is difficult to throw a man out on the street, any man in a difficult situation. Especially when it concerns your boyhood friend. Everyone has sides to their personality. It was the empathetic side of Michael that stopped him throwing Noah's bags onto the sidewalk, then and there.

Charlotte rolls over in bed. 'What was that all about?'

'Noah was out of painkillers.'

'Has he got any Tylenol?'

'He's fine. Go back to sleep.'

She murmurs in a dreamy voice. 'Sometimes he sounds vaguely English, don't you think?'

In the nursery of the neonatal and the ark of the needle, Noah releases the tourniquet. He has a good feeling welling up inside. It is good to be in the know; it is good to be the Noah.

51

IT WAS NINE O'CLOCK in the morning. Michael arrived at the precinct. Brooke was waiting in the foyer.

'Good morning.'

'Coffee?'

'OK, so let's get out of here.'

Michael and Brooke sit in the café courtyard under a white oak tree, empty of leaves but full of birds that missed their migration. A swirl of crisp brown leaves lifts and falls around the two agents' feet.

'So what's up?'

'Too much is up.' Brooke picks a glazed cherry off the Danish and pops it in her mouth, like red fruit candy, then another. 'You're not going to believe what I am about to tell you.'

'You're doing that fudging thing again.'

'The prison Psychiatrist at the maximum-security prison phoned.'

'And?'

'He wants to meet with us and stressed the word *urgently*.'

'What's so urgent?'

'It's about Byron.'

'Byron was arrested in The Illuminati Hospital two months ago.'

'Yes, but the man they have locked up swears he's not Byron.'

'Crazy bastard, who does he think he is now, Percy Bysshe Shelley, or perhaps Thomas Love Peacock? '

'He insists he's your friend, Noah!'

'Show's how crazy Byron is because Noah's staying at my house.'

'The problem is the Psychiatrist doesn't think this guy is crazy.'

'Even my unborn children know he's crazy.'

'The Psychiatrist said, if it is Byron, he's had a complete change of personality.'

'Byron is a brilliant psychotic. He can mimic any mindset to fool psychiatrists. He gets a huge kick out of controlling a situation—he's a lyrical serial killer. Byron has a masters degree in English literature, that's why he's a self-professed master of rhyme. He reworked the poetics of Percy Bysshe Shelley *The Daemon of the World,* and the death poem, *When Soft Voices Die.* He's obsessed with Shelley's poetical philosophy—Shelley's view of transient things which leave behind transcendent effects. Such as the death verses he wrote for me: Odors, when sweet violets sicken, live within the sense, they quicken.'

'Disturbing he took it on himself to rewrite those particular poems and send them to you.'

'He'll rework any reality to achieve his purpose.'

'And so, how are you finding Noah? Must be stressful on you both.'

'That's a timely question.'

Just then, one of the technicians from the crime unit calls.

'Hi, Michael. I've checked your computer programs. Someone has tampered with your hard drive. In a bad way.'

'What?'

'They've created automatic pathways and links to the police airways and downloaded all your case sensitive files. Whoever did it has also linked you into deep cover porn sites. I'll write a detailed report and send it through.'

Doubts stacked up. The weight of thought started an avalanche of questions. Noah's character was so radically different now. Had Noah been into his computer? Noah's massive character change pushed anomalies forward in Michael's mind; he's addicted to drugs and violence, claims to be a chef but faked it with ready made food, and gave a glib answer about owning his so called restaurant. And the bedroom scene last night was plain weird.

'So Brooke, did you make a time to see the psych?'

'He said he would make time, any time.'

They headed to the prison, a trip that would turn into a head-on collision with a troubling head-case.

Michael and Brooke met with the prison psychiatrist. Outside the barred penitentiary windows, a solitary almond tree stood, a dark pattern of branches devoid of white blossom. The Psychiatrist sat behind a massive oak desk, and rotated his fountain pen around his fingers, then unscrewing the cap, drew fresh ink into the barrel before wiping the nib on a blotter. 'Byron took a voluntary lie detector test. And the findings support his story of innocence.'

'What about fingerprints?'

'His fingerprints have been obliterated by acid. You need to talk to him yourself.' The Psychiatrist presses a buzzer.

A short while later, Byron appears at the door. His face hard to see through thick, tight-wired, security glass. The Psychiatrist waves him in; the inmate walks in a restricted way, his gait compromised by chains padlocked to steel ankle cuffs, a security guard on either side. They sit him down on a metal chair. The prisoner stares with a medicated gaze, however, no cotton-flossed sedation would stop the plea coming out of his mouth.

'Help me, Michael!'

Michael contemplates the man in front of him. Narrow-faced; the bones strikingly narrow at the temples, as though pressed in from both sides, high-standing nose, an under-jaw with an angular set, clear-cut chin, heavy boned brow. His lips thin and the cupids bow sharp-cut. His blood glimmers through the pale skin, and with each pulse, the veins on his neck course blue blood. From the face to the thick hair, he is the perfect mug shot of Bryon. Yet, the eyes staring straight back at him, distressed, frightened, and bloodshot, are not the eyes of a cold killer. Is this a case of mistaken identity or not? Is he looking into the eyes of Byron? Or the eyes of his boyhood friend Noah?

Michael begins the interrogation.

'Who did you invite to the high school prom?'

'You know! Sandra!'

'And who did I invite?'

'You didn't invite anyone. Tania invited you.'

'What did we do the afternoon before the prom?'

'Played baseball.'

'Did I win?'

'It was an even score. You hit the ball over the old man's fence. And he came out and cursed us because it broke his window.'

'Did he tell our parents?'

'No, he didn't have to because you told them!'

'After the game, then what?'

'McDonald's apple pie and coke.'

'Then?'

'Shopping at Kirkland's store. You helped me pick out something for Sandra.'

'What was it?'

'A heart-shaped locket.'

Michael casually says: 'I remember. That locket took all the money from your paper round to buy.'

'It's me, Michael.'

'I know it's you.'

'You've got to help me, Michael.'

The guards lift him to his feet. His time is up.

'It's a complicated situation. We need something tangible to prove that you *are* you—beyond the shadows of doubt.'

'I have a daughter.'

'With whom?'

'Sandra!'

'You never told me she was pregnant.'

'You moved off to college.'

'Did you marry her?'

'No, she married an older guy.'

'And the baby?'

'I don't know if she kept her.'

'Where's Sandra living now?'

'Long Island.'

'That's a start.'

The Psychiatrist nods, and guards usher the prisoner out.

'What do you think now?'

'Yes, it's Noah. I'm sure. But he's had a complete change of face. How is this possible?'

'Surgery is always breaking new medical frontiers. They use cadavers for facial transplants. But surgery knows no bounds, it seems. So the surgeons who did this facial transplant are operating outside the borders of medical protocols. Dangerous territory, to be sure.'

Brooke said: 'Perhaps it's no coincidence Michael. Noah's arrest happened from an anonymous tip-off, traced to a public payphone in The Illuminati Hospital.'

'So who the hell is in my apartment with Charlotte right now?'

52

MICHAEL UNLOCKS THE APARTMENT door. Brooke takes out her revolver and slips down the hallway. She scopes out the master bedroom first: a half-full coffee cup, no mobile phone, or handbag, or car keys. Brooke glances at a baby magazine open on the third stage of labor. The baby's head crowning reinforces her choice to assume a forever childless position, instead of a birthing one. In the bathroom, a damp bath towel on the floor. The mirror has a hint of fog where condensation has been wiped away with fingers. Makeup, mascara and a tube of tinted moisturizer, recently used.

Michael checks the nursery: drawers in the blue bureau had been emptied, closet cleared of clothes. He reaches down into the wicker trashcan, picks out cigarette butts, a used hypodermic, and bags them for DNA.

Brooke comes in with a bag of used syringes. 'I found three on the guest bathroom floor, two in the shower stall, and five in the flower boxes on the fire escape. Your room buddy is a diabetic who's a serial litterer, or he is a serial killer who is a user.'

The front door opens. In walks Charlotte balancing a brown paper bag of groceries on the shelf of her pregnant belly. To her surprise, Michael and Brooke are coming out of the babies' room.

'Is this a police convention? What's going on?'

'Where's Noah?'

'No idea. He up and left.'

'So why are you two here?'

'I got no answer on your mobile, had a new dad panic attack, thought there was an emergency with the babies, so I rushed home.'

'What? And Brooke—you were going to be the midwife? Why don't I believe you guys!'

The last thing Charlotte needs to know is she's been sharing the apartment with a complete stranger. One who now understands the entire layout of the apartment, the security alarm system, right down to the broken lock on the bathroom window. A stranger who had cut a duplicate set of keys, counted the steps from the front door to the bedroom, and who can now find all the light switches in the dark. Someone who knows what time Michael leaves for work, what days Charlotte goes out, what time she comes home, and the nights Michael goes to the gym. An impersonator, who has gone to extreme lengths to observe the details of their intimate daily lives and why? For what purpose? Michael has to face the possibility that he and Charlotte are Byron's next targets.

'So what did the specialist say?'

'The routine check wasn't brilliant. The blood test came back with some elevations. The specialist told me to put my feet up. Take regular naps. Or else the babies and I will be at risk.'

The phone rings. It is Charlotte's Mom, Katie.

'Hi darling, how was your check-up?'

Charlotte wasn't going to tell her Mom what an awful morning it was. She had started the day wearing a baby-love pregnancy t-shirt with four baby handprints on the front. The checkout woman told her she looked ready to burst. At the local café, the older waitress told her she'd raised five kids, all boys, and said twins? You're going to have your hands full. The Italian guy running the newsagent warned her to get all the sleep she could before the babies arrived. What people said about her pregnancy annoyed the hell out of her. There are some things you shouldn't say to a pregnant woman, especially a woman expecting twins. Don't ask her if twins run in the family; is this a natural pregnancy; or was it fertility treatment? Not that it is anyone's business. The question that made her crazy was the one about fraternal twins—you're expecting twin boys, what a pity you aren't having a boy and a girl.

While Charlotte is chatting with her Mom, the doorbell rings. Michael checks the security camera before buzzing the main door open. A deliveryman stands holding a large bunch of flowers. Crimson roses wrapped in red tissue paper and tied with black satin ribbon. Michael reads the card attached.

Flower of this red dye
Cut with a knife
Sinks the three apples of your eye.

Michael tips the delivery guy and shuts the door.
'Who is that?' Charlotte calls out.
'Wrong delivery,' Michael is quick to say, looking at Brooke.
'I'll take these flowers over to forensics,' Brooke whispers, 'and I'll see you back at the precinct.'
Michael sees her out, and then checks his mailbox. Amongst the bills, there is a monthly statement from American Express, the card

they use for vacations only, and it had been months since he and Charlotte's trip to the beaches of Mexico. He tears open the envelope to find a wad of statements adding up to thousands of dollars spent on Stingray tracking devices, spy cameras, micro-surveillance cameras, hand-held thermal imaging devices, audio surveillance, and drones. Byron had charged them all to Michael's credit cards by either using the PIN or forging his signature. Byron maxed out the Diners Club card. Lobster, caviar and champagne at Maxim's. He purchased a new Harley with Michael's gold card, yet the most disturbing purchases were stockpiles of firearms, ammunition, and equipment to produce explosives.

Charlotte hung up the phone. Her Mom had invited her to come and stay. At this point in time, Michael loved his mother-in-law, Katie B.

Later that night, while Charlotte slept, Michael finds what he is searching for; the network of electronic surveillance devices planted throughout the apartment; in the bedrooms, bathrooms, kitchen, balcony, living room, and even the guest lavatory. The entire apartment had been bugged, and their personal privacy as a couple systematically defiled. Manipulation, complication, and intrigue heightened Byron's ecstasy. Once Bryon has taken the time to study all the surveillance, he will act out his plan to kill them.

MICHAEL HAD BEEN ON edge all night and is up before the sun. Blurry-eyed, he goes through to the kitchen and fills the Italian espresso pot with cold water, adds freshly ground coffee, and sets it on the gas flame. It is too late for a midnight snack and too early for breakfast, yet he opens both stainless doors overly wide until the refrigerator appears to yawn. Charlotte hated when doors were left open. The freezer might go into meltdown. Flies might get inside.

Byron had stocked the kitchen pantry and refrigerator, and charged it all to Michael's credit cards; salmon from the icy waters of Norway, orange juice from Florida, raspberries from Ireland, maple syrup from Vermont, pitted olives from Greece, stem ginger biscuits from Scotland, and green-tipped mussels from the south island of New Zealand. Like a well-stocked delicatessen, down to the rye bread and a jar of Swedish herrings in mustard sauce. However, there are only two eggs left, on account of Charlotte's recent craving for hard-boiled eggs, her need for zinc. Egg yolks are something Michael avoids. Except this morning he's cooking pancakes.

If Michael couldn't be a law enforcement officer, he'd make a great fast order chef, open a restaurant, long white tablecloths, and blackboard menu, cook what he wanted to cook when he wanted to cook it. He puts two cups of flour in a bowl, cracks in two eggs, double yolks—two eggs in the same shell, always a surprise. He adds two cups of milk and two tablespoons of melted butter in the recipe of twos. He's whisking the ingredients together when seven things happen all at once. The espresso machine hisses to announce morning coffee, the kitchen fills with the glorious aroma of roasted beans, someone pushes the morning paper under the door, a dog barks, a siren wails in the distance, the knob of butter sizzles in the pan, Michael's phone pings a message, Charlotte comes up behind and hugs him.

'It looks like you've been up for a while, or worse; you haven't been to bed.'

'Coffee's ready, and I'm making you pancakes.'

'Why don't you sit here with your coffee and read the paper, and I'll cook the pancakes.'

'Do I look that bad?'

'Not too bad.'

'Everyone needs to stay up all night, once in a while. Stay up once a night, once a month, and apparently it stops some hormone from building up and making you feel depressed.'

'So, you stayed up all night to avoid the blues? Why don't I believe you?'

'Cos you know me too well.'

'Ten years of being with you, and I can read you like a comic strip.'

'What comic exactly?'

'I don't know, maybe Phantom? So masked man, what has my hero been up to in the midnight hours?' Charlotte flips a pancake onto a plate and sets it down in front of him. Michael pours maple syrup over the pancake, and smiles at the seamless way their roles reverse, spatula in hand, her pouring the batter he had previously beaten.

'I take that to mean you'd like more?'

Michael's day was going to take more than flipping pancakes to come out sunny-side up.

54

Michael lifts charlotte's bags into her Audi hatchback. The bags are heavy as if she's packed the proverbial kitchen sink. Lucky she's driving and not flying to her Mom's, he thinks. If you have ever waited at an airline check-in where a woman is holding up the line in front, decanting armfuls of clothes from one bag to meet airline weight rules, it could have been Charlotte. She's one of those travelers who carry overweight cabin luggage and argues with the check-in crew. 'It doesn't make sense; you should weigh people along with their luggage, and things would even out.' Although she packed, unpacked, and repacked, she always got Michael to sit on the bags so she could lock them. Even the expandable ones bulged at the seams. But when on holiday, she was the one with the first-aid kit, the scissors, the sticking-plasters, and insect repellent. Her handbag was the same, a deep cave of a leather bag that held everything she needed, including a hundred dollar bill tucked in a secret compartment. Her 'just in case' cash. Traveling light is not in her vocabulary, Michael thinks as he maneuvers the last bag into the trunk.

He will miss her. Of all the people in his world, she is the most miss-able person, in all the small ways, the way she smiles at him in the mornings and how her hair falls on the pillow. The way she pulls the cover over him and her. And the way she leaves notes, or fills a small vase of scented flowers, like violets, and puts them on his side of the bed so he will pick up their scent in his dreams. That is the Charlotte he loves and the Charlotte he will miss. The next few weeks will be hard without her. Michael plans on ordering the double baby stroller with the chrome wheels, styled on a 1959 Buick, as a surprise for Charlotte's return home. An urban buggy he can see himself cruising behind.

'Got everything?'

'I think so! You know me!'

'Yes, I do know you, and I'm going to miss the hell out of the woman I love.'

'Don't go mushy on me, or my mascara will run, and then my eyes will go panda, and I'll look like a hooker, and I won't be able to see to drive. And then some special agent will pick me up for driving erratically, and take me to the station for questioning, phone you, and you'll have to fingerprint me. Then you'll want to keep me for questioning, and you won't let me go.'

'Sounds like a plan! Anyway, drive safely and call me.'

'I'll call you when I get there. Bye.'

Charlotte's car pulls away and heads towards the motorway.

If she had looked in her rearview mirror, she would have seen Michael waving goodbye. Also, she would have seen a man standing like a dark shadow behind him, watching them both.

55

CHARLOTTE WAS OUT OF the house and away to safety, thanks to her Mom. Michael needs to shake off the night. The lousy feeling he had was not going to abate. He puts on running shoes.

Running through the park-scape, sunlight filtering through the trees, morning fog rising off rooftops, kids shooting basketball in the far court, running clears his brain. Finding Byron is a fox and rabbit game, and Michael knows Byron is impossible to simply hunt down. In another corner of the city, Byron knows who has disabled most of his electronic surveillance system. Michael is on to him, but that doesn't matter. It just makes it more of a challenge.

A pair of ducks waddling along the path with ducklings following, makes Michael stop to let the feathered family cross the pathway in front of him. Gentle moments. Teal ducks and ducklings going about their duck business. The scene contrasted hideously with the street life he encountered every day—the gangs, the murderers, the rapists, and the criminally insane. The ducks finish navigating the cracked concrete path and disappear beneath a wire fence into the long grass of a vacant property.

Being a special agent wasn't his initial choice of career. His first career choice when he left college with a degree was to be a fighter pilot, flying the world's most advanced fighter jets. He made it through the final five hour exam on verbal analogies, math, and instrument comprehension. He determined aircraft altitude, speed, and direction solely on instruments, answered aeronautical concepts on the speed rate of different aircraft models, and passed the intense physical. He was a perfect fit at 77 inches tall when standing and 40 inches tall when sitting. He weighed more than 160 pounds and less than 231 pounds. He didn't have more than 20-24 percent body fat. He completed the push-ups, sit-ups, and finished a timed one mile run. The sky was unlimited for Michael. His experiences, accomplishments, leadership, and potential made him the ideal candidate, except for one thing. He had impaired trichromatic vision, which made pink appear muted gray. He became a special agent by default when he took the brakes off thinking about a career. It was more like that.

Michael hears the whining of a giant mosquito and feels a sharp sting on his neck. The last thing he sees is the drake's eye, a wet black bead in a rainbow of blue-red-violet feathers. If the duck had been a female with gray feathers, the last thing he would have seen was a pink duck before his world went black. Perhaps.

Michael is seconds off choking. An unconscious person can't maintain airways as a conscious person can. His tongue is set to kill him. The tongue with it's history of private memories, French kissing, tip-of-the tongue, tongue-in-cheek, sometimes a tongue about to say something, but doesn't. Brown vomit was collecting in his pharynx. Michael is suffocating as regurgitated espresso and pancakes are drowning him. Stomach contents begin flowing to his throat and down to the lungs. Soon the stomach acid will start burning the lungs' inner linings. He is dying. A dying man feels nothing. Michael doesn't feel his body being rolled over into the unconscious recovery position, his arm being bent at the elbow, placed at a right angle to his body with his palm facing upwards. He doesn't feel someone tucking his hand under the side of his head until his palm is touching his cheek.

His lifesaver is a fellow jogger who pulled the hypodermic dart out of Michael's jugular vein. Jeff, in his capacity of precinct medic, may have saved Michael's life. He had moved Michael into the recovery position, and alerted the NYPD.

'We have a man down in Central Park. Agent Michael Steel.'

He checks the pulse on Michael's neck, rapid and erratic. Michael's face is red and his lips have turned blue.

'Michael, can you hear me? Charlotte needs you; your kids will need a dad.' He detects a slight pressure from Michael's hand.

'That's it, Michael, stay awake.'

Emergency response vehicles clear a path through morning rush hour traffic. In each commuter driver's rear vision mirror, the word ECNALUBMA reverts to the word AMBULANCE as the rescue vehicle swerves around them. In convex vision altered by light, reverse words make more sense than accidents. A young woman driving in front of the ambulance who has been awake most of the night crying because her husband has asked for a divorce, is driving her kids to school, both kids point with delight at the ambulance and police vehicles. The sound of sirens makes adults flinch, the sound we hope to avoid throughout our lifetime, the danger, the dying, and death. She pulls over and watches the ambulance pass by with a sense of relief. It's not me. It could be me. But it's not. I am safe right now; we are all safe. The emergency is about someone else. It's not our turn yet. Emergency vehicles flash past her, the batten-burg, checkerboard, chevrons patterns and stripes, and reflective lettering.

The ambulance arrives in the emergency bay. At the hospital, Jeff notes the doctor's look of concern, a look you could miss if you weren't on the lookout for it. Is Michael going to make it, or not? If not, who is going to tell Charlotte? Will I have to?

Michael is lying on the gurney in the emergency department, an oxygen mask on his face, IV drip in one hand, the other hand placed over his heart. He now appears as pale as the moon through a curtain. Wave after cold wave of anesthetized blue crashes over him. Four hours later, when he opens his eyes, he sees Jeff standing there.

'Good to see you're back in the land of the living.'

Michael's lips feel Novocaine numb as he blubbers out, 'What the hell happened?'

'Remember, you went for a run in the park?'

'Yes.'

'Do you remember anything after that?'

'A pink duck and a mosquito.'

'I don't know about the duck, but I'm sure the 'mosquito' was a hypodermic dart primed with enough sedation to knock over a raging bull elephant. Someone wants you dead.'

Michael pulls off the oxygen mask. 'Well, they're fresh out of luck with that idea,'

Brooke walks into the emergency department.

'What the hell happened to you?'

'Someone took a long shot at me.'

'Are you up to going to Long Island?'

'What do you think?' Michael stands up, rips the plaster off, and pulls the IV drip out of his arm.

THERE ARE TWO THINGS about Long Island Brooke knows: The Long Island medium who lives there. And that the Long Island iced tea claims to have been invented either by Chris Bendicksen, or by Robert Rosebud Butt. On the long drive to Long Island, and by the time they get to Sandra's apartment, Brooke will tell Michael everything she knows about Long Island; about Robert Rosebud Butt's original recipe for a Long Island iced tea, a mixture of five alcoholic beverages including; tequila, vodka, light rum, triple sec, gin, and a splash of cola, and that some highball variants have names such as; Three Mile Island, and Adios Mother Fucker, but whatever the name, the coloring of the cocktails appears to look like iced tea. All have a high alcohol concentration, around twenty-two percent, higher than most highball drinks due to the amount of mixer used. And she will tell Michael about the reality TV show, 'Long Island Medium', starring Marcia Sarno, a psychic medium, her cost of a private thirty minute consultation at four hundred dollars.

Michael tells her about The Long Island Killer. One of the most disturbing unsolved serial killer cases in crime history. In a private seaside community of seventy-two houses; there were seventeen murder victims, bodies on the beach and marshlands, the focus on one man in Oak Beach, a wealthy middle-aged bachelor with an appetite for paid sex; rumors of orgies, torture, and sadistic sex-addicted cops, and sex workers who partied in Brewster's house. And not forgetting the girl who ran through the gated community in Oak Beach, after phoning 911, screaming at the operator, 'They are trying to kill me.' Her dismembered body was found in brackish backwater. The Long Island serial killer has never been captured.

Michael parks the car outside a 1930's Art Deco apartment block. Brooke presses the door buzzer. A woman's voice filters through the intercom grill.

'Yes, can I help you?'

'Is that Sandra Fabienne ?'

'Yes, who's this?'

'Agent Steel.' He flashes his FBI badge at the security camera. 'This is my partner Agent Fullerton. We would like to ask you some questions.'

Michael and Brooke take the elevator to the second floor, opening into a grand entrance hallway with burr-wood and walnut paneling. The apartment door has a dark heart ebony wood trim. When Sandra opens the door, Brooke can't believe what she sees. The interior is 1300sq feet of luxury, carefully sourced Deco period furnishings and light fittings that could double as a film set for Gatsby or Poirot: Vogue-inspired murals, even a hand-painted Lempicka.

Michael can't believe what he sees. Sandra is as beautiful as ever, and he can understand why Noah had fallen in love with her: deep blue eyes, long blonde hair, particularly attractive features, high bridged cheekbones, and refined nose. Her hair pulled back behind one ear in casual perfection. He remembers why he had a crush on her back then. Her look turns from apprehension and concern to one of surprise and confusion when she sees Michael standing there.

'Michael, it's wonderful to see you after all these years.' She hugs him and kisses him lightly on the cheek. She smells like summer, as if her clothes were dried in the sunshine on a breezy day. Her sweater, pale blue, and when she presses into Michael, the warmth of her breasts reminds Michael that he kissed her once upon a time, a crush he held decades before. But Noah was the one she took to the high school prom, not Michael, and he could never figure it out until now. The reason Sandra and him were never an item is that he was destined to meet Charlotte. That is the fate of life.

'I've just made Lapsang Souchong tea. Would you like some? If you want coffee, you're out of luck, we don't have one coffee bean in this apartment.'

Michael realizes the connection. 'Fabienne teashops! I've just put two and two together.'

'Yes. Julian Fabienne is my husband.'

'You mean the captain of the cycling club in high school?'

'Yes, he didn't stop there. He went back to France and cycled through Asia. I bumped into him on a beach in Goa two years later; I mean, what are the odds. There was something magical about swimming in the Arabian Sea. We thought we both fell in love. Came back to New York, and the rest is our private history, as the cliché goes.'

Thought we fell in love. Michael did not miss her tenure. The way she said the phrase was like an overwritten valentine card, recycled for another lover.

'Michael, this is no high school reunion, so tell me, why are you here.'

'I need to know if you and your husband had a baby?'

'No, we don't have any children.'

'There was a rumor that you had a baby in high school?'

'If you weren't a friend, I'd ask you to leave. And if you are a friend, you'll change the subject. The fact is, I can't have any children. I find this 'did you have a baby' conversation stressful. Actually, it's none of your business.'

'When did you last see Noah?'

'What is this, Michael?'

Brooke interrupts. 'There is a problem with mistaken identity. Noah's in jail. If we can locate your child, we can prove Noah's identity through DNA testing.'

'What do you mean, prove his identity?'

Michael explains the situation, and Sandra's face turns pale.

Brooke saw her color change. 'You'd better sit down before you pass out. I'll get you a glass of water.'

'The thing is, I did have a baby with Noah. A baby girl, 7lb 4 ounces, she was beautiful. But there was a problem.' Tears welled up in her eyes.

'Was she sick?'

'No, she was perfectly healthy, an angel in fact.'

'So what happened?'

'My Mom didn't want me to keep the baby, and I did, so I was on my own. But when she was four months old, the milk and the money dried up.'

'What did you do?'

'I was persuaded to adopt her out. The nuns' wouldn't take her unless I signed final adoption papers.'

'I see.'

'Don't think I haven't regretted every day without her. I have no idea where our child is. My husband and I can't conceive a baby. We have tried IVF, everything. If he finds out I conceived a child with another man, but not with him, I don't want to consider how he would react.'

Sandra pours the tea she'd almost forgotten. The Lapsang, barely warm, poured from the teapot's sterling silver spout, a brew dark in the cups, over-steeped to the point of bitterness. She adds more boiling water. As she bent forward, Michael saw the flash of a heart pendant on a mini belcher chain.

'Sandra, I see you still have Noah's locket.'

'This one?' She touches the locket at her throat.

Michael leans forward to get a closer look.

'Wait, there is something.' Using a tiny silver key disguised within the embossed pattern, Sandra opens the locket. Inside there is a lock of fair baby hair tied with a pink satin ribbon.

'This is all I have of my little baby girl.'

'We can get a DNA sample from this hair. If it's a match, will you sign a legal declaration with regards to Noah being the father?'

'And if I don't do anything?'

'You could hold the key to Noah's life. Without your help, he'll stay locked up forever.'

She took the locket off and kissed it before handing it to Michael.

'Tell him I want to see him again.'

Something else caught Michael's attention. A purple and yellow mandala, a half-circle of bruises, the pattern of bleeding under the skin caused by pressure from a finger grip on her arm. She'd not been in the grip of spiritual love. Someone had grabbed her and held her by force. Is her husband an abuser?

57

On the way back from Long Island, the sun was framed in the passenger window, setting like a golden jello. An anomaly came back to Michael—a flash of Noah in the café before the couch fell from the sky. How Noah had asked on that fateful day, 'Do you believe everyone has a double in this world?' He was adamant he'd just seen his double in the men's washroom. Then Michael had another thought. He feels under the dashboard, until his fingers touch a small object attached like a limpet, and he rips out a satellite responder. 'Byron's been tracking us and listening in the whole time.'

'Byron?'

'I'm sure of it.'

'If he is as insane as you say, Sandra's life is at risk just because we visited her.'

Michael picks up the squad cars on the VHS and clicks the open channel. 'This is Agent Steel; I need immediate police protection for Sandra Fabienne, Apartment 2, Birchwood Lane, Long Island, as of right now.'

The response team replied, 'Officers dispatched. Estimated time of arrival is twelve minutes.'

'Thank you.'

Brooke pulls the unmarked police vehicle into a diner car park. She glances in the rear vision mirror, a double-take, as she checks her lipstick and checks for danger at the same time. They sit down in the last seat in the diner, near the kitchen, their backs to no one and a clear view of the front door.

The diner is famous for its steaks. Not one vegetarian bite on the menu, not even coleslaw or a chef salad. It is all about thick meat, the place for carnivores.

The waitress arrives at the table. 'Hi, what's it to be?'

'Two black coffees, thanks.'

Michael passes his phone to Brooke. 'What do you make of this?'

Because you will fall apart
A burning room in death's house
The carrion crows await the time
Solomon and the shrine
Icarus waxen journey to the sun
You will never hold your sons
For your name is written on the door
You will come back no more
Once death finishes what I have begun
Your name will be on page one.

'Catchy text.' Brooke scrolls down and reads one line at a time. '*The burning room in death's house*—death in a house—*Your name is written on the door*—that could mean your house—*Your name will be on page one*—news worthy deaths are on page one of the newspaper. So, he's out to make a burning man of you.'

Michael pays the bill. 'Byron's the one who's going to get burned.'

As they approach the squad car, low-throated 1,500cc Harley leaves the main road and roars into the parking lot notoriously loud, announcing its existence with kamikaze power, but slows down to a throb as it passes the squad car. The biker sheathed in black leather, the jacket has no gang patch, the bike has no current state license plate. The biker is about to park but then accelerates suddenly, as if he has changed his mind. Michael keeps his eye on the bike as it roars back up the carriageway, weaving in and out of traffic, with more than joyriding on his mind. Michael saw it first—a mobile phone blinking on the roof of their car.

'It's a bomb!' Michael pushes Brooke away from the blast with its incendiary fireball. Debris floats down slowly, like deciduous carbon, leaving an eerie silence beyond the quiet. Brooke stands up and views the carnage with growing trepidation. Bodies lie under a shroud of dust; one appears crumpled on the ground in a fetal position, covered in debris.

Brooke shouts into her phone: 'Agent Fullerton. We have three people down. Request immediate assistance.'

By the time the flashing blue and red lights arrive, Michael is standing, but the body of a woman who had been pushing a shopping cart, and a bystander, lay on the ground. Twenty-five meters away, next to the burning wreck of his squad car, Michael's mobile was hot on the asphalt, buzzing an incendiary text.

That was a blast
The king has got your number
There is no time to slumber

The gift of life is with Christ
And your numbers up if you don't get the gist
10-9-45 is the number to ponder
You've got one hour, so make it fast
Or it will be your last.

'A chess move. This is the madness of Byron,' Michael shows Brooke the text. He leans through a patrol car window and picks up the VHF phone.

'Agent Steel here, patch me through to Marcus Benson.'

'Hi, Michael, so what's happening?'

'Marcus, you're the chess player. Give me a few checkmate moves using the numbers 10-9-45?'

Marcus is a genius among other talents; he had won the chess nationals four years in a row and often played six players at the same time. 'I can think of two, but I'll get back to you.'

'Can you get back to me sooner rather than later. It's a matter of life and death and likely my death.'

'Well, if you put it like that, I'll be back to you before now.'

By the time the burned-out squad car is hoisted onto a tow truck, Marcus rings back with checkmate scenarios. 'The unpredicted checkmate will be a white bishop on nine and black king in the corner spot.'

'Thanks, Marcus, that makes sense.'

Michael turns to Brooke. 'Let's go.'

'Where to?'

'St Luke's Cathedral on 9th Avenue.'

'Why exactly?'

'The reference in the text to religion, the gift of life, and also the number nine—that must mean the cathedral on 9th street.'

'Now, why didn't I think of that?'

Stone staircases leading up to cathedral doors go on forever—endless processions of pilgrims on the pathway of righteousness. Sunday after Sunday, the weddings and the funerals under vaulted stone arches, the cathedral roof towers fifty feet over the hopeful and the hopeless.

The entrance doors are open for the faithful and the hopeful. Michael walks through the dusty light, down the main church aisle, between wooden pews carved from ironwood, the cross-stitch prayer cushions all Eden apples and doves, the shining brass eagle forged for the pulpit seems to rustle its burnished feathers. On the flagstones under Michael's feet, tarnished brass plaques engraved with names of entombed saints. Paschal candles are left burning next to the gold altar cross. The baptismal font filled with holy water, shimmers and reflects what Michael believes in. In family. In love. In higher forces. But in his job, he constantly wrestled with evil, and part of him felt contaminated. Death brushed against his nerves. Everyone walks in the shadow of death. If you are in a hurry in life, slow down, but if you slow down and wait, death catches you up—one way or another.

It is the flowers arranged in vases; funeral flowers that fill the church in uncanny abundance today. Funereal Casablanca lilies—flowers of the devil's breath. And an over-abundance of white roses, reminders of the earthly life.

Shadows tuck themselves into hallowed crevices; an organ blows cords of Mozart's *Requiem for the Dead*. A small message board in an alcove lights up in red neon.

Esteem a horse, according to its pace
But lose no wagers
On a wild goose chase
Turn to the eagle that stands in grace.

Michael recognizes the cryptic citation from Breton's poem, *'The Mother's Blessing,'* a poem penned in 1602, which alludes to chasing a killer will prove fruitless. The eagle is a notable bird of prey. He goes to the eagle lectern, leans between its wingspan, and glances inside the pulpit, a pair of eyeglasses left on a massive Bible. Michael does the cabalistic math on 1602, 1+6+0+2, adds up to nine, 3+3+3, a trilogy.

Oddly, Sunday's sermon had been carefully folded into nine white origami doves. Michael opens out the paper wings of each dove. Six are blank, and three have cursive writing.

Michael arranges the doves, their phrases of a riddle:

Kings IV the gift of life I give to you—in the puzzle of life you made the right move—your reward is four more hours of life.

Standing in the pulpit, like a weekday lay-preacher, he calls down to Brooke who is sitting in an elm wood pew.

'I chose bishop to king and came to this cathedral, only to find Byron acting as a demigod. He's deemed me four hours of life. That's his first mistake!'

Brooke was not the only one who heard Michael. The door to the rectory closed with the trespass sound of a church mouse, a scraping, and an unhinged squeak. One hundred prayer candles were blown out in unison as if by one almighty breath, or perhaps just a gust of wind in the belfry. Michael and Brooke pass through the cathedral doors, emerging from prayer light, both squinting into broad strokes of sunlight.

Michael makes a call to Marcus. 'The bishop to king was the right strategy. Do you have what we discussed in place?'

'Yep, my crew have practically wired you into the entire universe.'

BACK AT THE APARTMENT, Michael gets into the lion-clawed iron bath-tub. In his watery sanctuary, he sighs, sinking slowly until only his face and toes remain above the surface. It's a question of buoyancy and water displacement. Floating in the aqua zone, the heartbeat slows while the watch ticks time away, and the mobile phone on the wicker chair vibrates unheard. One minute, he's soaking the day off in the tub, next minute, a catastrophe no one sees coming.

An explosion faster than a scream rips through the apartment, blasting, splintering, and raining shattered glass on the street below. Rubble rain, more solid than heavy. The surveillance van on the street outside rocks with the force of the explosion. When the blast is over, the bathroom door frame stands like a lonely sentry on duty. The water in the tub has vanished. Iron beams left buckled overhead, wires fizz and spark like electrocuted glow worms. Blood runs down Michael's face as he lies encoffined in the empty tub.

Brooke slides open the side door of the van. A swat team emerges, and in no time are stepping through the destruction and chaos of Michael's apartment. Brooke calls out, hoping for an answer.

'Michael!'

She thinks she hears Michael's voice. Directing the beam of her flashlight, Brooke peers with trepidation over the rim of a bathtub, expecting to find a bloodbath. Brooke has never seen her partner in such a compromised position, lying naked like a big baby at the bottom of a tub. She wants to look the other way, but at the same time, she must check his vital signs.

'He's alive. Get the medics.'

'Get me a towel.' It was obvious he was naked. Michael covered his privates with his hands.

'Stay still.'

'I'm OK.'

'Seriously?'

'A headache from hell, and my ears are ringing like a bell.'

'Well, at least it's not a death knell. Someone above is looking out for you.'

Michael had saved the tub from the scrap heap during one of his fossicking expeditions, scrapped the rust off, resurfaced it, and repaired the four regal lion claws that grip the floor. Everything has a reason. The solid integrity of the mighty old tub saved him.

A young paramedic taped the cut above Michael's eye with two butterfly strips.

Michael spoke up: 'Do me a favor?

'Sure.'

'Turn around while I throw some clothes on!'

Michael shakes out all the rubble from his boxer shorts, then pulls on his t-shirt and recently distressed jeans before navigating through the devastation in the apartment. Firebombing is the destroyer of family dreams, wiping out precious memories, the wedding photographs and albums, things of inheritance, the heirlooms, including the baby shawls knitted by Charlotte's grandmother. Such a vast inventory of loss blurs the replaceable with the irreplaceable.

'Let's get out of here.'

On the sidewalk outside, Marcus hurries towards Michael, balancing an open laptop. 'Hell! Glad you're OK! You'll want to see this. I've got all the data from the scanners.'

The screen shows four views of the apartment and the surrounding area via satellite. 'Check this out.' Marcus pushes replay to show a quiet street scene captured by satellite right before the explosion. Then a sudden blinding flash of phosphorous green obliterates the scene.

'Play that again in infrared.'

Marcus changes the pixel size in the Quantum infrared mode and the explosion re-blasts.

'The bomb was definitely detonated using a remote laser beam. There, an electromagnetic beam from that blue saloon car across the street.' Marcus step-frames the explosion. 'See those car lights? The vehicle disappeared up 5th Street after the blast.'

'Are we still recording, Marcus?'

Marcus taps the computer keys. 'Yes, that same car is heading north.' He brings up more windows on his laptop.

Marcus and Michael jump into Brooke's car. Five squad cars fall in convoy behind them. Black Hawk helicopters track the vehicles below. The saloon car passes the Yankee stadium on the east side of town and heads in the direction of the Harlem River. A person in a getaway car must know where he is heading and why. The driver of the stolen car was an ex-member of the Harlem River Rat gang from the Bronx. His go-to place is the edge of the cliff, a place where in his derailed mind, he is still king of the Bronx and always will be. He earned the right. He passed his right of passage as a boy of thirteen, something you had to do to become a fully-fledged member of the toughest gang in the Bronx. They gave him two choices for the initiation. Beat or jump. He chose to jump instead of being beaten by the gang. While either induction occasionally resulted in a fatality, at least the gang gave him a choice—something his parents never gave him. The initiation he chose on that hot summer day was to jump one hundred and ten feet from the C Cliff rock ledge into the Harlem River. To him, C Cliff was about making a choice, then standing by the decision you made.

The thermal camera sends real-time images from the helicopter to Marcus's laptop. 'He's stopped.'

The suspect walks away from the parked vehicle, the radiometric imagery verifies each step he takes. Heat surveillance also shows two people complicating the scene by making out in the bushes, a hundred meters away. The Black Ops interrupt the lovers and order them away. The squad of sharpshooters moves in closer to ensnare by stealth. The trap sets. The person who gets ensnared does not notice others in the same place, at the same time.

Meanwhile, the bomb squad team, padded in gray body armor like android centurions, check the suspect's car for booby traps. It turns out that the vehicle is registered to a grade three teacher in Connecticut. Her vehicle had been pimped on a reality TV show episode; sprayed baby blue, upholstered in pink suede, accessorized with dual fat chrome exhausts and bookshelves fitted into the trunk were crammed with brainteaser books, Sudoku, and crossword puzzles—then stolen.

CHAPTER

59

THE GOLDEN BALL OF sun rises from a watery depth, a brief firmament of the horizon that has puzzled great thinkers through the ages, and the world of illusion remains in a world of questions.

The morning breeze of first light carries briny scent up the river—New York near the sea—a hint of fish caught in a net. Michael gets out of the squad car and walks along the cliff towards a silhouette of a man—a glow of final embers—the last cigarette. The man's profile comes into focus. Michael holds his Glock 23. Cold metal in hand. He approaches the silhouette. Something is very wrong. Has the man been expecting him all along? The man stares directly at Michael and his gun. Does he know this man? A delay of thought gives a definite advantage. The man takes one lightning step, grabs Michael, and hugs him close.

'Michael, it's me, Noah!'

'You're not Noah!'

Black Ops rise out of the gray rocks. From a distance, the two men look like two brothers. Both are even in height, of similar weight and physical stature. Even in the M-16 scope, the target cannot be clearly identified. It is Michael's back that is now in the firing line. The cliff edge, perilously close.

Byron breathes harshly in Michael's ear. 'This is your final right of passage, and I'm here to initiate you. I'm calling it, a shoot-out or a jump-in. Either way, get set to die.'

The sun flares.

As if by telepathy or is it psychic sympathy, the babies begin to kick inside Charlotte's womb, as she dreams the night away, a silent communication happens via the heart and the belly, her babies' hearts pounding like tiny drums. She sees Michael's face in amongst fluorescence glowing in the breakers, long silver-green strands wrapping around rocks in the ebb tide, unwrapping again in the flow. What the mind sees, the heart transmits, as if Michael is the sender and she is the receiver. He is in deep trouble. She knows it.

It is the smelling salts of wet seaweed rising from the river that awakes Michael's senses, and he breaks free from Byron's grip. Like the river rat he is, Byron shouts, 'I'm still the king, and here's the thing…' Black helicopters thunder up the cliff face, sharp shooters at the ready—Byron's cranium shatters, its viscous mess splattering Michael with macerated brain pulp, the gaping skull pouring out a river of bloodied prose, an end to the finale of rhyme.

60

MICHAEL WOKE TO AN insomniac cat purring on his pillow, but it was good to be awake and alive. He turned over, but the cat persisted on human company, curled up on his chest, face to face. Not the most comfortable night's sleep on Brooke's sofa bed, but the apartment blast had rendered him marginally homeless. Couch surfing was now the new norm. Brooke gave up her one-woman living room, not because she felt sorry that he was temporarily homeless, but she liked the company since her girlfriend up and left without leaving a note, taking the shared dog and clearing her personal stuff out when Brooke was at work. The split was inevitable because two feisty women in a small apartment made a PMS calendar from hell. Arguing and picking on each other until Kleenex tissues ran out as fast as tears—until Brooke was alone. The dog gone, and just the cat for company. One woman living alone was a lot more straightforward. Peace. Quiet. Tidy. Lonely.

Michael picks up the late edition newspaper off the coffee table.

He reads the front-page news about an apartment blast, their apartment, and the killing of a man, as yet to be identified. He reads the article below, about a four-year-old boy who fell down a twelve-foot cliff into the gorilla enclosure at the Cincinnati Zoo, coming face-to-face with the 400 pound beast. The gorilla soon became agitated, disorientated, and started behaving erratically. The dangerous animal response team made the decision to shoot the gorilla dead. Human, or animal, or a human acting like a wild animal, critical response teams make the decision to shoot to kill. The death of two animals on the same page, and only the gorilla mourned by millions. Just then, Brooke arrived back in the apartment, both arms filled with grocery bags, with a French baguette sticking out the top.

'Well, glad you're still here. I've got to say, it's nice to have your company.'

'Is there a chance of you two getting back together?'

'No, we never will.'

'What happened?'

'We fought a lot. But that wasn't the reason we split.'

They'd been planning a marriage for June when suddenly Claire up and left, claiming she was attracted to an Italian guy, a tour operator she met in a club.

'When I came back from work, she'd cleared out her side of the closet and taken my Jimmy Choo sandals. We had the same size feet, so I let her borrow them sometimes. But there she goes taking them with her.'

Michael's mobile rings. 'Chief!'

'We are expecting company from higher up. They want to speak to you. My office. One hour.'

Michael wonders, who is cracking the whip to make the Chief jump through hoops like a circus dog?

CHAPTER

61

MICHAEL SEES BLURRED OUTLINES of three people behind the frosted glass of the meeting room. When he enters the room, the situation becomes clear. The Chief is definitely irked. He sits opposite a man wearing tinted prescription glasses, who is seated beside a woman wearing a dark blue power suit. She has a perfect mannequin look, high necked white shirt, with a touch of lace on the collar, her fair hair tightly twisted in a French knot held by a silver clasp, a sparkle of crystal earrings, somewhat fake, glass with a diamond pretense. He observes her the way one person takes the other in on first impressions. She does the same with him; a confident, self-assured man, handsome too, but her eyes catch a flash of gold—married. The best ones are always taken, from her experience at least. Still, she is not a woman to let a small band of gold get in her way if she wants something badly enough, but Miller isn't sure if Michael is the man to give her what she wants right now.

'I'd like you to meet special agents Miller and Simpson. Miller holds out her hand, and Michael shakes it, an old-fashioned handshake where one person might reveal a hidden blade.

Tension hardwires the atmosphere. The Chief, who usually chairs important meetings, sits back, taking himself out of the picture or out of the line of fire. Two agents are conducting this meeting. CIA agents, sleuths ordered from the very top.

Miller speaks first. 'Congratulations Agent Steel on ending the reign of the infamous Lord Byron.' She glances at Simpson in a conspiracy of silence. 'We understand you had Byron living under your roof for months,' Miller never takes her eyes off Michael as she speaks, 'all the while you believed it was your best friend, Noah. Is this correct?'

Michael is about to say how identity isn't just about looks, how his friend's personality had changed, small things, but enough to make him suspect Noah wasn't the real deal. 'No, I believed...' Miller cuts through his sentence with a whip of words. 'One fact is clear, Byron fooled you. Even with all your past experience and knowledge, he duped you—perfect facial duplication is a reality.'

Without allowing Michael another word, she changes the subject abruptly. 'The DNA report from the silver locket of baby hair is conclusive. Noah Reddich will be released today. However, the surgery he requires to remove Byron's face will have to wait for some time. The Illuminati team who performed the surgery still have some questions to answer.'

Simpson follows with a statement that shocks Michael.

'We'll take it from here. Byron's body will be transferred into our custody today. Please arrange for all case files to be sent to CIA headquarters.'

Simpson stands up. End of meeting.

The special agents stand together, an incendiary combination, like bonfire and matches, then they were gone.

The Chief locks the door. 'I have something to show you.'

He spreads photos of international politicians, movie stars, princes, and Byron aka Noah, over the table.

'Take a look and tell me what they have in common.'

'They are all Biozen clients of Cutter.'

'Correct. However, Byron and Noah were the only recorded complete facial identity reconstructions performed by Illuminati surgeons. They kept detailed records of both surgeries but no other. The operative word is Illuminati surgeons. Keep in mind the hospital is owned by Christian Cutter. No medical records have been kept on any of Cutter's clients. But there are other players in all of this. There is one unidentified international corporation with links through Saudi Arabia, Paris, London, Rome, Sydney, and Hong Kong. This is bigger than cosmetic surgeries, facial transplants, or murder inquiries. Homeland security is at risk. And Christian Cutter, is somehow involved in all this. Take a look.'

One photograph is face down. Michael turns it over. 'The U.S. president?'

The Chief turns it back over. 'And that's the way it's to stay—face down. You have never seen this photo. Got it?'

He slides the photographs into a white envelope, and locks them away in his safe. 'Influential world leaders are very edgy about Christian Cutter's involvement. Nothing will be disclosed. You understand. This is a complicated matter and case sensitive. Today I've been given instructions that Christian Cutter is to be left alone, and not investigated, under any circumstances. He is untouchable. Is that clear? There is to be no direct contact, no surveillance, or harassment. I will regard any interference as insubordination, which carries the penalty of instant dismissal.'

'But Chief, why not quietly investigate Cutter?'

'The CIA, and Home Security are all over this. We no longer have jurisdiction. He's off bounds to us, and that's final.'

The Chief had his orders and was jumping through flaming hoops set alight by others. The meeting was over. Michael knew better than to push the Chief, at this time or any other.

'Send me your update on the Rose Garden Murder. We can't have this maniac on the streets either.'

FISHING FOR FRIENDS WAS paying off. The phone calls, invitations, tactful bribes came one after another. Christian Cutter was on the role of a lifetime; played his part, kept ahead of the players, knew how to associate himself with influential people, and developed his raft of social skills. Winning doesn't always mean playing by the rules. It means winning. Christian got ahead because he'd learned the side game. Bend the rules. Better yet, break them. Politicians and leaders learned this long ago. And fabricating the rules, keep you ahead of the game. Money talks. Even dirty money. Money was money. And in this connected and accelerating world, he got richer, faster.

And so it was. The World Wide Corporation arrange a meeting and send the latest jet for Christian. He will be the guest of honor.

His vision of sun and sky, arc of horizon, are clear to him today. The sun is shining through the plane window, there are no window blinds to bother with. Aviation glass adjusted opacity and shade, automatically. The female crew assistant brings out a chilled bottle of Moet, a three-liter jeroboam in a plated white gold bottle sheath, laser engraved with the Dom Perignon label. He picks up the flight phone and makes the call he can only do once a year.

'Could I speak with Mrs. Cutter, please?'

'Certainly, can I say who's calling?'

'Her son.'

'Of course, I didn't recognize your voice. You sound a long way away.'

'But never out of touch.'

He hears the weight of the phone placed on the sideboard in the communal dayroom, and Ma's soft slipper shuffle.

'Hello?'

'Hey Ma, how are you?'

'Christian, I was just thinking about you too. Happy birthday my darling boy.'

'Thanks Ma, and thank you for having me! You know it's Joe's birthday too.'

'Yes, of course I know. How could I forget? Is he with you?'

'No, he's not.'

'Too bad, darling, never mind. It's good to get a break, don't you think?'

'Ma, I'm up in the clouds. Your voice is fading out.'

'That's nice, dear. Storm coming your way?'

'No, Ma, I don't do storms.'

'Nothing but blue skies for you today then. Happy birthday my number one son.'

'Don't ever say that to Joe!'

The stewardess pours the champagne, hands Christian a chilled flute, and notices his brief sideways glance at her name badge.

'I've got to go now. Something's come up. Bye Ma.' Christian finishes one conversation and starts another.

'Celeste Bleu, won't you please join me? I hate to drink alone, and I'm guessing the pilots don't drink and fly.'

'Sorry, Sir.'

'Help me out with this vintage from France,' Christian said, with one of his all-encompassing glances that takes her in; her brunette hair pinned up in a neat French-style chignon, her blue eyes with long, dark eyelashes, a fusion of international beauty. She had refined features and polished skin, the creamy complexion of a bisque porcelain doll; more than a catwalk model, she is his type of woman.

'Sir, I am not allowed to drink on duty for safety reasons.'

'When do you come off duty?'

'After you open this.' Celeste hands him a sealed manila envelope with a smile. 'Happy birthday, Sir.'

Christian takes a mouthful of champagne. Effervescent bubbles tingling around his teeth, remind him to invent a Moet Dom Perignon mouthwash, as part of his claim to fame, and Moet in a toothpaste tube too, and Moet you can spread on toast instead of jam.

He opens the envelope. Inside is a card with a picture of a wild bobcat in a conical birthday hat. As he opens the card, Happy Birthday plays. When he closes it, the sound of a different tune—a recorded message.

There is more. Christian takes the stack of legal papers from the envelope, ownership papers for the one hundred million dollar plane he was flying in, and the official deed to the island he was flying to, extravagant showcase pieces that no one in their right materialistic mind could refuse.

The acquisition of this plane takes flying the skies to a new level. Christian walks up the spiral staircase with Celeste to the upper deck. The jet can carry up to twenty passengers; comfortably sleeps ten, kitchen with German appliances, bathroom with Italian designer fittings including gold plated basin and faucets; a conference room for doing business at altitude using state-of-the-art technology; direct Internet access, and satellite communications, a video room with a cinematic system, 52 inch flat-screen display, and a library.

Refuelling a million bubbles in the sparkling Christofle fluted glasses, Christian adds, before a smile, 'I need to celebrate. It's my party and my jet. I'm officially taking you off duty, *le ciel est bleu*, the sky is blue, I am going to rename this plane, C Bleu, after you.'

As naturally as Christian was attracted to people, by their beauty, by their wealth, and by their performance, or all three, the wealthy were as drawn to him, as Celeste was drawn into his arms. A two-way attraction happens just as inevitably as a powerful magnetic beacon brings migrating raptors and osprey together.

Christian and Celeste fly the line of the Equator together—in bed. Below them, the water, a sheet of unruffled glass, coral reefs, white-sand beaches surrounded by crystal clear turquoise blue water, palm-fringed coves, and private islands, where his soon-to-be neighbors, the mega-wealthy live and vacation.

Two hundred foot sailing boats lay at anchor on the blue playground of sea. The weather sunnier and warmer than anywhere else in the world. Even at night, if it turns cold, the rich can pay someone to burn hundred dollar bills to keep warm, because it's true, that's what big players can do. If they run out of firelighters for their barbeque, they just burn money, so when food is grilled and served up, even a simple lunch tastes rich and corrupt.

Seen from above, Christian's island appears like a sleeping dragon. Christian buckles up for the landing on a runway that ends at the edge of the Caribbean Sea. All the directors of The World

Wide Corporation wait for Christian.

He doesn't feel overwhelmed as much as over-welcomed. A bit of overkill, considering he's the only visitor embarking from the plane, but he likes it. Behind each director, a burly bodyguard stands, each guard packs an MK45 weapon on his shoulder, a full-size Ruger P-89DC pistol in a plaid leather holster, and a black and tan Doberman Pinscher restrained at the end of a tartan leash.

CHRISTIAN HAD GREETED THE rich and powerful, but now he is puzzled about just how he will shake hands with the main man. Steve doesn't miss the way Christian's eyes flick to Steve's empty sleeve where his right arm once was, and back to Steve's left hand. He likes the game of squirm because, with an amputated limb, you hold the rulebook on amputee etiquette. Sensing Christian's unease with an empty sleeve, Steve discloses, 'It happens. I was one of the lucky ones. I gave my right arm to an apex predator. They made a meal of it. Sharks have survived two hundred million years, and my arm was just part of the food chain, in case you were wondering.'

Christian considers his next move. He knows they are waiting for him to make a photo handshake, a firm handshake where one holds on for an extended time to show trust. But the right handshake wasn't an option. If he has bowed to Grand Empress Dowager, he will bow to the armless one. And so he does. He executes the deep bow, not too low to appear fake, but low enough to show respect.

After the official handshakes or lack of handshakes in Steve's case, the atmosphere changes to island style.

On the lawn, a local group of musicians perform an island reggae rendition of Happy Birthday. There are two birthday cakes. One is a replica of Christian's new jet made of white and blue icing. The other cake is his island, the houses, the sandy beaches, the ocean all built to scale in confectioners icing, right down to tiny brown marzipan coconuts in the little green almond paste palm trees.

Steve passes a Sakai knife to Christian. 'For cutting the cake. And you don't need to make a wish. We're in the business of making wishes come true.'

That afternoon, Steve gives Christian the grand tour of his newly acquired estate. His island, surrounded by the bluest seas in the world. There are four buildings on the five hundred acres. The main house has wide-planked indigenous hardwood floors and an infinity pool to the sea beyond.

Off the master bedroom there is a private plunge pool set in a calm lagoon, surrounded by tropical gardens abundant with heady flowering jasmine and frangipane, where wild birds of paradise with white trailing plumes, are sometimes seen.

All his life Christian had taught himself to be an island unto himself, an island no one could reach. Now he was home. Here he can play the castaway or king, and escape whenever he needed.

Next to the grass tennis court, rackets and balls are set out on a trestle table. The rackets are made of heavy wooden frames strung with catgut. Each tennis racket is a collectible in perfect condition, signed by consecutive Wimbledon champions. A game played the old-fashioned way is set to be a challenge.

Steve and Christian play singles, but Steve beats him on account of his wicked left handers. Game over.

'You impressed me with your serves Christian. The counter said

120 mph, yet you say you never play?'

'Not since I was a kid, and back then, it was volleys on the brick wall with my brother.'

'You should bring your brother to the island and your mother if she's well enough. I'd like to meet them both.'

How does he know about Grace? And I never mentioned Joe or my birthday, Christian thinks as he sets his voice to casual.

'Well, thank you.'

'I'm glad you like the place. You can think and do what you like here. Talk to the seabirds, and they will agree with you. Listen to the wind. No disturbances. Isolation focuses the mind. The bird-song and waves you hear are Alpha waves. Calming. You'll be as alone as you want to be. Imagine no other footprints but yours.'

Sea birds screech in the silence between sentences.

Then Steve got to the real point. 'We at The World Wide Corporation want you to focus on our business alone.'

'Very flattering, but I have numerous clients and a business to run. Focusing on one client is not possible.'

Steve over-rides Christian. 'And of all the men in the world, we have chosen you to help us because your products get results. Many of us in the company are older guys who will eventually be sucking soup through golden straws. But you've changed all that. With your help, we will outlive and outsmart anyone who stands in the way of our global business. We can buy countries if need be, but we can't make ourselves any younger. Age is the enemy of the future.' Steve changes tactics, 'The proletariat member you have been treating with longevity serum, happens to be a key member of the communist party responsible for the ongoing development of the controversial Chinese floating islands—military bases and airstrips in the open sea.'

'That's my private clientele.'

'The fact is we know who all your clients are, but that's not important.'

'To me, it is. I have an ultra-high-security password generator in place for all my clients. That makes my business impenetrable.'

'If that were the case, we wouldn't be having this conversation. You have a 256 bit security key with a 128 bit block cipher, right? Again, this is not the point. It's about global preservation. We would like you to do something for us.'

Christian takes another sip of his martini, fishes out the stuffed green olive with a cocktail stick, and looks far out to the horizon, knowing the line has been crossed and compromised.

'We are concerned about Chinese control. The establishment of mobile islands will create world instability and take China a step further in their quest for world dominance.'

Steve lets that sink in for a few seconds.

'There is a meeting of Chinese delegates in Peking, and before this, Yang Lee Vong is going to North Korea on a diplomatic tour.'

'Yes, I know this.'

Steve continues his monologue. 'On this tour, you have arranged to meet Vong at the palace of the North Korean leader. We know you intend to administer the serum to him in Korea as part of his routine treatment. Only this time, we'd like you to administer, not the Life Serum but the new AntiXserum.'

This is where silence is a useful tool.

Christian says nothing but measures the extent of the trap Steve is setting. He listens inside the silences of the latest proposition, dark-laced, treacherous with blackmail.

'If we are to continue with our relationship, we need you to deal with Vong.'

Vong had gone on about his military islands to Christian. Vong was an arrogant man, bragging about his islands. In fact, he said they would make the world bow down to the imperial red flag. But then, not every leader is born to be mourned.

'You do your part, and our organization will take care of the rest.'

'Let me think about it because to date the AntiXserum has only been tested on rats.'

'Yes, I know, and one of your rats has ended up in The Illuminati Intensive Care Unit, in a coma, on life support.'

64

MICHAEL SPENDS THE NEXT week gathering floor plans and scoping out real estate offers in the hunt for a new apartment. In a seller's market, it takes more luck than you think to buy a property exactly on budget that ticks all the boxes for space, view, bedrooms and a study, located in a quiet neighborhood with a park within walking distance. He is in the middle of negotiations with a tough seller, and Michael is not being helped by the commission-driven agent, when his mobile rings.

'Honey, I'm coming home tomorrow.'

'Great news darling.'

'But I'll need a pick up from Mom's. I'm lending her my car for the week.'

'No problem. See you there.' Michael hangs up the phone. He enters a number on his smartphone and holds it up to the real estate agent. 'This is my final figure.'

DRIVING BACK INTO the city with Charlotte, Michael turns right at the first set of traffic lights and drives in the opposite direction of their old apartment. Halfway along the street lined with chestnut trees, he stops outside a historic brownstone building.

'Let's take a walk.'

Charlotte eyeballs Michael, reading his face. 'Is there something you want to tell me?'

'That I love you?'

'Something I don't know?'

'Recognize this place?'

Charlotte opens the car door. 'Yes. This is the apartment we went through at the open home, with a price tag out of our ballpark.'

'Well, it's sold again.' With that, Michael walks right up to the front door and unlocks it.

'You bought it?'

'We sure did!'

Much to Charlotte's surprise, Michael scoops her in his arms and carries her, baby-weight and all, over the threshold. As soon as her feet touch the polished floorboards, Charlotte wonders how it is possible to feel so happy and at home. Then, thoughts change, as thoughts do, she has another feeling that Michael is holding something else back from her.

'I love this apartment, but why, without talking to me? Not that I'm complaining, but really this is a lot to take in right now.'

Michael senses her concern and decides to tell her the whole story: Noah's identity theft, Byron escaping and living with them as Noah, the explosion at their apartment, Bryon's death, and Noah's imprisonment.

Charlotte listens to it all. 'That's one scary bedtime story you're telling me.'

On the first night of a thousand nights in their new apartment, they snuggle together under the goose-down quilt. Michael looks across at Charlotte, her long lashes closed over her eyes, her face as beautiful as Raphael's Madonna. A honeycomb candle flickers warm shadows on the wall, and the moon casts a thin shaft between the drapes. In a heartbeat, he feels a shift in himself. For the first time in weeks, with Charlotte's warm body so close to him, his thoughts no longer racing. Sleep is coming.

CHAPTER

65

MICHAEL WATCHES BREAKING NEWS from Beijing. On screen, the fresh-faced news announcer, Jodi Summer, is standing in the cold. With every word she speaks, a puff of white mist frosts her syllables. Standing in the semi-dark, outside the main entrance of The Peking Union Medical College Hospital, in minus ten degrees, Jodi wishes the TV network gave her a more exciting topic than reporting on an old man dying in China. Why didn't she get to cover the royal wedding or fashion week in Milan? Jodi faces the camera, her eyes with an expression of false empathy. She wonders if viewers will see the ice crystals freezing the black mascara on her lashes or whether the length of them might look like her lashes were not real but fake.

'Cue me, hurry up; I'm freezing my tits off here.'

'You're live!' The cameraman mouthed.

She regains composure and commences her monologue in the

sincerest tone she can dispatch from her newsy repertoire.

'The military leader Mr. Yang Lee Vong was admitted to hospital this evening at 7 pm. Authorities are unclear why he was suddenly taken ill at the conference dinner. By the time he arrived at the hospital, doctors said his condition was deteriorating rapidly, and an hour later, he slipped into a coma. His condition is listed as critical. It is understood he will be unable to complete his diplomatic tour, consequently China's construction of one hundred new missile silos have been put on hold, awaiting Vong's recovery.'

By the time Jodi finished speaking, her eyes felt like two frozen balls in their sockets. She hated this job. Her mobile rang.

'You're fired for cussing on camera.'

'Who is this?'

'The man who listens to your every word.'

'Christian? Where the hell are you?'

'Over by the lion statue.'

Jodi turns to see a tall, familiar figure standing by the lion, an imported statue made of hard rock, combining the body of a lion and the head of a human, a Sphinx, the human and the divine, good over evil, the choices we make that create the direction of our existence. Jodi sees the man, and sphinx, and without further hesitation, runs towards them.

Christian and Jodi kiss each other like the fuck buddies they've been for some years. Aware of her body shivering, in a pragmatic gesture, but with a hint of romanticism, Christian removes his bespoke tailored coat, his modus operandi for winter with its four-figure price tag, drapes it over her shoulders, which leaves him standing in his black pinstripe suit; the gray slivers of thread running vertically in the cloth, are not silver, but stripes of pure platinum thread. She slips her arms through the sleeves and feels the double cashmere as he does up the last solid gold button, the one at her throat. The energy between them—high octane and thrilling. 'Back to my hotel to warm you up?'

Meanwhile, Michael is about to switch off the late news when the camera pans over the Asian crowd and focuses on the one and only European couple, standing by the Sphinx.

'Cutter! What are you doing in the city of red dragons?'

CHAPTER

66

IN THE LUXURY SUITE AT the Hotel Éclat Beijing; a phone rings on the ebony-wood bedside console. Christian puts down his glass and picks up a call from his Eastern personal assistant in the adjoining room next door.

'Christian, a Mr. Charles Council is on the other line.'

'Ask him to phone back. Trace the call when he does. I want to be sure it is him.'

Charles was about making money when the world was in crisis; tsunamis, earthquakes, floods, hurricanes, and landslides. Human-made catastrophes; pandemics, elections, shifts in international politics, war, and terrorist attacks. The phone rings. Christian picks up but waits for the caller to speak first.

'Mr. Christian Cutter?'

'Mr. Council?'

'Call me Charles.'

Christian pulls the covers over Jodi.

Charles heard the sound of silk caressing a naked body. 'What would you say to an informal get-together in Paris this week?'

'That is possible.'

'Excellent. I'll make all the arrangements then.'

After Christian hangs up the phone, he thinks about the name Charles, a Germanic word meaning 'man' but not just any man. Christian will soon meet an audacious autocratic man, a potentate, a self-appointed supreme ruler amongst the world of elite business leaders. What is it about Charles. The name Charles starts with the letter C. That particular letter has the numerical equivalent of the number three, creative energy, mercurial, profoundly talented and driven, very social, also able to be ruthless, and cruel, severely lacking in empathy, and exhibits extreme negativity, when it suits. Like attracts like. Christian and Charles were destined.

Christian studies Jodi, her face more angelic than he had noticed. Asleep, she is in her element. The paleness of her skin, bisque and beautiful on the silk pillowcase, silk loomed and embroidered in the old Chinese way of the Yellow Emperor; peaches to bring long life to the sleeper and crane birds to carry the soul away—should the sleeper die before waking. Then Christian dials room service and orders a chilled bottle of champagne. He has five hours before his next flight—time to make out in the warmth of woman, before stepping out into the cold again.

THE PRIVATE CHARTER PLANE lands in a quiet corner of Charles de Gaulle Airport, where a customs official and a limousine are waiting. The French official checks the passports, talks briefly to the pilot, and salutes as Christian enters the limo.

Charles Council is sitting in the back of the black limousine. A man in his early to mid-forties, no older, with a taste for film noir, his voice carries a mix of accents, French, American, the upper tone of a highly educated British university scholar, and the vocal timbre of a baritone. Oxford came to mind. His stare comes from onyx black eyes set in high arching brows. Dark curly hair, tanned skin. Like all successful men, his tremendous personal magnetism is evident as Christian shakes his hand, a well-manicured hand of unbidden success.

The venue is the famous Chez Georges, a 1920's era Bistro. The pursuit of wealth is a beautiful thing Christian thinks as he enters the bistro with its honest white tablecloths covering the bank of tables running the length of the room, with opulent mirrors along the wall behind. Not just ordinary mirrors but treasured antique mirrors, their ornate gilt frames surrounded by silvered cherubs and turtledoves. In mercurial Venetian glass, you see yourself in a richer light, while eating the richest food in the world.

Very smoke and mirrors, this place, but in a good way, Christian muses, noting that he and Charles are the only ones here.

'I thought you would like the best kept Parisian secret. I should qualify my statement here. Usually, it's packed at lunchtime, with a line of people waiting outside the door, all because of George the owner making the place what it is. The menu and wine list are superb. Right now, the place is ours.' Then who should walk into the room but Steve and the directors Christian had met on the island, that is, Christian's island.

There was no guessing the people of importance in the room. Charles said, in an even tone: 'Let me introduce myself officially. I am CEO of The World Wide Corporation.'

Born into an inglorious life, the less Charles's parents did for him, the more he did for himself and the richer he became. If all the world is a stage, The World Wide Corporation takes the money. As the afternoon progressed Christian gets on remarkably well with Charles. What's not to get on with? Loves caviar, and is one of the wealthiest and most powerful men on the planet.

The waiters pour vintage champagne before discretely backing out of the room and closing the kitchen doors behind them.

'I would like to propose a toast to the success of our ongoing business. Christian, as our guest of honor, we have another gift for you.' Christian stands up, and Charles hands him an ornate gold key. 'It's the key to our future relationship. It fits one lock in the world.'

'Is there anything specific you have in mind for me to unlock?'

'We know you are a man who likes to climb to great heights. The higher, the better, if I am not mistaken. The key opens the door to a private apartment on the summit of the Eiffel Tower. Gustave Eiffel's 1889 secret pied-à-terre, the one he built for himself.'

Christian guesses the weight of the 24 carat solid gold key in his palm. 'Thank you for your generosity of which I accept!'

The room fills with applause, except for one-armed Steve, who bangs his left hand on the table. Charles taps on his glass with a gold knife, cutting through the applause. 'Please enjoy the lunch, and thank you all for coming.' Charles sits back. 'I understand you like roses. You'll be at home at Gustave's place. The interior is in its original state, right down to the art deco wallpaper of blue roses. Not interior décor that suits everyone's taste, but I hear chintz roses and chrysanthemums are making a comeback. It's an enchanting room filled with wooden and leather furniture, a grand piano, and there's even a small laboratory Gustave used for his experiments, which we hope you'll make good use of.'

George, the bistro owner, dressed in the typical checkered garb of a French chef and lover of excellent cuisine, appears with his starched white hat over his salt and pepper hair. He dusts the flour off his hands and greets his luncheon guests as if they are his oldest and closest friends.

'Welcome back, gentlemen. Please enjoy our charcuterie, in honor of your American guest, petite Yankee hot dogs for entree with grilled onions, sweet pickles, and a special mustard.'

Charles stirs the yellow mustard and drops a blob on Christian's hot dog. Christian mentions nothing about the trespass on his plate.

'I understand you're into spicy condiments.'

Christian finishes the hot dog in one mouthful. He wipes the hot mustard from his mouth with the starched napkin.

Then comes the gastronomic food pairing Bistro Chez George is famous for, a degustation menu of eight courses with wines to complement each dish. Christian samples rich portions of the chef's signature dishes, each mouthful served on a sterling silver spoon; escargot with garlic butter, freshly shucked oysters, scallops in white wine sauce, roasted pigeon, and pan-seared duck. Christian's welcome wedge of apple tart is served on a Limoges bone-china plate. One fragrant bite takes Christian back to Joe and him in Ma's kitchen; the homemade pies she baked, the apples not too sweet or too tart, a sprinkle of sugar and cinnamon. And she'd cut shapes out of pastry scraps, not for the economies of baking, but like her grandmother once taught her, pastry rosebuds and leaves baked on the top. Christian took another nostalgic mouthful. He hadn't heard from her lately. And Christian hadn't heard from Joe. He wonders how she is and how Joe was.

'Let's get on with food for thought,' Charles says to Christian.

He signals the headwaiter. Liqueurs appear in shot glasses, a glory of distilled spirits flavored with fruit, cream, herbs, spices, flowers, or nuts, a sweet finale to the meal. Charles becomes rather verbose after his second glass of absinthe, as if the green fairy in the glass has awoken and stirred up an alcoholic sugar high. Charles taps his glass with a silver filigree spoon.

'Our company is the elite of the corporate world and the axis of the financial world. When we make a move, both worlds follow; that's our cause and effect. We make the changes others don't even begin to dream up. What we don't create will never exist. It is up to us to extend reality as it is known. Christian, you are a genius, you've rediscovered what great alchemists have known about for centuries. I salute you!' Charles lowers his choir-deep baritone, and adds discreetly: 'I want to discuss a private matter with you.' Later, a limousine takes Charles, Steve, and Christian to a private meeting at the Gustave apartment, the French civil engineer's pied-à-terre, kept just as he left it, right down to the drawing board, and the couch where he used to take naps. It was also where Thomas Edison once dined and where the two of them drew up a list of economic elites. Only people of the utmost prestige were ever invited to step foot inside Gustave's apartment. The view of Paris from such a height is stellar—a brimful of stars glazing over the City of Eternal Light. The fact that Charles had chosen to give this apartment to Christian sent a pointed message. He expected great things from him. Some men are gods, and some men are slaves. The dominant rule in this world, that's what he and Charles were born to do, rule. Christian's name is an open invitation to access the highest levels of international life. Celebrities and politicians welcome him to their private apartments. Time is a luxury. He can take his time, make time and take time out, and he waits for no one. His name brought him respect, and now, awe.

Charles glances down at his wristwatch, a watch with two faces then looks at Christian.

'We've observed you for a while and admire you. You are a man with the right aptitude and attitude to be a world player. We like how you operate, and we want you to make the Life Serum and AntiXserum, exclusively for us. And in return, you get to have anything you desire in the world.'

Christian kept his composure.

'You don't have to give us your answer right now, but we sincerely hope you say yes.' The need to do favors is part of the cost of doing business, but the devil is forever in the exact details. Right at that point, Christian is sure Charles gives him a malevolent glance, the evil eye, a long hard look of disquiet, disgust, and admiration. In this situation, Christian senses that he, as a businessman, has some power, but it is nothing compared to the power Charles and his loyal group of billionaires has. Fortunes can rise or fall at Charles's says so. Not one of these men dare oppose Charles because Charles is a black box—no one knows what is inside.

Christian's face remains impassive and watchful, like a witness listening to the devil's advocate. 'And if I say no…what then?'

'Life is only as long as a life is,' Charles slides on the mâché mask of satire, 'and we'll part as friends in the end, either way.'

CHAPTER

68

IT HAPPENED BEFORE HIS flight from Paris to New York. Christian got the chance to use one of the twenty-seven functions on his recently purchased Victorinox Swiss Tool. He was sitting at the bar drinking a twenty-one gun salute whiskey on ice. The busy bartender had handed a bottle of Perrier water to a woman, but forgotten to open it. Christian leaned over, flicked off the cap, and gallantly poured the sparkling water into her glass. The woman turned around.

'Christian!'

'Madison!'

What were the odds of meeting up with a woman he hadn't seen for more than fifteen years, in the bar of a transit lounge of all places, in one of the busiest airports in the world? Synchronicity fascinated Christian.

'You look as lovely as ever.'

He had met her at his first job out of university. Theirs had been a romance as long as the summer lasted. It had been an unseasonal Indian summer on account of the killing frost of fall. The bright sunny days in autumn had made bees swarm on the overripe figs. Blue Jays became intoxicated on concord grapes that had shriveled to raisins on the vines during the heat. Their blossoming relationship crossed over into different romantic pathways, and on the walk along the beach, silence found its way between them, both of them worldly enough to know the feeling of an ending as they kissed goodbye. Then it was ended.

Now here he was, pouring her a glass of sparkling Perrier. This was the point where Madison's boyfriend walked over, introduced himself, and put an ownership arm around her shoulder.

The intercom announces the couples flight.

'Nice to see you again Christian, let's not leave it so long next time.'

She departed out of his life again. He felt her leaving as a visceral departure. A sense of loss for what could have been. His love life was a revolving door, and Madison was the one woman he still wanted to walk back in.

THE FLIGHT BACK from Paris on his private jet was uneventful. Back on the ground, customs had already been cleared, so the jet taxied uninterrupted into the private charter lane. As soon as the jet parks and the side hatch opens, Christian feels released. He strolls across the tarmac to the waiting limo. His New York personal assistant, Emma-Jean, is waiting inside. She sits opposite him and arranges her long elegant legs to the side. Anatomically speaking, he will always be a leg man, and his glance tells her so.

'Seems like you have your own paparazzi now.' Emma-Jean hands him the New York Times. The front-page photograph shows him leaving the Parisian restaurant with the caption: 'Jet-setter Cutter has dinner in Paris and breakfast in New York.'

He discloses his next move with a smile. 'Actually, that's not quite true. I haven't had breakfast yet.'

'Would you like a croissant or something a little tartier.' She pours him a tomato juice with a generous splash of lemon vodka, and a swizzle stick in the glass. The Bloody Mary matches her lipstick and red leather skirt, and his eyes slide down her legs. She is dressed to impress, down to her red leather boots. Conscious or unconscious, her choice of red awakened the physical, red the color of sex, passion, and lust. Red gave him an appetite. He can have anything he wants, but right now, it isn't tomato juice, but red hot and within arms reach. He sets the remote window shades to privacy mode.

CHRISTIAN ARRIVES BACK in his neighborhood. A kid rushes past on a scooter, a dog runs behind, the barber waves from the shop doorway, the garbage truck arms hug trashcans. It is Monday, and it's good to be home. Leaving Emma-Jean to straighten herself out, Christian steps out of the limo and lets the chauffeur carry his bags to his apartment.

Inside his front door, while surrounded by all that is familiar, his homecoming feels decidedly uncomfortable. He needs advice he can trust. He needs to talk to family.

'Joe, are you there?' The echo emphasizes emptiness.

Where is Joe when he needs him?

He puts the bag of croissants down on the kitchen bench, just as Joe comes in.

'Bring these from Paris?'

'No, the Brooklyn patisserie on 14th.'

'Are these croissants as good as the Parisian ones?'

'Better, Brooklyn has everything we need.'

'So, why go to Paris?'

'That's what I'd like to talk to you about.'

Christian spreads a double helping of strawberry conserve on the buttery croissant, doubling the calories, but not caring.

'In Paris, I met some compelling people.'

'What happened?'

'They gave me an ultimatum.'

'What kind of ultimatum?'

'Be rich or be dead.'

'A deadline. What the hell! You don't need any more money, or to be dead! I understand the rich part, but why threaten you? Are they the Mafia?'

'No, they run the Mafia.'

'What do they want from you?'

'They insist on my compliance. I can have anything I want. But only if I produce the longevity serum and AntiXserum, exclusively for them.'

'And if you don't, they'll kill you?'

'One way or another, they will destroy me. Alive or dead.'

'Remember when our father Henry died? The door swung open, and we saw our future. We felt like it was a new beginning. Death was an awakening.'

Two brothers, held for years inside the stronghold of parental rule and dominance, until Henry's timely death opened the door to Christian and Joe's unusual kind of genius. And they both knew it.

'Christian, you alone discovered how to create the eternal cycle of life and death. It's your doing, and it won't be our undoing.'

'You're right. Fuck anyone issuing ultimatums.' Christian knew what he had to do.

'So what has the artist been up to while I've been absent?'

'I made a breakthrough in the last few sessions. The portraits speak to me; the eyes look back at me, they see everything, and beyond. It's uncanny how alive the paintings have become.'

'It's working then, the new materials?'

'Yes, the paintings have come to life.'

'I told you they would.'

69

CHRISTIAN GETS IN HIS car and drives to the office. He swipes his pass, and the glass door slides open. A pigskin jacket draped over the back of his black Aeron chair is a garment foreign to Christian. Someone in his office is disturbing the habitat of bookworms, blowing the dust off the top pages and replacing the books, one by one, searching for something. However, this intruder is neither concerned about the hazards of book dust nor is he cleaning the book collection to save specific volumes from being eaten by mites, and he is not in the least concerned by Christian's arrival.

Whatever his bookish habits are, Christian notes the intruder's shoulder holster packs a French military issue PA-15. A delayed blowback semi-automatic pistol—too lethal to be ignored. An intruder with a military build and a keep the fuck away from me persona, at the height of six foot four, definitely not pussy enough to be a cat burglar, and too complacent to be a book thief, but nevertheless, a purloiner who perplexed him. Christian remains nonplussed, but then, only for a minute—he is intrigued by the man's blatant belligerent audacity to be in his office in the first place and how did he bypass the state-of-the-art security system.

And where, for that matter, are Viper and Killjoy? The dogs should be tearing him to pieces. But here the intruder is, running his fingers along the leather cover of a rare book—a thousand thoughts of Man, scribed on parchment using the ancient language of symbols.

'Find what you're looking for?' Christian poised his hand over the security button. The man glances up unperturbed. Indeed the man has merely been waiting for him. The man doesn't say a word. He puts on his jacket, walks past Christian, and out the door.

Only after Christian hears the lock click does he speed dial Charles Council, who happens to be sitting by the pool in the Bahamas, a whiskey on the rocks in one hand and his other hand busy undoing the flowery bikini top of the woman sitting cross-legged in a lotus position in front of him. His bodyguard held the phone out to Charles, but with his hands already full, something had to give, the woman or the whiskey, his dilemma for the day. 'Tell him I'll call him back later.'

Christian hangs up the phone, and when he glances out into the topiary garden, he sees his two guard dogs lying near the yellow trumpet flowers of Gelsemium Elegans. He whistles through the glass to catch their attention, but they are dead asleep, flecks of bloodied foam around the edges of their jowls.

Both dogs are dead.

70

CHRISTIAN LEAVES HIS OFFICE and steps blindly into a yellow blast of sun, in contrast to sunshine's playful light in his garden where Viper and Killjoy lay dead on the lilyturf. He fumbles for his Armani sunglasses, only to find them useless; one arm had broken off inside his lapel pocket. It was turning into a day of accidentals. And he had never seen a stainless steel vending cart parked on the sidewalk in front of the Biozen building before, with its yellow carnival umbrella and cooking tools dangling. The heated hot dogs rollers wafting grilled smoked meat and sautéed onions, made Christian feel somewhat neurodivergent.

The Vietnamese vendor is after a sale. 'Hi Charlie, what can I do you for?'

'That's not my name.'

'All foreigners I call Charlie, easy for me to say. What you like?'

'I'd like to know what you and your cart are doing outside my office building? Do you have a hawker's permit?'

'Christian Cutter?' He jumps at the mention of his name.

Christian turns to face Michael, the last person he expected to see standing there.

'Sorry, I didn't mean to startle you. You should try one, the best in New York.'

'No thanks, I'm vegetarian.'

Michael's demeanor seems amicable, but Christian is on guard. The menacing mute man in his office rifling through his books, the death of his dogs, the sudden appearance of a hot dog vendor's cart, and Agent Steel outside his office eating hot dogs, adds up to being too coincidental.

'These hot dogs are iconic; only on the last bite does the fiery sauce kick in because the Tiger Carolina Reaper chili is grafted with the red habanero and the Pakistani Naga, chilies married for heat. Way hotter than a Trinidad Maruga Scorpion chili. The Reaper should come with a warning label!'

Michael notices how Christian glances at the hot dog cart more than once, how his breathing seemed a little shallow. His body language is completely different from previous encounters, more tentative than before, with an edge of defensiveness. I'll see what happens when I push him further and really unsettle him.

'I was coming to see you with some good news. Spencer, your partner, is out of his coma and making remarkable progress due to an eminent French specialist in toxicology, Dr. Belleau. Her treatment seems to have made a real difference in Spencer's recovery.'

The carotid pulse makes its appearance on Christian's neck.

'Tests conducted on Spencer identified the poison as a chemical mutation of Gelsemium Elegans, known as heartbreak grass. A highly toxic herb.'

The plant is of China and Asia genus, native to subtropical and tropical America, Honduras, Guatemala, and Mexico.

'Dr. Belleau is an expert who works with botanical poisoning cases. You may recall the Russian whistle-blower who fell down dead, while out jogging in Surrey, England, at the age of forty-four. And it was suspected the whistle-blower ingested the Gelsemium poison on a trip to Paris. His symptoms were the loss of muscle power and spinal cord paralysis. It was front-page news.'

'Can't say I read that article.'

Michael looks him in the eye, and continues his conversational trajectory, observing subtle physical changes in Christian. 'Then there was the case of the Chinese tycoon, Yang Lee Vong this month. Dr. Belleau told me that Vong was poisoned by a chemical and botanical serum, and the yellow flowers of Gelsemium had been added, for good measure, to a slow boiled cat stew. She also said, in lethal doses, the serum causes slow asphyxia followed by death.'

Trying to appear unconcerned about destabilizing rhetoric, and more concerned about time-wasters, Christian flips his wrist, to look at his diamond-studded watch.

'That's all very interesting for a cop, I guess.'

'Agent!'

'Yes, well, you must excuse me Agent Steel. I have an urgent engagement on the other side of town.' Christian is well aware that anything he inadvertently reveals to Agent Steel could be used against him. Even a sloppy smile can incriminate.

'One more thing, your name came up in a routine search of the priority access files to The Medici Library.'

How is that possible? Christian thought. Madison dumped the ledgers and erased the computer files. Unless she double-crossed him? 'So?'

'On your visits, did you see anything or anyone you didn't think

belonged there?'
   'No, sorry, I can't help you.'
   Michael makes a mental note of anomalies.
   Christian hails a cab. A man watches from angled shadows.

71

Opportunity turns to synchronicity in Christian's mind. Friday was one of those days. It began at lunchtime when he walked into Giraldo's, as he likes to do on rainy afternoons. Giraldo's Italian restaurant not only has the red-checkered tablecloths but a checkered past. There was a mortal line on the back wall where machine guns created a deathly arch in the painted plaster with peppered sprays of bullets until bodies on the bloody floor settled the depute between Mafia families.

Christian sits at his favorite table with Joe, mobile phone switched off, time to think, escape from a world where the negatives were more plentiful than the positives. He was being overtaken by a bad unnerving feeling, and he couldn't make it right. A disturbing time for Christian.

His dreams were unfathomable too. Christian shared his three recurring water dreams with Joe. 'In the first water dream I see waves coming; they don't bother me because I believe nothing can touch me. As I watch them in front of me, they turn monstrous and gain terrific momentum, bearing down. I change my mind, but it's too late; they hold me under. In the second water dream, I'm swimming in murky water, and I find myself in a house floating in a vast ocean. The house is slowly filling up with water to the window frames, then to the top of the door. Perilous to stop, the house starts to sink with you inside it. And in the third water dream, a massive Tsunami wave bears down and washes everything away. The whole coastline vanishes. These dreams happen every night. One dream follows another. As soon as I close my eyes, water overcomes me.'

Joe knew some things about astrology. 'You should pay closer attention to the stars. If the French Emperor Napoleon consulted with the stars and his astrologers before going into battle, then this is what you must do.'

It seemed that Joe didn't know.

Christian did glance over the morning horoscopes, but his star sign was clueless. So he had paid eighty dollars to a woman who inked his right palm and read nothing; a hundred dollars to a woman who gazed into a crystal ball; and fifty dollars to a woman who poured him a cup of black tea, then flatly refused to tell him what she saw in tea leaf dregs; then he had gone to the celebrity tarot reader on Long Island, who asked him to shuffle, and draw cards from the pack. Out of fifty possible cards, he drew the twins, the three cups, the card with two swords, and the last card—the hanged man—a man hanging from a tree with bolts of lightning falling from a dark sky. When he took a closer look at the card, the man looked exactly like Joe.

JOE LEFT BEFORE the pizza arrived at the table. Then who should sit down opposite him but Madison. Christian would never have guessed he would bump into her twice in two weeks. First in the departure lounge at Paris airport where she was flying to Florence with her Italian boyfriend. Now, here she was, only this time she was alone. Christian felt the same attraction, this powerful pull towards her, but stronger than he had felt before.

'Well, if it isn't you again!'

As soon as she spoke, Christian knew his heart had kept a corner for her.

'A small memento for you.' Christian unclips his Swiss Army knife from his belt and hands it to her.

She takes the knife and flips open the folded blades and gadgets one by one: a can opener, corkscrew, toothpick, bottle opener, short-bladed cheese knife, and one for cutting up apple or peach.

'Don't you know it's bad luck to give a knife as a gift? A knife signifies a broken relationship.'

'Well, if you have a dollar, you can buy the knife from me. That way it's a purchase, and not a gift.' She closes the stainless blade before handing the knife back, an act of self-closure.

'I've read a lot about you lately, Christian.'

'All good, I hope, Madison.'

'My Father was treated for burns at The Illuminati Hospital. He made an amazing recovery. Like a new man, he even appears to be ten years younger.'

'That doesn't surprise me. Good-looking genes seem to run in your family. You look stunning as always, Madison.'

'And you are even more handsome than I remember. I had such a big crush on you CC.'

'I often wondered what happened to us. We just kind of fizzled out, didn't we?'

'We were too young to know how good we had it.'

'Best summer of my life.'

'Sure was.'

'Tell me, why did you choose this place for lunch.'

'A whim!'

'I think synchronistic.'

'Christian, don't let me stop you eating your pizza.'

He admired her gorgeous curves in the red sheath dress. 'I've found an appetite for something else. As rich as tiramisu, more delicious than Sicilian cassata, and less calorific than gelato.'

'You haven't changed much, if at all.'

'Neither have you. I've got a gourmet kitchen at home. I'd love to show you around. What do you say?'

'Depends what you're cooking up!'

Christian pays the bill and leaves with Madison. Outside the restaurant, he clicks the car-remote, opens the passenger door for Madison, like a gentleman, and just as she is about to get in, their arms lock around each other. Neither one is letting the other go this time.

The public parking meter Christian had previously fed a handful of loose change to, buzzes a high-pitched electronic noise, ending their together moment.

AT DUSK, OUTSIDE CHRISTIAN'S apartment, a man watches through high-resolution binoculars from a vantage position on the rooftop opposite; a red car is parked outside, a woman sits in the driver's seat, a high top laundry van is parked next to the grocery store monitoring Christian's comings and goings. Inside the van, two men watch a closed-circuit surveillance monitor as Christian arrives with a woman. A red light flickers behind the silvered curtains in the window of the apartment opposite—someone lighting up a cigar? If you had no idea you were under surveillance, then a cigar was a cigar, a car was a car, and the van was just another van parked on the street.

Every clandestine act inhabits the domain of shadows. So much goes on behind one's back. While Christian was on an overseas trip, his apartment mailbox was tampered with, the envelopes steamed open, each letter unfolded, read, scanned, refolded, placed back in its respective envelope and carefully resealed, then reposted. The contents of his trashcan had been rifled through with latex-gloved hands. Two men in a fake telecommunications van had climbed a ladder on a telephone pole to tap incoming and outgoing phone wires. A series of surveillance cameras and listening devices were installed throughout his apartment.

If Christian or Madison had bothered to feel under the bed before kissing like frenzied mating animals, and tearing clothes off each other, they would have found the bug, no more significant than a half sucked pink peppermint heart candy. But they had other things on their mind. As they make love, Madison varies her sexy moves to what she knows he loves, Brazilian moves with a little bit of Ecuadorian. Why let her slip away from his life? They should be together forever, he thinks, as he kisses her nape.

Her scent makes him realize he wants this woman to be there in his bed in the mornings, to drink coffee together, read the Sunday papers together, and maybe have kids together, and have a normal life together. Why can't he be like Joe and have a love relationship instead of this on again, off again, love life? Why did Madison come back into his life? To show him what intimacy is, what love is? She planned this reunion. She wants him as much as he wants her. Christian loves the feeling of Madison, and while sexy centerfold stuff was happening on that rainy afternoon, all their intimacy was recorded in close up.

It felt good to wake up and see this beautiful woman, her dark hair cascading over the linen pillowslip. As Christian studies her face, she opens her eyes, remarkably amber, like cheetah eyes.

'Good morning handsome, find what you are looking for?'

'And more! You know it!' She wraps a thick white bath towel around her tanned body. 'First, I'm going to take a warm shower. Then I'm taking you for breakfast at my place. My treat.'

Christian brews coffee while Madison puts on her make-up. She checks her face in the mirror. She doesn't need much to enhance her features, just a light brush of dark mascara, a lick of honey brown lipstick, and an expensive French perfume on specific pulse points.

'That took you no time at all.' He liked a confident woman who didn't spend hours making herself up like a model on assignment. He'd had one or two girlfriends who became no more than one-night-stands when they took too long to get the tousled look. All they did was keep him waiting. Sure they looked a million dollars, but in the time it took to perfect an image, they lost a billionaire in the process. Christian was the kind of guy that didn't wait for anything.

Madison dresses for a casual weekend look: designer blue jeans, pale lemon linen shirt, and tangerine ankle boots in Portuguese leather. She slung her matching leather bag over her shoulder.

'Come on then, don't keep a woman waiting.'

He picks up his cobra skin wallet and flips the billfold open. First, he counts the hundred dollar bills. Eight hundred. Then he counts the fifty dollar notes. There were five. No money is missing, but his platinum, gold cards, travel cards, and his driver's license have been shuffled like a deck of cards and put back.

Madison stands watching him.

'Christian, if I were a hooker, you could check your money after sex … but hey! Is there anything wrong?'

Intuition is a valuable sixth sense we either act on or ignore at our peril. Christian left his apartment that morning with Madison lightly holding the crook of his arm like a hot new flame. They lost each other once, now they were two people walking along, intimacy rekindled, the fire between them reignited. One person belonged to the other. Christian had the feeling he'd been waiting all his life for Madison to step back into it. A rush of orgasmic sex and whatever those endorphins set off, he felt like a different man. Even the local pigeons had turned into white doves, in an act of magnificence, the smart drugs also helped.

They go inside Madison's apartment.

'We're practically neighbors.'

'Amazing the coincidence. I can see your place from here.'

'You have a particularly large telescope here … for?'

'Stargazing.'

'For stargazing?'

'And looking at the moon.'

'And here's me thinking, people who have a telescope in the city must be voyeurs and up to no good.'

'Christian, you're more suspicious than you used to be.'

'I disagree. I'm just a lot more cautious these days.'

Christian checks out Madison's apartment.

'I like your style. You're into art deco. Nice glass collection. How strange to have a material born of earth and fire decorating your living room.'

He picks up a vase, and instead of just looking through it, saw a frozen rind of ice on a lake.

'Well, it isn't mine.'

'What is it then?'

'It's inventory.'

'All this is inventory?'

'Yes. I am an acquisitions assessor for antique stores and auction houses.'

'Interesting.'

'People call me up to check out estates. Here and Europe as well.'

'So you're a freelance antiquarian?'

'I never thought of myself in that way, but yes.'

'So you travel a lot with your job?'

'Mostly France.'

'Paris?'

'Yes, in fact, I'm going again this month.'

'I have an apartment in Paris. Well, it's an old one, but new to me, it just came into my possession.'

'You are lucky then. I have things come into my possession, like this Lalique crystal vase and that Tiffany Blue Dragonfly lamp, but I don't own them.'

'Lucky maybe. But there's no guarantee that I can keep hold of anything that comes my way,' pulling her into him.

'How about me Christian, am I a keeper?'

Madison's mobile interrupts his reply.

'Hello? ... yes ... of course. I'll see you later, darling.'

'Who was that? I am guessing your Mom?'

'No, the man who you met at the airport.'

'Your boyfriend.'

'Was my boyfriend.'

'You broke up?'

'He's my fiancée now. Soon to be my husband. In three months we'll be honeymooning in Paris.'

'You didn't think to tell me?'

'You didn't ask.'

'And our night together didn't change your mind?'

'Christian, it entered my mind.'

'And?'

'But no.'

'No?'

'No, nothing will change my mind, once I commit.'

'So last night was just your final fling?'

'I guess so. Like a guy has a stag night.'

'You don't strike me as a user, Madison.'

'Christian, you've missed the point. You and I could have been an item, but you've never been the proposing type. Besides, even if you were, our timing's off. I've got someone, wedding invitations printed, guest lists, the wedding is on, arrangements are happening as we speak.'

'So why are you staying in New York?'

'Shopping for a bridal gown in the garment district. Then I'm meeting Alberto in Verona for the wedding.'

'Verona, City of Lovers.' Then under his breath he said: 'Or, star crossed lovers.'

'I would love you to be our guest. A June wedding.'

'Love to.'

Christian goes over to the telescope. 'May I?'

'Sure.'

He focuses on Cutters Delicatessen, sees the queue for the famous freshly baked bagels going out the door and around the corner. Then Cutters Drugstore fills his vision, Mr. Kravit, shooing away a dog about to pee on the fire hydrant. Stems Flowers comes into view, a sad man walks out with a funeral wreath. At Cutters Butcher, two deliverymen hoist flanks of kosher beef, each side of frozen carcass wrapped in a veil of white muslin with patches of blood seeping, here and there. He watches the men disappear into the store, the destiny of animals, to be butchered into eye fillets, topside, chuck steak, mince, and organ meats, kidneys, and liver. All the bible tripe and honeycomb tripe laid out with other offal displayed in the chiller cabinet for a passersby to see, garnished with fresh parsley, and plastic carrots, to make bits and pieces of dead animals as attractive as can be.

Madison ties the strings of her apron. Busy in the kitchen, she doesn't hear Christian talking on his mobile above the whir of the food mixer. The more distracted she is, the easier it will be to do what he needs to do. She scrapes black char off the sourdough toast, and pours the Béarnaise sauce over the soft poached eggs on their bed of chopped spinach.

'Does your future husband know he is getting such a great chef, as well as a sexy woman in the package?'

'You're not jealous, are you?'

'On the contrary.'

After the wedding was announced in newspapers, Madison receives an unexpected invitation to appear on the TV show, *Wedding Dress Love*, where the star of the show, Miss Madeline Love, will offer the bride to be a selection of designer wedding gowns to choose from. All Madison has to do is say yes to the wedding dress she loves the best.

The following Tuesday, Madison arrives at a converted warehouse in the Bronx. She was expecting a Bridal Atelier store, but this must be the television studio where they do the filming. She has a feeling, yes, that's what this is. A handsome man dressed in a dark suit holds the front door open for her. She steps inside and into another world.

Above her, antique ormolu chandeliers hang from a painted fresco ceiling. Gardenia scented candles are alight on a walnut and faux ebony table with gilded winged cherubs carved on the hips of the legs, and around the table a set of French Louis XIV Bergere armchairs, with carved wooden roses in gold leaf finish.

The whole place feels glamorous, but there is no one in sight. Not one camera, no film crew, and the doorman is nowhere to be seen. Maybe I've got the wrong night. She turns to leave. But there, on the antique French armoire, she spies an off-white garment bag with her name on it. She unzips the bag.

Inside is a beautiful cream silk sheath dress with a handwritten note tied to the silk straps:

Here is the first wedding gown.
But before you try this one on,
Look inside the white box
On the Rococo table.

Sifting through petals of white tissue paper, she uncovers designer bridal lingerie: silk knickers, French figure-hugging lace-up Basque, silk bridal stockings, and lacy suspenders, all in a soft palette of cream.

She changes into the lingerie and wedding dress in the opulent dressing room of grand proportions, with not one but two brocade chaise lounges. Standing in front of the mirrors, it's all about her in the cream dress. Madison views herself from every angle, twirling into a bridal narcissist.

Everything is right. Right size, right color, right neckline, right down to sleeves, and the train of the ethereal veil. Nothing needs shortening, lengthening, or altering. No puckering, bunching or bulging. The embroidery, exquisitely hand-sewn. She uses the hand mirror to see how the tiny covered buttons sit like candy drops at the back. Perfect.

'Yes to the wedding dress!' She says it louder, 'Yes to the wedding dress!' She expects the production team to appear. Instead, the floor-to-ceiling mirror in front of her opens like a door, and a man appears in front of her, like a well-dressed magician. He sits down on the couch. Looking startled, Madison exclaims, 'What are you doing here?'

'Speak up if you see anything you don't like—or forever hold your peace. This is your time to give in to bridezilla impulses, be as demanding as you like.'

'So all of this is your doing! Thank you! Everything is so special.'

A spider had found its way onto the silk gown as if to unravel the web. However, a spider on a wedding gown is a good omen. So, Christian crushes it deftly between his finger and thumb.

'How does it feel to sit down in the dress?'

'The bodice stays in one place while the skirt kisses the floor. What could be more perfect?'

'Champagne!' He pours champagne into two flutes, then from a red Cartier box, removes a pair of solitaire diamond earrings, and drops them into her glass.

'You only get married once, so here's to your special day, take care not to drink the diamonds.'

Before the next glass was poured, the diamonds in the lobes of her ears sparkled, and stars appeared in front of her eyes—after the final sip, tiny pinpricks of pink were popping like questions.

Why are the cherubs on the ceiling lifting my veil and taking my diamond earrings?

Christian props her up in front of the full-length mirror, pulls back her wedding veil, and kisses her. The flute slips from her limp fingers, and lead crystal smashes against marble.

'Interesting, you should drop your glass as if by bridal tradition. Every little thing you do means something although, you may not be so aware, the number of pieces the bride's glass breaks into will symbolize how many years she will stay married, and how many children she will have, that is, if the bride lives.'

Madison, unable to scream, as one by one, each silk button, from wrist to elbow, is cut from her gown, bouncing along the marble floor, the kinetics of buttons, like summer peas. Then comes the silent scream, born before death, primordial as blood bubbling through eons of bloodlines. The long arched blade of the filleting knife takes to her, slicing down the length of her arms, her veins, her thighs. And she screams on unheard, until the scarlet pooling of blood. Life is a messy business especially in silk.

She is tall, even so—the couture wedding dress bag is a perfect fit.

CHRISTIAN ARRIVED AT MADISON'S apartment to find the front door wide open and the apartment empty of chattels. No telescope, no furniture, no drapes, no crystal, nothing. The oriental rugs were gone; even the basil plant and rosemary bush, along with the lemon tree on the balcony, had vanished. The entire apartment had been forensically cleaned—traces of her had vanished. The removal was an erasure of all she owned, leaving nothing but a vacant hollow space where footsteps have permission to echo.

'May I help you, Christian?' His nerves jump at the sound of his name. It was Mrs. Kitts, dressed in black, as she had done for years since her husband, the fireman, had died, not in a fire, but lying next to her asleep. Local neighbors dubbed her the black widow on account of his mysterious death, but she didn't mind.

Standing here in an empty room with a clairvoyant is particularly creepy. The old woman knows things no one should.

Christian thought, What would Joe do right now? First, he would diffuse the situation with one of his jokes, and then he'd say, relax, don't take it all so seriously. Imagine you're standing here talking to your friend, only you're not; it's old Mrs. Kitts, a friend of Ma's. Then he would execute one of his diversions; the tactic of the three-legged stool practiced as kids, when you are under pressure, for example, let's say Henry is about to pounce, go for the kill, and when you thrust something at the beast—like a lie—the lion forgets to pounce.

'I've come to pick up my sweater. I left it here.'

But there is no sweater, and lioness Kitts is watching him, looking for the monster within, but all she can see is him.

'If you're looking for Madison, she's gone. Here today and gone tomorrow. Just like that. The removalists came on Wednesday, spent the day packing and loading up her stuff. I asked what they were doing, but all the man said was this: packing is about volume rather than weight. Then two cleaners in white paper suits came and left the place spotless.'

'Did she leave a note?'

'This was left in her mailbox with your name on it.'

Mrs. Kitts hands Christian a beige envelope.

He holds it up to the light.

'Expensive handmade stationary right down to the paper-makers watermark, must be the invitation to her wedding in Italy.'

Mrs. Kitts closes her eyes, and nods, as if listening to truth, a voice whispering in her ear. Christian leaves Mrs. Kitts and her craziness in the hallway, as the elevator doors open. A man in a blue suit stands aside. The suit is an expensive fabric, well-tailored, Christian thinks—clothes make a man, but this man is playing the part of an unfriendly person. Not only does Christian have to see him in close proximity, but there is a smell about him, some odd taint—opium. Sharing an enclosed space with the stranger gives tension. The hazards of an elevator; schmaltzy piped music, tinkling tunes on a loop. *The Girl From Ipanema*—coming from every direction. And the stranger.

The elevator stops on the second floor. The doors open, and another man wearing an identical dark silk suit enters. The men share an agitated conversation, one speaking Mandarin and the other speaking in Cantonese, but the punch Christian feels is international, a hard blow, it snaps two ribs, he doubles over. The Cantonese man answers his mobile, and holds up his hand to stop Christian groaning.

'Mr. Cutter, we have been sent to give you a message.' They shove Christian down and prop him against the cold stainless steel walls of the elevator.

'Look around you, Mr. Cutter, the walls are too drab, don't you think? Needs to be more like Christmas? Splashes of red?' The Cantonese man grunts as he punches Christian, splitting his cheek open. Not finished, he pulls out a silk handkerchief, and proceeds to dab Christian's bleeding cheek in a calculated manner. With Christian's blood there on wet silk, the assailant presses out a flourish of red chrysanthemum flowers, blooming blood-flowers painted on the wall, then admires his Oriental signature of blood. As if that wasn't enough for the day, the Mandarin speaking man reaches down and grabs Christian by the balls.

'You, you handsome man.'

'And you are fucking weird.' Christian shoves the delinquent hands away. But the kicks kept coming; precision kicks to kidneys, spleen, and already broken ribs. The elevator doors opened on the ground floor, the two men step over Christian, taking care not to slip on his blood as it pooled slippery on the floor. They threw his wallet at him. Daylight robbery? It's the wretchedness of being wealthy; you're a target, more to come after, more to steal.

'Rob me, you fucking thugs, tomorrow I'll still be rich, and you'll still be losers.' He checks his wallet. It is flush with five hundred dollar notes, his platinum and gold cards still there. Nothing had been stolen. A new black credit card with unlimited credit, had been added to his wallet. A limited edition issued by invitation only. Christian's name embossed in gold.

Christian stumbles outside as pain's delay kicks in. He falls onto the sidewalk, cold winter air biting his face. Pain is not a thought, it's an impossible feeling. Extreme pain makes you stare at nothing in particular; the hem of a cashmere camel coat, a small black dog on a pink leash, two white wheels of a kids bicycle, a yellow basketball hitting the sidewalk, a sheet of newspaper flapping against the curb, and a face on a billboard. The sea of people streaming past him diverted either side of his body, not touching him. He was an uninhabited island in an ocean of urban inhumanity. He's a sudden bloody tramp, a bum, a nobody. There's only one thing to do when you're down, pick yourself up. He stands up and leans against the vertical slabs of the building.

Christian stares over the busy road to get his bearings, and takes comfort in the sight of a tall building, one he owns. The building he bought for a steal, renovated the guts out of, but kept plaster deco cornices, grand colonnades, and iron balconies, to remember a bygone era.

He had given the new tenants naming rights, their logo in neon over the door, yet he had never sanctioned the billboard on the roof, nor had he authorized the giant photograph of himself on the billboard, his face printed larger than life, an advertisement for a funeral parlor. It read; *Life's a big party. So when it's parting time, call the funeral specialists. For the best final send-off ever.*

Christian dials the number from his mobile. The phone rings and clicks onto a recorded message. 'Leave your name and number, and we'll get back to you sooner than later.'

The voice belonged to Madison.

One way, or another, Christian gets back to his apartment, peels off his blood-clotted clothes, and stumbles into a steaming hot shower. The disinfectant soap lather stings, and the white face cloth turns bright red. He gingerly applies pressure to the cut on his cheek. Christian touches the broken xylophone of his ribs with the tips of his fingers. He had never broken a bone in his life, but his ribs were broken for him by professionals. Christian dries himself off. He needs stitches unless he wants scars. The last thing Christian wants is scars. In the dark hours, he puts on his darkest pair of sunglasses.

At The Illuminati Hospital emergency department, he pushes past patients at reception and speaks to the nurse at the desk.

'I need to see a doctor right now.'

'We have two triage emergencies and ten ambulant patients, and a line of twenty people before you. So wait your turn, and fill out this form.'

'Do I look like the form filling kind?'

The nurse checks his ID.

'Sorry, Mr. Cutter, come this way please. A doctor will see you immediately.'

A tetanus booster, IV pain relief of Morphine extraction, an x-ray and MRI scan of his chest, three rolls of white strapping tape for his ribs, cuts cleaned, ten sutures, and his cheek covered with sterile gauze. Christian was patched up, given a script of painkillers and was good to go. Good to go home to his apartment and order up a bodyguard.

75

BACK AT HIS APARTMENT, Christian slits open the envelope Mrs. Kitts gave him at Madison's apartment. Inside was a DVD. The cover is blank, no credits, nothing but a plain ordinary sleeve. It is the blankness of the unknown that makes Christian curious. He adjusts the volume on the Dolby sound acoustic system and sits down in front of the television screen.

An hour later, after watching the process in detail, he ejects the disk and takes to it with a cleaver from the wood block on the kitchen island. He lacerates the DVD, to obliterate its electronic face. He takes a pair of poultry scissors and cuts through brittle evidence, around and around, until there is one unbroken strip, as thin as the silver tinsel you hang on the bough of a Christmas tree. But this wasn't the Christmas season. This was no gift. He had destroyed the evidence, but surely this wasn't the only copy. There will be more to eliminate if he can get to the source.

'Joe, I could do with your help. Are you there?'

He listens for a sound. He needs Joe right now. Joe always has a different angle, a way of putting what Christian says through a kind of Joe filter. Two minds are better than one. Having Joe around is like having a confident, a soothsayer, a clairvoyant who can see things he can't, and most of all, he trusts Joe to keep his secrets and never lie to him.

'The Christmas decoration is a bit of overkill? Let me guess. The bulls-eye target on your back got larger?'

'You know Joe—I have what people want. I have more than most, more to come after, more to plunder. Am I climbing upwards or falling backward. Am I disposable? People are following me—do I imagine it? No, I see people moving in and out of the shadows. They conceal themselves in corners of the city, but I know they are there.'

Clandestine actions are insidious.

'They want to take me down.'

'And the problem is?'

Christian assumes the smile of control.

'Thanks, Joe.'

It is Joe who picks up the phone and dials Ma. If there was a way out of a situation, Ma has read about it.

'Hi Ma, it's Joe.'

Hearing Joe's voice unnerves Grace. Whenever Joe rings, it means one thing, Christian is in trouble.

'Joe? Can I talk to Christian?'

'No, Ma, I'm afraid that's not possible.'

'Why not, Joe?' Grace asks carefully.

'Ma, if only you knew.'

'If only I did.'

There are cracks in her sentences; cigarettes, coal fires, traffic fumes, and winters have weakened her voice, but not her mind.

'Put him on the phone, Joe.' Her voice tempered with an edge of anger. 'Sorry Ma, I can't. I shouldn't have called you. I'll explain later.' And with that, he hangs up. Grace is not a woman to worry, usually, but the less she hears from Christian, and the more she hears from Joe, the more concerned she becomes. Things were unraveling for Christian. She knew it as she hung up the phone, and heard the bell for dinner.

76

THE BEST THING ABOUT being rich is freedom, the freedom to do what you want. Stick a thumbtack on the world map and go, take a cruise, a flight, go places where the sun shines all day, and it never rains, where the sky is tropical blue, kick off your shoes and go barefoot, endless ocean waves breaking on the shore, and a hammock strung between coconut palms makes the world right again.

Today the sky is cloudless, the perfect day to fly. Christian walks around the side of the corrugated metal hangar. The aircraft tug carefully maneuvers Christian's Hawker jet out of the hangar; first, the aerodynamic nose of the plane emerges, followed by its twin-turbines, the latest aerospace technology from Rolls-Royce.

The World Wide Corporation had generously showed their appreciation. Christian had supplied the Biozen Life Serum to fulfill their orders, but that was as far as he was prepared to go. Despite recent extravagant gifts by Charles, Christian refused to reveal the formula, and he categorically refused to manufacture the AntiXserum for them. Lately, they had stopped making demands. Had The World Wide Corporation finally accepted that Christian was in complete control of his formulas? Were they getting off his case as a respectful course of action? The perverse violence and intimidation tactics that certain members had employed, ceased. Christian assumes what he wants to assume.

Two ground crew rotate the plane 180 degrees to face the wind. Christian walks alongside the jet, shading his eyes from the morning sun with one hand, as he takes out his Ray-Ban Aviator glasses with the other. The aviation manager comes out of his office and hurries across the tarmac.

'Morning Sir. Here's your updated flight schedule.'

Steps unfold like a metal concertina from the main cabin, and Christian steps up and into luxury with Joe. Christian walks through into the cockpit. He scans the instrument panel. 'Doesn't get much better than this, Joe.' He sinks down into the pilot seat, switches the jet engines on, and listens to the orchestrated whine of turbines rising musicality, in perfect pitch for takeoff.

'Hawker Alpha Whiskey to Air Traffic Control, ready for takeoff.'

'Cleared for takeoff runway zero-one, Hawker Alpha Whiskey.'

Joe looks out of the cockpit window to where green kudzu grass edged gray tarmac down to where the olive green mangroves entered the bay. If it were late summer, and grass had yellowed, it would contrast more with the green mangroves, but summer had come and gone.

Soon they were airborne, leveling out at 20,000 feet.

'You got a list going? What kind of a list?'

'A bucket list, one hundred things to do before you die.'

'The only bucket, or make that buckets in my life, are buckets that hold ice. Silver Champagne buckets. Seriously, we don't need a bucket list, unlike the poor sods that have no idea when their time's up. Not us. We live how we like, and we live as long as we want. The only time we have is the time of our lives!'

The sky turns into its version of heaven, empty blue, whispers of cotton wool clouds float on by, white and quiet, the world and its complications gone. But out of the blue, a man's voice interrupts the reverie.

'Hawker Alpha Whiskey, seems like you are enjoying your new jet.'

Blatant intrusions mentally blank out voice recognition.

Disconcerted, Christian responds: 'This is Hawker Alpha Whiskey. Identify yourself, caller!'

'Hawker Alpha Whiskey. I thought you would recognize my voice?'

On hearing the man speak again, it is clear Julian is speaking.

'My mistake Julian. I wasn't expecting to hear from you. Are you currently on the island? Over.'

'I wish. Have you considered the proposition we discussed in Paris? Charles awaits your answer, and I must tell you, he is not the most patient man. A fact you should be aware of Christian.'

Christian makes no response.

'I hear your silence. But don't worry. This airway has security clearance.'

'As I told Charles, I can't possibly release the formulae to be used outside my control. What part of no doesn't he get?'

'So be it. Enjoy your dive. I'll pass on your response to Charles.'

'How does Julian know we intend to go scuba diving today, and what's up with the Shakespearian *so be it*. But then, I pegged him as having an act.'

'Maybe Julian is a thespian? And it's no act.'

'You did right by us Christian. We own what we create. No one has the right to take that away. Here we are, the boys from a poor neighborhood who have everything we dreamed of, like Leonardo da Vinci or an Einstein or a Mozart, our chance to be remembered forever. It's our fate to be famous. To give our secrets away would be to give away our immortality, like Julian will, the one named after a dead uncle when he should have been named after a dead fish, dying unrecognized, not immortalized in the human race. You'd end up being another nothing, like the rest of the mortals—unremembered.'

Julian listens on.

Christian banks the plane to the left, and the noise of the turbines multiply. Suddenly out of nowhere, a jet fighter appears beside them, like a magician of the stratosphere—illusions of soft clouds reflected in the pilot's mirrored visor. The fighter jet dangerously close.

'Hawker Alpha Whiskey this is fighter pilot 47.'

The pilot's uniform has no visible military insignia, no brass stars or gold eagles, just black, with a matte black helmet and dark visor.

'You must return to your base immediately. You no longer have landing clearance on the island. Repeat, return immediately.'

'This is Hawker Alpha Whiskey. You have no jurisdiction here. This is international airspace, and the island is mine. I'm within my international rights!'

'This is your final warning Hawker Alpha Whiskey. Return immediately.'

The fighter jet glinted like a double-edged blade as it maneuvered into a firing position. Christian angles his jet towards his island, a lush green circle in a ring of white sand where coral reefs fan out in the transparency of blue sea. A phosphorous white light streaked past his cockpit. A Sidewinder missile, a million dollar warning, is a show of infinite power.

'This is Hawker Alpha Whiskey. Mayday! Mayday! I am under attack from an unknown fighter jet. Hawker Alpha Whiskey does anyone read me? Over.'

'Yes, this is the island. I read you Hawker Alpha Whiskey. Loud and clear.'

'I am coming in for a landing. Over.'

'This is Island to Hawker Alpha Whiskey. Permission denied. You're on your own.'

The fighter's heat-seeking lasers are now locked into position, set to activate the destruction of the Hawker, obliterating Christian in midair.

'OK! OK! I get it, Julian! Charles won't take no for an answer, will he?'

'So I take it as a yes?'

'Yes.'

'Then, so be it. Consider yourself free. Free to land, that is. Have a nice weekend. I'll see you in Paris in a fortnight.'

A sonic boom followed, as the fighter jet broke through the sound barrier and disappeared. If Julian and Charles thought Christian was about to give up everything he had worked for, and believed in, they didn't know Christian or Joe.

Christian lands on his island, or what he thinks is still his island.

77

AT THE POOL BAR, the island manager, Lance, is drinking a cold beer in the shade. 'Cocktails are ready by the pool.'

'You're fired as of right now! When I want to land, I land.'

Lance flashes Christian a smug look. Unmistakable. Christian steps closer, wanting to smash his fist into that smirk, and punch the pugilistic nose, but Lance's knuckle-duster hands, and steady stare, make Christian hesitate.

'It was Julian's call, not mine. Besides, I have everything prepared for your weekend, and then if you still feel like it, you can fire me on your way out.'

The dive boat leisurely swayed at anchor with a full rack of dive tanks and a dual of tuna rods. Lance was a real operator. He had the physical build of an athlete, the confidence of an enforcer, and the persona of a professional bodyguard. Lance and his dogs had managed more than luxury islands.

Lance acted as though nothing had happened. 'What say I get the boat. It's feeding time.'

A manager will make the week run smoother. Fire him later, thought Christian.

Sharks circle, and at each pass the circle tightens—Christian waves the bloodied head and skeletal frame of a skipjack tuna to entice the sharks closer. Black sharks eye him from every watery angle. They fixate on Christian, the tuna frame he holds appears to be an extension of his arm. Every thing is bait. A shark attacks its victim faster than it takes a human eye to blink. Five rows of teeth can sever a man's leg off, tear kidneys, heart, and lungs out—bite by fatal bite. Some people would argue, some men deserve nothing more than a good devouring. One shark darts in and rips the tuna from Christian's meshed glove. Its eyes closed in a primal attack. Once the bait was taken, Christian had nothing left to give. The apex predators circle. Christian, blinded by the sting of saltwater seeping into his mask, tips his head back and blows air out to clear the salty brine.

Christian ascends slowly through the blue, suspended between the sharks and the surface, the hull of the boat still sixty feet above. In that vulnerable space, one shark comes in search of more food. A sharp jab on the nose with the tip of a speargun is all it takes to show that Christian is no easy meat.

On the surface, he spits out his regulator and swings his empty air tanks and buoyancy compensator onto the back transom of the boat and climbs aboard. Lance stows the tanks and weight belts, hangs up the regulator hoses to dry, fires the triple engines, and soon the powerboat is cutting through the liquid highway towards a lunch of fresh caught tuna and a glass of cool wine beside the infinity pool.

One brilliant day followed another. Nothing less than it should be in paradise. Swim. Swam. Swum. And more sun. Until at the end of the week, New York called, and it was time to go.

Christian gave Lance a wave from his cockpit as he taxied down the runway. The Australian stood barefoot on the lawn in his board shorts and faded blue t-shirt. He nodded back. The Aussie was OK.

The jet was back at 20,000 feet in less than three minutes. Should be a quick flight home with this following wind, Christian thinks, watching the elongated shape of a large Magellanic cloud from the cloud atlas. The white cloud rose until it hit the tropopause, then spread out like angel wings. 'That reminds me, Joe, we have to arrange the deaths of some significant people, and none of them are righteous angels.'

MICHAEL CAME OUT FROM the library into bright sunlight. He squinted at a passing jet flying across the blue square of sky. A flight of pigeons swirled in synchronization before landing like flotsam on the plaza.

Pigeons have their own legends. Rothschild, one of the wealthiest families in the world, amassed a fortune by setting up pigeon lofts throughout Europe, then sending only white homing pigeons, the symbol of wealth and sacrifice, to carry private information between financial houses. Therefore obtaining crucial facts ahead of the competition.

And so dynasties grow.

Not every man believes in birds, but lately, Michael was noticing more, and taking note of what he saw. Two tourists with cameras and 'I love NYC' embroidered on baseball caps were sitting on a park bench side-by-side, throwing wild birdseed by the handfuls.

Michael hails a yellow cab. The cab veers in front of a white Ford Bronco and cuts through the stream of cars blaring an irate fanfare. The cab driver pulls into the curb like a bright yellow bird, coming in for a handful of coins, the seeds of a fare.

'Where to?' The taxi driver asked.

'Drive around and tell me when the fifty dollar flag drops.'

Michael needed time to think, and a fifty dollar fare in thickening traffic would buy him that time. Images flash by the cab; a billboard, a jeweler, a theater, cars, people, a billboard, people, a billboard, a repetitive urban monotony. Michael's mind drifts back to books he had read in the vaults of the rare book library. Cabalistic numbers with multiple meanings: number one means God, wisdom, and creation. Number two means female, reproduction, and spiritual development. Number three means power, everlasting life and is owned by the Devil. There's something in every number, and the killer is doing something with the numbers. But what? The meter clicks over. At $30 on the meter, the penny drops.

Michael phones Brooke. Two rings later, she answers.

'What's up?'

'The serial killer is instigating the Cabalistic number three. Three murders, three mortal wounds, and three months apart. Three is the number for everlasting life. Symbols are clues, and the clues are symbols. The serial killer is enacting an ancient death cult. It's as ritualistic as it is real.'

'You got a secret guru?'

'The vaults of the rare book library, it's all down in black and white.'

Brooke had her own library in her apartment. She was a collector of first edition comics and kept hundreds of comics, individually sealed in cellophane bags away from dust and book mites.

'Did you see The Green Lantern while you were there?'

'Close, more like The Phantom on steroids. I nearly bumped into Cutter, I'm pretty sure he saw me, but he was in a hurry, got in his car, and drove away.'

'I'm not surprised. My women's intuition tells me he has a love interest. The librarian.'

'She's no longer working there!'

As the flag fall hits $40, the taxi cab suddenly brakes, abruptly breaking his concentration. 'Talk later, Brooke.'

The cab driver was worrisome behind the wheel. He speed through an intersection thinking of another time; the sun glinting off the horizon, of picking black grapes, and smiling up at a young woman on a wooden ladder, her hair tied in a blue scarf matching her eyes, the ladder wobbling, catching her in his arms, then a jolt and the rapid smell of gasoline. Blinded by love is the same language in any country. The poorly paid foreign cab driver, with a medical degree, has driven smack into the back of a car.

'You ran the stop light,' Michael shouted. 'What the hell were you thinking?'

'Thinking it's not good here in USA. This place has no heart.'

'You know, that concertinaed sports car is going to cost you your license, your job, everything you've got.'

'My wife, I've got nothing without her.'

Through the shattered windscreen, Michael glimpses another scene unfolding. Christian Cutter is out of his car, assessing the damage. Cursing, he shouts at the cab driver but doesn't see the backseat passenger inside the cab. Michael watches the short fuse of Cutter, how his agitation fires off into a tantrum.

Neither Christian, nor the cab driver, sees Michael drop a fifty dollar note on the front seat, then exit out the back door of the cab. A beautiful woman has captured Michael's attention. There is a twenty-foot graffiti portrait of a bride painted on the façade of the Colonial Insurance Building. A delicately painted Guipure lace veil half covers her face, a Mona Lisa without the smirk. But in a surrealist way, the woman in the painting watches. She is the clue he is searching for. Call it a hunch, intuition; he knew the portrait of the woman was connected to the murders. He takes a snapshot of the portrait with his phone and sends it to Brooke. She phones back immediately.

'Can you run an identity match on the bride.'

'Got it. I'll get back to you.'

'One other thing.'

'What's that?'

'I ran into Cutter again today.'

'But he's off-limits.'

'Purely by accident.'

'How's that?'

'My cab rammed the back of his Porsche!'

'What are the odds?'

'Yeah, oddly synchronistic.'

A building is nothing more than a temporary canvas. A light rain begins its drift over the city, bringing its shower of acid rain to dissolve the veiled bride. No man can stop the rain, but rain drives Michael to break the padlock and trespass into the dilapidated building. The General Fire & Insurance building was vacant, closed to the public for renovation, elevators out of order. He jumps over a pool of stagnant water to avoid a spaghetti tangle of electrical wires dangling from black gaps in the ceiling.

On the third floor, he jimmies a window, pulls out his pocket-knife, and scrapes the blade through the woman's painted lips. He leans further out of the window to gain greater perspective, to comprehend the magnitude and difficulty of creating a painting on a fifteen-story building. To scale these walls, you would have to be insane. He backs into the empty room to gain another perspective.

Rain falls and continues to fall, as only rain can do. In the erasure, the bride in the painting appears to be bleeding out, blood-red and yellow ochre streaming down the white facade of the building, pooling into gutters.

Michael phones forensics. 'I want DNA scrapings of all known Chalkman portraits around the city.'

LUNCHTIME—MICHAEL WALKS into the precinct office to the symphony of six phones ringing and no one answering. Brooke is the only one manning a desk. He hands her a knife in a plastic bag. She holds the sealed bag up to the light, observing the deep red smudge on the silver blade. Brooke looks questioningly at him.

'Dried blood?'

'Red paint. It's a sample taken from one of Chalkman's paintings.'

'What do you hope to find in a scrape of paint?'

'I want to know if it contains human DNA.'

Michael pulls the forensic photo files of the ritual serial murders and spreads the grizzly images over his desk.

Brooke comes back from the forensic laboratory. 'The lab will inform us of the result in four or five hours.'

Michael arranges the photos of the murder scenes side by side. The Inflatable Murder: a naked man in a pool lounger. The Rose Garden Murder: a woman lying on a bed of roses. And The Mirror Murder: a woman in a wedding dress. He takes a deep breath to find some oxygen.

'So what are you thinking.'

Michael stands back from the photos. 'The autopsy reports state that victims were drugged but remained conscious throughout. The torture was specifically meant to terrify, not kill.'

'So you think it's not just about the act of killing.'

'Yes, but there is more to it.'

Michael turns to the computer and types in pineal gland. He scrolls to a paragraph on the medical website: pineal, a pea-sized conical mass of tissue behind the third ventricle of the brain. The pineal controls hormones, but now scientists have discovered two unique crystalline forms in the pineal.

'Research of serious crime deaths revealed greater intensity of hormones and Calcite deposits than death by untimely accident.'

'So what you're saying Michael, is that he increases the potency and saturation of pineal chemicals and hormones by the process of fear. The question is, what is he using all this for?'

'For making paint pigments, pastels, and fine art chalk, but that's just the beginning.'

C H A P T E R

79

A MAN OF STATURE walks up the steps to Christian Cutter's apartment. On the second floor of the apartment opposite, one drape moves, not by the wind, but by Mrs. Kitts. If she had been on the other side of Christian Cutter's door, she would have seen a black leather gloved hand post something through the slot. Instead, Shadow the cat pounced on the envelope. If it had been a mouse, it wouldn't have stood a chance.

Christian opened what remained of the clawed embossed gold envelope, to find an elegant hand-scripted invitation to The Paris Bistro De, from Charles. Not every invitation is inviting.

Christian stands in front of the plate glass window, and asks Joe about the implications of turning down the invitation. In the past month, he had been beaten up and nearly killed. A jet fighter was prepared to evaporate him in mid-air. FBI Agents raised questions about his personal life. And, an anonymous person had sent an incriminating CD. He was sure Julian orchestrated this harassment under Charles's direction. And he was right. A man like Charles could either scare you half to death or have you killed, depending on what you had to offer, or what you refused to offer.

A covert in the fourth-floor window had Christian caught in the crosshairs of an infrared scope, a red dot centered on his forehead. They knew Christian would give up his formulae—eventually. He would have no choice.

Sensing he is being watched, Christian presses the automatic blind control. Privacy rolls down, dismembering his reflection, to the point where the covert can no longer see into his apartment. The man removes his audio listening headphones, packs the sniper's rifle into its case, and switches on a mobile phone. 'I delivered the invitation. Cutter was talking to a guy named Joe. A lengthy discussion. Cutter sounded upset. At first, he considered not coming; then he said he was going to Paris after all.'

'Good. Stay with it. Cutter may be bluffing.'

'Something else, he said.'

'Yes.'

'He invited this Joe to Paris.'

'OK, we'll look into it.'

CHRISTIAN FLEW TO Paris with Joe. Christian wears an Armani suit because he maintains the idea that he is too well dressed to be anything less than highly successful.

At the Armenian market in the seventh arrondissement, Joe buys seven black t-shirts, seven pairs of black jeans. Christian buys a mille feuille pastry, and a new Laulhere handcrafted Basque beret. The Laulhere factory has stood on the same spot, a landmark in the arrondissement, for one hundred and seventy years. The blue-black wool beret was to be a gift for the enigma of the true artist,

Joe. Leaving his platinum card in his wallet Christian pays in cash.

By the time Christian walked over the Siene Bridge and along the Boulevard St Michelle, the Parisian moment changes. Paris news stands are emblazoned with Christian's face. Vicious headlines threatening to unmask the billionaire and reveal his hidden life. He buys a paper and reads so-called revelations that could ruin him. A tourniquet of secrets and lies, more tabloid than truth, a litany of false allegations. Some said he had accessed a deep pornographic snuff site, that he was having an affair with the Vice President's wife and there were photographs to prove it. Another said they had proof he was a user of Sticky Rice, the Asian male hook-up app. More crass for the masses, but who was feeding the tabloids such gluttony of gossip?

By the time Christian had taken a taxi to Bistro De, he was half an hour late. The restaurant was fully staffed and booked out for just the four of them. As soon as Christian comes in, Charles, Steve, and Julian smile in social unison.

'Christian!' Charles shakes his hand warmly. 'So pleased you could make it.'

Steve greets Christian with an inscrutable bow.

Julian wondered if Christian was going to tell the story: 'Was your flight satisfactory?'

'Trouble free as you'd expect. No jet fighters on my tail.'

'A terrible misunderstanding.'

Christian didn't miss the underlying tone; the French emphasis on 'terrible' sounded like tearing to shreds or tearing apart.

'Well, we don't want any more misunderstandings, do we?'

'My exact sentiments.'

After the main course, Charles folds his white napkin, crease upon crease until the napkin-origami is identical to the one he had undone at the beginning of the meal. Julian hadn't used his napkin.

It remained folded throughout. Christian, not a man to put things back together, left his napkin crumpled.

'Now, let's go where we can talk in private.' Charles indicates a door to a room with a past. Presidents and Kings had sat in the same room at the Bistro De, discussing situations and making decisions on the states of things; the state of the economy, the state of the nation, and the state of their marriage and extramarital affairs. It was a room where significant matters of state were settled.

The desserts, brazen in calories, petit fours, citrus tarts, dark chocolate mousses, and sugared almonds, all deftly arranged on the mahogany sideboard.

Charles takes a cigar from the humidor case, ceremoniously unwraps the gold band, and snips the end with a cutter. 'I know you don't smoke, but do you mind if I do?'

The question is, what part of Charles's thousand dollar cigar was to mind? The mainstream smoke exhaled through Charles's teeth, or the side-stream smoke from the end of the cigar, either way, Christian was about to take in pricey toxic chemicals, like it or not.

Charles rolls the cigar between his thumb and index finger. 'I can't resist a good Cuban.'

Julian lights up. 'Neither can I.'

'Me neither,' Steve says, lighting up with Julian's help.

Charles taps the ash into the crystal art nouveau ashtray.

Puffs of a Cohiba Behike cigar, handcrafted by Elie Bleu, with a glass of Remy Martin's Black Pearl Louis XIII in your hand, make someone the center of attention. Thousands of dollars of burning tobacco leaves fill the room. As the smoke clears somewhat, Charles says in a conspirative tone, 'The woman in the bride dress was a nice touch. I thought. Though some thought, you were a little over dramatic at the end.'

The three men wait for Christian's reaction. Christian remains tight-lipped and expressionless, allowing him time to think.

Julian leans forward. 'We filmed it all, every slice of your filleting knife. It was easy to gather incriminating evidence on your activities, which shows how vulnerable you are.'

'What are you talking about?' Christian's eyes give a paranoid flicker in the day of exposure.

Charles scrapes around the dessert plate with a fork of irritation, then takes a shot of Remy on the rocks to clear marauding crumbs from his throat.

Christian waits for what is coming next.

'We do know that the FBI, and, in particular special Agent Steel, has more than a passing interest in you. For a time, we've managed to curtail recent inquiries into your activities. Steel was close to convincing the justice system to put a warrant out for your arrest. We stopped that. Officially he can't do anything about you right now. And we hope to keep it that way, with your co-operation, that is. To that end, we want to put forward an offer.'

Up to this point, Christian believed he was untouchable. His meteorite global success had given him an innate sense of security.

'You've been a little indecisive of late, haven't you? But this should help you make up your mind.'

With that, Julian hands Christian a black leather compendium. The exact opposite of a gift. Inside is a dossier of covert surveillance. The more Christian scrutinizes the photographs, the more he realizes how much his intimate privacy has been violated. Negative scenarios have a way of doubling and tripling; nothing reverts back to beginnings. What Christian doesn't know is that Charles has arranged for Joe to take the fall for Christian.

Charles leans forward to top up Christian's balloon glass with a little more Black Pearl. Charles is a man who can add or subtract the zeros and make nothing exist that he doesn't want to exist.

Christian watches two hundred fifty dollar puffs of smoke go up in the air. Charles is a third of the way through smoking his cigar, but not entirely through explaining the plan for Christian's exile and exodus. The pressure is on to accept the bailout package. If this is a sweet deal, Charles is the honey scorpion delivering it. A few points were fictional, but the overall plan was to package Christian up and make him disappear without a trace.

Anything with strings attached pulls you this way and that. The more people take control, the more you lose control of your life.

Charles is a reader of minds. 'We have set up three laboratories in unregulated countries. These are countries where money rules; where we can ensure the police and government won't touch you. You get out of the public eye and out of the hands of the law. We're prepared to invest hundreds of millions of dollars into your ideas so you'll be free to follow your destiny of greatness.'

'No one but us knows about your life interests, and we want it to stay that way,' Julian said.

Charles adds, with a sweep of his cigar: 'But the final decision is yours.'

'And what's the price that I pay?'

'You keep the fame in your name, but you give us the formulas.' Christian's golden parachute has become iron manacled. He signs the deal; his pen, oddly missing, so there is no choice but to take what Julian offers—a black onyx pen, heavily engraved. As he signs his name, Christian feels a foreboding, enough to make him doubt himself; a first time for everything.

'We are with you, Christian. We've planned for your safety and ongoing research for as long as you wish. When you go back to New York, don't raise concerns, especially with Agent Steel.'

'I can take care of Steel, in my own way,' Christian brags.

'Arrangements have been made for Agent Steel, and they can't be interrupted or altered. All your affairs will be taken care of.'

'What affairs would those be?'

'The sale of your cars, and disposal of all assets—the contents of your apartments, your boat, your jet, the island, real estate, and share portfolios, cellared wines, gold, precious stones, jewelry, paintings, and artworks—it's all part of the deal. We have someone in mind for it all. Within a week, you will simply disappear into another life with a new passport and identity. And you don't need to worry. Your mother Grace, will be taken care of for the rest of her natural life.'

'What about my laboratory?'

'Yes, we'll take care of that as well.'

In the back of the limousine, on the way from the New York La Guardia Airport, Christian pours himself a Jameson on ice. Back at his apartment he spends the rest of the evening killing off his email accounts. He spends Sunday morning wiping out his social media, until he is dead to the world of paparazzi and glitterati. Dead to everyone but Joe.

80

WHILE OTHERS WERE MAKING plans in Paris, Michael was in New York with a plan of his own. Michael took Brooke to see the apartment. As they settled in the back of the cab, Brooke says, 'I take it the insurer paid up for you to afford a new place?'

'Down to the last dollar. The insurers paid for all the damage; including furniture, appliances, electronics and personal effects, at full replacement value.'

'That's unheard of. Insurance companies notoriously drag out their payouts. I had a bag stolen from a hotel room once, a cabin bag stuffed with clothing. It took months before I got a pathetic compensation check.'

'That's what I always believed. But the insurance assessor came one day, accepted the claim on the spot, and cash was electronically deposited into my bank account the following day.'

'You're kidding! You must have friends in high places.'

'I'm not complaining. We are talking a million dollars of damage plus. Not only. When I phoned the baby store about payment and delivery of the nursery items I'd put aside, the store manager said the account had been paid two weeks prior. Not by me.'

'An anonymous person. I've heard of that. A generous gesture, but there's always a payback. It happens around holiday time, philanthropists paying off accounts at stores like Kmart to help people in need. But you're hardly a needy guy.'

'In need? Yes I am! I need to find out who is trying to set me up. I've got forensic accountants on to it.'

Michael opens the front door. Brooke surveys the interior, impressed with the style.

'This must have cost you an arm and a leg.'

'Yes, but at least they are still attached.'

The apartment has the same layout as the one that Byron tried to kill Michael in, only much more spacious.

'Your old apartment was built for newlyweds and memories. A family of four would have been cramped. But now, this is much larger, with a great view over the park. Everything brand new, for new beginnings. Fate sure has a way, doesn't it?'

'Sure does. Hey, come and check this out.'

Brooke follows Michael to the nursery.

'I called in specialist baby decorators who design everything for the baby, or babies in our case. It's what Charlotte wanted in the first place.'

'Did you have a color therapist?'

'Charlotte did. I'm jaded over color therapy.'

'How come?'

'Since my last prison visit when I asked the prison psychologist how violent offenders were controlled within penitentiaries. He said one of the ideas was to use color therapy to help the violent offenders stay calm. The color therapist advised the State that pink was the right color. Then said, I'll show you the pink day room.'

Brooke said: 'Pink! That would make it bright and gay.'

'And then, I looked through the window of the violent offenders' day room. For the most part, it was still institutional green. The only pink I saw, was near the ceiling. I asked, how come they didn't paint the entire room? He replied, they did, but the inmates hated the color so much, they peeled off what they could reach by hand and ate it. Their point was, they are what they are, and no color was going to change them.'

Michael opens a door to a fresh white and lemon sherbet space with a kid-size tub. 'There's even a kids' own bathroom.'

'Sumptuous, if I could fit in there, I would. Lucky babies!'

Michael's phone rings.

'Sally, from forensics.'

'What did you find?'

'Chalk scrapings from the bride portrait show the presence of three sets of human DNA. As you suspected, there are also traces of semen in the sample. But there's more. Samples from other portraits around the city show other female DNA. At this point we have cross-matched the victims of the Mirror Murder and the Rose Garden murder to the street art. Each victim is portrayed on a separate downtown building. Interestingly, the same two sets of male DNA show up in each portrait. And now we're waiting for results from Paris Interpol on the Pharaoh Murder.'

Michael hangs up just as the doorbell rings.

'Agent Michael Steel? Please sign here.'

'Who sent this?'

'Doesn't say. Just needs your signature, Sir.'

'More baby stuff?' Brooke asks.

'Doesn't look like it unless Charlotte's enrolled them in art classes.' He unwraps the package to find a wooden box made of balsa, and on the lid, a graphic of the yellow Eye of Horus in a blue triangle. Inside the box, there is a rainbow of colored chalk pastels, each with a small label wrapped around it. Printed on each label, a tiny image, again the Eye of Horus. The same symbol Michael had seen on an antique box on display at the *Great Bodies of Art* exhibition.

The note read: *A gift of the finest art pastels should ring a few bells. Good hunting. Charles.*

'Charles who? Who the hell is Charles?'

Michael flips over the packing slip.

'No name, just a local address you'll recognize. This is about to get a lot more macabre. If these art pastels are what I think they are, it's the breakthrough we've been looking for.'

Michael picks up the phone and dials the Chief.

'We have enough forensic evidence to arrest Chalkman for the serial murders. Chalkman makes his own art materials and is using human remains in his pigments and chalks. Forensics have matched at least two murder victims. We need a search warrant for his apartment.'

'Consider you've got it, but wait for my call.'

IN THE UNDERCOVER car, Brooke and Michael act like a couple doing life around New York. Brooke swerves around a white pigeon as it lands on the yellow centerline. She parks the car outside Cutter's address and turns off the ignition.

She unzips a chocolate bar and drops the foil wrapper at her feet. She is one of the sixty percent of drivers in the city who eat food in their cars. If anyone took swabs from a steering wheel, they'd find it twice as dirty as the buttons of an elevator, and six times nastier than a smart phone screen.

When Brooke finishes her mouthful, she says, 'Detectives have interviewed the neighbors already. They say, sometimes a man comes out of the apartment in the early or late evenings—some thought he must be a night worker. A man in his early to late thirties, above average height, athletic, dressed in running gear, or dressed in black. To one neighbor, he was known as the man on the run because he always seemed in a hurry. Mrs. Gibson from apartment 5A said she'd seen a young woman coming and going from his apartment recently but hadn't seen her in recent weeks.'

On the dashboard, the second hand of the analog clock ticked ahead of itself.

'And if you talk to the locals, they all know Cutter. It must be funny to grow up in one neighborhood and live there all your life. Me, I did the math once; I've moved twenty times in my life, so far.'

'Cutter owns this whole place. Even the widow Mrs. Kitts knew him as a small boy. Christian was a close friend of her son's before his accident.'

'Let me guess. He died?'

'Yes, he did. Spencer Kitts and his brother were in the back alley with Christian when Josh Kitts fell off his bicycle, and cracked his skull open on the gutter.'

Michael and Brooke filled in the minutes, waiting for the Chief to phone back with the all-clear on the warrant to arrest Chalkman and search his apartment. They watch customers come and go from Cutters Delicatessen, the place known for comfort food, as much for families as it was for one person, eating alone. The leaves of the maple trees threw dappled light onto the brown cobbled sidewalk. People were sitting outside the deli drinking coffee. In the window, traditionally dried salamis hang, jars of kosher pickles lined up behind baskets of freshly baked artisan loaves. An Italian wedding cake on a silver plinth, stacked in three ascending layers of confectioners cream, with icing falling in folds, decorated with fondant cherubs, and bluebirds nestled amongst swirls of cream ribbons. A cake to catch Brooke's bridal imagination. 'See that wedding cake in the deli window? It's not real.'

'Why do you say that?'

'The whole thing is made of plaster. You can tell. So much is fake about weddings, even the cake. But I guess it's just made to give you an idea of how exciting the one big day in life will be. A fairytale template for some to follow, but not me.'

Michael's mobile rings before the conversation shifts into same-sex marriages.

'Chief.'

'You've got it. You're clear to go in. Back up is on its way.'

'Thanks, but hold them back at a distance. We don't want to spook this guy cause we know he's a runner.'

Michael and Brooke conceal their weapons inside their jackets. From the outside, it was a casual look. A passerby on the sidewalk would have no clues. Michael and Brooke could be friends visiting, or religious hawkers, or a couple meeting a real estate agent to look through an apartment for sale. They walk up to the front door. Michael uses a skeleton key to open the warded lock. They enter and conduct a quick scope of the apartment before radioing in.

'Suspect is not on the premises.'

And so it happened, Federal Agents, four women, and six men raided the apartment at 4:15 pm. The District Attorney entered the apartment carrying a search warrant issued under the Crimes Act.

Michael shook his hand. 'Tate, this is my partner Brooke. Brooke, this is Tate from the DA's office.'

Tate said: 'What have you got so far?'

'Too early to say. We're doing a thorough sweep of the building.'

As one set of agents sifts through the trashcan, another searches for mobile phone records, photographs, diaries, notes, anything they can forensically scrutinize. Brooke opens all the cupboards in the designer kitchen. 'Nice place, but it feels propped, like a show home.'

'Check the fridge?'

'Empty.'

'And the pantry?

'Nothing fancy.'

'Liquor cabinet?'

'A few spirits. None drunk.'

'No food. No garbage. No dirty dishes or dirty laundry.'

'It doesn't look like anyone lives here.'

Brooke finds a British Airways holiday brochure and drops it into an evidence bag. 'Or they've gone on vacation.'

'This place has been professionally cleaned. And I don't mean by a maid, housekeeper, or commercial cleaner; it's been forensically cleaned. We're not going to find anything here. The whole place is propped and staged. He knew we would come.'

On the top of an antique Japanese kimono chest sit three remote controls, neatly aligned, but modern technology is out of place on aging cedar wood. Michael picks up the white remote. The monitor shows the front door and a panoramic view of the street. Michael changes remotes and the monitor switches views. 'Every room is under 24 hour surveillance.' So it was. The investigation was being recorded while they were fingerprinting, photographing, and forensically going over every inch of the premises. 'We're being monitored in real-time from somewhere outside.' He picks up the red remote. The halogen lights dim, the massage chair undulates, the gas fire flares up, the TV turns on to the sports channel.

'Catching the baseball game? Toys for boys. Entertaining stuff!'

The room appears out of proportion for a building of this era.

Michael presses the yellow button on the black remote, and the dark side of the building's architecture reveals itself. The wall slides back to expose a hidden studio, more substantial than a crawl space but smaller than a living room. Portraits hang around the walls painted in chronological order of death. A series of faces with dead eyes, staring open like dolls' eyes, fixed and unfocused. Each portrait has a Polaroid photograph taken at the murder scene. All were pinned with entomologist preservation pins, turning the dead into a kind of specimen. The dead, fluttering against the wall like moths. More canvases lean against each other, stacked in dim corners. Paint dried sadly long ago, like an impressionist fait accompli, a done deal.

Michael and Brooke photograph the portraits and send them for face matching. A response comes back in minutes—no portraits of the living.

Michael tentatively touches a painting sitting on an easel. 'The paint is still wet on this one.' A match for a missing person.

Brooke notices the potpourri of roses coupled with love notes beside the portrait. 'They were lovers by the look, and he's made a shrine. And look at this pregnancy test wand. A positive.'

There was a map of New York City pinned to the opposite wall, covered with photographs of vacant buildings. Michael notices handwritten notations. 'There are eleven marked buildings. By my reckoning, that's a victim's portrait on each building. He's even got satellite images and color printouts of weather patterns, and dates—the past and the future.'

'Chalkman's painting the town red in a sick-fest of slaying,' Brooke said, looking horrified. 'So where is he right now?'

Michael points at a building on the map. 'This building is labeled Alexis, with today's date. He's going to paint again tonight.'

The sun is about to set. When the crucible moon lights the sky above the city, evil has configured, to scale the walls below. Time is crucial. Michael and Brooke leave the apartment and head down-town, leaving the forensic team to catalog the findings.

81

AT THE INTERSECTION BROOKE brakes suddenly as a Porsche runs an amber light. Two blocks back from the target, the back alley is wall to wall with police vehicles. She parks behind the line of squad cars. 'What has the Chief organized for backup?'

'Stealth helicopters, and on the ground, half the precinct.'
She and Michael enter a communications vehicle packed with law enforcement personnel. Although the NYPD has jurisdiction over the whole operation, Black Ops, special units, FBI and CIA are there. Everyone wants to take down this guy.

The briefing takes thirty minutes, and at precisely 8:35 pm, the teams take up their assigned positions around the block. Above them, helicopters turn on night vision cameras with heat seeking monitors; green lights scan the buildings below. Nothing can move on the ground without detection. Darkness makes seeking complicated. Finding one person is more of a lucky strike in the dark.

Shadows flit over a car rusted on its axles, a masterpiece of urban abuse. Then the power grid loses its grip. It starts as a brownout, a sudden drop in voltage. Then comes a total loss of light. With the network down, the helicopter pilot sees the city block as a powerless black island in a sea of city lights.

Meanwhile, Michael and ten Swat Team members go on foot across the vacant lots towards the intended building, navigating by night vision in pitch darkness.

With the blackout as his advantage, Chalkman climbs the highrise walls of the night by using forgotten wrought iron fire escapes as ladders. He stops on the steel meshed landing—runs his hands over the walls to see if the surface is suitable, plaster over concrete, a good surface to paint on. Only the wind stirs above him as he takes his chalks and begins to draw Alexis back to life.

Time and reality are suspended in the world of creativity.

He brushes her hair, the color of blonde. He opens her sleeping lashes until her vibrant green eyes entrap him in her gaze. By the time he draws the line of her oval face in the velvet night, the arch of her red lips smile back at him.

The storm enters the city from the west. Dark clouds roll in as only dark clouds do, while the universal power of the lightning storm recharged the atmosphere, electrifying the sky.

Helicopters in ghost mode cut through sleepers' dreams. On board, thermal imaging picks up solo movement.

'Suspect is moving on the west side of the building. Hold on. He seems to have vanished. Where did he go?'

The pilot, swift as a hawk after prey, flies the helicopter to the south side of the building.

On the ground, Michael speaks to his team in a quiet monotone, 'Suspect has disappeared off their screens. We're going in.' The front door of the once-grand but now abandoned building had buckled. Homeless and drug users had levered their way in. The stench of acrid urine blanketed the team in the underside of neglect; a stained mattress spewed its filthy snow of kapok. Michael's night vision glasses catch wild rats' eyes, eerily emerald. The wind in the upper floors ghosted pane-less windows, no more than transparent openings. Michael steps around gray shapes of derelict furniture, a desk, a chair, and walks through the frames of skeletal walls. Outside of the twelfth-floor window, tell-tale sounds—the rubbered scrape of climbing shoes dragging against brick and the aluminum jangle of ascender clips.

'He's here.' No sooner had Michael spoken, strobes from the helicopters turn the night to pseudo-white daylight, highlighting the climber.

In the next block over, directors, film stars, and the media attend an annual red carpet event. Most switch their attention to the light show happening around the abandoned building. A carousel of blue and red flashing lights. In the sky above, black ladders drop from the belly of a stealth helicopter; dark anonymous figures slide down through a blue-black sky, bruised by the storm. With that much action, the red carpet event paled in contrast. If this was a movie, who would want to miss it?

It started with a director leaping into his limo, followed by his lead actor and production crews. The entire red carpet event descended on the crime scene; dressed in couture evening wear, Graff diamonds bedazzling.

The faceless stars in the heavens were being replaced by billowing storm clouds. Black helicopters hover. Michael edged toward the window. White strobes rove the building, as camera crews set up to capture the unfolding drama. Spotlights in a brilliant act of wandering, shine in blinding fashion. Chalkman is startled, then awed by flashing lights. If social media is the cinema of the world, the moment in crisis is the moment of fame. For in the moment of creation, the artist's spark comes from the universal power, and creating art is the only way to ignite the eternal spirit. Christian was right—genius never dies. It is time for the truth to be revealed—suspended in litho light, Joe reaches out, pointing upwards to the almighty specter of God in the heavens, in the same position as Michelangelo's *Creation of Adam,* fingers almost touching. Lightning cracked almighty and struck a metal spire. Then, Zeus throws Joe a lightning bolt out of the heavens, down his out stretched arm, until his body arcs in white electric, his body a perfect four-pointed star. His hands, his feet, all connected, all of them a point of the perfect pattern. Joe, at the center of both the circle and the square, truly the *Vitruvian Man* of Leonardo da Vinci; two superimposed men, a second set of arms and legs. A divine connection between man and the universe. The artist becoming—a reality and a fantasy, life and death as inseparable.

In the space of the fall, the street artist is the image of the perfect man, but then, no man has the right to survive such a fall from grace. Searchlights follow the harrowing fall of the man.

Spectators hold the sound of one man's skull smashing open on the sidewalk, as an indelible memory. A falling star, unable to be caught, or a man falling to his death? One way, or another, Joe's death as an artist will remain forever in the memory of the people, perhaps.

The police secure the crime scene with yellow tape as the specialists move in, a white laundry of forensics, their blue gloves placing red number pegs on evidence; crime by color, crime by numbers, working the forensic grid, piece by piece. The broken body lies face down, blood spreading like telltale forensic ink on a blotter of black clothing, pulpy brain matter with white bone protruding. But it is the outstretched hands; the palms dusted with white chalk as if the body was that of a gymnast, that catches Michael's attention. A bag of white chalk attached to the waist had burst open, giving the body its own fatal forensic chalk outline of a dead man—a chalked man.

A cold drizzle fell out of the blackened nightscape. City lights danced on the rain-slick sidewalk where boxes of colored pastels had exploded on impact. The rain, having nothing else to do, set about dissolving a spectrum of magenta, orange, and blue, mixed with red arterial blood; colors that should never share the same palette fizz and dissolve together in disharmonic spillage around the body. A psychedelic drama—smashed pastels give off a rainbow of acidic gas bubbles, colors popping, spitting and hissing like bicarbonate of morbid sherbet, until the polychromatic patterns turn the death scene into a bizarre abstract street painting on the gray sidewalk.

Michael said: 'Rain is activating the lime in the Calcite chalk. Cover the body immediately, or there will be nothing left of it by the morning.'

When the body is turned over, there was Joe, colored chalk had feathered around his corpse like a multicolored corona, a kaleidoscope of wild colors formed a broken halo—a twisted smile on his lips, while his pastel aura streamed to the gutter, and away to the farthest realms of municipal drains. So they erect a forensic shelter, a white nylon tent to cover the nomad spirit. Its walls light up as shadows loom and play across its surface, crime investigation shadow dancing on another death. At 2 am, a few squad cars remain, blue and red lights revolving slowly as the ambulance pulls away, and the emergency dissipates. There is a point when you are so tired, nothing you think makes the slightest sense. Chalkman is the killer, but with the finding of two male DNA's in the telltale semen, who and where is the other man, Michael wonders.

82

NEXT DAY, MICHAEL RETURNED to the crime scene. He was not immune to death, anyone's death. It happened right here, he was a witness, as much a part of last night's unfolding drama, he was one of the players. Death was as haunting as any place in which you find yourself altered by trauma. He looked down at bunches of flowers, handwritten notes, and candles as a memorial for the street artist that Chalkman was. New Yorkers' never forget a New York moment.

As the sun warmed up the morning, a chunk of metal glints in the sunlight. Michael picks up a fob of keys from the gutter. When he presses the central lock on the keypad, rear lights flash, and doors unlock a car parked opposite the alley. He strolls over and opens the trunk. The stench of rotting meat forces him to take a step back. The source appears to be more than just butchered meat, which should have been refrigerated. Perishables that go off, produce their own distinctive rankness; a fillet of Norwegian salmon, Greek acidophilus yogurt, wedges of Gorgonzola, Stilton, and Camembert cheeses, a bag of pigs cheeks, and dog bones—the awkward stench. Underneath it all, a melted tub of vanilla bean ice cream. What gets Michael's attention isn't the rotting groceries but the boxes of art pastels amongst the grocery bags. When Michael unlocks the passenger glove box, he is in for another surprise. He scrutinizes the driver's license and the vehicle's registration papers. Michael hits fast dial on his mobile and phones the precinct. He talks to the officer on duty. 'Can you run a vehicle check on a set of plates, CCJC4563?'

'The vehicle is registered to a Mr. Christian Cutter.'

'Has the owner reported a yellow Porsche as stolen?'

'No, nothing is reported on that vehicle.'

'Get me a tow truck for a vehicle at'…looking across the road he sees the street number of a music store, '1069 East on Stratton.'

It was the forensic report on the contents of Christian Cutter's car that prompted the Chief of Police to upgrade Cutter's status from a missing person to a person of interest. And why he called an emergency briefing.

Once coffee found its way into bloodstreams, and sugar-glazed donuts added a finale of carbohydrate infusion, the room became a drone of intense conversation about the past forty-eight hours; the investigation of Chalkman's apartment, the stakeout and Black Ops operation, the bizarre lightning strike on Chalkman and the latest revelations about Christian Cutter, and the ongoing question of his whereabouts. Chief brings the room to silence. 'The blackout for investigating Christian Cutter has now been lifted. Bring Cutter in for questioning.'

Michael turns to Brooke. 'Let's pay Mr. Cutter a visit.'

WITH A SEARCH WARRANT in hand, Michael arrives with Brooke at Christian Cutter's apartment. Across the street, Mrs. Kitts peers through her drapes. The flimsiness of the sheer fabric allows her to draw her own line between nosiness and curiosity. As soon as she sees agents going up to Christian's door, she picks up her phone and calls her oldest and dearest friend, Grace.

'Grace, something's happening at Christian's apartment. He's got a lot of visitors going in. Have you heard from him?'

'No, I haven't heard from him for four or maybe five days.'

'Then why don't you call him? I'm sure he'd like to hear from his Mom,' Kitts says, trying not to cause Grace alarm, keeping her voice calm, as she watches armed law enforcement officers position themselves along slated rooftops.

Michael knocks on the door, a deliberate hard knock so it resounds to the back of the apartment. No answer. He holds down the intercom buzzer. No response. He opens the front door with a skeleton key. Just then, a phone rings from inside the plastic bag Michael has in his jacket pocket. It's the one piece of evidence from Cutter's car that Michael had clearance to retain. The caller's name is Ma. So, Ma, you'll have to wait, while we see what your son's been up to.

The search begins, room by room; the L-shaped dressing room has shirts lined up by colors, dozens of suits zipped in individual black garment bags, a meticulous and organized closet, the state of a man's closet reveals the man's state-of-mind.

Brooke finds a neatly organized syringe kit.

'A diabetic?' Brooke drops the syringes into an evidence bag.

'Or using! If this is what I think it is.' Michael opens the bathroom cabinet to find neatly aligned rows of pristine vials full of clear liquid. 'This is his life-long addiction.'

The living room is as expected, for a bachelor billionaire's place of residence. Brooke thumbs through the collection of glamour and business magazines, featuring Christian on the front covers. She flicks through article after article about the man; a famous, self-made man, fame and fortune evident, it crosses Brooke's mind that the lavish lifestyle, private islands, private planes, boats, travel, real estate, designer clothing, is merely a front for a man with dark secrets.

It is the black oriental cat mewing at the window that disturbs her concentration, it's feline persistence to be let inside, a creature of habit and habitat. Brooke opens the catch on a sash window. Without hesitation, the cat jumps inside, rubs itself against her ankles, and purrs. A needy Velcro cat all fuss and demands. Brooke preferred polite cats, ones that wait for feeding time. In fact, she preferred dogs.

In the hallway, blocking access to the rest of the house, Michael is in a stand off with dogs. He has never seen this aggressive breed of dog before, and nothing had backed him into a corner like this. But here they were, two drooling, growling, salivating American Bandogge Mastiffs, one hundred and fifty pounds apiece. A canine cross between a Pitbull and a Neapolitan, bred for protection and trained by Cutter to kill. A total of three hundred pounds of killer dogs. Michael pulls his gun. Brooke comes out of the kitchen, and the dogs turn their attention to the new intruder.

'Hello boys! Are you hungry?' She tosses rump steaks in their direction, which they attack with relish, before they turn on Brooke. Big canine tongues licking her face isn't appreciated. 'I think they're going to lick me to death. I wonder when these poor babies were last fed,' she said, tentatively leaning away from the dogs' slobbering jaws.

'Cutter had been on his way home with their dinner,' Michael said, remembering the 40lb bag of premium dry dog food in the trunk. 'But where is he, right now.'

'Judging by the size of these brutes, they wouldn't have lasted home alone for long.' Brooke phones the police animal station. 'Stand-by to take two massive dogs and a cat! No, they are not under arrest.' Brooke hangs up. 'Smart ass newbie down at the pound.'

They get into the elevator, and Michael pushes the fifth floor. Nothing happens.

'The trick with cage elevators is the mechanism,' Brooke remarks, closing the cage door. 'The two magnets, the male sprocket and female counterparts, must ultimately connect together.'

The lift ascends into the hidden life of Christian Cutter and his high-tech laboratory—special agents follow.

84

THE LAB WAS A SAFE biological area: centrifuges, cold storage, micro-biological incubators, nucleic acid purification system, pumps, flow-meters, vacuum concentrator, a wireless monitoring system, a compound microscope to measure mass in micrograms. Still, for all this paraphernalia, Christian hadn't managed to hide the laboratory as well as he should. Michael touches the tempered glass door. Cold but not freezing. The pressurized door duly unlocks. Michael and Brooke walk into a chill of a white room. An autopsy table harbors the lingering smell of formaldehyde.

Liam, the coroner, inspects the instruments displayed on the steel trolley. 'How impressive. Gigli Saw Amputation Knives—a number 3 and a number 4, dissecting scissors, Halstead Mosquito Forceps, Volkman Retractor, a Frazier Ferguson Suction Tube, Luer Bone Rongeur, Liston Bone Cutting Forceps, and let's not forget the Putti Bone Rasp. There's enough surgical equipment in this room, to dissect a good section of New York City!'

Michael has a particularly uneasy feeling. On the far wall, a six-foot stainless steel tank stands in front of a bank of drawers. But thankfully, both the tank and the corpse drawers, when he checks, are empty.

Beside two electric blenders on a bench, there are plastic bags of fine white powder, zip-lock bags, like the kind of bags a mom would put her kid's peanut butter and jelly sandwiches in for school.

Michael opens the bag of white powder, dips in his knife blade, licks his finger, and tastes it. It wasn't cocaine. On the stainless bench, a five-tier electric fruit dehydrator is set to automatic. The kind you can buy on sale in Walmart, Brooke thought. Adjustable temperature, digital timer, and automatic shut-off up to twelve hours. 'All this tech equipment, and he's drying fruit! What next?'

Liam lifts the lid of the dehydrator. A dank odor makes him step away. 'Dried pineal glands.'

Brooke holds down the urge to retch.

Michael contemplates the dried glands, the industrial blender, and the white powder. 'Fuck!'

He runs to the stainless steel trough, rinses, and gargles whatever disgusting residue is left on his tongue; not satisfied, he scrubs his teeth best he can with his fingers, dries his tongue on a red terry cloth towel, then a quick check to see if he has turned into some kind of cannibalistic monster. Brooke watches Michael reviewing his tongue in the mirror, and holds back a smile. 'You've done some daring things, but none as daredevil as this.'

Michael wipes his mouth with the back of his hand. 'Cutter's been officially missing for twenty-four hours. Checked his private jet?'

'Still in its hangar.'

Michael holds Cutter's mobile phone to ransom. Cutter's driver's license, passports, and the keys to all his cars were at the precinct.

'We've got his vehicles. He can't have got far. Unless he has other identities, he's here in the country still. We'll check every road, bus, train, ship, and all airport routes out of the city, out of the State, and out of the country. We'll get him.'

Forensics continue. Smears of blood and droplets of fluids come alive. Walls are alight with ultraviolet and infrared, and dustings of fingerprints ghosting bricks throughout the apartment. With the dogs taken away to the precinct, Michael, Liam, and Brooke check out the living room. Brooke sits down on the leather chair and presses a keypad. The chair squeezes her calves while shiatsu balls pummel up and down her spine.

'You should try this!'

'I would if I wasn't supposed to be trying to find evidence here!'

The remote controls on the coffee table appear identical to the ones in Chalkman's apartment next door. Michael picks up a black remote and pushes the yellow button. The apartment wall slides aside to reveal a room between Cutter's and Chalkman's apartment. Inside, there is an odd collection of old apothecary jars. Some empty, but most are filled with a tarry brown substance.

On the bench, an industrial blender, newer than the one found in Cutter's lab, a dozen heavy-duty dust masks, bags of French chalk talc, and boxes of latex gloves, all housed in a strip of space between. A no man's land of no rules. The connection between the two apartments was proving to look like a co-conspiracy between Chalkman and Christian Cutter.

'I'm sure forensics will find these two were operating together, Michael.'

'Cutter is no longer classified as a missing person. He is, as of now a wanted suspect. I'm going to put out a murder warrant for Cutter's arrest.'

The search of the apartment continues. Hanging on the wall

amongst a collection of Romantic and Impressionist paintings, is an oil painting by Delacroix in a heavily gilded frame.

'A room filled with this amount of artwork could be mistaken for an art heist.'

A data check to determine whether any of the valuable paintings were listed as stolen, reveals an interesting fact. Recently listed for sale at the Sotheby's Winter Auction, the Delacroix fetched a record-breaking eight figures, purchased by a Mr. Christian Cutter. The major artwork had been painted in browns using pigments from ground-up mummified bodies. According to the National Art Gallery, in this Delacroix, the hue of mummy brown was haunting, a deep, rich brown that gave subtlety and depth to deep shadows.

On the wall, a framed photograph in sepia showed the pastel maker Griuik Cutter with the painter Eugene Delacroix. An entry in Delacroix's diary, penned so eloquently, noted that: *There was nothing like Griuik Cutter pigments to complete the picture.*

On an elm wood art table there are ancient leather-bound books of symbols and archaic writings belonging to the Cutter family of the 15th century.

Curtis, the criminal psychologist, delicately turns pages over.

'I've never seen anything like it. There's an obsession here. Either Chalkman or Cutter, or both men, have deciphered and connected a sequence of symbols that span centuries. Whoever did this is beyond smart, a genius. I would surmise it's Cutter, who sees himself as the inherited master of the Cutter dynasty. I think he's a loner obsessed with the ancient death cult that believed eternal life was found through the eye of death. Look, this is the symbol.'

Curtis holds a parchment page up to the light, and as he does, a watermark is revealed. 'If you superimpose this eye of death watermark, over Cutter's drawing of a dissected brain showing the pineal gland, you'll find an exact match. That's the connection Cutter has made to eternal life in the twenty-first century.

Michael said: 'Whereas, Chalkman on the other hand is an enigma, there are no photographs or personal papers amongst the belongings. Nothing to lead us to his true identity.'

'Not surprising, staying anonymous and hidden is an important part of the psychotic's fantasy life.'

Brooke glances at the portraits and the apothecary jars of mummy brown. 'An artist who makes a killing through art.'

'Dental records will throw some light on who he was.' Michael thought about the connection between the two men. The reclusive artist, and the businessman Cutter, who is most definitely not a reclusive character. If anything, he is a leading light in society, a star of today, not a hidden man, but maybe a deceptive man. He and Chalkman had been sharing something deep and dark.

'Cutter knows who Chalkman is.'

Surveillance has the surrounding streets covered. There is a chance that Cutter might turn up. Liam searches through dark corners of Chalkman's laptop and finds the HTML of a deleted website. The site banner reads, *The Alexis Series,* boxes of fine art pastels for sale—price on application. 'Didn't you say one of the victims was a woman called Alexis?'

Brooke pitches in, feeling angrier than she should. 'He's been selling her on the Internet—body, and soul. Now she's cadmium yellow, magenta, and cobalt blue.'

Curtis, hearing the conversation, leans over to see. 'Death as part of creation, that fits. This guy thinks he's made her immortal in the pigments, and now possesses her after death.'

Michael's phone rang.

Chief asked: 'What have you got?'

'We've got more than one serial killer.'

'Yes and?'

'The strange thing is Christian Cutter is involved.'

'Why do you say that?'

'He shared part of the apartment building with Chalkman.'

'You mean he rented out part of his apartment?'

'No it appears they lived together.'

'As in a relationship?'

'No. I think Cutter and Chalkman killed together.'

'Any leads on Cutter's whereabouts?'

'No, but we've got his vehicle, mobile phone, passport, private jet, and secured his apartment. We have alerts at all the entry and exit hubs around a three hundred kilometer radius of the city.'

What Michael doesn't know, is that the Chief has been getting calls about Cutter's disappearance since 5 am.

International celebrities, social media influencers, royalty and politicians want him found, and it isn't for murder. People who make the world spin on its axis are turning up the heat and making the Chief's life spin out of control. People are in a panic. Without Cutter's serum, some of the beautiful, rich, and powerful people will turn jaw-dropping wrinkled overnight, and age far beyond their chronological years.

'Keep me up to date.' Chief clicks off.

Cutter's mobile rang in Michael's pocket. Michael pulled the mobile from the evidence bag just as the call dropped. The call was from Ma. He spooled down to see her address—St Margaret's Convalescent Home and Respite Center. 'Time we visited Ma.'

CHAPTER

85

Michael and brooke arrive in time to see an over-happy nurse aide pushing a tea trolley down the bright hallway, stopping at every door announcing with a happy Irish lilt, 'Tea, anybody?'

She pours Earl Gray tea from a blue and white Japanned pattern teapot and serves the brew in delicate bone china cups; with sugar lumps, milk or slices of lemon. Chocolate chip cookies and pecan butter cookies are heaped on a large floral plate for patients to help themselves. But combinations of cookies sharing the same plate is disturbing to the few who like to take things one at a time, and even the sight of a double up sends their day into a spin. But such bakery intricacies never bothered a woman like Grace.

Grace Cutter, aka Ma, was sitting in her room, a large corner room, windows with chintz curtains in glazed cotton, and a view over the park. The blue and white wallpaper was printed in a repeated French pastoral scene of a shepherd boy holding a lamb next to a haystack. Grace knew how many boys and sheep were in her room, one hundred and fifty-five and a half, to be exact. She had been here enough months to count every one, except, architraves and corners bothered her, the way the wallpaper had been misguidedly cut, and half a boy and half a lamb thoughtlessly glued together. It's things to do with people that bothered her in life. She kept a list, which amounted to one hundred and twenty-three things, to be exact.

Over the past few days, the list had grown formidable. Christian had forgotten to call her, and that worried her, especially since yesterday was her birthday, and he never forgot her birthday. But yesterday, not as much as a phone call. How can a son not phone his Ma on her birthday? She had phoned Mrs. Kitts to ask why. All Kitts said was, there's a lot of toing and froing at Christian's place. The police are there. Maybe something's gone missing, or is amiss. Then Kitts said she had to go and hung up the phone. That worried Grace, even more.

It was unlike Kitts to cut conversations in half and leave words hanging. Enough to give her a sleepless night again, until the staff nurse gave her a sleeping tablet at around 3 am, then she slept the sleep of the almost dead and missed breakfast. No matter. Sweets are like a lovely drop of medicine, sugar helps take the edge off anxiety. Her son, Christian, had brought the sugared almonds back from Paris a few weeks ago. She likes to suck the sugar coating off sugared almonds. She keeps two jars. One is half full of blue and pink sugared almonds, the other half full of nuts she had sucked.

Michael introduces himself and Brooke to Mrs. Cutter, who is particularly taken with their shiny Federal Bureau badges.

'Mrs. Cutter, do you mind if we ask you a few questions about your son?'

'My boy, the famous scientist, he's always on the television, he's a good boy, visits his Ma, sends me things, and pays my bills, takes care of everything I need. I never have to ask. People can over-ask you know, but I've never asked anyone for anything. He's a truly generous person, always has been, even as a small boy.'

Slipping a word between Grace's word-stream is difficult. Grace kept her mind sharp, even if it seemed at times like she wasn't the sharpest knife in the kitchen drawer. Her shelves were packed with well-thumbed books, classics like Faulkner, Dostoevsky, Mary Shelly's Frankenstein, to humor like 'Dirty Jobs', by the writer Christopher Moore.

'We are trying to locate your son,' Brooke said.

'Good. Well, when you do, tell him to call his Ma.'

'So, you haven't seen or heard from him lately?'

'He forgot my birthday yesterday. What kind of a son forgets his own Ma's birthday, I ask you!'

'Is this the first time?'

'Yes.'

'When was the last time you saw or spoke to him?'

'Has something happened to him?'

'Not that we are aware. We just need him to help us with some inquiries.'

'I see. Would you like an almond?'

'Don't mind if I do.' Grace shakes a handful into Brooke's palm.

'Mrs. Cutter, may I ask you about Christian?' Brooke crunches on an almond.

'Of course.'

'Does Christian share his apartment with anyone?'

'You mean, does he live with anyone? A woman? No. No one. He lives by himself, except for—I shouldn't really tell you this, but his brother is there.'

'How long has he lived with his brother?'

'Always.'

'Mrs. Cutter, how many children do you have?'

'One. I wanted more, but it wasn't to be. When I was pregnant, I was told I was expecting twins very early in the pregnancy.'

'Let me get this straight. You were expecting twins?'

'Yes, for a while, but only one was given to me. The other baby vanished. It happens. See that book on the shelf? Plato said people are conceived perfect but then are split in half by Zeus.

'Learn something new every day. Mind if I borrow the book?'

'Sure, Agent Steel.'

'So, you're telling us, Christian is an only child but lives with his brother?' The clock on the wall ticks on. Grace takes her time to answer Brooke's question.

'Yes. The doctor said when a twin disappears, the surviving twin might feel that an important person is missing. Not my Christian. As soon as Christian said his first words, he began talking to his brother. He always talked to him. He said his brother was afraid of the dark; his brother also did a lot of bad things. A dead twin attaches its soul to the living twin. Plato said that too.'

Grace stares at the wall, a little distracted.

'Does he have a name, this brother of his?'

'Joe. He calls him Joe.'

Brooke and Michael look at each other and back to the distracted Grace.

'Have you ever heard of the name Chalkman?'

'Chalkman?'

'He's a well known street artist.'

'No, can't say I have. A few more nuts?' Grace holds out the jar to Brooke. She has seen how much the special agent likes nuts and how her clothing makes her look manly.

'Are these almonds from Vermont? They taste of maple syrup.'

'No, no, my dear, Paris, France. They're French, sugar-coated that's the sweet taste, I only like the sugar coating though. I don't care much for the nuts inside—my family was dirt poor. When I was a child my Christmas present was always a sock, someone's sock, with an orange from the fruit bowl stuffed in the heel, and raw almonds wrapped in brown paper, crammed into the toes.'

'So ...' Michael articulated slowly, looking at Brooke. 'You suck the sugar coating off first, and then you put the nuts in the blue jar?'

Grace says, smiling with the first and only set of false teeth she has ever possessed in her life.

'Yes! I suck the sweet stuff off and save the nuts because there are some people in the world who like them.'

Brooke makes a run for the trashcan outside in the hallway, spits out almonds, and rinses her mouth at the water cooler.

The cafeteria aromas of fried onions and heavy brown gravy crept along the linoleum corridor and under Grace's door.

'That's the bell for lunch. Do you want to stay?'

'No thanks, another time. Agent Fullerton and I must go.'

'Too bad, Mondays are my favorite.'

On her way out, curiosity makes Brooke ask the nursing sister, 'What's for lunch today?'

'Liver and onions. Monday is official offal day. Mrs. Cutter gave us the recipe. I don't fancy it myself, but most of our residents love it.' But she is speaking to the unconverted. The two agents walk hurriedly down the linoleum corridor and out the exit.

Brooke negotiates her way out of the St Margaret's car park, and narrowly misses an abandoned Zimmer frame, before she swerves around an elderly gentleman carrying a bunch of daisies.

'You'll be in safer territory once we hit the freeway.' Michael phones forensics. 'Sara, get me the DNA results of Chalkman.'

'No problem, the autopsy has been completed.'

'I also need a DNA sample from Grace Cutter. She's a resident at St Margaret's. If I'm right about the DNA findings, Christian Cutter has disappeared.'

'We'll need a warrant to get the DNA, so it will take a couple of hours.'

'Thanks Sara, be careful out there. Keep an eye on the nuts.'

Brooke backs into the car park at headquarters. 'Nice of you to warn her of the nuts,' running her tongue over the nutsy bits still in her teeth.

The alarm she'd set on her mobile beeps a timely reminder from the cavern of her leather handbag, not that minutes matter after all this time when you are meeting an old friend. 'Gotta go. I have a story of my own to turn a page on.'

'I'll call you later once the DNA results are in.'

BROOKE SHOWERS AND dresses in a black dress that hugs her curves in an unselfconscious way, as only a designer dress can. Brooke walks to Brendan's Irish Bar with expectations. She was an FBI agent, a dedicated law enforcement officer, today Brooke would solve another mystery, in her off-duty hours.

Brooke had not seen or heard from her college friend Emma for years, and her whereabouts had become a conundrum. She missed her. The blow-in from the Emerald Isles, the woman whom she'd once loved with a passion, because she was so different, and could play a jig on the fiddle. Irish as Irish is. She found four-leaf clovers, and wanted to believe in rainbows with their pots of gold. She'd gone back to Dublin after graduation, and the letters Brooke wrote her got stamped return to sender. Now, as fate has its own way of determining the future, Emma is back for an international law conference and has looked Brooke up.

Brooke is nervous but excited about catching up with her former room buddy. As soon as she enters the pub, Brooke recognizes the flaming red hair and those sapphire eyes. They hug in an extended lost and found greeting, and settle down at the bar.

'How long has it been?'

Emma was never good at counting time. Brooke knew it was ten years and five months and two weeks since they had parted. Where was she living, did she live with anyone, what aspect of the law did she go into. They chatted, drank, chatted, and drank some more.

'I am the defense attorney who works to get the accused released, and you, the law enforcement officer, who works to bring criminals to prosecution.'

'They say opposites attract.'

'They're right about that. If there wasn't someone prosecuting, there would be no one to defend. Isn't it funny how we strangely complement each other.'

'Let's go eat,' they say, in unison.

The tone of their laughter, lyrical, as they walk arm in arm down the street.

Michael knows Brooke's emotional life is edgy right now, so he hesitates before contacting her in off-duty hours, but once you're in law enforcement, commitment never stops. And phones find a way of interrupting everything.

Brooke's phone rings in the fumble of her bag.

'Are you ready for this?'

'Did you get the results from forensics?'

'Are you sitting down?'

'Not yet.'

Brooke and Emma find a quiet table in the bay window.

'Go.'

'The DNA tests on Grace Cutter came back 99.99% positive that Chalkman is Grace's son!'

'So Grace lied. She does have two sons! Christian and Chalkman. They're twins.'

'Not exactly.'

'How exactly?'

'Forensics found Chalkman had two sets of DNA.'

'What did you say?'

'Chalkman had two sets of DNA.'

'Two sets of DNA in the one man? How is that possible.'

'Genetically, it's extremely rare. Chalkman was a chimera.'

The cafe clatter made it hard to hear the details.

'What! You're saying he's a Chinaman?'

'No, a chimera.'

'How does that happen?'

'One twin is assimilated by the other in the womb, early on in gestation, which then leaves only one living baby. Then when the surviving baby is born, that child carries both sets of the twins DNA. And can have two different blood types at the same time.'

'Chalkman a chimera! What are the odds?'

'Most chimeras remain undetected and are discovered only by accident, especially if both zygotes are of the same genetic sex.'

'Can you tell a chimera just by looking ?' Brooke asks, writing the word chimera, with her index finger into the fog of the window.

'Yes. If the twins are of the same sex, the chimera might have eyes of different colors. And the autopsy confirms Chalkman had one brown eye and one blue eye.'

'What color eyes does Cutter have?'

'I wondered when you were going to ask that. Cutter's passport and driver's license all state that his eyes are blue.'

'Remember those boxes of blue contact lenses in Cutter's bathroom cabinet?'

'I remember they were non-prescriptive. So if he wasn't wearing them for long or short-sightedness, he was using contacts to make both eyes blue.'

'Yes. And there's more. The forensic samples from Cutter's hairbrush are an identical match to Chalkman's DNA. And wait for this—a match to the mother, Grace.'

For a short time, Emma ceased to exist; to allow Brooke's brain to rewire and recap clues.

'So, while we've been wasting our resources searching the subway stations, and airports for Cutter, he's been in the morgue all along. Christian Cutter and Chalkman are the same person.

'Yes. Christian Cutter was the living chimera.'

'Now the deceased chimera.'

'Yes. And Cutter, the chimera, was the one and only serial killer in this case. There was no Joe. He was Joe and Joe was him.'

Cups crash sharp white from the kitchen. By the time Brooke hangs up the call, the condensation on the café window had erased the word—chimera.

CHARLOTTE'S BAGS HAD BEEN packed, ready to go to the hospital for months. She had read all the popular baby books and attended antenatal classes, but some of what she read, or was told, didn't apply to her. At times she felt left out, until she happened to join a multiple birth specific group. She also did ten classes to learn hypnosis birthing, and read five books on raising twins rather than a single baby. As the due date approached, she arrived for her usual prenatal appointment. Charlotte felt worried.

Her specialist reassures her about the birth. 'Just because you're carrying twins doesn't mean the labor will be twice as long and twice as painful.' But all Charlotte hears are the words twice as long and twice as painful. During the ultrasound, the specialist turns the monitor around so Charlotte can see the amniotic choreography of her babies floating as the twins. Their heartbeats monitored and their position in the womb checked.

Charlotte steps out of the examination gown and back into her maternity clothes before taking a seat in the specialist's office. His desk had photos of his own children arranged in silver frames, three pairs of baby shoes cast in bronze, a father of three, but a deliverer of hundreds of babies. But a man who was about to deliver news she wasn't expecting.

'Both twins are heads up, which means neither can be born the old-fashioned way.'

'You mean a cesarean section? When?'

'Now, but don't worry. Everything is looking good. I have no concerns for the babies at this stage.' He picks up the phone and books her in for surgery.

Charlotte calls her Mom to pick up her grab bags for her hospital stay, and then calls Michael.

'Where are you? Is everything OK?'

'Yes, and no. I'm just talking with the specialist. The babies are positioned heads up, so the only way out is a C-section. We'll meet our twins in a couple of hours.'

'I'm coming now.'

THE DELIVERY SUITE is crowded with pediatricians and nurses ready to assist each newborn baby. Charlotte has one support person who is scrubbed up, dressed in a sterile blue gown, a paper theater cap, and wearing paper shoes. When he walks, he rustles like a paper cowboy. Michael is ready to stand and deliver—well, ready to watch the deliveries, cut the umbilical cords, and during the entire birthing process, try to stay upright and not let emotional gravity take over. How much should a man be involved in the birth of his children? Michael has often contemplated this. He read that childbirth used to be a woman's business, usually carried out at home, and the man could be found in the kitchen boiling saucepans of water and miss the actual event. He read that laboring women need to let thinking take a back seat to allow primal unthinking to take over. How can anyone stop thinking? Two out of five partners want to be at the birth, and so here he is, one of the two, a modern man holding Charlotte's hand, with a lot on his mind.

Charlotte is quiet, unnaturally so for her, and so is Michael. He smiles, but it's the kind of smile that feels slapped on, a smile that doesn't belong to how you think, one of those expressions that you want to wipe off and redo.

Michael had read that one man watching his wife give birth fled to his hometown of Rome, and never returned. Delivery, apart from a box of pizza, wasn't for everyone. He had mentioned to Charlotte, once, he had thoughts about being a waiting room dad, instead of a deliveryman. Boy, did she spit the pacifier! But now, by Charlotte's side, all he wants to do is be there with her in this unrepeatable moment of their life history together.

'Relax Michael,' Charlotte squeezes his hand. 'You're going to be a dad any second!'

And there they were.

'You've got two beautiful babies … but.'

'But what? Something's wrong with the babies?'

'No problem at all, it's just that …'

Michael takes one look at the babies and smiles.

'Everything's fine! It's just these babies are not what we were expecting! We've got a boy and a girl—not two boys!

'Let me see them!'

Michael and Charlotte watch four tiny feet being foot-printed for the records. Each baby with its own identification band attached to its cherub-like ankle.

CHAPTER

87

BOTH BABIES ARE MEASURED, checked and weighed in their first natal examination. Both babies have twenty fingers and twenty toes between them. While the nurses make Charlotte comfortable, Michael slips out of the delivery suite to phone the families. The doctor, still in his operating scrubs, comes up to Michael.

'Congratulations, a boy and a girl. Despite technology, nature still delivers her own surprises.'

'Thank you for everything, Dr. Connelly.'

'My pleasure. Perhaps there will be other deliveries in the future?'

'Maybe! Doctor, do you have a minute? I want to ask you about twins.'

'Sure. You have healthy full-term twin babies. Studies say twins are famous for closeness that begins in their mother's womb and can share bonds throughout their lives.'

'Yes, we are just over the moon about that.'

'A twin pregnancy can be complicated and does not always end so well. In fact, 90% of twins cease to be viable in the early gestation stage. That means there is a one in three chance we had shared a womb with a twin. One would never know.'

'I understand. But what is the difference between that and a human chimera?'

'You've been doing your research. But it doesn't apply to your twins. It is known as the vanishing twin syndrome. A pair of twins is conceived, one embryo dies in the womb, the surviving fetus completely assimilates its dead twin. The baby is born with its own DNA, as well as its twin's DNA. A rare event because the odds of being born a chimera are one in five million.'

'Can you tell me something. How is the surviving chimera twin affected emotionally and psychologically?'

'That's a wide-open question. We usually think of a human body as containing only one person. Certainly the surviving baby has some of his twins cells secreted away inside him. He will likely experience loneliness, the desire for lost perfection, and a life long search for a twin soul, a soul mate. They may suffer a conflict of identity, like the material self versus artistic self. They can be prone to antisocial personality disorders, and are likely to live with an imaginary friend, not just in early childhood, but throughout their entire lives.'

Charlotte is left quietly alone, with her precious newborn babies, together for the first time. The hormones of love peak, she forgets the world, her babies are everything; she makes contact with their skin, traces their perfect features with her fingers, counts their toes, and takes in the sweetness and pure innocence of them. Michael comes back into the room, and together they hold the bundles of babies, the miracles of multiples right there in their arms. The baby girl with brown eyes, and the baby boy with blue eyes.

EPILOGUE

At the bukistan border, after a grueling 16 hour bus ride through the mountains, a man gets off the bus, pulls his dust-covered duffel bags down from the roof, and walks over to the border control. A red striped metal arm attached to the sentry box makes a shady line between one country and another. A defining line where people are either walking towards or walking away from something—a place in the dirt between the past and the future.

The man knew what his past was and what led him to this place, to this point on the map.

The guard at the border wonders why this handsome, well-dressed American man would have a twenty year visa for the underworld of the world, or as he thought, the asshole of the world. But he doesn't bother to ask the man why he has come during the dog days of summer, and what he is planning on doing here. Instead, he stamps the foreigner's passport, and goes back to reading the personal classified ads in the local Bukistan paper, where women advertise to make every man a happy man.

The night was falling fast. The stars about to blink. The traveler walks through the border gate, looks up at the evening sky and breathes deeply. The star Sirius, twice as massive as the sun, twice as bright as any other star, Sirius the Dog Star, shines in the dusk over the purple mountains. A white limousine waits, and so does she—the woman he met on the subway train. What are the chances? But, then nothing happens by chance.

Spencer smiles—life goes on.

www.ingramcontent.com/pod-product-compliance
Lightning Source LLC
Chambersburg PA
CBHW061214190726
48288CB00001B/186